Dean Maureen
   Thanks so mu...
support of my debut novel,
Thanks for helping me change
the convers...

The

Anniversary

"What do you do when life has you in checkmate?"

JJ Winston

The Anniversary © 2017 by JJ Winston.

This book is a work of fiction. However, names, characters, businesses, organizations, places, events and incidents either are the product of the author's imagination or are used fictitiously. Any resemblance to actual persons, living or dead, events, or locales is entirely coincidental.

For information contact:

info@uptownmediaventures.com

Book design by Uptown Media Joint Ventures

Cover design by Leonard "LC" Collins.

ISBN: 978-1-68121-040-7

First Edition: March 2017

10 9 8 7 6 5 4 3 2 1

Dedication

This book is dedicated to my God, significant other, mother, children, grandchildren, family and friends. It is also dedicated to those individuals and their families who are suffering with a behavioral health disease.

Page intentionally left blank

Acknowledgements

Ionce watched an episode of the *Oprah Winfrey Show* where Oprah encouraged her audience to create a bucket list of one hundred tasks to complete before you die. Writing a book of fiction was at the top of my bucket list. After all, fiction often imitates life and I want my fiction to inspire individuals and their families to believe that when we fall down, with the help of the Lord, we get up.

I want to thank my God for giving me the strength to write *The Anniversary* over a three year period. I would also like to thank my editor Marianne Eggleston for the countless hours that she spent on editing my work. I would also like to thank my publisher Ken Kelly McElroy of Uptown Media Joint Ventures for believing in my work and for giving me a vehicle to tell Grandville and Juliette's story. Special gratitude to Leonard "LC" Collins for creating the art for my book cover.

A special thank you to Everett Prewitt, author of *Snake Walkers* for taking the time to read chapters from my manuscript and for giving me invaluable advice. Much thanks to Melissa Stallings, Terry Winston and the Honorable Judge, Pinkey S. Carr for proof reading my work and for their love and encouragement. Much gratitude to Beverly Byers for her efforts and assistance with marketing *The Anniversary*.

Lastly, I would like to thank my family, including my mother, significant other, my children grandchildren, and my friends for their love, advice, encouragement and support.

Page intentionally left blank

Table of Contents

Prologue

"What's happening to me? Who are you? What do you want? I don't believe you. Momma wouldn't do that. She wouldn't lie to me."

Grandville found himself in the bathroom with the door closed and looking in the mirror talking to himself. He realized that he was talking out loud again, and it scared him because Juliette could have been listening. He couldn't tell her he was hearing voices inside his head, who were telling him lies about his mother. Juliette wouldn't believe him. Nobody would believe him.

When it first happened he fought back and wrestled with the voices and they left him alone. But, now they were starting to come and go whenever they wanted. It was getting harder and harder to make them stop talking to him and telling him stuff which he didn't want to hear or believe. I can't think straight anymore, and I need to tell somebody but who can I tell? Greta is going through the same issues I am since mom's death. I don't want to burden her.

"I have to talk with Franklin, but he's my business partner. I can't. I have to keep my personal life out of the office. He may understand, but I can't talk to Franklin about this. He may try to take over our business," the voices said.

"Why you say that? Franklin would never do a thing like that to me. We're best friends."

"Well, you know what your mother said don't you? Keep it all to yourself and don't tell nobody," the voices said.

Grandville peaked out of the door to make sure Juliette was not in the bedroom. He tip-toed across the room, laid down and stretched out across the bed feeling exhausted, because he couldn't believe what had just happened again. Facing upward he looked at the ceiling. He then closed his eyes and the voices were gone.

Chapter 1
Tragedy

Grandville awoke to a beautiful sunny August morning which seemed to hold the possibility of promise. Juliette, his beautiful wife, was in the bathroom taking a soothing warm bath in their Jacuzzi tub.

As Grandville lay in their bed, he reminisced about the night before. He thought about the way they made love, and it touched him deeply. He and his wife had become one, over and over again. He had not been intimate with Juliette for a number of weeks and to remember how she touched him and his insatiable need for her body made him tingle.

Ever since the night his mother died he had not been able to pull it together, and he felt guilty for the way that he had neglected Juliette and his family. Juliette had always been his remedy for every problem which plagued him. He hoped her touch would eradicate the voices which had started to invade his head since his mother's death.

Grandville had been so depressed at the loss of his matriarch. The disturbing news which she delivered on her deathbed made it so that he could barely look at Juliette, let alone touch her. However, last night while the voices attempted to communicate with him, he ignored them while he drank Vodka. He caught a glimpse of Juliette when she was getting ready for bed and his body went crazy. He suddenly remembered what he had temporarily forgotten, that she made him feel things no one else had. While he made love to his wife he noted the voices had left his head.

Grandville raised himself up and was mentally preparing to face his day when the voices started to whisper to him again. Their message was clear, that he was worthless and he didn't deserve a wife as good as Juliette. He had lied to her about his past and because of his omissions his family could be hurt. He closed his eyes again and drifted off into a light sleep, hoping that when he woke the voices would be gone.

Soon, the smell of bacon frying and the coffee aroma in the air woke him out of his slumber. It led him downstairs where he found Juliette and their kids seated around their dining room table.

"Grandville sit down. I made breakfast. Here's your plate. Do you want some coffee, baby?" Juliette asked. Grandville looked down at his plate. Juliette had prepared him bacon, scrambled eggs and toast with strawberry jam.

"I can't believe it. This is the first time in months you've made coffee. So, you know, I have to have a cup to go with this delicious meal.

"Aah, thank you darling."

"Honey, I'm sorry that I slept so late and didn't make your Java like always."

"Grandville it's okay. You slept in because you needed the rest. It's Saturday and it's okay to take a little time off. You've been working too hard and you're still dealing with your mother's death."

The voices chose that moment to start whispering to Grandville and try as he might, he found it difficult to focus on the words Juliette was speaking to him.

"Grandville are you listening to me?" Juliette asked.

"Yes, but I missed the last thing you said."

"I said, I think you need some time to relax, so I'm going to take the kids to the Mall. I promised Jessica I would buy her a new outfit. If I am going to buy her an outfit, it's only fair I let the boys pick-out an outfit too."

"I want Daddy to come with us Mommy," Jessica said.

"I know you do, but we're going to let your Daddy relax. When we get back home you can show him your new clothes," Juliette said.

"No mommy, I want my Daddy to help me pick a pretty dress," Jessica whined.

"Jessica, Daddy is not going to come with us. Now, I want you and your brothers to go and wash your hands and meet me in the front hallway. We're going to be leaving in a few minutes."

"Oooh, Maaaa, alright."

The kids left the kitchen to follow their mother's directives leaving Juliette and Grandville in the dining room alone.

"Hey lover, I loved what you did to me last night, and I am hoping that we can do again real soon," Juliette said in her sexy way.

"I enjoyed you too baby. Sorry I've been neglecting you."

"Grandville you haven't been neglecting me, you are grieving and I understand. Losing Mother Stubbs has been a big blow and I think you've been overdoing it. It's a beautiful day so spend it doing whatever you want. I'm going to keep the kids out of your hair for a while."

Juliette kissed Grandville lightly on the lips, got her purse and the kids and walked out of the house towards her SUV. Soon, Juliette and the kids were gone, and Grandville was all alone with the whispering voices in his head.

He tried to take Juliette's advice and relax, but he couldn't seem to sit still with the voices reminding him of all that he was not. He needed relief, but the only time the voices didn't bother him was when he was sleeping or when he was drinking. Today, he had slept in and wasn't tired, therefore going back to sleep was not an option. So, he decided to sit on the back porch in an attempt to relax.

The porch overlooked a large yard which was very lush and green. It was filled with beautiful flowers, and a slight smell from the roses on the nearby rose bushes blew in from the mild southerly breeze.

Grandville inhaled the scent. Then, he noticed the bushes that framed the backyard, which he kept meticulously trimmed, were growing out of control.

He wanted to do what Juliette had implied; sit still. But, gazing upon the back yard reminded him, since his mother's death, he had neglected more than just his wife and children. The condition of the bushes reminded him, that he had also neglected the up-keep of their home.

The voices continued to whisper to him. So, Grandville decided to try and quiet them by doing what he always did when he wanted to silence them, he started drinking. The Grey Goose Vodka, chased with Cranberry juice tasted refreshing in the summer heat. Grandville sat on the back porch consuming several drinks while waiting for the Vodka to do the trick and quiet the voices.

His wife, nor his family had any idea that he was hearing voices in his head which no one else seemed to hear. Besides, he didn't know how to tell his loved ones what was going on with him. If they knew about the voices would they believe he was crazy? If his job found out would he be terminated from his employment? These were the questions which he pondered while he consumed his drinks.

This time, the Vodka didn't seem to have the same effect on the voices like it had in the past. Instead of the voices becoming quieter, the whispers in his head seemed to get louder. Grandville decided that the best way to deal with the voices was to focus his mind on something else. At that moment, he decided to cut the backyard hedges. It wasn't long before Grandville had his chain saw in hand and plugged in.

As he watched the green limbs fall to the ground he spotted a vision of Gina, his deceased cousin. Gina was dead, and had been for several years. So, when he started seeing Gina in the corners of his mind, he knew the visions were not real and what he was seeing was a figment of his imagination. The voices and the visions had started tormenting him shortly after his mother's death and

Grandville was at a loss as to what to do to make them go away permanently.

He was using the chain saw to cut the hedges and the visions of Gina, when he heard a scream. He realized the scream wasn't in his mind and the voice had come from outside of his head. He looked down and saw red splattered over the green limbs which were lying on the ground. His eyes focused, and he saw his beautiful daughter with a hole in her neck, and he realized he had cut her with the chainsaw.

Grandville dropped the saw and immediately fell to the ground next to his injured child. "Jessica, Daddy is so sorry he hurt you. Please wake up." Grandville sobbed over his unconscious and bleeding daughter. Grandville spotted Juliette running towards him crying and yelling. He couldn't make out her words, and he couldn't quite comprehend what happened.

Juliette and the kids were at the Mall. How could his daughter be lying in front of him bleeding. He was confused and the voices continued to torment him in his moment of grief.

"You're a fraud and you're worthless." The voices whispered. He watched as Juliette ran at top speed towards their house. He couldn't move, and he didn't want to leave Jessica. So, he continued to talk to her, begging her to get up. He was telling her over and over how sorry he was for hurting her. Soon, Juliette had returned with several white towels which she placed against the gaping hole in Jessica's neck. He watched as the towels turned a bright red from Jessica's blood soaking through them.

Grandville was in shock and as he heard the wail of sirens which seem to get closer with each passing second, he couldn't understand exactly what happened. His only daughter was lying in a pool of her own blood and he became incensed. He rarely spoke out loud to the voices as he didn't like to acknowledge their presence, however, at that moment he began to yell at them.

Grandville yelled out at the top of his voice with a whaling scream, "Look what you made me do!!! You made me hurt my baby. Why did you make me do it?"

He didn't notice the look of disbelief on Juliette's face as she watched Grandville carry on a conversation with himself. Juliette took off in a light run when she spotted the police and the ambulance as they pulled into their driveway. Several men in uniform ran to meet Juliette and as she directed them towards where Jessica lay.

The EMS techs ran to Jessica and began trying to treat her wounds, but it wasn't long before they announced Jessica had expired. They said, "There's nothing else we can do Mr. and Mrs. Stubbs. We're so sorry for your loss. Can you tell us what happened?" the policeman sympathetically asked them.

Grandville said, "I killed her. They made me do it." "Who made you do it? There's nobody here but us," the Police Officer said. Grandville ignored the policeman's questions. He began whispering to himself and the police and EMS techs realized they were dealing with a mental health emergency. One of the policeman went over to where Grandville was standing and gently put hand cuffs on his wrists and led him to the police car.

As they led him away, he looked back at his wife and his home, and he wondered if he would ever see either again.

Chapter 2
Locked Up

Grandville had made only one friend at the Oakhill Prison. Oakhill was a private facility which was contracted with the State of Ohio to incarcerate individuals who had been found guilty of a variety of crimes. The prison operated a ward for inmates who admitted that they were mentally ill and voluntarily consented to serving their time in a facility where they could receive treatment.

Montell Jarvis had been living in the prison for one year prior to Grandville's arrival at Oakhill and his cell was located right next door to Grandville's. When Grandville first arrived at the prison it was late in the evening. By the time the institution had processed him and moved him to the special floor specifically for inmates who were mentally ill, there was only one hour left before the lights in the facility were turned off.

Grandville was led to a solitary cell where his wrist and ankle chains were removed. The guard who was an older, middle aged, white man, shoved a scratchy wool blanket and permanently stained sheets into Grandville's arms and then closed the cell door. Grandville noted the only furnishings in his new cell was a bed with a thin mattress which had lumps, a metal toilet, and a small metal sink.

By the time Grandville made up his lumpy little bed he was nearly out of his mind. The voices which sometimes plagued his mind competed with the voices from the inmates in the prison. Montell who was in the cell next door, could hear Grandville's shouting out to the voices inside his head. Montell's soothing words carried to Grandville through the paper thin walls, "It will be okay man. Don't listen to the voices inside your head listen to my voice."

Grandville attempted to focus on his new neighbor's words and over the course of the night the voices in his head began to fade. The next day when it was time for Grandville to leave his cell he was nervous because he didn't know what to expect. He didn't know how his fellow inmates would receive him, because most of what he knew about prison is what he learned from watching television.

Many would assume as an attorney, Grandville would know the system and prison setting, but this was far from the truth. In reality Grandville was a civil attorney. The most he knew about the criminal side of the law is what he had learned in his criminal law and criminal procedure classes in law school and what he saw on the television show *Law and Order* and the old HBO show series *Oz*.

Grandville quickly began to figure out the prison routine. The other inmates on his cell block got to have a shower every Monday and Thursday morning right after breakfast. On Grandville's first full day in the institution he headed down to the showers right after he had eaten one of the worst meals of his life. The eggs which were served with breakfast were literally green and the oatmeal was hard and lumpy. Grandville ate the meal, because he wanted to keep his strength up. He knew if he didn't eat, his body would grow weak and make him prey for those inmates who were abusers.

Each prisoner had been issued a mud brown, flimsy, bare thread robe that buttoned on the side. The inmates were given the robes to keep, and they were to wear them along with the prison issued plastic sandals every time they went to the shower area. Two guards directed each inmate to come out of their cells and to walk in a complete straight line as they were escorted to the shower area. As the prisoners entered the congregate shower stalls they were told to disrobe and to wash themselves. The guards then left the area to stand outside of the shower entrance.

Grandville had been an involuntary patient at the State of Ohio's Psychiatric Hospital for five months prior to arriving at Oakhill when Franklin and his lawyer came to see him. They had reached a plea deal with the Lake County District Attorney's Office.

Grandville would go to Oakhill Prison to be involved in a special program for offenders who had committed violent, heinous acts but were determined to be suffering with a mental illness when the act occurred.

All the inmates in the program voluntarily participated in therapy and other programs aimed at rehabilitation. According to the deal, how much time he served at the facility would depend on his progress in respect to overcoming his mental health issues. In order to be released from Oakhill he would need to convince two separate Psychiatrists that he was sane and no longer a threat to himself or society.

Grandville was no fool, he knew this deal was the best chance he would ever have to one day regaining his freedom, his wife, and his family; so he agreed to the plea deal with no hesitation. His legal team explained to him that he would be moved to Oakhill immediately, but it had taken Grandville more than two days to arrive at the facility. As a result of being moved from different holding cells in various local city jails; he had not taken a shower in days.

He was standing under the spray of the water, thinking about her, with his eyes closed shut, when he felt a presence standing behind him. Grandville opened his eyes to find a large, massive, bald, African American man in his personal space. Grandville tried to control the fear which was threatening to fill every pore of his body, he was tense and rigid as he prepared to fight for his dignity and respect if necessary.

"Hey Sweetie you are one fine thing, look at your cute butt and your wavy hair, my friends call me Big Joe."

"What? You talking to me?" Grandville said.

"I got the feeling that you and I are going to be very good friends," the bald man declared.

As a teenager Grandville had taken years of Tae Kwon Do and self-defense lessons, and he knew how to defend himself, but in that moment he was frozen. He felt as though he was a character in the scene of a very bad prison movie. Before Grandville could speak again or react, a man whom he had never seen before, emerged from the corner of the shower stalls and said, "Joe, knock it off."

"Come on Montell just let me hit it once. He is so pretty and I just want a little taste," Big Joe replied.

"No! Now walk away," yelled the unknown naked man.

Big Joe turned as if he was walking away, but then out of nowhere, he charged the unknown man. The man realized Joe was trying to grab him, and in one fluid motion kicked him in the groin and punched him in the face. Joe was momentarily stunned, but he still managed to reach out and put the unknown man into a massive bear hug while lifting him off the floor. Big Joe screamed out, "I need some ass, maybe I can get some from you!"

Grandville sprang into action and delivered several punches and kicks to Joe's back. The kicks were so powerful Joe immediately dropped the unknown man and turned towards Grandville and said, "I am going to kill you."

Grandville positioned his body into a defensive stance in preparation to defend himself against Joe's attack. Joe reached out to grab Grandville and Grandville delivered a karate chop to a pressure point in Joe's neck, and then a fast front kick to his groin. Joe hit the ground hard and Grandville kicked Joe in his face with all the weight and force in his body. He then stepped around Joe's hulking body to turn his attention to the unknown man who had risked bodily harm to help him.

"Thanks for helping me. Are you okay?" Grandville quickly asked.

The man sprang to his feet and then said, "Come on we have to get away from him before the guards come back." Grandville followed the naked, unknown man to the back of the showers.

"Just stay cool and don't volunteer any information if the guards ask you what happened," said the unknown man.

About three minutes later the water in the showers turned off, and the prisoners were lined up to leave from the shower area. Big Joe's face was visibly bruised. When the guards inquired about what happened to him, he told them that he had slipped and fell in the shower. Grandville could see the awe and respect in his fellow inmate's eyes as he quietly walked in the single file line back to his cell.

Grandville wasn't a very big man as he was only about 5'11 and weighed about 180 pounds, but despite his size, he had shown that he would fight before allowing anyone from the prison to victimize him. Grandville knew how it felt to be a victim, and he vowed a long time ago that he would never let anyone make him feel that way again without a fight.

Grandville was delivered back to his cell to get dressed and prepare for the afternoon count where the prison staff counted each prisoner to ensure each inmate in the institution was accounted for. After the count, the prisoner's cell doors were opened, and the inmates could leave their cells and go to the library or visit other inmates who were also on the unit. Grandville didn't want to go to the library and he did not know anyone at Oakhill, so he went back into his cell to lay on his lumpy little bed and to think about her. He was lost in thoughts of his beloved Juliette when he heard a voice outside of the ones in his head. He opened his eyes to see the unknown man from the shower standing over him.

Grandville's first reaction was to attempt to get off the bed into a fighting stance. He didn't know if the man came in peace or if he had come to try and hurt him.

"I'm not going to try and hurt you. I just wanted to come and introduce myself. My name is Montell Jarvis, and I live in the cell right next door to you," Montell said.

Grandville attempted to relax as his body was in a state of fight or flight. He took a deep breath and said quietly, "Hi. My name is Grandville Stubbs. I want to thank you for helping me out earlier."

"You're welcome. I don't know if you remember me but we've met before. You used to do my sister's taxes," said Montell.

"What's your sister's name?" Grandville asked.

"Amanda Landis."

"Of course I remember Amanda. How is she doing?" Grandville inquired.

"She's doing great. She's making crazy money and her daycare center is remaining full," Montell responded.

"That's great, I'm glad to hear it. Please tell your sister I said hello when you talk to her again," Grandville said.

"I'll be sure to do that. She comes to visit me here from time to time. Grandville, I know when you were on the outside you were a big time corporate attorney and a tax whiz, and it's my hope you were also a chess player," Montell said in a questioning tone.

"Yes, I know how to play chess. Although I don't think I am very good at it, but I do know how to play," responded Grandville.

"Do you know Chess Notation?" Montell asked.

"I understand its concept, but to be honest, I have never played using it before."

"It is pretty simple. The rows on the chess board are numbered from 1 to 8 horizontally and A thru H vertically. Basically, each square on the board has a corresponding number and letter," Montell said.

"Okay, it seems like you're really into Chess," replied Grandville.

"It helps pass the time. I'm hopeful you and I can play sometime. I'll teach you chess notation so even at night, after lights are out, we can still play," said Montell.

"Okay that sounds alright," replied Grandville.

"I have a few connections here, and I have arranged for you to have a complete chess set delivered to your cell. You should get it tomorrow," Montell stated.

"Okay, but if the board costs you any money, please allow me to reimburse you for what you pay and for your trouble," said Grandville.

"No that won't be necessary. You probably haven't played in a while, so I'm going to have to take it easy on you. I can teach you chess notation while you become reacquainted with the game," Montell said.

"Okay," replied Grandville.

"Grandville, I really want to thank you for getting Big Joe off of me. A few months ago he and I got into an altercation, and I had to beat him down. I can't stand how he tries to intimidate the younger, weaker inmates. He must have really been into you, to try and violate you in front of everyone. That hasn't been his style since I beat him up the last time he attempted to attack an innocent kid in the shower. Now days he usually only inflicts his sexual perversions on the willing, and please believe me, there are plenty of guys in here who are willing. You know what it means to be on the down low. Well, here in Oakhill, some of these brothers are right out in the open, but act like they haven't been switch hitting when their wives and girlfriends come to visit. I'm so glad that you know karate, and you are not afraid to fight, because if you hadn't intervened Big Joe may have tried to rape me. Then, he would have been the second man I would have killed," Montell angrily stated.

From the time Grandville arrived at Oakhill, he and Montell had become very good friends. They were both from Cleveland, were close to the same age, and they knew many of the same people. Over a game of chess Montell shared his story regarding how he found himself to be housed in a prison.

"In the outside world I was a police officer. I like you, am married and I have a teenage son. You know how it is when you become a husband and a father. I was working hard trying to provide for my family, and I admit that I put in a lot of hours, closing cold cases and working undercover. I wanted as much overtime as possible so I often volunteered to work late. I tried to give my family a comfortable lifestyle. I wanted them to have some of the finer things in life.

When you work "Vice", you get to see the seediest side of America, and you also get to witness what happens to the weak by the vultures who prey on the innocent. I wanted my son to be strong and able to protect himself, so I put him in martial arts. Even though I was busy, I made time to take him to his classes and to pick him up. I also went to his tournaments and encouraged him.

Monty was never really any good at team sports like football or basketball, but he seemed to excel at martial arts and quickly moved up in rank. Monty was always a smart, quiet, sensitive kid, who did well in school, but didn't have a lot of friends. It didn't seem to bother him as much when he became friends with the other kids from his karate class.

One day I was working an undercover assignment that ended early. I had talked to my wife earlier in the day, and she had indicated that Monty had his martial arts class. She was going to drop him off so that she could run errands. I decided since I got off early, I would surprise Monty and come to his class. I am the one who got a surprise.

When I arrived at the building where the classes were held it looked like the place was deserted. I saw Eric, who was Monty's karate instructor's car in the parking lot, but his seemed to be the only one there. I thought maybe Monty's class got cancelled, but I decided to go on ahead inside. The door was open, but no one was in the front room where the class was generally held.

I was getting ready to leave when I spotted Monty's book bag propped up against the wall. I walked through the back door to where the bathroom was located and I heard moans. When I opened the bathroom door I saw my twelve year old son gagging on Eric's penis while that motherfucker ejaculated in his mouth.

That is the last thing I remember before I woke up in the State Psychiatric Hospital. I have been told that I pulled my son off of Eric, and blew Eric's brains against the walls with my service revolver, right in front of Monty, who is to this day traumatized. The doctors in here say I suffered what is known as an episode of Brief Psychotic Disorder. I know I should be sorry for what I did, but honestly I feel absolutely no remorse. I don't remember a damn thing. But I do know, I gave that motherfucker an ending, but his was not a happy one.

The bastard deserved to die, he was a cancer who needed to be cut out of society so the rest of us can survive. I trusted Eric with my most precious commodity, my only son. I was out busting my ass trying to put monsters in jail, but I left my only child with a demon. I am disappointed with myself for not seeing what he was before he hurt my son.

My wife hasn't divorced me yet, but I have a sinking suspicion she will very soon. She's a very physical person, and the lack of sex has to be driving her crazy. I'm sure she's getting her bump and grind on with someone. She still comes to see me at least twice a month but she has grown distant.

Now, whenever we are together, our whole conversation seems to be centered around Monty and how bad he is doing with his nightmares and how he is doing in therapy. I can't help him, because I'm in here, but as the Bible says, this too shall pass," Montell stated.

Grandville admired Montell even more after he heard his story. Even though Montell did not remember killing Eric, he stood up for his son. Grandville knew how it felt to have your innocence stripped away. He often fantasied about how his life would have been different if someone had come to his defense earlier. Grandville suspected that as Monty grew older, he would become grateful for the love Montell had for him. Montell's life was destroyed when his mind snapped, and he killed Eric. However, with what he witnessed Eric doing to his son, Grandville suspected just about anyone, including himself would have done the very same thing.

Grandville had shared much of his story with Montell, but he could not bring himself to share everything, because some of his story was too shameful and much too personal to repeat.

Chapter 3
It's So Hard to Say Goodbye to Yesterday

Juliette Stubbs looked at the wedding photos which were displayed on the mantel above her family room fireplace. She began to reflect back to a time when she and her husband Grandville Stubbs were happy and the envy of their friends.

Then, the phone rang, and she did not hesitate to pick it up.

"Hello," Juliette said into a cordless phone.

"Hey Juliette," Samantha Trunk said.

"Hello Samantha," Juliette replied.

"How are you?"

"I was thinking about him again. Our wedding was one of the most beautiful days of our life. Samantha, we were so in love with each other."

"Juliette, and you still are. You just have to help each other through the good times and the bad times."

"I'm not sure what's going to happen to us."

"Listen, that's why I'm calling to check in on you. I want to make sure we are still on for dinner tomorrow evening."

"Yes, it's going to take everything I have inside of me to not break down, but I'll make it."

"I know. It's been our tradition to go out to dinner on the Anniversary, and I think it will be good for you to get out the house. Tara is going to go with us."

"Okay", Juliette said as she looked down at the number on the phone's caller ID.

"Tara said, she can have Tabitha babysit the children while we are out. I'm not taking no for an answer," Samantha declared.

"I don't need Tabitha to babysit, because the kids are in Columbus with my mother. What did you have in mind?" Juliette asked.

"Well, I was thinking we could go down to Shooters. It's supposed to be 77 degrees tomorrow evening and clear. It will be relaxing to sit by the river and have dinner. We can watch the sunset and chill," Samantha replied.

"Okay, but I want Greta to come. I don't want her to be alone tomorrow either," Juliette stated.

Samantha sucked in her breath but for once she held her tongue. It was not lost on Juliette the level of disdain which Samantha seemed to hold for Greta, but what always puzzled Juliette is why Samantha disliked Greta so much.

Greta was Grandville's twin sister, and in the past nine months had relocated home to Cleveland from California after enduring a nasty divorce. Greta had been married to Rayshawn Robinson, a Black Basketball Association (BBA) Superstar who is one of the LA's number one players. Greta did not have any children of her own and with the exception of Grandville, Juliette and their children, they were the only family Greta had who are still living. There was no way Juliette would let her be alone on the Anniversary, as she also needed a distraction from the memories.

"Okay, what choice do I have? If I want to hang out with you, I have to deal with her, but you know that I can't stand her. Some yellow chicks think they are all that," Samantha replied.

"What time are you guys coming to pick us up?" Juliette inquired.

"We'll be there at about 6:00 PM. That way we can have a cocktail before we leave. I'm going to need one, maybe even two if I have to deal with Greta," Samantha said.

"Okay, I will see you tomorrow evening," Juliette stated.

After Juliette disconnected the call, she went back to gazing at her wedding pictures and reminiscing about her past life. She looked breathtaking in her off-white formal wedding gown, complete with a long train which stretched behind her, and it gave her the appearance of a Princess.

Grandville was dashing in his black tuxedo, accented with an off-white vest; her very own Prince who gazed lovingly into her eyes. Another Anniversary was almost upon her, and she couldn't help but remember what she once had and what she so wanted again.

Many would think she was out of her mind and as crazy as her husband, if they knew what she was thinking. She missed her husband and wanted him back despite what he had done. She dreamed of his caress daily, and she had only let one man touch her in an intimate way since her husband had been away. The guilt which she felt for participating in the act of infidelity was crushing her heart.

Juliette thought about the first time she had laid eyes on Grandville. They met at a small coffee house located down the street from the Cleveland Law School. She was having a cup of coffee and going over the cases which she had briefed for her corporations class when she noticed two attractive brothers walk into the door.

One of the guys was about 5 feet 10 inches tall, with light brown skin, hazel brown eyes, and wavy dark brown hair which was tinged lightly at the corners with gray. He was looking at her with such an intense stare that she suddenly felt self-conscious. She looked down at her notes and attempted to ignore his eyes as they seemed to bore into her soul. A few minutes later, she felt him before she saw him walk up to her table.

"Excuse me miss, but do you have the time?" the unknown man asked.

Juliette looked down at her watch and replied, "It is 4:45."

"Thank you. I couldn't help but notice the corporations law book that you're studying. Are you at the law school?" the man inquired.

"Yes," Juliette replied.

"What year are you?" the man questioned.

"I am a second year night student," Juliette responded.

"Excuse me, I don't mean to be rude, but my name is Grandville Stubbs, and my friend who is up at the counter is Franklin Lowe. May I ask your name?" the man inquired.

"My name is Juliette Jamison," Juliette replied.

Grandville reached out and shook her hand. The electricity which shot through her body from his touch almost made her pull her hand away. Grandville felt it too, and it made him look deeply into her eyes. Their connection was broken when Franklin walked over from the counter with two cups in his hand. He was a tall, deep chocolate colored brother whose wavy hair was cut in a low fade which framed a handsome face and a beautiful smile.

"Hey Grandville, I got your tea. Are you ready to go?" Franklin asked.

"Sure, but before we go let me introduce you to Juliette. She's a second year student at the law school. Juliette this is Franklin," Grandville stated.

"It is nice to meet you. When I was in law school, they didn't have students who looked like you." Grandville looked at him straight in the face.

"Grandville, we have to go now or you are going to be late. Don't you have to be there at 5?" Franklin questioned.

"Juliette, I hope to see you again very soon," Grandville said. Then he turned around and was gone.

Juliette watched him as he quickly walked out of the coffee house. She wondered exactly who Grandville Stubbs was and why he had affected her the way that he did. During her life Juliette had dated a lot of men. She was considered to be a beautiful woman. She knew that her unconventional style, along with her shapely body and her blemish free mahogany skin, magnetized her to have a lot of attention from the opposite sex. Juliette was young, attractive, and educated which was a mix that gave her an opportunity to meet some of Cleveland, Ohio's most eligible bachelors. She had never heard of Grandville Stubbs before and tried to forget how his touch had affected her while she continued on with briefing her cases.

At 7 PM, Juliette walked into her tax law class after already having attended her 5:30 corporations class. At the age of 26, Juliette had a Master Degree in Social Work from the prestigious Case Western Reserve University's Mandel School. Now, she was more than half way finished with her law school education. She was taking tax law and corporations as two of her law school electives, because it was her plan to run a non-profit association aimed at helping those with social problems - specifically children. Juliette wanted to know everything which she could about these subjects to ensure that she understood how to keep her endeavor afloat when and if she was given an opportunity. Juliette was a very bright young woman. Tax law was no longer on the Ohio Bar Exam. Juliette had taken the class anyway, because she knew without money her ideas would never become a reality. She wanted to know all that she could about how to use the US Tax Code to her advantage.

When Juliette walked into her class, she was shocked to see Grandville Stubbs at the front of the class sitting with her professor. When he saw her come into the room he smiled, and she experienced the same feelings which she had felt earlier when she met him. She wondered if she would be able to concentrate on the tax law material with Grandville so close by. Juliette felt an immediate and overwhelming attraction to Grandville and she didn't know why. He was attractive, but he wasn't drop dead gorgeous. Her thoughts were interrupted by her professor's loud booming voice.

"Class. I would like to introduce you to Grandville Stubbs. He was one of my many students when I taught at Cornell School of Law. Mr. Stubbs turned down several lucrative offers of employment on Wall Street to return back to Cleveland, which is where he was born and bred to work for McPherson, Waterhouse and Smith. He specializes in the area of Corporate Tax Law. Mr. Stubbs fancies himself as a Professor in training, and I thought it would be fun and educational to have him come in and teach today's class. I would like the whole class to join me in giving Mr. Stubbs a huge applause."

Juliette couldn't believe it. Grandville Stubbs was an Attorney. She wondered how old he was as it was virtually impossible for her to tell. He had gray at his temples, but his skin was smooth and unlined. She could tell that he would look even more sexy and distinguished as he grew older. Juliette realized that she had not been paying attention to Grandville's lecture as she was so caught up in wondering about him. She shook her head ever so slightly and attempted to focus on his words in relationship to tax law.

Soon the class was over, and the primarily Caucasian class was applauding Grandville's lecture. Juliette was gathering her books and notes to depart the classroom when Grandville walked over to her desk.

"Juliette, do you have a moment?" Grandville asked.

"Sure," Juliette replied.

"I would be most appreciative if you would have a cup of coffee with me. We could go back over to the coffee shop where we met earlier today if you would like? This was my first time giving a law school lecture, and I was hoping you could honestly critic my delivery," Grandville asked.

Juliette couldn't bring herself to go home before talking more in depth with Grandville. She had run into him twice in one day. She felt the Universe was trying to tell her something, and she didn't want to turn a deaf ear to the calling. Soon, Juliette was seated across from Grandville in the very same coffee house which they had met in earlier during the day. However, the two of them didn't talk about Grandville's lecture. Instead, he spent their time trying to get to know her better. He was asking questions about her likes and dislikes, what she enjoyed doing in her spare time and places that she always wanted to go. They made plans to see each other on the upcoming weekend. Soon afterwards the two became inseparable.

Chapter 4

Set Adrift On Memory Bliss

Grandville and Juliette made plans to go to the movies on Friday, and she was so excited when the phone rang and it was Grandville.

"Hi, are you ready?"

"Yes, how long before you get here?"

"I'm two minutes away."

"Oh, let me grab a jacket."

"See you in a minute."

Juliette felt herself letting go and her guards were down all the way. There was no turning around for her either. She had been in love before and at this time in her life she was not afraid to love again.

They had planned to go see a movie. She had not been to a movie theater on a date in a very long time and was excited. As she moved closer to cuddle up with him while watching the movie, she realized his warmth and tenderness with her. It felt nice to touch his arm, and she was so into feeling his body energy next to hers, she got lost in his touch.

Even when Grandville made love to her, he caressed her whole body, and he made her feel adored and worshiped. He was a man of character, and he had proven this in so many ways. When she was with him he reinforced the fact that he could be counted on.

Her son, Jabari's father Jack, had been her first love, but the feelings she had for him paled in comparison to the love that she felt for Grandville. Her love for Jack was borne out of lust. She met Jack at a nightclub when she was a junior in college, and her attraction to him was initially based on his extremely good looks. The two had very little in common besides their instant almost animal sexual attraction for each other.

Jack had a quiet magnetism which drew people to him and she was no different. When she was with him she was like a moth to a flame. He was a bad boy, the kind you brought home to your parents when you were ready for them to know that you had become a woman, in every sense of the word.

Juliette's plan was to use Jack to become more skilled in the art of lovemaking. She wasn't very experienced but what she lacked in knowledge, she made up with enthusiasm. Jack was an exciting teacher and she was a willing student. What she didn't expect was to get caught up in her feelings. Jack made her body feel amazing; things that she had never felt before. The more time they spent together in bed pleasing each other, the more she learned about him, and she couldn't help herself from falling in love with him.

Jack had been removed from his parents, who were both heroin addicts, when he was five years old. While growing up, he had been placed in numerous foster homes until he ended up in a residential facility where he lived until he aged out of care. He was then placed into an independent living program where the County provided him with his own apartment and a small monthly allowance.

Jack realized early on that he wasn't going to college. He had no money, no family, and no supports. Plus, he didn't get the educational foundation many of his peers received because he had been moved around so much. Jack had common sense and learned his talent was cutting hair and with the State of Ohio's tuition assistance and his hard work, he graduated from barber college. After he finished school Jack was able to obtain his Barber's Certification which gave him the ability to cut hair legally for money in the State of Ohio. His dream was to own his own barber shop. He was laid back, engaging and talented and his customers loved him and his business grew.

Juliette had been the first constant in Jack's life and when Juliette found out that she was pregnant, she thought that he would be thrilled, but instead he was angry.

"I don't want any kids right now, so you're going to have to get rid of it," Jack angrily declared.

"Jack, I cannot believe you don't want your child after all you've been through," She snapped back at him.

"I just opened my barbershop, and I can't afford any distractions which could derail my dreams. This just isn't a good time for me to have a kid,"

Juliette was more than heartbroken, because she had fallen in love with Jack and wanted to have his child. She had respect for how he had made it in the world on his own without any family assistance and very little support.

She wanted to give him a present, one that could only be given by a woman to a man when she carries his seed. She wanted to give him the gift of his own family and to know what it meant to live in a world where he was bonded to someone by blood. Juliette wanted him to experience the feeling of having someone which he could count on besides himself.

"I didn't plan this pregnancy."

"Well, I didn't either. That's why you have to have an abortion as soon as possible."

She learned from her doctor that her birth control pills had been rendered ineffective after she had taken antibiotics for a bronchial infection.

Juliette was about to graduate from college and start her master program, and having a baby wasn't in her plans. Sometimes God has a greater plan for your life, and Juliette believed the Lord had a plan for her unborn child too.

"I am having this baby with or without you. I didn't plan to get pregnant, and as you know I was on birth control. I agree that right now is not the best time for me to have a baby, but for some reason the Lord believes it is the right time," Juliette shouted.

"Now you want to bring the Lord into this. It wasn't anything Godly about what you did to me to find yourself in the position to be knocked up," Jack sarcastically replied.

"I agree. I sure as hell didn't get myself pregnant. That was something you did all on your own, and I am not having an abortion so you can just forget about it," Juliette angrily stated.

"I can't make you have one, but I can let you know that if you decide to do this, I am going to step out of the picture," Jack advised.

"It sounds like you are saying that you don't plan to help me through my pregnancy?" Juliette questioned.

"Look Juliette, I don't want my kid to get put through the things I had to go through when I was young."

"You are not the only one who has gone through hard times as a kid."

"I just want to be established financially and married before bringing a child into the world. Neither one of us is ready for a child right now," Jack explained.

"Well I suggest you get ready, because like it or not, you will be a father in approximately seven months," Juliette stated.

From that moment on, things were never the same again for Juliette and Jack. By the time she was six months pregnant their romantic relationship was over. When she went into labor her mother phoned Jack who came to the hospital and helped her deliver Jabari, and he also signed the birth certificate. Juliette looked into Jack's eyes shortly after she delivered their son and saw the pain, regret and love he had for her and their new child. But, she was not moved, because she was hurt that Jack bailed on her when she was most vulnerable.

In almost every animal species the male protects the female when she is pregnant, and she would never forgive Jack for abandoning her when she needed him the most. In her mind he had proven that he would always jump ship when a crisis arose. She wanted a man who would be there when things got rough. She knew that in life there would always be storms, and she wanted a helpmate who would be there to help her navigate through them. Jack's actions proved that he was not that man.

After Jabari was born, she treated Jack with indifference, letting him know their relationship could never be what it once was. She never got the chance to forgive Jack, because two months after giving birth to their son, she buried him. Jack was murdered in front of his barber shop by local drug dealers, because he had asked them to stop selling drugs in front of his barbershop. When Jack died, he did so alone, and the only family he had to mourn his loss was she and Jabari.

Grandville was the first man Juliette dated seriously since Jack. She accepted many dates, but she had not let anyone touch her intimately for more than three years until she started seeing Grandville exclusively. His lovemaking was slow and intense and his touch was very different from how Jack used to touch her.

Before Juliette, Grandville had experienced a string of bad relationships. When he met Juliette he was only 30, and he had already been married and divorced. He was glad that he did not have any children with his ex, but he was starting to long for them.

He would see other men with their kids and his arms would ache. He realized that he was getting older and he had grown tired of the dating game. Grandville was looking for someone he could count on, who wanted a family and someone who was willing to work hard so they both could advance. He had started to re-evaluate his choice in women, and had put a lot of thought into where his marriage went wrong.

His ex-wife was not educated and had no interest in anything except cooking, cleaning, and catering to him; and trying to figure out ways to spend his money. He realized, he wanted a woman who would take care of him and his family, but he needed a woman who also had her own ambitions and interests.

Grandville's and his ex-wife were only married a year before their relationship completely fell apart. She became unhappy due to his long work hours. He tried to explain to her he needed to work long hours so he could advance them financially. But, her complaints became louder and more frequent. He doubted if he ever loved her, but instead she made him feel needed. He had started dating his ex-wife right before he graduated from law school and thought she would help him to complete his picture of success: beautiful wife, white picket fence, and 2.5 kids would fulfill his portrait of the American Dream. Instead, what he thought would be his dream life was in reality a nightmare, and he realized he should never had married his ex-wife. Grandville didn't love her or respect her, and the combination proved to be a recipe for failure.

Grandville had been divorced and dating for the past four years, and was a lot more careful not to get caught up in the superficial. In the words of the R & B group Bell, Biv, Devoe, he didn't easily fall for a big butt and a smile. However, he was anxious to find a woman who he could plant roots with; someone he could build something with.

When he met Juliette he instantly felt like she might be the one that he had been waiting for. He was looking for a mate who was beautiful, inside and out. He also wanted a woman who was educated, trust worthy and loyal.

On his second date, Grandville set out to woo Juliette and treat her the way a woman who is both beautiful and special should be treated. He took her to lunch at an exclusive restaurant. He knew that his attraction could be intense, and he did not want to scare her off. That's why he had decided to take it slow and to take her to lunch on their first date.

During lunch, he learned that she had a two year old son, and the child's father had been murdered by street drug dealers when he asked them to stop selling their illegal product in front of his barbershop. Juliette explained, she and her son's father had broken up shortly after she had become pregnant, but she still felt grief due to his death. Her son's father grew up in a residential facility, and he had been removed from his parents when he was very young. Therefore, Juliette had to carry the burden of raising her son alone with little financial assistance from social security and no support from her son's father's family.

Juliette was working full time, attending law school, and raising her young son with the help of her mother and extended family. She was a woman of character and his attraction for her grew beyond her beautiful face and outstanding body. Once he learned her story, he grew to also respect her.

Juliette told him about her work as a therapist in a residential facility for teenage girls, and he could tell that she really enjoyed what she was doing. Juliette was funny and passionate. He admired how much she seemed to care; she had heart and she was tough. She was the kind of women he needed by his side when things went wrong, and during his short life he had learned, despite the most careful planning, things will always go wrong.

Finding out she worked so hard made him want to make her life more comfortable. He could tell she was a woman who believed that she had to do it all and he wanted to take care of her. He wanted her to know she didn't have to be a superwoman, because he wanted to be the man who would help her achieve her goals, whatever they might be.

After the lunch date, Grandville invented excuses to see her again. He took her to the movies and he took her and her son, Jabari, to the zoo and to the Cedar Point amusement park where they spent time together like a family. He focused all of his attention on cultivating his relationship with her and advancing his career, so he could give her and her son the life that he felt they deserved. He really liked her son, Jabari, as he was a cute little rambunctious boy who looked a lot like Juliette.

At the beginning of his relationship with Juliette, Grandville had just started his own tax preparedness business with Franklin, who was both a licensed Attorney and a certified public accountant.

Franklin was also one of his best friends and fraternity brothers. Together he and Franklin made a lot of money doing taxes for their families, friends, and small businesses. For Grandville, this was his side hustle. But for Franklin this was a full-time gig and together the two of them had a thriving tax practice. Grandville used the money he made from this venture, along with the money he had saved from his quarterly bonuses for his work at the law firm. He invested his savings in a startup dot.com which specialized in Android technology.

Grandville had done his research and felt strongly that smartphones and tablets would be the next big thing. He held onto his shares for several months, and then sold them at the height of the market just as android technology and smart phone development exploded. As a result, he made close to two million dollars in profit.

Grandville was a smart man. He knew money like this could be spent quickly if he did not focus his priorities on smart investing. So, he decided to put the majority of the money in a trust. He made a decision to use only the interest generated on the money and to never touch the principal. He continued to live in the two bedroom apartment which he was renting and decided to keep his old car. He told no one, including Juliette, about his windfall, and he decided to maintain his lifestyle with very few upgrades.

Juliette didn't seem to mind his long work hours, because she was also busy attending law school, working and caring for her young son. Grandville did notice, no matter how busy they both were, when he and Juliette did get together, they spent quality time. Together, they developed a routine. Juliette's mother didn't work, and she loved having her grandson around. So, on Friday nights after Juliette hung out with her best friend Samantha, she spent the night at his apartment with him. On Saturday mornings, he would wake her up with breakfast in bed, and then she would go and study at the law school.

On Saturday evenings, he would take Juliette and Jabari to dinner. Sometimes they would watch movies or just play around doing nothing but hanging out together.

On Sundays, she and Jabari would sometimes attend Mass with Grandville. He also went to her church with her a few times, but he hated the long service, and privately admitted to Juliette that those parishioners who got filled with the Holy Spirit during the service scared him.

Grandville's church was different from the one Juliette attended; it was quiet, solemn and ritualistic. Also, the service never lasted more than one hour and fifteen minutes, and the time that the service began and ended was convenient for him. He was raised Catholic, and attended Catholic schools until he graduated from high school. As a child, he had thought about becoming a priest, but quickly abandoned this thought when he found out that priests must take a vow of celibacy. The church he attended had many black parishioners. So, the church had praise dancers and a pretty good choir which put a soulful twist on the quiet songs located in the hymn books.

Grandville felt comfortable with the religion of Catholicism, he found peace in the repetition of it all. He understood the rules and he knew what was expected of him. As he grew older and learned more about science he wondered if God even existed. He felt the stories in the Bible were put there to remind people, they should treat people right and with respect because that is what separates us as people from other animals. He knew right from wrong, and he tried to always do the right thing. However, he was human and that meant sometimes he made mistakes.

His secret about how much he was worth would be one of many which he kept from his beloved. He now regretted and viewed this as a mistake. He should have trusted his instinct and told her the truth right before they got married. At the time, he made the decision, he felt that he was doing the right thing. In his mind his motivations were pure. He wanted to be one hundred percent certain Juliette wanted him strictly for himself, and he didn't want the money to become a distraction.

After he and Juliette had been dating for about six months, she decided she wanted to buy a house. Juliette was fearful that when she graduated from law school, she would be denied a mortgage due to her high student loans. She felt that it would be prudent to purchase her home before she graduated from law school. As luck would have it, she found a home which needed work and was being sold by the owner who lived in another state and was unable to take care of it. The owner was looking for someone to assume the mortgage on the home and was giving all the principal paid on the home to whomever purchased it.

The five bedroom, three full and two half baths, brick colonial house was located in Willoughby Hills, Ohio. The house was on the border of Cuyahoga County in nearby Lake County but was only about twenty-five minutes from Downtown Cleveland, Ohio by freeway. The neighborhood boasted an excellent school system, and the property sat on an acre of land offering privacy from her neighbors.

The house had a finished recreation room, an attic with a kitchenette, and a full bathroom, which meant she could rent it out to a college student if she ever needed money. Juliette was required to put down $700, and her mortgage was less than the money she was paying to rent the small house which she and Jabari had been residing in. The home was very large and had more space then she and Jabari needed, but she wanted a home that would grow with her. She also wanted to have enough space for her numerous relatives who might find themselves in need of temporary shelter.

When Juliette approached Grandville about buying the home she did so with the request that Grandville act as her Attorney regarding the matter. Grandville was so impressed by her drive to better her and her son's situation, he decided to do much more for her. The first thing he did was ensure the home had no liens or other encumbrances attached to it. Once he learned the property was free and clear except for the mortgage she was trying to assume, he advised Juliette that if the property's plumbing, electrical, structure and foundation were in good shape, the property may be a good investment for which to proceed.

Juliette brought in professionals who determine the home's structure, plumbing, electrical, furnace, and water heater were in good workable condition. When Juliette's credit was determined to be strong enough to buy the home, Grandville prepared all of the transfer paperwork, and refused the money she offered him as payment for his legal services. He also refused her request that he see the home prior to her completing the purchase. Grandville wanted Juliette to know that he trusted her judgment, so he decided to wait until she actually owned the home to see it.

When the home transferred into Juliette's name, Grandville accompanied her so he could see the house for the very first time. As Juliette had reported, the home needed a lot of cosmetic work, but he was impressed with the home, as it was a rare find that she had gotten for a low price. As Grandville toured the home, he wondered if the home had hard wood floors underneath the carpet. He could see beautiful moldings, leaded built in cabinets and architecture which could not be replicated in today's new homes. Much of what made the home special and unique was hidden behind layers of paint.

Grandville emerged from the house after he finished touring it and joined Juliette in her new backyard. "Juliette, you were right. This house does need a lot of work but all in all you got a great deal on this property. I am proud of you, you did real good here," Grandville honestly stated. Juliette gushed as she basked in his compliment.

"I took two weeks off from my job. Right now I'm on a short summer break from the law school."

"What are your plans?"

"I want to paint the inside from top to bottom and clean the place up so me and Jabari can move in."

"Yes, a good paint job and a little cosmetic work here and there, and the place will be beautiful."

"I can't afford to pay the rent where I am staying at now and the mortgage on this place, so I'm on a very tight timeline. My two brothers are going to help me and my mom said she would also help," Juliette said.

"Well, guess what. . . . I'm going to help you too."

"Oh, Grandville. I greatly appreciate your offer."

"The Independence Day holiday is coming up, and I took three weeks off from my job at the law firm."

"Really . . ."

"Also, Franklin and I have closed our tax office until November. So, I am all yours. I suggest we start by having you pick out what colors you want in each room. Also let me give this to you before I forget," Grandville stated.

Grandville reached into his pocket and pulled out a folded receipt. He put it in into her hands and then said, "I paid the conveyance taxes for you and please don't insult me by suggesting you will pay me back. Consider it an early birthday present."

"But my birthday is not until the end of January, and it is only the end of June," Juliette replied.

"Juliette I know when your birthday is. I love you and I want to take some of the stress off, so let me," Grandville said.

"Okay but you know that you are ruining me for anyone else," Juliette playfully stated.

"That is my plan precisely," Grandville teased back.

What Grandville failed to tell Juliette was that he possessed a hidden talent. He was practically a master carpenter. He single handily could do just about everything associated with fixing up her home. Grandville spent his whole three week vacation with Juliette and her family working on the inside of her house.

The original kitchen in the property was old and dated, so Grandville installed new cabinets, counter tops, and put in a new kitchen floor tile using his own money. He convinced her to allow him to replace the kitchen by telling her, they would work out a repayment plan later.

Even after she returned to work and school, he continued spending virtually all day and night working on her house. He helped her brothers paint the inside of her new home from top to bottom. Then, after seeing the wood floors under the carpet in the family room and living room were in good condition, he removed the carpet and sanded and stained them and they gleamed.

By the time Juliette and Jabari moved into their new home, it was very beautiful. Her mother was very impressed with Grandville. She had met him on several occasions, but she had never spent any extended time with him until he helped to fix up Juliette's house. She couldn't get over the fact that he spent his whole vacation working on Juliette's endeavor.

She was at her mother's house visiting when her mother said, "That guy Grandville that you're dating is a real man."

"Mom, you're falling for him too?" Juliette giggled.

"He seems to be in love with you, because only a man in love would put that much time and work into fixing up your house."

"You make a good point."

"I hope you hold onto him because he seems like the whole package. He is very easy on the eyes and seems to be financially secure and educated."

"Mom, I have waited such a long time to find a man like Grandville. He's everything I've ever wanted and more."

"Also, he knows how to do repair work, and his actions have saved you thousands of dollars."

"Mom I love him, but I'm taking our relationship day by day. He seems to be a man of his word, and he is very good to both me and Jabari but I am still a little hesitant.

"Don't let this man slip out of your hands I tell you. Another women will snatch him up so fast it will make your head swim."

"You know what happened with Jack. I question if I am a good judge of character when it comes to romance and maybe what I think I see in Grandville is only what I want to see," Juliette confided.

"Girl I always taught you to look at what people do, not necessarily what they say. Actions speak a hell of a lot louder than words.

"But, I am not looking at the work he put into the house. I'm looking at his heart too."

"This man did all of your home transactions for free. He gave up his whole vacation to fix up your new house using his own money, so that you and your son would be comfortable when you moved into it. I say his actions indicate that he is in love with you. I think that you are a great judge of character, because you did damn good when you brought him home," her mother declared.

"Okay, okay. . . I am holding on to Grandville and will never let him go. I think I'm in love again." Juliette's mother looked at her with a slight smile, and only hoped her daughter had enough sense not to lose the love of her life.

Chapter 5

Shackles (Praise You)

Grandville Stubbs looked out of the bars of his small cell. His body was rigid and tense with adrenaline as the voice in his head whispered the same thought it did every day for the past almost three years. "Maybe today would be the day I will hear from her. Maybe I will receive confirmation from a letter, a visit, or some other communication. I need to know my previous life wasn't a dream - that what we once shared wasn't a figment of my broken imagination. Why did this have to happen to me?" He said out loud, as he found himself talking to himself again.

Later, as he was lying on his lumpy little bed, Grandville closed his eyes and began dreaming of green grass, a lush golf course … and of her standing in the distance. He took in a deep breath and could almost remember the smell of a soft summer breeze in the air. He could almost feel the heat of the sun beating on his skin while playing golf. He closed his eyes tighter, and there he was, transformed, sitting next to her in Utopia in the VIP Room of the clubhouse. She was with him. Her beautiful dark mahogany skin, her straight white teeth, her full perfect shaped lips, her long soft flowing hair and oval shaped eyes with long lashes.

"Stubbs," Emerson one of the prison guards at Oakhill called out. His fantasy was abruptly interrupted and without a warning Grandville had to slip back to the present and the lumpy bed that held his lithe body. His mind was still a little drowsy from the deep state of his imagination and clear visions which he was interacting with before he heard his name called in the distance.

"The nurse is here with your medication," Officer Emerson stated.

Grandville got off of his bed and walked to the cell door. He put his hands through the bars so that Emerson could slip the handcuffs on his wrists and open the cell door which trapped his body away from the rest of the world. The nurse, obviously new to the detail, looked him up and down, appraising him from head to toe. Noticing his light brown skin, his wavy salt and pepper hair, and light brown hazel eyes. It was not lost on her that the man standing before her didn't look like a man who should be serving time in a penal institution due to psychiatric problems. With the exception of the mud brown jumpsuit and haggard expression, he looked more like a successful stockbroker or a banker.

Grandville took the cup filled with medication from the nurse's outstretched hands and swallowed the pills without the benefit of water. The nurse took the cup from him and he stepped back into his cell. The medication helped to stop the demons from consuming his brain and taking over his body. It quieted the voices in his mind that commanded him to do terrible things.

Grandville laid back down on his bed again and glanced at the calendar which he kept on the sparse dingy wall. His mind, which was sometimes jumbled and confused with voices, noted that the next day he would have to deal with the "Anniversary." This was another reminder of all that had went wrong with his life and with his mind. It all would have been too much to bear if it wasn't for the faith he had in her. He willed himself to believe after all of this time she would grant him the opportunity to reveal himself to her. He knew that he had committed a most unthinkable sin, but what they had once shared was so beautiful and so real, despite his crime, he felt one day she would come to him and allow him to explain what was almost inexplicable.

The thought was not lost on Grandville that Anniversaries are supposed to be a time of remembrance, a time of celebration. What had occurred could not be celebrated; should not be remembered, but it also could not be forgotten; particularly in his damaged mind. The Anniversary was important, because it signified exactly what he had lost.

On that warm, humid, sultry day he had completely lost his mind and then his daughter. But, his actions were the catalyst to him regaining some sense of sanity, because it forced him to receive the help which he so desperately needed. He would give anything to be insane again. If this would somehow bring back his daughter who was a little miniature of her mother. He adored her, because he helped to make her, and in his heart he felt that he had given her the very best of him. However, he could never truly forgive himself for what he had done - for what he had taken. He knew, his request to the love of his life was unrealistic. Why would she come to visit him in his small private hell? She was already in a hell of her own which had been provided by him. No, he was certain she would want to forget and not remember him. Yet, he had no choice but to continue to hope the love which they shared before that ill-fated summer day had not completely slipped away.

He tried to stop his thoughts from wandering back to the day when the demons in his head could no longer be controlled. The voices had started talking to him the very next day after his mother had passed away and seemingly appeared out of nowhere. They talked to him about terrible things and on that horrible day he tried to block the voices; to quiet them. So he drank a bottle of Vodka but the voices got louder instead of quieter like they had done on previous occasions when he drank alcohol. It was too painful to remember, so Grandville shook his head and tried to clear his thoughts back to her, his one and only true love.

He remembered her comfort, her sex, her kiss, and her smell. He was about to lose himself in her again. In the deep, deep depths of his mind, when he heard the voice of one of his fellow prisoners announcing mail call. He used to rush to his cell door in anticipation of her letter, but he learned over the years that mail never came to him. So, he continued lying on his tight little lumpy bed. He poured his will into drowning out the mail call shouts which were destroying his fantasy. Then, he heard the words that had never been spoken to him before while in his cell.

"Stubbs, you have a letter."

Grandville jumped up and went to the cell door and anxiously reached out his hand for the letter. The inmate gazed deep into Grandville's eyes, looking for signs of vulnerability, for a weakness that he could exploit. However, Grandville was not easily intimidated, because he knew the danger which came with living in a psychiatric prison. He had committed a most terrible crime, one which he could never forgive himself for.

He was a man who lived with demons in his head. A demon from the outside world would never be a threat to him, but the demons which lived in his head would always be most dangerous to everyone. He was prepared to tear through the cell doors and commit murder on his fellow inmate if he was not given what he had waited so many years for, and his eyes and body manner conveyed this reality. The inmate holding the letter in his hand, sensing his determination slipped the letter though the cell bars into Grandville's waiting hands.

Grandville could not contain his excitement. He closed his eyes and offered a silent prayer which was something he rarely did anymore. Please let the letter be from her, his love, his wife. "Please forgive me for I have sinned and ask for forgiveness." He spoke softly under his breath.

The letter had been opened as this was the customary practice of the prison and this angered him. He didn't want some prison guard reading words meant for his eyes and his heart. Staring at the envelop, he knew before he saw her distinct handwriting, that the letter which he held in his hands was indeed from her.

He pulled out the white crinkled paper and unfolded it. Her smell invaded the air in his space. Grandville closed his eyes. Then, he deeply breathed her scent into the furthest reaches of his nose and into his lungs. He wanted to savor the smell and the letter. The anticipation of what she had to say. He had waited so long, but felt he could wait a few moments longer before hearing her words finally speak to him.

So, he put the letter on his bed and went over to the metal wash bowl. He turned on the faucet and watched the fluid turn from a rust color to cloudy. Then, he cupped his hands to put the tepid liquid on his face in an attempt to focus. Maybe it was the medication which made him feel as though he was in a daze; or it could have been that he had finally had his wish fulfilled. After all this time she had responded to him. He wanted his mind clear and sharp when he read her long awaited words.

After washing his face he sat on his little bed and picked-up the wrinkled letter. He could tell by the many creases in the paper that she had read and re-read the letter before putting it in an envelope to mail to him. He examined the outside of the envelope and found the return address which indicated she was still residing in their home. This gave him hope, maybe her words, in written form, would convey that she still loved him, still cared, and that she could actually forgive him. He focused his eyes on the paper, re-reading her words over and over again.

When Grandville received his letter from Juliette, Montell was the only person he wanted to discuss it with. After reading the letter several times he went to Montell's cell but he wasn't there. Grandville eventually located him in the library reading a newspaper.

"Hey Montell," greeted Grandville.

"What's up Grandville, I am just here trying to keep up with the news so I am reading old newspapers. The world continues to change while we are in here. All kind of crazy things are happening," Montell stated.

"I know, I stopped reading the paper my first year here because it is too depressing. What's the point of knowing what's happening in the world, when for the most part, we are not even participants in society as long as we are locked away in here?"

"We still need to keep up with the world as it continues turns whether we're inside or outside Oakhill. You never know how it could affect you."

"You're right, but they can't help me right now. I need to get my mind fixed."

"Yea, we are both in that situation. I guess."

"I was looking for you, because I wanted to let you know that I got my very first letter from Juliette and her words in written form have lead me to believe there is hope, and maybe she could one day forgive me."

"Prayer really works man. You believed and it happened."

"She even told me that she still loves me, but in her words it's clear she is also afraid of me," Grandville said.

"That's understandable, of course she would be, based on all that has happened."

"She has to know I loved my daughter and would never hurt her."

"Grandville you are just going to have to work harder to show everyone here at Oakhill you're better, and you won't hurt anyone else," Montell urged.

"I'm trying. I only seem to hear the voices when I am under extreme stress but the medicine is helping. My counselor wants me to start attending group therapy, but I have enough problems. I'm not really interested in hearing everybody else's issues," Grandville replied.

"I think you should attend the group, and I believe you hearing what some of the other inmates have endured might help you to put your problems into perspective," advised Montell.

"I'm going to give it some serious thought. Montell, I just can't believe she wrote to me. Almost when I had given up any hope she would communicate with me, she wrote to me. You kept telling me she would write, and she did, how did you know?" Grandville inquired.

"I didn't know, but from what you have told me about Juliette, I believed she would write. Life is a whole lot like the game of chess. Every piece on the board has a specific role. The queen can move like every piece on the chess board except the knight. Her job is to protect her kingdom and her king. Everything you have shared with me about Juliette indicates she is your queen, and she will attempt to protect you, despite what happened. Your job is to get better, so you can return to your life and get back to your queen and your kingdom," Montell replied.

"Montell, the Anniversary of Jessica's death is tomorrow and I'm probably going to have a bad day. I have asked to be placed in Solitary Confinement starting at midnight. I don't want to go off like I did last year," said Grandville.

"Are you sure you want to do that, it seems a little extreme?" Montell questioned.

"I know, but extreme actions call for extreme measures. I want to get out of Oakhill, and I want my family back. I long to be the man that I once was, but everything changed for me three years ago when my mind snapped. I need to be alone because I can't guarantee that I won't go off tomorrow. I want the prison staff and my clinical team to know I have insight into my illness so they will consider one day letting me out of here. I want them to know I didn't forget about what happened last year," Grandville replied.

"Last year was bad, but in fairness, you were provoked," stated Montell.

Grandville's mind strayed back to the day he almost killed Big Joe after Big Joe tried to attack him in the shower. It was the second Anniversary of Jessica's death, and Grandville was out of it, quietly conversing with the voices in his head.

It was shower day and Grandville stood under the spray of water trying to ignore the words that were amplified in his brain and Big Joe saw his opportunity. Big Joe had noticed sometimes Grandville appeared to be talking to himself, but Montell was always around to run interference. Big Joe noticed Montell was not around for the very first time, and he decided to take a chance to take what Grandville had denied him. Montell was not in the shower, because he had an appointment with the infirmary for his yearly physical and as a result missed the whole incident.

Grandville was under the weak spray of warm water with his eyes closed when Big Joe walked up behind Grandville and grabbed him without warning. His massive arms squeezed Grandville's body so tight he could hardly breathe. Big Joe's erection pressed into Grandville's back indicating his excitement. Grandville was in a state of shock but waited while Joe grinded his body into his. He relaxed his breathing and threw his rear end out towards Joe to make him believe that he was a willing participant.

"I knew you wanted it. You are so pretty, you remind me of my first bitch here at Oakhill. He rode me so good that I could pop my cork just thinking about it. Now bend over and let Big Joe please you. I promise it won't hurt," Joe gruffly stated.

Grandville acted like he was bending down, but suddenly threw his head backwards, with all the force in his body into Big Joe's face, breaking his nose on contact. Blood gushed everywhere and before Big Joe could react Grandville had turned around and began hitting and kicking him in his face, stomach and private area.

"You evil demon. Stop it, Stop it, Stop it," Grandville huffed and yelled. In Grandville's warped mind, Joe was the voice in his head.

"Aaaaaaah . . . .," Big Joe whaled in excruciating pain.

"You made me do it, you made me hurt her!!" Grandville yelled at Big Joe who had fallen and was on the floor of the shower attempting to crawl away.

"Why did you make me do it? Why!? I'm going to kill you so that you can't make me hurt anyone else!" screamed a deranged Grandville.

The water in the shower had stopped and the guards came into the area to line the inmates up and found Grandville hitting and kicking Joe, who was on the shower floor almost unconscious. The Guards called for backup and restrained, a naked, fighting Grandville. Then, the Guards transported him to the padded room located in the infirmary. Grandville was shot full of medications and was left in the room alone to calm himself down. Big Joe's nose was now crooked, and he had not even glanced at Grandville or uttered one single word to him since that day which was a good thing.

But, Grandville really didn't remember the beating he inflicted on Joe. Instead he could only remember just how badly he wanted to hurt Joe. It was to the point where he had lost all control. Just thinking back to that day made Grandville know he was making the right decision.

Montell watched the raw emotion which was etched in Grandville's face.

"Grandville you got to do everything the professionals advise in order to get better. With getting help, maybe next year you won't be here on the Anniversary, maybe you will be home," Montell stated.

"That's what I'm afraid of Montell. Until I deal with my issues, home is the last place I need to be," replied Grandville.

Chapter 6
Keeping Secrets

Juliette sat on her screened sun porch and looked out at her lush backyard. Over the past couple of months, she had started using the sun porch more often. At one time, she could not bring herself to go out on it, as it brought back too many painful memories and was a constant reminder of what she had lost. The rose bushes in her backyard were in full bloom and the fragrance from the flowers filled her nostrils as she nostalgically remembered back to the first time that she brought Grandville to see this house.

The first-time Grandville laid eyes on the house it was in a state of serious disrepair. However, he was able to see past how the house looked when she first purchased it to what it could look like with a makeover. Juliette appreciated all the support Grandville had given her during her home buying process. She remained in the back yard smelling the roses while Grandville was inside touring her new home alone. Over the eight month period they had been dating, she had grown to respect him and his opinions. She had the occasion to see him work in his role as an attorney and while he operated his tax business. Sometimes she couldn't help but overhear the phone conversations he and Franklin would have regarding their business. She noted, he was a shrewd business man, but he was still a genuinely nice guy. He treated her and her son very well and at that very moment, while she was smelling the roses in her backyard, it dawned on her, she was in love with Grandville.

Juliette almost didn't hear the front door bell from her spot on the sun porch. She wasn't expecting any company, so she rushed towards the front of her house to see who was at her door. Juliette looked through the peep hole and spied Greta who was pacing back and forth on her front stoop. Juliette opened the door and said,

"Hey Greta what a surprise, I wasn't expecting you until tomorrow."

"I know but I was shopping at Willoughby Commons and decided to take a chance and see if you were at home. Do you mind if I come in?" Greta asked.

"Sure, I am just sitting out on the sun porch. Can I get you something to drink?" Juliette asked.

"Do you have any wine?" Greta questioned.

"Sure, I have White Zinfandel, Chardonnay, Moscato, and Riesling," Juliette replied.

"I will have the White Zinfandel," Greta stated.

"You can go out to the sun porch. I will be out there in a minute," Juliette directed.

Greta went to the back of the house where the sun porch was located while Juliette went into her dining room China Cabinet and got two wine glasses. She then took some grapes and sliced cheese from the refrigerator and crackers from the pantry. She arranged the items on a serving tray along with the wine glasses and the bottle of wine. Juliette carried everything to where Greta was seated on the sunporch and placed the tray on a table next to the love seat which was positioned to overlook the lush backyard. Juliette noticed Greta was wringing her hands and she looked kind of nervous.

Greta was the spitting image of her brother except she was a girl so her features were softer. She had long, thick, wavy, salt and pepper hair that she had tied into a ponytail, and a light honey colored complexion with light hazel brown eyes. Too many she was considered to be a beautiful woman, but Greta, like Grandville, always seemed to be almost oblivious to her very good looks. Considering the fact Greta and Grandville were twins, and her husband's only sibling. She should have gotten to know Greta better then she initially did. Juliette didn't get to know Greta well until Greta moved back to Cleveland from Los Angeles and started spending large amounts of her time helping her with the kids. Juliette poured two glasses of White Zinfandel and gave one of the glasses to Greta who immediately took a large gulp.

"Juliette, I am sorry to barge in on you like this, but I didn't want to be alone considering tomorrow is the Anniversary. Where are the kids?" Greta inquired.

"With my Mom visiting my sisters in Columbus. I thought it was a good idea for them to have a change of scenery," Juliette replied.

"How are your twin sisters?" Greta questioned.

"They are fine. Jatina and her husband just built a new house right down the street from where Jamaya and her husband live.

"What a nice plan."

"My Mom thought it would be a good time for her to take a road trip to visit them. She felt it would help to take her mind off of what happened, and to give me a chance to deal with my grief without having to deal with my kids.

"Your Mom is so right, because you need to be able to release any negative energy during this time."

"Also my nieces and nephews can distract the kids by playing with them."

"The kids should build a strong bond as they grow-up together. Having a close knit family is what's helping all of us deal with this situation."

"Yes. Plus, Mom can have a chance to spend some time with my sisters and distract herself from me," Juliette explained.

"I was hoping to talk to you alone, so it looks like I came at the right time," Greta stated.

"Greta, what's on your mind?" Juliette inquired.

"Have you talked to my brother?" Greta asked.

"Why, have you talked to him?" Juliette inquired.

"No, I have not talked to him in almost three years and you know that," Greta replied.

"I don't know anything anymore. All I know is that one day I was living the dream, and the next day I was in the midst of a nightmare that I haven't been able to wake up from," Juliette stated.

"I know it's been a hard road, but there is something I wanted to tell you. There is more to Grandville's story then what meets the eye."

"Oh Greta, please help me to understand what he's going through, because I really don't know what to think."

"My brother is basically a good man who did a very bad thing, and I know for a fact he loves you and his kids more than anything."

"I know this too, but what am I supposed to do or even say about this mess we're in."

"I promised myself when I came back to Cleveland, I wouldn't say anything to you ever about my brother. But, recently I have started to reconsider."

"Well, I'm glad you did, because you can help me put the missing pieces of this massive puzzle together,"

"I've been watching you, and I know you are still in love with him despite what he did."

"Greta, girl please don't make me cry right now, because I did not want to tell anyone how much I still love and miss my husband."

"You were probably sitting back here reminiscing about him when I pulled up," Greta stated.

"Yes . . . tears began rolling down her cheeks. She couldn't hold them back any longer.

Juliette looked down at the floor and attempted to wipe away the look of guilt which quickly flashed on her face.

"Juliette you don't have to hide your feelings."

"I'm sorry, but how can I still love someone like him after what happened?"

"You and my brother shared a special kind of love and what he did blindsided you. It has been devastating for all involved but there is a lot you don't know," Greta advised.

"Like what?" Juliette straighten-up, wiped her face and questioned.

"Juliette I can't tell you, because I made a promise to my brother. I keep my promises at all costs."

"So, why bring it up if you are not going to tell me what I need to know to understand Grandville?"

"I just need you to understand that there is more going on then you know. But, I can't tell you because I made a promise, I have even kept the promise I made to you. If Grandville ever finds out he will be furious with me," Greta stated.

"Greta I am confused. You haven't asked me about your brother in the three years Grandville has been away."

"I know, I know . . . ."

"According to you, you have never even visited him, so why are we having this extensive discussion?" Juliette asked.

"Because you're stuck in limbo. I am Grandville's sister, so that makes us family."

"We've always been family, so . . . ."

"I also consider myself to be one of your friends and I am your sorority sister. All that I am trying to say is, I love you and I can't stand to watch you jogging in place."

"Greta, you know my love for you and Grandville runs deeper than the ocean."

"If you would had filed for divorce or got a new man, I would never have even mentioned Grandville again to you, because I would see that you had moved on."

"I'm still a married women, and I took a vow to love my husband through thick and thin. So, I'm just trying to hold on to that truth."

"I know, because you have barely even looked at another guy since Grandville has been away."

"I read 1 Corinthians 13 often. It's the scripture about true "Love", and it makes me remember the bond Grandville and I shared as husband and wife."

"You and I both know Grandville has spoiled you and that for you there is no other man."

"As the word says, he showed me the most excellent way to love him, and I haven't been able to let that go so easily."

"My brother has some serious skeletons in his closet which contributed to what happened on that fateful day."

"I know he's not a beast inside. He was a good man, until the day that Jessica passed."

"All I'm suggesting is for you to reach out to Grandville. Ask him to address his issues, so the two of you can recapture what you once had," Greta quietly and compassionately replied.

"Why haven't you been to see your brother?" Juliette questioned.

"Because I believe if he sees me it would hurt both of us more than it would help us. I also can't bear to see my twin locked away like an animal," Greta replied.

"Well, have you written to him?" Juliette asked.

Greta took another large sip of her wine and then said, "No, I haven't written to him, and he has not written to me either. There has been no communication between us."

"You of all people should be communicating with him and helping him. Especially, if you know his deep dark secrets, Greta."

"Sometimes words are not necessary when there is nothing that can be said."

"There is always an encouraging word which can be spoken to someone who is in need of help."

"The question is have you written to my brother? I know he has written to you. If I know Grandville as well as I do, you have received a minimum of at least one letter a week since he has been gone," Greta stated.

"Actually I wrote to your brother for the very first time two weeks ago," Juliette disclosed.

"What did you say to him in the letter?" Greta asked.

"I told him that he had to deal with his past if he ever wanted to see me again," Juliette replied

Greta poured herself another glass of wine and popped a few grapes in her mouth. After chewing the grapes and taking another gulp of her wine she said, "How do you know his problems stem from his past?" Greta questioned.

"Come on Greta, I am a trained clinician, and I have come to know you and your brother pretty well"

"Really . . . ."

"I too consider you both family, and a friend, but even Stevie Wonder can see something from your childhood has screwed you and Grandville up pretty bad," Juliette honestly replied.

"Is it that obvious?" Greta questioned.

"No. It wasn't at first blush. I can see it more in you then I could in him."

"I have tried so hard to live a normal life, but what is normal with so many skeletons in the closet. They want to get out one way or another," Greta said then holding her head down in the palms of her hands.

"Human nature wants you to be free from holding guilt in your heart and mind. You can't hold bad stuff in without talking to someone about what happened to you."

"Juliette, we were taught not to tell anyone what's goes on in the family. What happens in the house, stays in the house."

"Though, I did think it was weird Grandville really never talked about his childhood. I guess he got pretty good at hiding his pain."

"I guess . . . I was not hurting inside as bad as Granville."

"Like we behavioral health professionals love to say - if you don't deal with your pain, it will deal with you," Juliette replied.

"There have been fewer true words ever spoken. That's why I am asking that you give Grandville a chance."

"Greta, I'm trying."

"I wouldn't be mad at you if you decided that you could never be with Grandville again. Considering all that has happened."

"Well, I haven't made that decision yet."

"But, if you make that decision no one would even blame you, but I think you love my brother in spite of what he did."

"It's the fact, that I know Grandville, and he would never willingly hurt his daughter for any reason."

"I remember the first time that I heard about Grandville dating you. My Mom called me the next day after Grandville introduced you to her. She was so excited Grandville had met someone whom he had described as the love of his life."

"Don't make me cry again . . .!"

"She told me that she could see why Grandville had fallen in love with you. I remember the first time you and I met."

"You were so high class," Juliette said trying to smile behind her tears.

"Do you remember when Grandville brought you to LA to go to Rayshawn's game?"

"Oh my goodness, we had so much fun that weekend."

"We had seats in the LA's private lodge where we had all the food and drinks we wanted."

"Now, you're talking about five star. Most people never get a chance to experience the finer things in life like we did."

"Then, after the game we went back to my house and stayed up all night talking about movies."

"I remember it like it was yesterday. It's funny how we hold onto memories in our mind."

"That was the first time we hung out, and I knew right then and there why my brother had fallen for you."

"Greta, I'm a simple person, who loves the simple things in life. Like loving my family and taking care of our children and our home."

"Juliette, you are very different from the other women my brother has brought home in the past. He would usually bring home women who were weak and did not have an original thought of their own in their heads."

"Ahhhh, that's not fair to say."

"I'm telling you the truth. Most of them were only interested in him because of what they thought he could do for them. Some were overly caught up in his looks. Others were in to him, because he is a lawyer and they saw him as a good catch."

"Some women can be money hungry."

"You are strong, have your own mind, you're beautiful and ambitious, and you seem to love my brother for himself. You are not superficial and those who spend time with you can see that you help make Grandville a better man. When you are with him you also make him happy. Grandville really does deserve some happiness in his life. Mom and I loved you for giving him that," Greta stated.

"Thanks for telling me all of this, it does help some. I just can't seem to get it together. I miss Grandville so much. Then, I feel guilty, because I should hate him for what he took from me and our family. I talked to my therapist about it, and she tells me that it's okay for me to forgive Grandville.

"It's good you're talking with someone about this situation, because you cannot get through it alone."

"I know I should forgive him, because he was sick and out of his mind. I can't help but to remember all the good times we had together, and I so want that life again."

"Hold onto the part which you can and never let it go. You can get through all of this together."

"I can't afford to want what we once had, because what we had no longer exists. I just don't know what kind of relationship Grandville and I can have now."

"If you truly believe 1 Corinthians 13, you'll keep no record of wrongs against Granville."

"Greta, I haven't seen him in three years and the only communication we've had between each other are the numerous letters he's sent to me."

"I know . . .

"You must really know your brother well, because I have so many letters from Grandville that I could publish a book."

"All I really know is, I can't be around Grandville unless I have empirical proof that he is better. Even then I will probably be hesitant to be in his presence," Juliette advised.

"You have every right to feel that way," Greta stated.

Greta looked out into the yard and then said, "You know this is the first time I have ever sat back here. It is very peaceful."

"At one time I couldn't bear to sit back here, but in the past few months I have been sitting out here more. I feel closer to Jessica back here," Juliette replied.

"I know tomorrow will not be the best day for us, so what's the plan?" Greta questioned.

"Well, Samantha just called me a little while ago. She and Tara are going to come over and have a drink with us. Then, they're going to take us down to Shooters, we will have dinner and watch the sunset. So, make sure to be at my house by 5:30," Juliette said.

"Are you sure you want me to come? I know Samantha hates me, and I don't want to be the reason why the two of you fall out. I am telling you right now, I will not allow her to disrespect me, especially tomorrow. I hope she understands that I am mourning too," Greta exclaimed.

"Of course I want you to come with us tomorrow. Samantha Trunk is my best friend, and she's been my friend for the last twelve years. What I want to know is what's the deal between the two of you? Why don't you like each other?" questioned Juliette.

"Hey Juliette, I don't have anything against your girl. Actually I admire her and she is also a member of our sorority. I have always been impressed with what she is doing professionally, being she is only the second black female County District Attorney in the history of Cuyahoga County. Your girl is the one who hates me, because she dislikes lighter skinned black women. Hell, I don't even think she likes the lighter brothers. I think she has an issue with blacks who have lighter skin period. You might as well admit it, your girl is a real witch who has self-esteem issues," Greta declared.

"No she is not, and that's not a very nice thing to say," said a flabbergasted Juliette.

"Maybe not, but you and I both know what I say is true. Simply put, your girl is color struck. It really bothers me, because both of us are African American women who share many of the same struggles. You got to know my mother before she died, as she considered you to be her daughter, and like you, she was a beautiful dark skinned sister. Mom raised me and Grandville not to get all caught up on skin color and complexion. Light skinned blacks get dogged by White America too. We're all part of the same race and we really shouldn't divide ourselves," stated Greta.

"I know Samantha and she is not that petty. I have to believe your beef is a little deeper than that," Juliette replied.

"Ok, so here's the deal, one of her friends used to date Rayshawn when we were in college. Her girl is a beautiful chocolate sister that Rayshawn used to sneak around with when he thought I wasn't paying attention. Samantha is just jealous. She thinks the reason Rayshawn married me is because of how I look. The funny thing about it is, she is probably right. Rayshawn is a shallow man who only wanted me so I could be his trophy wife. It took me a long time to see it because I really loved him. Grandville and I knew Rayshawn before he became a big time baller. He grew up in our neighborhood, and we all went to junior high school and high school together.

I thought I knew him, but he changed when he became a member of the BBA, and the fame went straight to his head. In college, I allowed the cheating, because I refused to have sex with him until we were married. I told him, once we were married his running around had to stop. You know, it didn't and I wasn't going to keep forgiving his indiscretions. I believe, I have a lot more to offer then just a pretty face.

I'm a college graduate with a degree in accounting. I am also licensed as a CPA, but Rayshawn didn't want me to work. I spent most of my time volunteering with the other BBA wives, and working with Rayshawn's Charity. The truth is, most of them are flakier than a Pillsbury biscuit. When I would get the chance to be around you and Grandville, I was reminded of the kind of love that I also wanted but didn't have. That's why I never had any kids with Rayshawn. I didn't want to bring a child into our mess. I was miserable, but from the outside it looked like I was living the life. Seeing you and Grandville's love was one reason why I didn't come home more often."

Juliette sat back wine glass in hand listening to Greta rattle on about Rayshawn.

"Then, after thirteen years of marriage, I realized that I was wasting my life. That's when I decided, I couldn't live that way anymore. I waited until I caught Rayshawn cheating again and then I was out."

"I wondered what made you end your marriage so suddenly after all that time."

"Luckily, California is a community property state so I did very well in the divorce. Another reason Samantha doesn't like me is, because now that I am single again, she sees me as potential competition in her endeavor to pull a man," Greta remarked.

"Why didn't you tell me you knew Samantha from College?" asked Juliette.

"Because I didn't. I went to Ohio University and she and Donna went to the University of Bowling Green. I said her girl Donna used to sneak around with Rayshawn who went to Ohio State. I never said I knew them personally. Rayshawn and I were in an alleged exclusive relationship and as his woman it was my job to know who the other chicks were. Rayshawn was never serious about Donna, or any of those other girls that he was cheating with. He used those other women for a good time. By the time I had finished college he had a five carat diamond engagement ring sitting on my left ring finger and we were married," Greta stated.

"Wow . . ."

"This is why Samantha may see me in a different light."

"I have met a lot of Samantha's friends but I don't recall a Donna. All I know is tomorrow will be another difficult Anniversary. I have counted on Samantha for the past couple of years to help me make it through the day. She makes me laugh, and she is thoroughly entertaining. Last year she distracted me so much with her jokes and stories that I made it through the Anniversary without barely thinking about Jessica and Grandville and what happened. I was depressed but not as much as I was the year before last. Samantha has been a good friend to me and I love her like a sister. All I ask is that whatever is transpiring between the two of you be put on hold until after tomorrow," said Juliette.

"Well, would you please talk to her about how she treats me because I have never had any beef with her. Last year I saw Donna in the airport and I wouldn't have known who she was if she had not introduced herself to me. She said that she had heard about me and Rayshawn's divorce, and she wanted to apologize for sneaking around with Rayshawn when we were in college. Rayshawn has cheated with so many women since college that she was but a mere faint memory. She said she knew how I looked, because the tabloids was always running stories about Rayshawn's scandalous affairs. She is married to a rich investment banker and has three kids. She told me that she couldn't be happier. Apparently she fell out with Samantha, because though she didn't say anything negative about Samantha, her body language indicated they were no longer close. Your girl is juvenile to be holding on to a grudge from years ago regarding a situation that doesn't even concern her," Greta declared.

"Okay I will talk to her, but promise me, you will be on your best behavior." Juliette replied.

"I promise to be good, but for everyone's sake, have that talk with your girl," Greta advised.

Chapter 7

Can We Talk?

Juliette opened her eyes, and adjusted her vision to the sunlight which filtered through the blinds in her bedroom. It was a beautiful sunny morning, but she struggled to get out of the bed. She, like so many other Clevelanders, loved the warming sun rays and the mild weather that can be a rarity in Cleveland. She wanted to put her head back under the covers and to skip this day completely. That way she could make believe that what happened didn't, and that things were like they used to be. Juliette knew being in denial wouldn't change anything, so she got out of her bed, and went into her attached bathroom to get ready for the day. She had a nine o'clock appointment with her therapist and she didn't want to be late.

Juliette had started seeing Emily McHall, who was her therapist, six weeks earlier and she appreciated the fact that Emily rearranged her schedule so that she could make Juliette's appointment her very first of the morning. Juliette had tried to deal with her grief with regards to losing Jessica, and her issues around Grandville, on her own but realized she needed professional help and someone unbiased who she could talk to.

Finding an African American female therapist was not an easy task, even in a city as large as Cleveland. Juliette didn't have anything against White female therapists, but she wanted a Black female, because she felt a "Sister" would better relate to her life experience. When Juliette approached Emily about her becoming her counselor, Emily graciously took Juliette on as client, even though her practice was full, and she didn't really have the space to see anyone else.

After showering, dressing and putting her makeup on, Juliette ate a banana and drank a cup of coffee. She then jumped into her

Volvo SUV and headed towards the east side suburb of Beachwood where Emily's office was located. After both women settled into their seats, Emily began their session.

"I know today is a difficult day but how are you doing?" Emily questioned

"I am doing the best that I can, considering the circumstances. I am sure that I will start to cry as soon as I leave your office. I am going to go over to the Rooming House and do a little paperwork to try and keep my mind busy and off of what today represents. I plan to go and cut some roses from my backyard and put them on Jessica's grave as soon as I leave here," Juliette replied.

"That's good. That will be therapeutic for you. Have you started writing another letter to Grandville?" questioned Emily.

"No, and I don't know if I am ready to write another letter to Grandville just yet. I poured my heart out in the last letter," Juliette replied.

"How are you sleeping?" Emily asked.

"Sometimes I have nightmares, but mostly I'm so busy taking care of the kids and running my business that at night, I am so exhausted I fall into a deep dreamless sleep. The kids are out of town with my mom this week, so I have more free time on my hands than usual. Last night I had a dream about Jessica. It's the first one I have had in a long time," Juliette responded.

"What happened in the dream?" Emily asked.

"It was a bright sunny day like today, where the sun sits high in the sky, and Jessica was in a pasture surrounded by beautiful wild flowers. She was running and jumping through the flowers and laughing. I was so happy to see her that I tried to run to her, but try as I might, I could not reach her. Jessica could see me too, and she said, 'Hi Momma, I am with God and we love you and my daddy.' Then, I woke up," Juliette responded.

"Juliette, what do you think the dream meant?" Emily asked.

"I don't know. Maybe the dream is Jessica's way of trying to let me know she is okay," replied Juliette.

"Some people think dreams are a way for our unconscious mind to deal with issues. Today is the Anniversary of Jessica's death, and it seems probable that Jessica would be on your mind, but maybe the dream means more," Emily stated.

"Like what?" questioned Juliette.

"Well, for one thing you said that in your dream Jessica tells you, she is with God. Then, you said in the dream Jessica, said she and God loves both you and Grandville. Could this be your unconscious mind telling you despite what Grandville did, you believe God still loves him?" Emily asked.

"Do you think Jessica is trying to tell me to forgive Grandville?" asked Juliette.

"I don't know, but maybe that's what your unconscious mind really wants," replied Emily.

"I still love Grandville, and I suspect I always will. I have been thinking about him and Jessica a lot in these past few weeks. We were so happy, everybody said so. How could I have been with Grandville for all those years and miss how sick he was?" Juliette questioned.

"Sometimes extreme stress can bring on an underlying mental illness. Was Grandville under stress?" asked Emily.

"Yes, his mother died a month before everything happened. Grandville was also under a lot of pressure at work. He was on the partnership track and was working on a big case for the firm when his Mom passed away. He was due to be in court to handle the case the day after his mother died. He had to give his case to another associate attorney, so that he could deal with all the details around his mother's funeral," replied Juliette.

"Was she sick or was her death sudden?" asked Emily.

"She found out that she had cancer six months before she passed away. I think Grandville was in denial about her illness because he was still working like a slave. He would be up half the night, preparing tax returns, writing memos, briefing cases for the partners, and preparing for the trial. Right before his Mom died, she called Grandville over to her house, and he was with her when she went home to be with the Lord. Greta and her ex-husband Rayshawn were on their way home, but they didn't make it in time to see Mother Stubbs before she passed. From the moment his Mom passed away, Grandville had been a little off, but that was to be expected," Juliette stated.

"Before all of this happened what kind of husband was Grandville?" Emily asked.

"Grandville was a great husband, provider, and father, who treated me and the kids like gold," responded Juliette.

Juliette could no longer hold the tears which had been creeping out of the corners of her eyes. She wiped her eyes with tissue which Emily kept on the table near where she was sitting, and then said, "I am so confused. I am still in love with the man that Grandville used to be, and I don't know if he will ever be that man again," Juliette declared.

"Grandville has an illness which may have caused him to commit a terrible crime, but underneath it all, he is still the same man he was before all of this happened," Emily responded.

"I feel so guilty," Juliette confided.

"Juliette, what happened was not your fault, so you shouldn't feel guilty," Emily responded.

"I feel guilty because I should hate Grandville for what he did to Jessica, but I can't find the hate in my heart. I often wonder if Grandville lied to me and didn't disclose his condition to me before we got married," Juliette remarked.

"What makes you think he lied about his condition? Did he conceal something else from you?" Questioned Emily.

"Yes, I recently found out Grandville has a lot of money that he never told me about," Juliette replied.

"How do you know?" Emily asked.

"Because Grandville's best friend Franklin came over two months ago with a cashier's check for fifty thousand dollars. When I asked him what it was for, and where he got it, he explained that it was money from Grandville's rainy day fund which Grandville wanted me to use to take care of the kids and the house. When Grandville was first put in jail, Franklin gave me a pass book to an account which Grandville had at a bank I was unaware that he had an account with. The account had a hundred thousand dollars in it. Now, Franklin comes over with more money, and he refuses to tell me how Grandville had that kind of money saved. It's a lot of money, but I was under the impression it was all the money Grandville had. I can't figure out how Grandville raised fifty thousand dollars when he has been locked behind bars," Juliette stated.

"Isn't Franklin the man who Grandville had his tax business with?" Emily inquired.

"Yes," Juliette responded.

"Well maybe it was money Grandville set aside for his business," Emily suggested.

"Yes maybe, but I sensed there is more to the story but Franklin wouldn't tell me. Of course I took the check. My business is doing well, but sometimes finances are rough. That money gave me breathing room, and I was able to use some of it to begin therapy with you. Also Greta, who is Grandville's twin, and only sibling came over yesterday, and for the first time we had an extensive conversation about Grandville. She urged me to find it in my heart to forgive him. She thinks that I am still in love with him because I am. Emily, I just don't know what to do," Juliette admitted while she continued wiping the tears from her eyes.

"I know it can be confusing, but you can do what you want to do in this situation. If you decide to try and make your relationship with Grandville work, that it is okay; and if you want to forgive him, that's okay too. You can also choose to move on without Grandville, and if this is your decision, then that's okay also. The only advice I can offer is for you to find it in your heart to forgive Grandville. No matter what your decision is regarding your relationship, because in my experience those who can't find forgiveness in their hearts are the ones who are emotionally tormented," Emily advised.

"What do you mean?" questioned Juliette.

"Juliette, I don't know how it feels to lose a child, nor do I want to know, but I have worked with many who have experienced loss. I have seen people destroy their lives, because they have become consumed with revenge, bitterness and hate. Those who work through their stages of grief fare much better," Emily advised.

"I want to forgive Grandville, and one day I hope he can find it in his heart to forgive me for the mistakes I've made too," Juliette stated.

"What mistakes? From what I have been able to gather you have been an exemplary wife and mother," Emily questioned.

"I did something so terrible, I am even embarrassed to talk with you about it," Juliette responded.

"Juliette, this is a safe environment where you can tell me anything without judgment. Further, I am bound by the rules of confidentiality. So, unless you are about to tell me you're about to commit a future crime, then what you say here, stays here," Emily reassured.

"To speak what I am about to tell you makes it real for me. I have never talked to anyone about it and the guilt is eating me alive," admitted Juliette.

"Juliette, you don't have to tell me what you feel guilty about today or ever, but you know as well as I do if you don't put it out there we can't deal with the problem. Therapy is all about you. I am here to help guide you through your feelings and emotions so you can arrive at a place where you can feel comfortable to make decisions," Emily responded.

"Your advice is sound, and I do trust you because before I chose you as my therapist I vetted you. Your reputation is stellar and you are known to keep the confidences of your clients. What I am about to say weighs on my conscious daily but I hesitate to talk about it. I have made several mistakes which could make Grandville sicker if he ever knew. If I am to recapture what we once had, I know I must reveal my secret. I just don't know if I could ever look him in his eyes after what I have done. I need to make sure we have enough time left in our session, because I may only have the strength to tell this story once," Juliette stated.

"I took the liberty of scheduling you a two hour session, because I felt that with the significance of the Anniversary you might need more time to talk, and I didn't want you to feel rushed. You have another hour with me," Emily advised.

"Thank you Emily. Over the past couple of weeks I have been reminiscing about my time with Grandville. This week I looked at our wedding pictures and remembered how happy we were together. I reflected on how he courted me and how happy we were on our wedding day. Marriage means something to me. I stood before God and two hundred of our family and closest friends and made a commitment to love and cherish Grandville in sickness and in health. I made a commitment to never forsake him. We made a covenant to each other, a contract ordained by God. I violated my vows and everything I believe in, and I disgraced myself before the Lord, when I slept with Grandville's best friend," Juliette confided.

"Franklin?" Emily questioned.

"Yes," Juliette replied.

"When?" Emily asked.

"About two months after the tragedy. I don't know what happened. Franklin picked me up and took me to Grandville's pre-trial. This was the last time I have ever laid eyes on my husband. He looked disheveled, and his eyes were red, so I knew he had been crying. I had been crying too, my daughter was dead, and my husband was locked up. I wanted to look into his eyes, I wanted to see if he was insane like Franklin kept insisting. However, Grandville never looked up, and he didn't seem to know we were even there. He was whispering to himself and he looked scared. My heart was broken, even after what he had done. I just wanted to walk up to him and put my arms around him and tell him everything would be okay. When Franklin and I walked out of the courtroom, I broke down in tears. I cried for all of us, Grandville, my kids, Franklin, Greta, and most of all myself.

When I got home I was still crying, and I was such a mess that Franklin walked me into the house. The kids were with my mother and Franklin made us both a drink in an attempt to help me calm my nerves. I drank my drink down quickly and continued to cry when Franklin put his arm around me and told me it was okay for me to cry. All I know is, one minute I was crying, and the next minute we were kissing and in each other's arms, caressing, and making love to each other.

It was quick and primal, and the act which we engaged in wasn't about love, or even lust. It is the last time I have ever been touched in an intimate way. When you are receiving sex on a regular basis, you take it for granted. You never anticipate the last time you will make love, it just happens, and it's usually due to some unforeseen event. I am sad that the last person who I allowed to touch me intimately wasn't my husband, but his friend Franklin.

After it was all over Franklin and I were both remorseful about what we did. We promised to never speak of it and to never tell Grandville. Franklin was in tears and apologized to me over and over again. He told me, he had always been attracted to me. He said, he would have asked me out the first time he met me if Grandville had not gotten to me first. Franklin told me, he loves Grandville like a brother, and he would do whatever Grandville needed or anything he felt necessary to make his situation better. He kept telling me Grandville didn't have a guilty heart or mind and he was sick with a mental defect.

I should have talked to Samantha about this, but I can't tell her. She has a big crush on Franklin, but he has never given her the time of day. When I would suggest to Franklin that Samantha was interested in him, he would say that she was very physically attractive, but he could tell she wasn't the woman for him. He said, he felt that their personalities would clash, and he wouldn't say much more. It has always puzzled Samantha as to why Franklin never seemed to acquiesce to her charm. She speculated maybe he is only attracted to light skinned women or that maybe he is gay. I have seen many of his women friends, and they have all been African American. They range in complexion from light skin tones to darker hues, so I knew that wasn't it. Believe me, when I say there is nothing gay about Franklin.

If Samantha ever found out what happened between Franklin and I, she would never forgive me. She would feel betrayed just like Grandville would. She confided in me on numerous occasions her feelings for Franklin. Samantha doesn't have a lot of family who live here in Cleveland and as a result we are so tight, she is like my sister. My younger sisters are fraternal twins, and they are very close to each other, and my brothers are very close. I am the oldest and though I know my siblings love me, I have always felt like the odd man out. After I met Samantha we formed a sisterly bond. She has always been open and honest with me about her attraction to Franklin, and don't forget to add in the fact that I am married," Juliette replied.

"Juliette, maybe you are underestimating Samantha. She is your best friend, and as such I would think you would be able to talk to her about anything," advised Emily.

"At one time I would have agreed with you, but recently I haven't been so sure. A couple of weeks ago Samantha and I went out to dinner. We were having a great time when we saw Franklin come in with a pretty woman who I have never seen before. His table was on the other side of the restaurant from where we were seated and he didn't even see us. As soon as Samantha spotted Franklin with the mystery woman she instantly got mad and insisted that we leave. Granted we were done eating but I couldn't understand what the rush was all about. After we paid the bill she asked me if I have ever said anything negative about her to Franklin. I didn't even respond to her comment but I was pissed that she would think that I would do such a thing. Samantha really likes Franklin and if she finds out that Franklin and I slept together she will think that I purposely sabotaged her."

"I'm glad you shared your story with me, because with everything out in the open we can focus on the work which needs to be done. I'm going to give you two assignments, and I would like for you to complete them for our next session. The first assignment is for you to write a letter to Samantha, and tell her everything you would want to say if you were talking to her about how you feel. It's okay to be angry in the letter, and it is okay to use profanity. The goal is to allow you an opportunity to release your anger towards her. Once you've completed the letter, we'll review it and talk about it. The next assignment is to research Bipolar Disorder as this is the disease which Grandville is suffering from. I know you are a Licensed Independent Social Worker, and you may have learned about Bipolar Disorder in your master program, but you need to go further in depth for a deeper understanding of how your husband has to live with this illness. I also think it's important you know all you can about Bipolar Disease," Emily advised.

"Ok, when is my next session?" Juliette asked.

"I want to see you back in three weeks. You're going to need a little time to complete these assignments. Also, call me if you are having any problems with dealing with the Anniversary. I may not be able to talk to you right when you call, but I promise that I will get back to you," Emily stated.

"Thank you Emily, I will see you in three weeks," Juliette replied.

Chapter 8

Reminisce

Grandville adjusted his eyes to the darkness of the dark hole which barely fit his body. He didn't know what time it was, but he knew it was the morning of the Anniversary and one of the worst day of his life. Grandville had met with his prison counselor Bill Bolden right before he was taken into the hole. Bill was a tall white man with red hair, freckles and a slight Southern Ohio drawl.

"Are you sure you want to do this? It seems senseless to punish yourself for events which you cannot change," Mr. Bolden stated.

"I need to be all by myself with my thoughts. I need time to reflect on the actions which put me in a place like this," Grandville stated.

"Grandville you are here because you did something while you were in the midst of a psychotic breakdown. You were not in your right mind, and I'm sure you experienced some kind of underlying stressor which pushed you over the edge. Since you're determined to do this, I suggest while you are isolated that you reflect on those events which put you under the kind of stress which caused you to suffer a psychotic break. You're going to need to be painfully honest with yourself and remember things you probably would rather forget. I suggest you start with trying to remember your first bad memory. When you come out of the hole we can talk about the work which needs to be done to help you overcome your issues," Mr. Bolden advised.

Now, Grandville was lying on a cot in a small cramped space. He was trying to do what his therapist had suggested - to remember events which he desperately wanted to forget. He decided to take Mr. Bolden's advice, and he focused his mind back to a time when he was five years old.

He could remember the ding dong sound of the doorbell like it was yesterday. He and Greta were in their separate rooms asleep, when the ringing doorbell woke him up. He had to go to the bathroom anyway, so he got up out of his bed, and tippy toed his five year old body out into the hallway. He peered down the steps and saw his Aunt Genevieve and his cousin Gina come into the house. He crouched down to listen to what they were saying without being seen, because if his mother found him up listening to grown folks conversations she would spank him.

"Genevieve, what are you doing here and why isn't this child in bed? Do you know what time it is?" His mother asked.

"Yes, I know what time it is," Genevieve replied.

"Genevieve why is this child crying? What the hell is going on?" Grinda questioned.

His Aunt reached into her purse and pulled out a gun and then said, "You know exactly what is going on Grinda. I bet you didn't think that I would ever find out?" His aunt angrily stated.

"Genevieve what is wrong with you and why do you have that gun?"

"I want you to look me in my eyes and tell me the truth."

"The truth about what? Look at how upset this child is, you're scaring your daughter now stop it!" His mother demanded.

"I believed you when you told me that the twin's father ran off. I don't know how I could have been so blind. How could you have betrayed me the way you did? I'm your only sibling. When our parents and grandparents died in that car accident, I took you in and raised you like you were my own child rather than let you go into the foster care system, and this is how you repay me," his aunt cried.

"I was sixteen when we lost our family, not a small child, and you are only five years older than me, and I don't know what you are talking about. Now put that gun away," his mother directed.

"You are going to have to live the rest of your life knowing what you did to me," Genevieve declared.

"What I did was try and take care of your husband and daughter while you were locked up in the mental health ward at the hospital. Now, I want you to put that gun away right now. You're scaring me and Gina," Grinda again demanded.

"You should be scared, but not for you, but for me."

In one quick motion Aunt Genevieve put the gun to her temple, and blew her brains out in front of her sister, her twelve year-old daughter, and her nephew, who unbeknownst to everyone in the room had witnessed the whole ordeal. The urine Grandville had been trying to hold poured out of his body through his pajamas onto the hallway carpet, and he immediately fainted. When he woke up he was lying in his bed in new dry pajamas, and his mother was staring down at him. His young mind hoped what he saw his aunt do was part of a bad dream.

"Grandville are you okay? Does anything hurt?" His mother questioned him.

"My head hurts a little bit," replied Grandville feeling very groggy.

"Here take this medicine, it will help you with your headache."

Grandville's mother put the pills in his mouth. Then, held the glass of water to his lips, so he could try and wash the taste from the medicine off of his tongue.

"Grandville, I don't know what you heard or saw, but don't tell anyone about tonight. Don't even tell Greta. If anyone asks you where you were when Genevieve came over, you tell them that you were in your bed asleep. I need you to be a big boy and do that for me," his Mother stated.

"Ok Mommy".

"Now your Mommy wants you to try and get some rest. I will be back to check on you in a little while," his mother said.

Then she was gone, leaving him alone to try and figure out what happened. Grandville was traumatized and tried to make sense of the events of that night. He remembered the blood and the look his aunt had on her face when she died. At the age of five, he didn't really understand what being dead meant. He remembered during that same year in the spring, a baby bird had fallen out of its nest in their backyard. His mother had explained, that the bird was dead and had gone to be with the Lord. She also explained the bird was not coming back and it was gone forever.

Grandville wondered if his aunt was dead, and if so was she in heaven with God, and if she would be gone forever like the baby bird in his backyard. Grandville learned later that his Uncle Greg, who was Aunt Genevieve's husband, and his aunt were like that bird, they were both dead, and as a result were never coming back.

Aunt Genevieve had killed her husband Greg before coming to his house. Then, she had taken her own life on that fateful evening, and the police ruled the tragedy as a murder/suicide. Grandville attended the double funeral along with his small family and tried to make his young mind understand what had happened. As a result of losing both her parents, Gina, who was twelve years old moved in with Grandville, Greta, and Grinda.

Grandville, nor Gina, ever received any professional help to assist them in dealing with the trauma of watching his aunt kill herself. Neither of them ever uttered a word about that night, not even to each other. During those days when horrible events occurred you just didn't talk about them. Being Black was hard enough, and when you had problems you went to church to talk to the Lord. Growing up, he often suffered nightmares where he relived that awful night over and over again in his head. However, he kept his word to his mother, and never disclosed to anyone what he witnessed. He did his best to forget it had even happened.

His cousin Gina seemed to form a bond with him which she didn't have with Greta. She seemed to sense he was present when her mother took her life. She would read to him and spent more time with him then she did with Greta. Grandville was crazy about her and would do just about anything she asked if it would please her. She looked a lot like his mother and his aunt, and had deep, mahogany colored, blemish free skin. Greta and Grandville were both light completed, with wavy hair, and hazel colored eyes, but they had the same features as their mother, like her eye shape, lips and face structure.

As he grew older, he watched his mother work two jobs to support her small family. Gina often babysat him and Greta, while his mother worked the night shift in a machine shop. When he turned ten, Grandville started to question the love which he held for Gina, because she started to touch him in ways which made him uncomfortable.

The first time it happened, his mother was working the night shift at the machine shop, and Greta had fallen asleep while they were watching movies. Gina suggested that she and Grandville play a game. He was excited, because he was getting to play with Gina without the interference of Greta, who competed with him for Gina's attention. Gina put a blindfold over his eyes and led him into her bedroom.

At first Grandville thought they were about to play hide and seek, but then Gina pulled down his pants and put his private part into her mouth, as he struggled to get free. Gina who was both bigger and stronger than Grandville put her weight on him, and held him down, while she performed oral sex on him. Grandville couldn't control the wonderful sensations which flowed through his body. He didn't understand what was happening to him. The stiffness in his private area was startling, and the white pee which shot out of his privates into Gina's hot mouth left him spent. All he knew, he was ashamed and embarrassed, because he knew what Gina did to him was wrong. He knew that no one except the doctor was supposed to touch him down there.

After Gina was done assaulting him she said, "You better not tell anyone what we did tonight. If you do the authorities will take me away from Aunt Grinda, and she won't have anyone to babysit for her while she works. That will be bad."

Grandville often overheard his mother on the phone, talking to the various bill collectors who were always calling their house. He knew his mom needed to work in order to afford the modest home they resided in, and he believed Gina's threats. As a result, he never told anyone about how Gina would come in his room in the middle of the night when he was fast asleep, put her weight on him, and force his penis into her mouth, while she sucked until he exploded.

Grandville felt victimized, and he felt as if he had nowhere to turn. There was no one which he could talk to about what was happening to him and his feelings about the whole situation. He couldn't understand how his body constantly betrayed him, because in his mind he didn't like what Gina was doing to him. Anytime she would put her mouth anywhere near his penis, it would stand straight out, ready for her hot tongue.

Grandville reflected on how during that time, he would sometimes fantasize about who was his and Greta's father. According to his mother, the twin's dad cut out on her when he found out that she was pregnant. Grinda never said much more, and she never even told the twins their father's name. Grandville would sometime imagine who his father might be. He constantly wondered if his dad was a millionaire, or a movie star, or even a professional athlete. He also wondered if his father was a bum or a derelict, or worse. He wondered if this was the reason his mother had not disclosed his identity to him or Greta. Grandville wondered if he had a father around would he have saved him from the wickedness of Gina's touch? Late at night, when Gina wasn't in his room molesting him, these were the thoughts which plagued him and destroyed his peace. Over time, he figured out that his mother would not provide him with the answers to his questions about who his father was, so in time he stopped asking.

When he turned thirteen Gina stopped putting his penis into her mouth and started putting it in her vagina. By this time he had learned about sex in school, and he knew what he and Gina were doing with each other was wrong. He almost fainted from the pleasure he felt when he entered the tightness between her legs.

88

Grandville always felt a constant inner turmoil. He went to a Catholic school and had been taught that sex was okay between a husband and a wife, and it was not allowed under God's rules by those who were not married. He also knew it was against the law to marry your first cousin. Even when Grandville attended confession, he refused to utter a word about what was occurring between him and Gina to the priest. He was in constant fear of going to Hell for the sins which he was committing, but the pleasure he felt between Gina's legs often made him cry out in ecstasy. After the sex acts were completed, Gina would remind Grandville to never disclose their sexual relationship to anyone.

"Remember to never tell anyone about what we do," Gina reminded him.

"Gina why do you keep coming into my room in the middle of the night? We can't do this anymore. We are cousins and you could get pregnant," Grandville stated.

"You are going to do whatever I want you to do. You better not tell anyone and if you do tell, I will say that you raped me. You are bigger than me now, and you know that you love how I make you feel so let's cut the crap. If Aunt Grinda ever finds out what has been going on between us when she is not here, it will break her heart and you could go to jail so keep your mouth shut," Gina replied.

Grandville couldn't understand why Gina didn't have a boyfriend as she was a very attractive young woman. She was about 5 feet 7 inches with small apple sized breasts and a tight shapely body. She had a beautiful deep dark complexion like his mother, deep dimples, and long hair which came down to the middle of her back.

Grandville noticed whenever they were out, men would admire Gina. They would even attempt to talk to her, but she seemed immune to their advances. She only seemed to have eyes for Grandville, and she would gaze upon him lovingly when she thought others were not paying attention. Grandville felt immense guilt for what he was doing with Gina. On one hand he was like any other teenage boy, he was fascinated with women and their bodies and the act of sex. However, on the other hand, he knew that he shouldn't be engaging in those acts with his cousin. Grandville couldn't understand how his mother and sister appeared to be clueless as to what Gina was doing to him, and he tried to find ways to channel his anger. He often went to the basketball court in their neighborhood to play pickup games in an attempt to burn off his frustrations.

As a teenager Grandville was the kind of guy who kept to himself, and he didn't have many friends. He was quiet and didn't have much conversation for anyone with the exception of Gina, Greta, and his mother.

When he was fourteen, he was outside playing basketball when he met a new kid who had recently moved to the neighborhood named Rayshawn Robinson. The two played a pickup game against some other kids on the court, and he and Rayshawn beat them like they stole something. Right then and there, the two cemented a bond which took years to break. Rayshawn seemed to really take to both Grandville and Greta and spent a lot of time with the twins.

Grandville really liked Rayshawn and started going over to his house after school and hanging out. Rayshawn's father owned a small, construction company, and sometimes Grandville would help Rayshawn and his father work on homes. Hanging out with Rayshawn and his dad is how Grandville learned how to repair wood and how to paint and to do other repair jobs. Rayshawn was an only child, and Grandville was his best friend, and over time they became close like brothers. Rayshawn's father was also a part time karate instructor who held two black belts and every day after school when they didn't work on houses, Grandville accompanied Rayshawn to his father's gym to take martial arts lessons. Rayshawn's dad never made him pay for the lessons because for some reason he really liked Grandville. One day after karate practice Mr. Robinson started talking to Grandville.

"I have been watching you and I can see that you're a good kid. What kind of grades do you get in school?" Mr. Robinson asked.

"Mostly A's and B's," Grandville replied.

"What's your grade point average?" questioned Mr. Robinson.

"Three point eight," Replied Grandville.

"I want you to continue working towards earning your black belt, you are a natural and as long as you keep your grades above a 3.5 and keep working hard, your karate lessons with me are free. I want you around my kid, you and your sister are a good influence on him. Since we moved here, Rayshawn has been doing better. He is a talented basketball player, and he could go far but he needs to get better grades. Do you know what association brings upon assimilation means?" asked Mr. Robinson.

"No, what does it mean?" questioned Grandville.

"It means when you associate with someone you will pick up their traits. I want you to continue to study hard, but I want you to get Rayshawn to study with you. The more Rayshawn is hanging out with you, the more of you will rub off on him. Do you think you could do that?" asked Mr. Robinson.

"Mr. Robinson I will try, but you know I can't make Rayshawn do anything he doesn't want to do," Grandville stated.

"I know you can't, but keep talking to him, because he really values your opinions," Replied Mr. Robinson.

Grandville did get Rayshawn to study once he learned Rayshawn's weakness was Greta. The twins often studied together, so getting Rayshawn to the library was easy once he learned Greta would be there. Rayshawn soon started to excel in school along with his basketball game. His grades improved and he began testing better.

Rayshawn became very popular, mostly because of his basketball skills, and Grandville became popular too just because he and Rayshawn were such good friends. All of sudden all kinds of girls were throwing themselves at him. Grandville was a very attractive guy who was unaware of just how handsome he was. Unlike other teenage boys, Grandville didn't think about sex all the time because he was getting more than he could handle at night with Gina.

One night when Grandville was sixteen Gina came into his room, and he was having sex with her in his bed. His mother was working the night shift and Greta was asleep. He was pounding Gina from behind with all the force in his body when he looked up and he saw his mother standing over him with a look of pure horror on her face.

"What the hell is going on in here? Hell no! I know you didn't bring some fast tailed girl up in here. Who the hell is that under you in the bed that I paid for?" his mother angrily questioned.

Gina attempted to hide her face under the cover as Grandville attempted to hide his body from his mother who, walked over and yanked the cover off his bed.

"Oh my god, Gina. How could you? Get your ass out of Grandville's room right this instance," his mother demanded.

"Aunt Grinda he raped me, he forced himself on me," Gina declared.

"You are a lying Jezebel, and it sure didn't look like you were getting raped. You should be ashamed, you have corrupted my child. Now get to your room and we will talk later," his mother directed.

Gina scurried out of his room with his bed sheet wrapped around her body while Grinda stared through Grandville as he attempted to cover himself with his blanket.

"How long has this been going on?" questioned Grinda.

"Since I was ten," replied Grandville.

"What? You mean to tell me when Gina was seventeen she was having sex with you. Why didn't you tell me?" his mother questioned

"She said that she would tell you I raped her. She also made other threats and I believed her. She said Greta and I would be removed from you and placed into foster care," Grandville replied.

"Grandville there is nobody more important to me then you and your sister. You shouldn't have believed her threats and you should have told me," his mother stated.

"I didn't know what to say, how was I supposed to tell you that I was being forced into sex by my female cousin? I didn't think you would believe me," Grandville honestly replied.

"Gina is my niece and we are the only family she has left, but she has to go. I am going to move her in with Ms. Forester from our church. She wants her to stay in her home, but she needs someone to live with her to do errands like grocery shopping and light cleaning. It's high time for Gina to get out on her own. Don't talk to anyone about what has been going on between you and Gina, not even Greta," his mother advised.

Grandville did what his mother said and never disclosed to anyone what Gina had been doing with him since he was ten. Gina moved in with Ms. Forester, and Grandville did not see her again until his graduation ceremony from high school at the small party his mother had for Greta and Grandville.

Gina was polite but still looked at him lustfully when she thought others were not watching. His mother seemed to see what she had not seen before and purposely kept them apart. After she caught them together, she did not allow Gina to come to their home but instead would visit her at Ms. Forester's house. Grinda did share with Grandville that Gina had become like the daughter Ms. Forester had always wanted but never had. The two had become close and Gina seemed to be relatively happy.

Grandville kept on living his life and hanging out with Rayshawn who had evolved into a huge high school basketball star. All kinds of women were after Rayshawn, but he was in love with Greta who only saw Rayshawn as a friend.

"One day your sister is going to be my wife, and you and I are going to be brothers in the eyes of the law," Rayshawn declared.

"Do you think you are ever going to change Greta's mind? She's always telling me, she sees you as only a friend," replied Grandville.

"Grandville you have to be friends with your woman if you expect for the relationship to work out. Sooner or later I'm going to make your sister mine. Wait you'll see," Rayshawn said.

"It's cool with me, but you better not ever hurt her," Grandville replied.

"Man I love her, and I promise you, I will treat her good. She will live the life others dream of," Rayshawn stated.

Rayshawn had all kind of groupies who were constantly around, and they were willing to do whatever he wanted just to get close to him including having sex with his friends. Rayshawn told Grandville, they needed to practice having sex with women, so when they got married they could physically satisfy their wives. Rayshawn also suggested, Grandville take advantage of the opportunity the groupies were offering, as practice makes perfect. With Gina no longer available to him, Grandville's body was going crazy. He was used to a sexual release at least three times a week, and thanks to Rayshawn's groupies, there were willing females who wanted to make sure he got the release he wanted.

After Gina, he made sure to never touch a woman sexually, without the benefit of a condom, no matter if the girl told him, she was on the pill or not. He didn't want to catch a sexually transmitted disease, because he wanted to go to college. He also didn't want to risk getting someone pregnant and having a kid before he was married, because he knew having a kid before he was ready would make it harder for him to succeed.

He and Greta understood, their only shot for them attending college was by winning a scholarship, because their mom could not afford to send either one of them, and there was no way she could pay for them both to go to college. They constantly pushed each other to succeed and as a result they both earned top grades.

Grandville decided to take one of the scholarships offered at a small liberal college out of state, while Greta opted to stay closer to home. Grandville was like most men who did not want to have kids to soon, he had safe sex with many willing women. What made him different was his religious upbringing, and his conscious tore him apart every time he sexually touched a woman who was not his wife.

As the years went by, Grandville buried the memories of what Gina did to him deep in the recesses of his brain. He never told a soul about what happened between them and because he didn't see Gina anymore, it was easy to put the memories out of his mind. After he graduated from high school, he left home to attend college in Upstate New York and did not return home, back to Cleveland, to live until after he and his first wife divorced. He had worked so hard and had been so busy after leaving home, that what happened with him and Gina was never to be thought of or discussed.

After Grandville's divorce from his first wife he came back home to Cleveland and had been home for one year when his mother called him and told him that Gina was very sick, and the doctor's suspected she had pneumonia. What he didn't anticipate was that Gina would die at the age of 35 from a lung infection that millions have recovered from. Grandville and his small family took Gina's death hard. Grandville realized that despite what Gina had done to and with him, he still loved her, and they had shared some good times together. Grandville had never told Juliette about what happened between them, and it was one of the things which he regretted not sharing with her.

When his mother was on her death bed, she called him over and told him news which still had him reeling.

"Grandville I don't have long, the Lord is about to call me home, and there are some things you and I need to talk about before I depart this world," his mother whispered.

Grandville was barely holding it together, his mother wasn't even sixty-five years old. He was convinced spending her life working so hard to take care of him, Greta, and Gina was why she was dying so early. Grandville hounded his mother for years to quit working after he started making great money and could pay most of her bills. Greta had started hounding her years before he did, as her marriage to Rayshawn made her an instant millionaire. However, it was not until about nine months before she died that they were successful in getting her to retire. He had plenty of money from his trust, and he used some of the money from the interest payments, along with Greta's large contributions to subsidize his mother's social security check so she could live a very comfortable lifestyle. His mom became sick three months after she retired and barely got the opportunity to enjoy her freedom from work.

"Mom you should save your strength," Grandville advised.

"Grandville I don't have much time left, so I need you to listen closely to what I want to tell you," his mother hoarsely whispered.

"Okay mom what is it?" Grandville asked.

"I'm about to share something with you that will distress you, but I can't go home to the Lord with this on my conscious," his mother shared.

"Mom, you have been fantastic, and whatever it is I can handle it," advised Grandville.

"Grandville, I haven't been honest with you and Greta. You know how the two of you would always ask me about what happened to your father, and I would tell you he left me when he found out I was pregnant? Well that isn't really accurate," his mother confided.

Grandville started to feel nervous, because he knew that whatever his mother was about to say would forever change his life.

"Mom what are you trying to tell me?" questioned Grandville.

"What I have to say is difficult, but I can't leave this earth with this heavy burden on my heart. I owe you and Greta the truth. I want you to know I am sorry for lying to you all these years but at the time I really didn't know what to do. I could have made different decisions, better choices, but I chose to never deal with my secrets and this will result in a lot of pain for you and Greta," his mother stated.

"Mom you have me feeling a little nervous," Grandville replied.

"Grandville, I am sorry but what I am going to tell you will hurt you, and that's the last thing I want to do. When I die, I don't want you or your sister to have unanswered questions, because I never told you who your father was, so here goes. Your Uncle Greg was your biological father," his mother confessed.

"What! . . . Who was my father?" asked an exacerbated Grandville.

"Honey I'm sorry. I wasn't planning to ever tell you, but when you are dying you tend to re-evaluate your life and the choices you have made," Grinda stated.

"So that's what Aunt Genevieve was talking about when she came over that night?" questioned Grandville.

"Yes. Greg and I were together only once when Genevieve was in the hospital suffering from mental health problems. Greg loved her, and I loved her too. We were crying over Genevieve and how much Gina missed her, and it happened. Actually, I was in love with another man, but we broke up when he found out I was pregnant. We had never consummated our relationship, so he knew for certain that he was not your father.

After our breakup he went back home to Florida where he was from. It was easier for me to let everyone believe he had gotten me pregnant then left me. I never even told Greg or anyone else that he was your father. I believed that if Genevieve ever found out it would break her to the point of no return and she was already very fragile. She never got over the loss of our parents and grandparents, and she suffered horribly with major depression. I didn't talk about it much because it hurt so bad, but we lost our whole family in that car accident.

After our parents and grandparents died, all Genevieve and I had was each other. What happened between Greg and I wasn't planned, it just happened. We were comforting each other and it somehow got out of control, and it only happened once. When I found out I was pregnant, I felt like I had no other choice but to have you, because abortion is not allowed in the Catholic Church. My only other option was adoption, and I didn't want to do that. I am so grateful God blessed me with you and your sister, despite who your father was, and the two of you have brought me great joy.

I simply can't imagine how my life would have been without the two of you in it. Since you were the first boy in our family, you were special to us, and we all kind of doted over you. I don't know how Genevieve found out about me and Greg, or that he was your father. You look like me, but you and Greta have Greg's coloring and hair, maybe that's how she figured it out. We don't know where you and Greta got the hazel eyes but it was probably from Greg's side of the family. All that's left of our family is you, Greta, and your kids. Please make sure you take good care of them," his mother advised.

Grandville felt like he was going to be sick. All those years he thought he was having sex with his cousin, when Gina was really his half-sister.

"Did Gina know?" asked Grandville.

"I am not sure. She was there as you were when Genevieve took her life. She heard what she said, but every time I would try to talk to her about her parents she refused to discuss them or what her mother did. I feel like I failed her because I should have gotten her some help. Maybe if I had, things would have turned out differently. After she moved in with Ms. Forester, I learned Greg had been sexually abusing Gina, and Genevieve found out about it. I'm not sure how long Genevieve knew about what was happening to Gina before she snapped," replied Grinda.

"Mom what else? I know there is something else you're not telling me," said Grandville.

"What made me come home early from work that night and come into your room when I caught you and Gina is, I had noticed

Gina was putting on weight. She never went out, and she didn't have any friends, male or female. I suspected she might be pregnant, and because you were the only male around her, I decided to do my own investigation. Unfortunately, my suspicions proved to be correct on both counts," his mother confessed.

"Mom, what are you saying? Are you telling me that Gina had a baby? My baby?" questioned Grandville.

"Yes, Gina gave birth to a son. We put the baby up for adoption, because you nor Gina were in a place where you could take care of a baby. You had been through so much I just couldn't tell you. I told Gina if she ever told you, I would never speak to her again and I would disown her.

She corrupted you, stole your innocence, and she owed you that much. You deserved the opportunity to be happy, and to make a life for yourself, without more excessive baggage. I had planned to take this information to my grave, but while I have been laying in this bed, I was thinking about how you would feel if the child one day found you. I am positive Gina put your name on the paperwork as the father, and because you were a minor, the adoption agency allowed me to waive your rights as your legal guardian. I have come to believe it would be more devastating if you learned about this from someone you didn't even know existed, than if I tell you the truth while I am still able," his mother confided.

Grandville could not hide the tears which were falling from his eyes. Everything he believed about Gina, his mother and his paternity had been a lie. He didn't know what to do with this new information, and he didn't have a way to process it.

"Grandville do you see those little kids on the floor sitting around my bed?" his mother asked.

"Mom there are no children sitting around the bed. You're probably having side effects from the pain medication," Grandville responded.

Grandville held his mother's hand and tried to wipe away his tears. He was so tired, and after receiving the news he and Gina had created a son, it was like his brain just shut down. He closed his eyes and dozed off for a minute and when he woke up his mother was gone, along with his illusions of who he thought he was.

Chapter 9
Tomorrow
(A Better You, A Better Me)

After leaving her therapy session, Juliette spent an hour at Jessica's grave where she cried until there were no tears left in her for which to shed. Juliette decided to stop by her rooming house to try and get some work done before she went home. After Juliette and Grandville were married, Grandville made it clear that Juliette could work if she wanted too, or she could become a stay at home wife and mom. Juliette decided, she still wanted to work, but she also wanted flexibility, and the ability to set her own hours. Since she didn't yet know how to make her dream a reality, she continued to work at the job she held since before she had met Grandville.

Shortly after their first wedding anniversary Juliette learned that she was pregnant with twins, Juliette worked up until the day before she delivered the children. Juliette had completed law school, and passed the bar exam, shortly after she and Grandville were married. Since she was now a licensed attorney, she was promoted from her job as a residential therapist into the agency's Risk Management Unit drafting and executing the agency's contracts with various vendors and funders. Her new job paid well, but the work was extremely tedious and boring.

Juliette longed to own a business where she did something which helped to change young women's lives for the better. In college and graduate school, Juliette wanted to focus her career on working with troubled children, but her focus shifted when she realized kids grow up to be adults. Juliette decided that helping young adults was where she wanted to concentrate her career. When Juliette worked as a therapist, she heard horror stories from her young clients who were placed on her caseload. Many had been raped, abused, and neglected by the very same people who had a duty to protect them.

The abuse triggered some of the young ladies to experience mental health problems, or to become involved with drugs and alcohol. Some became extremely promiscuous, where others became lesbians who hated men. After Juliette received her promotion she didn't see the girls as often. However, some of the young ladies which she worked with in the past would seek her out at her new position, and they would talk to Juliette about how hopeless they felt with no future.

One day after putting the kids down for the night, she and Grandville ate dinner together and talked about her job drafting contracts, and how boring she thought her new position was for her. Juliette had mentioned to Grandville in passing that she wanted to operate her own business and she had started coming up with ideas. Juliette explained to Grandville that many of the young women in her agency's residential program had nowhere to go after they had become adults and had aged out of the system. Many ended up on the street, forced into a life of prostitution, crime, and poverty. Juliette wanted to develop a program that could help change their fate. She wanted to teach them how to be successful young women, armed with tools, like a trade or a skill which the young ladies could use to market themselves.

Grandville who was quiet and reserved by nature, was always more talkative when he was with Juliette. Juliette explained that she was thinking of opening a home for young women who had aged out of foster care.

"I only have one question. If you had a home for young women who have aged out the system, would you be able to make a profit?" Grandville asked.

"Yes, but I would need to own the property where the girls live, and I would need to have about eight girls paying at least eight hundred and fifty dollars per month a piece to turn a profit. The fee which the young ladies would pay will include meals and laundry service," Juliette replied.

"Where would young women get that kind of money?" asked Grandville,

"Well some of them get a social security check, and if they worked a little bit on the side then they could afford it. The most cost effective venture would be to open a rooming house. I could rent a room to each girl at a cost of four-fifty a room, but I would not be responsible for preparing meals or washing clothes. I would actually put in a couple of coin washers and dryers to help pay for the cost of the water and sewer bills. I would make a rule, that in order for a young lady to receive a reduced rent rate, it would be mandatory for the young lady to participate in our social service program," Juliette said.

"Sounds like you have some good ideas, maybe you should put some of this down on paper and see where it takes you," Grandville advised.

"You know you may be right. I'm going to take your advice," Juliette replied.

Juliette began working on an extensive business plan at night when the children were sleeping and Grandville was up in his third floor office working. He had turned the finished attic into a very nice study, equipped with everything that an office would need. At the very same time that Juliette was creating her business plan, she was also dealing with extended family problems. Two of her younger first cousins had become addicted to heroin, and her whole family was in a crisis. Juliette's mom was babysitting for her every day, but often found herself trying to help her two sisters deal with their daughters. On those days when her mother had to help her sisters and couldn't watch the kids, Mother Stubbs stepped in and babysat, because she still worked the night shift in the machine shop which she had been employed in for twenty-five years, and was available during the daytime.

Juliette was in a tizzy as to what to do, because she was juggling working full time, dealing with three kids, two of which were infants, and running a household. Grandville was working hard, practicing law, and running his tax business, and she didn't want to burden him with the stress which she was feeling from trying to do so many things at once, when Grandville again saved her day.

It was her third wedding anniversary, and Grandville had made arrangements for the kids to spend the whole weekend with his mother. When she arrived home from work, she found a note on the table, in her foyer, directing her upstairs to their bedroom. When she went upstairs she found rose petals on the floor leading to their jacuzzi tub that was filled with fragrant vanilla bubble bath and rose petals. Candles illuminating the bathroom and soft romantic music teased her eardrums. She undressed and got into the tub where she relaxed to Jill Scott's melodic voice, while she scrubbed her body and hummed along with the music, anticipating the night to come.

After Juliette soaked for forty five minutes, she got out the tub to find a large gift wrapped box on their bed, with a hand written note in Grandville's distinct handwriting, directing her to open it. Inside, contained a beautiful white strapless sundress, along with beautiful, matching, white shoes. After putting on the dress, and the matching shoes, doing her makeup, and fixing her hair, she descended down the steps and into the main part of their house.

Juliette did not know what Grandville had planned for her, but when she entered her dining room she gasped. Her dining room table had been transformed with white linen, silver serving trays, and a silver candelabra that was lit with nine candles sat in the middle of the table. Grandville came out of the kitchen, dressed in a black suit accompanied by two African American males who were dressed in matching white tuxedo's, with matching white gloves.

"Juliette you look lovely, Happy Anniversary," Grandville said, before kissing her on the mouth and turning her around to meet a tall, older, African American man in a black tuxedo.

"Juliette, I want you to meet Chef Rico," Grandville said.

"Hello, it is very nice to meet you. Whatever you prepared smells delicious, and I don't think my table has ever looked this beautiful," Juliette complimented.

"Thank you, it is my hope that you will enjoy the meal which I have created for you and your husband. Grandville wanted a special dinner, and I aim to please," said Chef Rico.

Chef Rico out did himself, and had prepared a spinach salad with blue cheese crumbles, pineapple glazed duck with risotto, asparagus, and a fresh homemade cherry pie with vanilla ice cream for dessert. She and Grandville drank champagne from silver champagne flutes and enjoyed each other's company. Each course was served by the young men who wore white gloves. The atmosphere was romantic and Grandville had jazz music playing in the background, and the sounds of recording artist Boney James, filled her ears.

During dinner, Grandville explained that he and Franklin had come to know Chef Rico, because they had been preparing his business taxes for several years and learned that he would come to a private home and prepare a meal in the owner's kitchen. Juliette thought that the personal chef for a night concept was a brilliant idea and she was happy that Grandville had planned an intimate evening for the two of them, where they didn't have to leave their house. She was also happy that Grandville was supporting an African American business. After Chef Rico and his staff cleaned up the kitchen and left, Grandville gave Juliette a small gift wrapped box.

"Grandville you can't possibly be giving me another gift, not after all of this. This has been one of the best nights, ever," Juliette declared.

"Just think baby, the night isn't even over yet, now open your gift," directed Grandville.

"No, not until you open your gift first," responded Juliette.

Juliette went over to Grandville and gave him a slim rectangular box which she had hidden in the small white clutch that she had paired with her outfit. Grandville tore open the box to find a gold watch that was engraved with the words, *'thank you for being my soul mate'* on the back of the watch.

Tears of happiness threatened to fall from Grandville's eyes, as he grabbed Juliette in a strong embrace and kissed her passionately.

"Juliette I love you, thank you so much. Now it's your turn to open-up your gift," said Grandville as he gave her a small box.

Juliette shook the box, but didn't hear anything, but she fully expected the box contained more jewelry. On their first wedding anniversary, he gave her a set of one carat diamond ear rings. On their second anniversary, he gave her a two carat diamond bracelet. She thought, he had gotten her a three carat diamond necklace, but the box wasn't big enough to contain that. She couldn't control her excitement anymore and tore the paper off and opened the box to find a key.

"Grandville you didn't get me another car did you?" questioned Juliette.

"No baby, do you want another car?" Grandville asked.

"No sweetheart, there is no reason for us to make another bill. The Volvo SUV is paid for and it drives like a dream. So, if this isn't a car key, what does this key fit?" Juliette questioned.

"It goes to your new property, you are now the proud owner of your very first rooming house," Grandville stated.

Juliette was almost speechless. "What! Grandville I am confused?" Juliette responded.

"Don't be confused, let me enlighten you. One of the lawyers that I know in passing works for the Catholic Diocese of Cleveland. My firm represented them on some charitable trust issues. As you know, Catholicism in the United States is way down and there are fewer Convents. The Catholic Church is one of the biggest landowners in Cuyahoga County and the church has been discretely selling some of their unused Convents. I was able to purchase one at a price which we couldn't refuse.

The building is in decent condition and located on a quiet residential street in Euclid Heights, Ohio. Each room has an attached half bathroom, and there are fourteen separate rooms where the young women can sleep. The house also has a large congregate shower area, a large living room, a dining room, a full basement which could be finished, a study, and a small apartment located on the top floor. There is a full kitchen and all the appliances including the electrical, heat and plumbing are in good working condition. I have the deed right here and a cashier's check for Ten thousand dollars. I want you to quit working and start your dream. The money should be enough for you to purchase all the incidentals and consequential which you might need like comforters and curtains for each room, and it should be enough to get you started. But let me know if you need more, and I will see what I can do," Grandville stated.

Juliette could barely contain her excitement. Tears of joy streamed down her face as she hugged and kissed her husband. She showed her appreciation to Grandville all night long and woke up happier than she had been the day before. Her business, "A Better Tomorrow", changed her life. Juliette was able to put together a phenomenal social service program for young women which offered her the ability to spend more time with her children. It also provided an opportunity to make a good living while aiding in helping to change the course in the lives of the young ladies who resided in her rooming home.

On Monday after their wedding anniversary, Juliette did not hesitate to give her job a two week notice and begin the task of ensuring that her new rooming house was ready to be operational. Juliette spread the word about her new venture and ensured that each applicant to her new program had references that checked out and only accepted those young ladies who were committed to making their tomorrows better than their yesterdays.

Her very first resident in the rooming house was a young lady named Violet who had spent the majority of her life residing in foster care homes and various residential facilities. Violet was nineteen years old and she had no family or other support systems. Juliette sat down with Violet to interview her before allowing her an opportunity to participate in the program. During their interview Juliette learned that Violet's main interest was cooking.

Violet shared with Juliette while growing up in various residential facilities she hated the food and described the taste of the food as bland and dull. Violet had a high school diploma and was receiving social security, because she suffered with Bipolar Disorder and was unable to hold a steady job. A year earlier, Violet had aged out of the residential facility where she had lived from the age of thirteen until she aged out of foster care at eighteen. When Violet left the residential facility, she found a new residence in one of Cleveland's homeless women shelters. Violet was receiving a check for seven hundred and ten dollars a month. However, she was afraid to try to get an apartment, because she didn't want to put herself in a situation where she wouldn't be able to afford to pay her bills. When Violet added up all of her bills and what it would cost her to rent an apartment with utilities, it was more than her meager check.

Juliette knew Violet's mental health social worker, Lala, personally. Lala had the task of trying to get Violet and fifty other homeless mentally ill people off the mean streets of Cleveland. The two had attended college together and had kept in touch over the years. Lala had called to set-up a lunch date for the two of them when Juliette told her about her new venture.

"Listen, I got the perfect young lady for your new program. Her name is Violet, and she's a nice girl who I would love to see get off of these streets. She is a good kid who can go far with the right intervention," Lala stated.

Once Juliette learned that Violet could afford to live in her boarding house and after receiving a glowing verbal recommendation from Lala, Juliette agreed to meet with Violet. Now, four years later Juliette was reminded that making Violet her very first resident was one of the best decisions she had ever made. Violet soared through Juliette's social service program and was a recent graduate from the Culinary Arts Institute at Cuyahoga County Community College. Juliette did all her financial aid paperwork and found a private benefactor who paid for Violet's books for the whole two years while she was in the program. Juliette helped Violet to see that having Bipolar Disorder can also have its blessings.

Violet loved to cook and clean, and Juliette taught her how to use those times when she felt manic to channel her energy and to do just that. With Juliette's help, Violet set up a thriving business where she cooked and cleaned for others for a fee. When Violet finished Juliette's program she allowed her to continue to reside in the rooming house at half of the price which she charged the other residents. Violet now lived in the small apartment located at the very top of the old convent and was Juliette's eyes and ears of the facility. She knew everything that was going on with the women and would report back to Juliette what she heard and saw.

In order to be a resident of A Better Tomorrow each young lady had to agree to apply for food stamps. Each resident then gave their card to Juliette, who along with Violet, brought groceries for the Better Tomorrow Facility every two weeks. Each resident pays Juliette four hundred dollars to reside in the rooming house, which includes all the utilities, and each pays an extra fifty dollars a month to have their food prepared by Violet. Juliette and Violet in turn split the money which the residents paid to have their food prepared in an even fifty-fifty split. Juliette felt the arrangement was fair because Violet was using both her appliances and utilities to prepare the meals.

With her Social Security check and the money which she was making on the side, Violet was able to live quite comfortably for a young lady who was only twenty six years old. She even had her very own Honda Civic which she had purchased with money that she had made from her business. Most of the work which Violet did was under the table, and as such, did not affect her Social Security earnings. Violet also made extra money by transporting the other residents of the rooming house who didn't have cars to their various appointments all over town for a fee. Violet was a bright young lady, who had an understanding of how to make the system work for her. Which was why she kept a locked safety deposit box that held the bulk of her money as to ensure that she never exceeded the resource limit for her Social Security benefits.

After leaving Jessica's gravesite, Juliette arrived at a Better Tomorrow around 1pm. She was immediately struck by the delicious smells which were wafting through the Convent from the kitchen. She found Violet in the kitchen cleaning the lunch dishes and stirring a large pot which was on the stove.

"Something sure smells good in here," said Juliette.

"Oh, hi Ms. Juliette. I'm just making some greens for dinner. I also have both baked and fried chicken and some cornbread. Are you planning to stay for dinner?" Violet asked.

"No, I am not going to be able to stay tonight, I have to get home," Juliette replied.

"Okay, we had chicken salad sandwiches and fresh fruit for lunch. Did you have lunch, and do you want me to make you a plate?" asked Violet.

"No I haven't had lunch, I will have a plate if you have enough to share," Juliette responded.

"Of course. There's plenty," Violet stated.

Juliette could not get over how good the food Violet prepared was. Violet never purchased chicken salad from the store. Her salads were prepared fresh.

Violet sat down with Juliette at the large table, and Juliette devoured the food.

"Violet, your food is delicious," Juliette said.

"Thanks Ms. Juliette. I have some freshly squeezed lemonade would you like some?" Violet offered.

"Yes, and thank you," Juliette replied.

"You're welcome. I went to the West Side Market yesterday and brought a bunch of fruits and vegetables. The new girl Esther didn't get her food stamp card yet so her payee paid for her first month food bill in cash. I did just like you taught me, I went to the Market yesterday right after the new trucks came in, and I waited and went into the stalls at 3:30pm right before the market closed and the vendors were practically giving the food away. I was able to get some fantastic deals, including the lemons which I made the lemonade with and these greens," Violet stated.

"Violet that's great. You're doing a great job with the meals, keep up the good work. What else has been going on over here?" Juliette questioned.

"Ms. Juliette, I know today is not the best day for you, and I don't want to upset you and it can keep until tomorrow," said Violet.

"Violet spill it. What's up?" questioned Juliette.

"I overheard your cousin talking on her cell phone yesterday. I think she owes some drug dealers a lot of money," Violet replied.

"Why, what was Melinia saying?" asked Juliette.

"I kept hearing her say that she needed more time, and she kept promising whoever she was speaking to that she would pay back everything that she owes. She also said she didn't have the tape. I have no idea what she meant by that. When she hung the phone up she seemed to be scared. I hate to tell you this today," replied Violet.

"Violet, you absolutely did the right thing by telling me. Where is Melinia?" asked Juliette.

"I don't know. She left yesterday right after she got off the phone. She was dressed very nice and she had her hair pulled back into a bun and she had a cute dress on. Maybe she had a job interview, and then a hot date, because she wasn't at dinner last night, nor was she at breakfast today," informed Violet.

Juliette did not want Violet to know just how nervous and worried she was about Melinia. She hadn't really wanted to put Melinia in her program, but her mother practically got down on her knees and begged her. She reflected back to that conversation.

"Come on Juliette I have already promised Mabel that you would allow Melinia to be a resident of you rooming house. You have helped so many strangers, and I don't understand why you wouldn't want to help your own flesh and blood," her mother remarked.

"Mom, I do want to help Melinia, but I just don't think she's ready to be in my program. I mandate that all the women who move into my rooming house prove to me with written documentation that they have been sober and working a recovery program for at least six months if they've had a past drug or alcohol problem. Melinia has barely been clean for two months. I don't want her to bring any extra drama to what I am trying to do and if she's not ready that's exactly what will happen," Juliette replied.

"Juliette, if you were the one with the problem, I would expect everyone in our family to help you in any way they could. Melinia was a bright young lady who had a golden future until she got hooked on Oxycotin after dental surgery. Once her Dentist found out she was addicted to the medication which he prescribed to her, he cut her off, and that's how she began using heroin. Melinia is a college graduate and her future could be bright again with your help," her mother stated.

Juliette thought hard about her mother's request. Her family had strict rules about helping each other out. Her people had a rule about keeping the money in the family. Juliette and Grandville were the only attorneys in Juliette's large extended family, so anything which is remotely legal was bounced off her and Grandville first. Juliette or Grandville would then refer the case, or take it themselves, and sometimes they would receive a referral fee if they sent the case to another attorney. The fact-of-the-matter was that her mother was right, she had an obligation to Melinia because they shared the same blood.

Juliette went against her own internal warning, when she allowed Melinia to enter her program three months earlier. Melinia was only twenty-five years old, and she had already fallen hard for the drug known on the streets as "Horse," "Smack," and "Junk." She went from snorting heroin, to shooting it, in a matter of weeks, and after spending two months in a drug rehabilitation facility, she professed that she was ready to live a complete drug free lifestyle. In Juliette's experience, it took most people multiple attempts before they kicked the habit completely. But, Juliette prayed nightly that Melinia would be the exception and not the rule.

There was little else which Juliette could do about what was going on with Melinia until she returned to A Better Tomorrow. So, Juliette decided to get some work done before going home to get ready to go out with Samantha, Greta, and Tara. Juliette had turned one of the small rooms on the first floor of her rooming house into an office which was off limits to everyone but her. She had decorated the office with a small desk, a computer and printer, a small file cabinet, and book case. Her college degrees and her professional licenses were proudly displayed on her walls, along with her sorority paraphernalia. Juliette had written several grants in her small office which had helped the young women who were residing in her rooming house.

One of her grants allowed every new resident of A Better Tomorrow to receive a welcome package, which included a set of sheets and comforter for their bed, face cloths and towels, and each package also included toiletries such as lotion, a toothbrush and toothpaste, toilet tissue, and bars of soap. Each welcome package was purchased from a mental health agency which employs some of their clients who suffer with various types of mental illness. The employment programs offer those suffering with mental illness the opportunity to learn new skills and to earn money which helps to supplement their modest monthly checks. The agency was making a profit from the endeavor and the money made from the project was used to help more people.

Juliette was proud of what she had been able to accomplish in a very short period of time with her A Better Tomorrow program. Almost every woman in the program was involved in an educational program or working. Every evening there was an Alcoholic Anonymous meeting or a Mental Health Anonymous meeting which was held at her rooming home, and the women were mandated to attend one of the meetings at least three times a week. After she paid bills for the program, and accounted for all of the finances, Juliette logged onto her office computer and checked her email. After responding to several emails, she got up and prepared to leave, but decided to try and call Melinia on her cell phone. The phone went right to Melinia's voicemail but Juliette couldn't leave a message because her mailbox was full.

After locking up her office she went to look for Violet. She found her in the kitchen, which was exactly where she had left her earlier in the day.

"Violet, I am getting ready to get out of here," Juliette advised

"Okay Ms. Juliette, call me if you need me," Violet stated.

"Actually, Violet, I do need you to do something for me," Replied Juliette.

"What do you need me to do?" questioned Violet.

"As soon as Melinia comes back call me. I don't care what time it is," Juliette said.

"Okay Ms. Juliette," Responded Violet.

Chapter 10

Sooner or Later

Grandville was at the end of his stay in the hole. He didn't know exactly what time it was, but he felt like he had been trapped away from the rest of the general population for days and his body was cramped and tired. Remembering traumatic events from his childhood had taken a mental toll on him. He fell back into a deep sleep where he dreamed about Greta. In his dream, she did not speak one word to him and he woke up in a cold sweat. He reflected on his memories and realized in order for him to find peace, he would need to speak with Greta. He had to tell her the ugly truth about everything from who their father was, to what happened between him and Gina.

During the years which he had been confined to Oakhill, he had not once communicated with his twin who was also his only sibling. Not one letter, not one call, and it was his fault as much as it was hers. He could have written to her, but he had not, because he did not know where to start and what he needed to say to her just couldn't be communicated in a letter. For a long-time he was dead set against her seeing him while he was behind bars, locked away from the rest of the world, like an animal. For Greta to see him in the condition he now found himself in would bring them both pain, and they had both been through enough. However, he did recognize that Greta had also not made any attempts to see him, which meant she didn't want to visit with him behind bars.

His only real link to the outside world and his former life was Franklin, who came to see him once a month for two hours. The standard duration of a visit was one and a half hours. However, Franklin could stay longer, because he was listed on Grandville's paperwork as one of his Attorney. Also, when they did get an opportunity to visit with each other, they got to do so in a private room away from the prying eyes and nosey ears of the guards and other inmates.

Through Franklin, Grandville learned that Greta had permanently relocated back to Cleveland and was spending a lot of her time with Juliette. He was hopeful the two women which he cared the most about in this world were helping each other out. He felt guilty for not communicating with his sister, and he didn't even know that Greta and Rayshawn had broken up until he saw it on Entertainment Tonight. No one at Oakhill, except Montell, knew Greta was his sister, and Montell was with him when Entertainment Tonight ran the story of Greta and Rayshawn's divorce. After the show went off-the air, the two of them quickly went back to Grandville's cell to digest what they had heard.

"Damn Man. Have you talked to your sister?" Questioned Montell.

"No, not since right after we buried my mother." Grandville replied.

"Well, have you tried to call her or write to her?" Montell asked.

"No." Grandville responded.

"Man, I know you have been going through it, but it seems like your sister has been catching it too. Maybe you should try and reach out to her," Montell advised.

This conversation between himself and Montell took place more than one time before, and Grandville had yet to take his advice. He knew part of his healing process would include having a needed conversation with Greta. For the first time since arriving at Oakhill, he felt ready to make that conversation happen. Franklin had made plans to come and see him at the prison the following day. Grandville planned to give Franklin a letter, requesting Greta to come to Oakhill to visit with him in person. Grandville was confident that Greta would not deny his request and would come as soon as he summoned her.

Grandville and Greta had a complicated but strong relationship which some would not understand. Greta would never come to Oakhill unless Grandville personally requested her to do so, and he wouldn't ask her to come, until he felt that he had something to say. Even locked away, he felt a kinship with her which only close siblings could relate to, and he was glad that she had returned to Cleveland after her breakup with Rayshawn. He had no doubt that she was doing everything possible, to lighten Juliette's load on his behalf.

He often wondered what caused the split between Greta and Rayshawn. He and Rayshawn had been the best of friends from the beginning of Junior High school, and the two had remained tight well into their adulthood. Grandville was even Rayshawn's Best Man at he and Greta's wedding. Grandville had to give it to him, Rayshawn did what he said he was going to do, he gave Greta a lifestyle which most people could only dream of. Their house in LA was a ten thousand square foot mansion equipped with everything from a movie theater, to a full gym, and a basketball court located in an exclusive gated community. It was excessive, and opulent, and Greta never felt comfortable with all the glitz and glamour.

However, it's the type of life style which came with being Rayshawn's wife, and although Greta put on a great act, Grandville could see right through her. She was not happy, and she had been miserable for years. Rayshawn's cheating was notorious, and some of the groupies which were common place to the BBA, were so brazen. When he was at away games with his team, they would even sneak into his room and the rumors were rampant. Grandville knew all about the alleged affairs, and they had finally taken their toll on Greta, even though some were true and others were not.

Over the years, Rayshawn and Grandville had grown apart which was in some way due to the distance between where they lived and because of their busy schedules. It was also due-to-the-fact some of the rumors were in fact true. As Grandville adjusted his body to the cramped space he remembered back to a time shortly after Greta and Rayshawn were married. Rayshawn was a rookie in the BBA and he and Greta had moved to LA. Rayshawn called Grandville, who was away at Law School and told him that he missed him. Rayshawn asked him to meet him in New York City because the LA's were playing the New York Stars. Rayshawn who was a second-round draft pick from Ohio State had signed his first five million dollar contract to play the point guard position. Rayshawn was getting one of his first starts, and he wanted Grandville to be there with him to help cheer him on in hostile territory. Greta was working on decorating their new home and had a meeting with a big time interior decorator which she could not reschedule.

Rayshawn made all of Grandville's arrangements and picked-up all of the expenses for the trip, including the flight for Grandville into New York City, and his stay at a five-star hotel. He even gave Grandville two thousand dollars to have as pocket money and to go shopping for some new clothes. Grandville was a second-year law student, and at that time during his life he was struggling to make ends meet. He could not have afforded to travel to New York to watch the game in person if Rayshawn had not footed the bill.

Grandville was having a great time when Rayshawn did something which knocked the sails from under him. He was in his hotel room relaxing after watching Rayshawn's team destroy the Stars. The two teams were in different conferences, but were having an exhibitionist game and the media had made a big deal about it. Rayshawn had scored twenty-two points despite being one of the shortest players on the court with a height of 6'4. His performance was excellent, and Grandville was looking forward to partying with him to celebrate the win. Rayshawn had explained to him that after every game, he had to attend a quick team meeting. Rayshawn instructed Grandville to take a cab back to their hotel, and he would come through to Grandville's room after the meeting was over and then they would hang out.

When he heard the knock at the hotel room door, Grandville fully expected that Rayshawn would be alone. However, when Rayshawn entered the room, he had a woman with him who looked like she had been soliciting on the streets of New York. The woman had very light skin and long hair and was dressed like Rayshawn had picked her up from the corner of Hunt's Point, which was the local hoe stroll in the Bronx's. The area was made popular due to the HBO documentary, "*Pimps up, Hoes down.*" The unknown woman was wearing a black cat suit with holes all through it which left very little to the imagination.

"Grandville meet Katilinia." Rayshawn said.

"Hello Katilinia. How are you?" Grandville asked.

"I am great, but I will be much better once you are inside of me. Rayshawn you were right, he is fine. I can't wait to taste you while he hits my spot." K replied.

Grandville couldn't believe that any self-respecting woman would lower herself in the way which Katilinia did. He had never seen her before, but she was willing to give him her most precious commodity, her body. She basically was under the mistaken belief that Grandville was about to do her, while she simultaneously gave Rayshawn a BJ. Grandville was disgusted and decided that he wouldn't even touch Katilinia with somebody else's penis.

"Rayshawn, let me holler at you for a minute. Katilinia please make yourself comfortable. Help yourself to the mini bar while I talk to my man," Grandville said.

"Okay, but don't take too long, because mama has an itch that only you can scratch." Katilinia sexily replied.

Grandville pulled Rayshawn into the bathroom.

"Rayshawn what's up? Why did you bring that trick to my room?" Demanded Grandville.

"I can't get rid of her. She waits for me after every game. She wants me badly. I tried to explain to her that I am married but she won't take no for an answer. So, I told her about you and now she wants you, but she wants to give me a BJ while you do her," Rayshawn nonchalantly replied.

"I gathered that and you know that I am not down," Grandville stated.

"I am not going to have sex with her, I am going to let you hit that. It will be like old times," Rayshawn explained.

"First off, the last time we rolled crazy like that was when we were in high school and it was before Greta was your woman. Now she's more than just your girlfriend, she is your wife. When we were young we were stupid, we know better now, and incidentally letting someone give you a BJ constitutes as sex and we don't know this girl's motives. She could be trying to set you up, and later say that you raped her so that she can get paid. You made a promise to me, you said you would never hurt my sister. If you are running around letting strange chicks suck you off, you are hurting Greta, and she deserves better," Grandville declared.

"Grandville I love your sister, but even Jesus would have a hard time turning down all the women who are coming after me," stated Rayshawn.

"Man, I don't know what to tell you except that I want that trick out of my room. Now you go out there and get rid of her while I brush my teeth and pull myself together so we can go out," Grandville demanded.

"Ok man I hear you," replied a chastised Rayshawn.

Rayshawn left out of the bathroom while Grandville proceeded to brush his teeth, wash his face and made sure he looked presentable. When Grandville came out the bathroom the first thing he saw was Katilinia on her knees sucking Rayshawn's penis like it was food and she was an Ethiopian refugee. Rayshawn was trying to push her off of him but she had a vice grip on him. When she finished lapping up his orgasm like it was the last supper, she looked up at Grandville and said, "I hope you see what you could've had with no strings attached. I heard what you said and trust and believe that only a trick can clean a plate like I just did. If I can do that with my tongue, imagine what I can do with my box. Too bad that you will never know. Please give my regards to your sister. I will see myself out because as you know, tricks don't receive an escort." Katilinia nastily replied.

Katilinia quickly walked to the door, opened it and walked out slamming it behind her while Rayshawn struggled to fix his clothes. Once Rayshawn straightened up his clothes, he sat down on the bed and put his face in his hands.

"Rayshawn what the hell was that!?" Questioned an angry Grandville.

"Man, this is what I have been trying to explain to you. These groupies are ruthless; they want the opportunity to say they did something sexual with a professional athlete. When I came out of the bathroom she was on her knees hiding next to the door. She ambushed me, grabbed my penis and squeezed it and forced her mouth on me. Man, I was raped, and it is not like I can tell anyone." Rayshawn replied.

"Come on Rayshawn cut the crap. You brought her to my room with the expectation that we would both do her," stated Grandville.

"Grandville you don't understand, the groupies from high school and college have nothing on what I am experiencing in the BBA. Katilina has been following our team all around the country. She loves group sex, and is known for what she lets the players do to her. I have been trying to get rid of her for months. I thought if I let you do her, she would be satisfied and would stop bothering me. I didn't expect her to attack me that way because she has never pulled anything like this before. I love your sister and I am trying my best to faithful to her," Rayshawn replied.

"That woman just put your penis in her mouth, a woman that you claim loves group sex. How do you know that she doesn't have Herpes on her lips? In which case if she does, you may now have Herpes that you could potentially transmit to my sister. Man, I thought you were better than this and stronger than this. I am really disappointed in you," Grandville heatedly stated.

"Grandville, man I'm sorry. I'm going to get it together. I promise man," Rayshawn responded.

"I've heard that before Rayshawn. I'm telling you, don't hurt my sister. If you can't be faithful to her, let her go, so she can have an opportunity to be happy and to find someone who will be faithful to her," directed Grandville.

After 12 years of marriage Rayshawn and Greta had finally called it quits. Grandville was sure it was in some part due to Rayshawn's philandering cheating. Greta finally got fed up, and like the words of a famous R. Kelly song, "*it wasn't nothing that Rayshawn could do about it.*"

To Grandville, Greta was a beautiful woman both inside and out, and he felt that their attending Catholic schools and her involvement with the Church helped to shape and impact her personality. She was devout and went to mass and confession daily. He was almost positive, she was a virgin on her and Rayshawn's wedding night. He also knew his twin sister had very little experience with members of the opposite sex. However, despite her sweet disposition, Greta was someone who would stand-up for herself if she felt she was being wronged, and she had a wicked tongue which could cut sometimes worse than a physical assault.

Grandville suddenly thought about his family home, the one which he had grown-up in and his mother owned up until her death. Grandville and Greta did everything they could to try to get their mother to move out of the small house which was located on the far East side of Cleveland, close to Lake Erie. It was a tough neighborhood and their mother refused to move, she stated that she would never leave her home. She died in the very same bed which she had spent more than thirty years of her life sleeping in, and Grandville had not been back to the house since his mother's passing.

Franklin had informed him that Greta was now staying in their family home and he could not figure out why. He knew that Greta had done very well for herself when she and Rayshawn divorced. On top of the several millions which she received in the divorce settlement, she was also receiving a huge alimony check.

When Greta came to Oakhill to visit with him, he planned to talk her into moving out of their family home into a condo in one of the Bratenahl area's gated communities, as the exclusive suburb was close to where they grew up. He worried about her, because their old neighborhood had become rough with lots of crime.

"Grandville it's time for you to come out of the hole." Emerson's familiar voice brought him out of the memories of his past and back into the present.

"How long have I been here?" Questioned Grandville.

"You have only been in for about twelve hours. However, your counselor wants to see you so I'm going to take you to him," Officer Emerson stated.

"Will I be coming back to the hole after my meeting with Mr. Bolden?" Grandville asked.

"I don't know, I only do what they tell me to do, nothing more, nothing less, and we need to go right now," Officer Emerson stated.

Grandville followed Emerson to his Counselor's office and tried to figure out exactly what was going on.

"Have a seat Grandville," Mr. Bolden directed.

"Okay Mr. Bolden, but why did you have me pulled out of the hole?" Asked a curious Grandville.

"Because the Warden told me to. It would appear there are a few important pieces of information missing from your file that you failed to mention," stated Mr. Bolden.

"I don't know what you are talking about," Grandville replied.

"Grandville, you have a visitor who is waiting for you in the Warden's office." Mr. Bolden advised.

"I have never had a visit with my Attorney in the Warden's office and he wasn't due to come until tomorrow. What is going on?" Grandville questioned.

"It isn't your Attorney who is here to visit with you," Mr. Bolden replied.

"Is it Juliette, my wife, is she here?" Asked Grandville.

"No, I am afraid not," replied Mr. Bolden.

"Then who?" Questioned Grandville.

"Your brother in law, the one you have never mentioned. The famous LA's Point Guard, Rayshawn Robinson," Mr. Bolden replied.

Chapter 11
What About Your Friends?

Juliette put the last touches of her make up on and stared at herself in the mirror. She had done a fairly good job of hiding the swelling and puffiness around her eyes which had come from her crying earlier in the day. The white jeans that she wore, along with her very cute white top, showed off her curvy pop bottle figure, and the bright colors of her outfit contrasted well against her dark mahogany complexion. After putting on her lipstick, she went into her living room to have an adult beverage before Samantha, Tara and Greta arrived at her home.

She went into her dining room area and mixed her signature drink, Skyy Vodka and Cranberry juice, in a tall glass and tried her best to pretend everything was okay knowing full well that it wasn't. She was a little apprehensive about the whole night, due to the drama Greta and Samantha were having with one another. Juliette never did get an opportunity to speak to Samantha about the tension which always seemed to be present between she and Greta. She decided, that she would have a conversation with Samantha later. Juliette was already stressed due to the Anniversary, and she didn't feel like dealing with anything else that could potentially upset her.

Her ringing cell phone caught her attention, and she saw the name Tara Moran flash across the screen.

"Hey Tara," stated Juliette into her cell phone.

"Hey Juliette, I wanted to let you know, I am on my way to pick up Samantha. I am running a few minutes late," replied Tara.

"Ok," said Juliette.

"What are you doing?" Questioned Tara.

"Nothing, just sitting here having a drink and waiting for you guys," replied Juliette.

"Alright, well I will chat with you later. I probably should focus on the road," stated Tara.

"Ok, I will see you when you get here," responded Juliette.

Juliette hung up the phone and thought briefly about Tara, who in the past year had become closer to her. Tara was very opinionated, loved to debate and had a wicked sense of humor. Juliette had made her acquaintance due to another one of her friends whose name was Toya. Juliette and Toya had attended graduate school together. Juliette would occasionally hang out with Toya when Tara was around. However, she had gotten to know Tara better, due to Tara's friendship with Samantha.

Tara worked as a Domestic Violence Advocate for a private agency which contracted with the DA's office to assist victims of domestic violence with prosecuting their abuser, as a result Tara's agency had placed her in Samantha's office, and the two had become very friendly. Samantha had started inviting Tara to join them when she and Juliette went out. Juliette didn't mind, and she was cordial but she kind of kept Tara at arms-length until recently.

There were a lot of qualities about Tara which Juliette admired. She appeared to be hard working, a good mother and loyal. The qualities which she didn't like about her was that sometimes Tara was extremely too opinionated, and she could be downright rude to those outside her inner circle for no apparent reason. Tara also seemed to bring out the worst in Samantha, and the two sometimes fed-off-of each other's negative energy. Tara was several years younger than both Juliette and Samantha and could be a lot of fun because she was both loud and funny.

Juliette believed in friendship and had known many of her friends for a number years. She was somewhat leery of new people, believing that most people weren't genuine and had ill motives, like the words of the Canadian Rapper, Drake, *"No New Friends"*, had always been her motto. So, for the most part, Juliette kept her acquaintances on a superficial level. When she did invest her friendship in someone, she evaluated them first to see if their negative qualities outweighed their positive ones. She and Tara's relationship changed when Tara shared her life story with Juliette. Tara didn't hold back and told her about the details of the years of sexual abuse which she suffered at the hands of her older Sister.

Juliette was very cognizant of the fact that Tara could be manipulative. At times she could also be mean, nasty and cold, but she ignored the negative parts of Tara's personality and tried to focus on the positive. She attributed Tara's negative qualities to the years of abuse which she suffered from her older Sister. Juliette felt there was a lost, beautiful woman, underneath her tarnish, and she was determined to help her find the woman who was hidden beneath the years of abuse and pain.

Juliette was looking forward to hanging out with her friends but then remembered back to the last time she and Samantha had dinner. They were having such a good time until they saw Franklin. Samantha seemed to take it out on her that Franklin was out with someone else, but Juliette had to admit that Samantha had been acting nicer recently and she appeared to be working on her attitude.

The ringing doorbell brought her back to the present and Juliette opened the door for Greta. Greta looked stunning in a short black sundress, and wedge heels that showed off her amazingly long legs. She wore her hair loose, and it hung past her shoulders, her make-up was applied flawlessly and her smoky black eye shadow and liner accented her hazel brown eyes.

"You look beautiful, come on in. Tara just called a few minutes ago, she's on her way to pick up Samantha and they're running a few minutes late. Are you drinking tonight?" Juliette asked.

"Of course I am, and I am smoking too," Greta said.

Greta pulled out a huge blunt. "Give me one of whatever it is that you're drinking. I'm going to go on out to the sun porch and have a few puffs of this. You can have some too if you want," Greta stated.

"I'm drinking Skyy Vodka and Cranberry. I also have Hennessey and Jack Daniels, because I know how much you like dark brown liquor."

"You know that's right. I like my liquor like I like my men, tall and dark. I will have a Jack and Coke."

Greta proceeded to walk through the family room to the sun porch and Juliette went into the dining room to make the drinks. Soon the smell of marijuana wafted through the air and Juliette lit some incense to help mask the smell. Juliette smoked occasionally and this was one night which she planned to indulge. She just wanted one night where she could escape and not think about all the problems which were plaguing her life. After giving Greta her drink, and an ashtray, she took the blunt from Greta and inhaled several long puffs. The calming effects of the drug immediately took hold and Juliette leaned back into the couch.

"How are you doing Juliette?" Greta asked.

"I am here. I have been trying to keep myself busy to keep my mind off what today represents."

"You have too."

"I went to see my Counselor, then I stopped by the rooming house and did some paperwork."

"Girl you never stop working, do you."

"Well, you know that my cousin Melinia is now a resident of A Better Tomorrow, and she hasn't been back to the house in more than twenty-four hours."

"That can be alarming."

"I am starting to get a little worried. Apparently she might owe some drug dealers a lot of money.

"What . . ."

"I haven't had the chance to talk to her yet so I really don't know what is going on. I tried to call her but her phone is going straight to voicemail, and I can't leave a message because her voice mail box is full," Juliette replied.

"Well don't get yourself all worked up just yet. Maybe Melinia has a new man that she is hanging out with."

"Well she shouldn't be dating anyone right now. She shouldn't start any new relationships in the first year of becoming sober," Juliette advised.

"Juliette don't start tripping. You have enough to worry about, so don't add anything else to your pile before you know if there's even a problem with your cousin," Greta replied.

"You're right, I'm about to go and make myself another drink."

"Okay, but don't over-do it. Remember, you just took a couple of drags off this blunt, and this here is some powerful stuff. My girl who also happens to be a sorority sister from LA came to visit me a couple of weeks ago and she brought me an ounce as a gift. She and her husband drove cross country in an RV, so they could get a chance to see the United States from a different perspective. They stayed with me at Mom's house for a night and got back on the road the next day. She has a prescription in LA for this stuff and this particular-mix is known as purple haze. Smoking it makes me miss LA just a little bit, because when I lived there I puffed, puffed, everyday just to get through the humiliation of being the wife of the famous, cheating, Rayshawn Robinson."

"Greta, sometimes you need something to help you release all of the hurt inside."

"Then, after everything that happened with both my mother, and with Jessica dying and then what's happened with Grandville, without my best friend Maryjane, I don't know how I would have made it through most days."

"I can relate, but I hardly get the opportunity to indulge since I spend so much time taking care of the kids and running my business."

"How are you doing on finances? I have quite a chunk put up, and I want to give some of it to you as a gift."

"Greta, just like I told you the last time that you offered, I am good."

"Juliette, you drive me crazy, what's the point of being a millionaire if your family won't let you spoil them a little."

"You're spoiling me now."

"You won't let me buy the children gifts, and I understand you don't want the kids to grow up acting like entitled brats, but damn girl, can't you be like other people who have a rich relative and tell me what you want and let me get it for you."

"Greta please save your money. I have told you, the children and I are set on finances and besides Grandville has been having money sent to me through Franklin."

"That's my brother, he is a provider and he even does it while being locked up."

The doorbell rang again and Juliette got up to go and open it for Samantha and Tara. Samantha was dressed in a pink sun dress which had a split going up one side and showed off her lean figure and long legs. She also wore her hair down and ringlets of curls framed her pretty, ebony face. Tara had on a matching red and white capris outfit and both ladies looked very nice.

"Hey guys come on in. You both look beautiful. We're sitting on the sun porch. What would you ladies like to drink?" Juliette asked.

"Do you have any Tito's Vodka? You know that's my drink. It has less calories than most Vodka," Tara said.

"No Tara, I only have Skyy Vodka," Juliette replied.

"This kook tells us about Tito's every time we get together for a drink," Samantha chuckled.

"I know, and I need to buy some for the house."

"Juliette, I will have any kind of top shelf Vodka you have as long as it's not Absolute. You know, Absolute gives me an absolute headache. You know I want my drink chased with just a touch of tonic." Samantha said.

"Okay Samantha. Tara, I also have some Jack and Hennessey." Juliette said.

"I am going to have a Skyy and Tonic just like Samantha," Tara said.

Juliette quickly mixed more drinks and all three ladies went out to the sun porch where Greta was sitting. Samantha looked at Greta and said, "It smells like you ladies started the party without us."

"Don't worry we have more of the party favors." Greta replied.

Greta pulled out the blunt that she and Juliette had been smoking and relit it. After taking two puffs she passed it to Samantha who took three long drags and then passed it to Tara.

Tara took three long drags and said, "This is some real good stuff. It's strong and I'm feeling the effects of it already. I'm the designated driver. I'm feeling okay to drive right now but I better not have anymore," Tara advised.

"Tara are you sure you're okay to drive? I'm not trying to have you kill us in a car accident," Samantha asked with a questioning look on her face.

"Samantha, I've been driving you around for the past year, and we haven't been in an accident yet and you know I smoke just about every day."

"I'm just checking."

"And I'm just saying, it usually takes me a whole joint to feel like I do after two puffs off of her stuff," Tara replied.

"It's called Purple Haze, and I got it from one of my sorority sisters who has a prescription for it in in LA. It's very potent," Greta said.

"It's potent, I will give you that, but trust and believe, I'm okay to drive. There's pending legislation in the Statehouse to legalize Maryjane for medical purposes here in Ohio. I sure hope it gets passed, because if it does I'm going to get me a prescription for this here Purple Haze. I am going to tell the doctor I have Athletes Foot or something." Tara laughed.

"Good luck with seeing it implemented here in Ohio. The legislation may pass but the law will never go into effect. The old boys in Southern Ohio are against it. My office is against it as well. We're afraid children will be influenced negatively, and it will serve as a gateway to harder, more dangerous drugs. Most people are too stupid to stop with a drink here and there and a little Maryjane occasionally. We are also concerned that all kinds of people who have serious jobs will be under the influence while at work. You know how conservative this State is and the further South you drive the more religious the people become. As long as our State is controlled by Republicans, the Bill even it does pass, does not have a snowballs chance in hell of ever going into effect." Samantha said.

"Those Republican assholes kill me. More people are dying of Heroin overdoses here in Cuyahoga County and in Northeast Ohio then of anything else including Car Accidents. Why doesn't the establishment not see that prescribing of legal Opiates like Percocet and OxyContin is why so many are abusing illegal drugs like Heroin and not because of a little Marijuana. I have yet to meet the guy who wanted to rob me so that he could buy some Maryjane. However, I know a lot of people who will rob me to buy Cocaine, Heroin and OxyContin." Greta said.

"Well it's a good thing that we have some good stuff right here and don't have to worry about getting a prescription today." All four of the ladies squealed with laughter at Tara's joke.

"Juliette how have you been doing today?" Samantha asked.

"I'm okay Samantha. Just trying to hang on in there."

"Well your girls are here, and it's our goal to get your mind off whatever is ailing you."

"Thanks guys. What time is our reservation?" Juliette asked.

"They don't allow people to make reservations at Shooters, but I've been assured we will not have to wait for a table. Being a VIP does have its privileges," Samantha said.

"Cool so when do you guys want to leave?" Juliette asked.

"There is no rush. Let's hear some music and enjoy the drinks that you have prepared," Samantha stated.

Samantha jumped up and took everyone's drink glasses. "Juliette you just relax. I'm going to make us more drinks, and I'll also turn us on some tunes. Greta what are you drinking?"

"I am having Jack Daniels and Coke. Do you want me to help you?" Greta asked.

"Don't worry I am not going to poison you," Samantha replied.

"Damn Soror. I didn't think you would, I just thought trying to carry all the glasses would be difficult."

"No, I'm cool. I worked in a restaurant when I was a teenager. You just relax and hang out with the girls." Samantha replied.

Samantha headed towards the dining room, and a few minutes later the sound of Rap music filled the sun porch. Grandville had installed surround sound all throughout the house and the music sounded great as it floated out of her Boise speakers.

Samantha returned with a tray filled with drinks and asked, "Do you guys like the music? I brought this CD from DJ Emory. He's one of hell of a DJ, and he knows how to mix the old school with the new school in a way that makes me want to get up and dance." Screamed Samantha.

Samantha suddenly jumped up and start dancing and rapping along with the lyrics of Digital Underground's *Humpty Dance*.

"Juliette remember when we went to Regionals in Pittsburgh and we strolled to this song? We had a great time." Samantha said.

"I remember that. We met that cool Soror from Pittsburgh who showed us around the city. I also remember the White Cowboy who tried to holler at Samantha. The guy had on a fifty-gallon cowboy hat, a vest, a belt with a huge buckle and some cowboy boots with actual spurs in the back. He was looking at Samantha like she was steak and he was starving. We were in line for breakfast and he was standing right behind us. He asked, if he could join us for breakfast. Samantha looked at me and said, 'Why is this white man talking to me?' I almost busted out laughing right in the poor man's face as I tried to ignore this crazy fool right here," Juliette laughed out loud.

"Juliette knows how I feel about it. When I'm out of town, I can say what I want, because in other cities nobody knows me. It gives me an excuse to act a complete fool, but Juliette checks me when I get too far to the left. Also, I would never date a white man. I can't get past that fact that we were forced into sexual acts with white men during slavery. I won't voluntarily give it to them besides, I like my men tall, dark and handsome and he was the total opposite of that." Samantha said.

"I'm your BFF and that's one of my jobs. To stop you just before you cross the line," Juliette said.

"How touching. Don't start French kissing each other right in front of us. Do you guys want some privacy?" Tara teased.

"Forget you Tara. You're the Lesbo out of the group." Samantha remarked in jest.

All the ladies laughed and began to get into groove of the music. *Fight the Power* by Public Enemy followed by Master P's *No Limit* had the women out of their seats dancing like they were in a night club.

"Samantha, you're going to have let me hold a copy of this CD. Old boy really put some classic cuts on it. This is the music that made me fall in love with Rap. I can barely stand the garbage this

134

younger generation is putting out today. Now all the new Rap music seems to be about convincing our young black queens to become strippers and whores." Greta suddenly broke out rapping, "Hey bitches, hey hoes, drop your britches and get your butt on the pole and shake your ass for a dollar and some change. Now twerk."

The women roared with laughter.

"Greta, I agree. Some of this new stuff the younger generation is listening to is horrible and an assault to my ear drums. Lil Wayne for example is constantly putting out some crazy lyrics when it comes to our young ladies. Always talking about sex and oral sex and putting broom sticks in us, his lyrics are degrading to women, and it's so disappointing when you look at how talented he really is. I mean, in order to rap you have to have some command of the English language. Some of these young rappers are helping to tear the race down instead of helping to build it up. You know what makes it worse is, our young Queens actually dance to this music and try to convince themselves the Rappers are not referring to them." Juliette said.

"Juliette you and everybody else here has to agree, influences from our generation is the reason why the Rap is the way it is today. It started in our generation with Whoodini and their song, "*I'm A Hoe.*" Then, the group NWA took rap to a whole new level, and let's not even talk about Eaze E who loved to call women Bitches and Hoes. Hell, the brother had sex with so many chicks unprotected, he died from AIDS. Even Biggie, Eminem, 2Pac and Jay Z who are considered some of the greatest Rappers of our generation sometimes uses disparaging lyrics when they refer to females. I never take it personally when I'm called a bitch. Hell, it can be considered a term of endearment," Samantha said.

"Samantha, I have to disagree. I don't want my kids listening to half the crap that's out now. With technology, the way it is today, it's almost impossible to censor everything they see and hear. There is only so much that I can do," Juliette said.

"Okay ladies this conversation is becoming way too heavy. I say we go ahead and move the party to Shooters," Tara said.

"Good idea Tara. We don't want to be too intellectual tonight. Despite everything we are going to try and have some fun. I want to take a drink with me. Juliette, do you have any plastic cups?" Samantha asked.

"Yes, they're in the kitchen cabinet. You ladies can head towards the kitchen while I lock the house up and set the security alarm," Juliette said.

Juliette walked around to the front of the house and ensured all the windows were down and the doors were locked. She then went to the kitchen where Samantha and Greta had just got finished making drinks and set the alarm. Tara who was the designated driver decided not to indulge in any more alcoholic drinks until they had dinner.

The ladies piled up in Tara's old Ford Explorer and headed towards 90 West which is one of the freeways that would take them to Route 2, because it leads to Shooters in the Flats which is located on the West Bank of Cleveland's famous Cuyahoga River. After parking the ladies entered the restaurant where they noticed people both standing and sitting around the lobby. Everyone appeared to be waiting for their names to be called so they could get a table. Samantha marched up to the desk to give her name. The Maître d took one look at Samantha and immediately knew who she was, "Hello DA Trunk. How many in your party?" The Maître d' asked.

"There are four of us and we want to sit outside by the water." Samantha replied.

"No problem let me show you to your table," the Maître d' replied.

The ladies followed the Maître d' out to a large table which had a large umbrella in the middle of it, and was situated on a dock which sat on the river. He picked up the reserved sign and handed them each a menu, "Your server will be with you shortly," the Maître d' responded.

Juliette looked at the shimmering, calm water and relaxed. She was feeling the effects from the marijuana and the two Vodka's which she had consumed before leaving home, and she was feeling mellow.

"They have some great things on the menu. Juliette. Do you know what you want?" Samantha asked.

"No, I am torn between the shrimp and the Walleye, but I am going to see if they have a combo. Have you decided?" Juliette asked.

"You know I'm going to have the grilled chicken salad. Where the hell is our server? I want to order our table a round of drinks," Samantha declared.

"She'll be here in a minute. This was a good idea to come here. It's so beautiful and peaceful out here on the water. Greta, have you decided what you're going to order yet?" Juliette asked.

"Yes, I am going to have the pork chops," Greta replied.

"You're actually going to order swine?" Tara asked.

"Yes, Tara I am. I don't know what you've been told, but Pork is the other white meat, and we as African Americans would not have survived slavery without it. I know you won't be ordering any pig, but what are you going to eat?" Greta inquired.

"I am going to have the steak. You know I'm a meat and potatoes kind of girl."

Soon the server made it to their table. "Ladies I am sorry it took me so long to get over here, but it's a little crazy in here tonight. Can I start you out with dinner cocktails?" Asked their waitress.

"Yes, we are going to have one Skyy Vodka and Cranberry in a tall glass and two Skyy Vodka's and tonics in the regular short glasses and a Jack Daniel and Coke on the rocks," Samantha said.

The server left the table and the women chattered amongst themselves making jokes, shooting the breeze and gazing at the water. A few minutes later their server returned with their drinks, and then took their dinner orders. After going to the kitchen, she came back with a folded piece of paper which she gave to Greta.

"Is that the drink order bill? If so pass it to me, so I can pay it and you can get the next round," Samantha said.

"No, Samantha it's not the bill it's a note."

"Well who is it from and what does it say?"

Before Greta could respond a tall, dark, extremely handsome man walked over to their table and stood next to Greta.

"Greta Robinson. I can't believe it. I noticed when you walked-in, and I knew right away it was you. I never thought I would ever see you again. What are you doing here?" The man asked.

Greta stood up and gave the attractive man a long hug. "Oh my God Derek it's good to see you. Let me introduce you to my friends. This is Juliette, Tara and Samantha. Ladies this is Derek."

"Hello ladies it's good to meet all of you. Greta, you didn't answer my question, the last time I saw you, you were in LA what brings you to Cleveland?" Derek asked.

"Derek, I live here now. After I left LA, I came back home. I'm a Clevelander, born, bred and raised so don't start talking junk about my hometown. I've heard too many people refer to my city as "the mistake by the lake" and most of those people have never even been to Cleveland."

"Why would I talk junk about the place where I was born? I guess, I never got a chance to tell you that I was raised here in Cleveland. I have been away for years, but I was recently offered a job with the Cleveland Avilers. I took it so that I could come home. I was tired of LA and all the fake and phony people who live out there."

Tara was looking at Derek like he was a tall, drink of ice cold water and she was dying of thirst.

"Derek Dolan. I can't believe it. I haven't seen you in years," Tara said.

138

Derek took his gaze off Greta to glance at Tara. The look on his face gave-away the fact that he had no idea who Tara was.

"I am sorry but I don't recall meeting you in the past," Derek said with a puzzled look on his face.

"That's because the last time you saw me I was thirteen. You and my older brother Tim were very good friends, and you would come over to my house and hang out with him just about every day."

"Is your brother Tim Moran?"

"Yes."

"Yes, now I remember you. How is Tim I haven't talked to him in years, but I did see him at the last class reunion?"

"Tim is well. He is married and has five kids. He moved to North Carolina several years ago."

"I am glad to hear that he is doing well and please tell him that I said hello," Derek said.

Derek then turned his attention back to Greta. "Greta I don't want to lose touch with you again. Since we are both living in Cleveland now, I'm fully expecting us to get together. I put all my contact numbers on that note, and I am looking forward to a call from you."

Greta blushed, smiled and said, "Okay Derek I will call you."

"You better. I just finished having dinner with some of the other members of the Avilers front office and we are on our way out the door.

"I know you have to go. It was great seeing you."

"You ladies have a fantastic dinner and Greta you make sure you call me," Derek said.

Derek then leaned down and kissed Greta on the cheek, turned around and headed in the direction which he came from.

"Damn, that's one fine man right there. Greta how do you know him?" Tara questioned.

"Derek used to work in the LA's front office. He worked closely with me when I coordinated a LA's Date Night. Eligible LA's Girls and Players would go out with the highest bidders and the proceeds went to Rayshawn's charity. Derek helped me to recruit the single players and cheerleaders who participated in the event. We raised a lot of money and were able to offer three graduating high school seniors from Cleveland a full ride to Ohio State on behalf of Rayshawn's charity," Greta replied.

"Greta that's phenomenal," Juliette said.

"Thanks Juliette."

"I can't believe Derek Dolan was just here. I just can't believe it," Tara said.

"Is that the guy you told me about?" Samantha asked Tara.

"Yes Samantha it is."

"What about him?" Greta questioned.

"Derek is the guy who Tara has been in love with since she was a teenager."

"Ok Samantha. Don't embarrass me."

"The two of you looked pretty friendly, so why don't you use the numbers on the note he gave you to put in a good word for her," Samantha said.

"Tara no disrespect but Derek doesn't even seem to remember you," Greta replied.

"I know, but I remember him. I knew when I was a kid, he would grow up to be somebody important. I had such a crush on him. He and my brother were good friend. Then, one day after he and my brother Tim graduated from High School, he was suddenly gone and I didn't see him anymore. He's everything I want in a man," Tara said in a low whispering voice.

"Tara, I don't know how you could make such a declaration if you haven't seen him since you were a young teenager, but when I talk to him I will inquire if he's interested in you," Greta told her.

The waitress returned with their food and the ladies proceeded to eat dinner while Samantha entertained them with her stories.

"I was at an Ohio Democratic meeting the other day and one of the Ward Leaders, who also happens to be one of my Sorors, was talking to me in the bathroom. She has the biggest ass I have ever seen on anyone. Both of us were in the bathroom stalls doing our business, when it became apparent she was doing number two and these loud farts were echoing off the walls. Do you know this chick kept talking like nothing was happening. I on the other hand was doing everything I could to get out of that bathroom before the stench killed me," Samantha started laughing so hard. The women almost choked on their food due to laughter and tried to control themselves, so they could hear more of Samantha's tales when out the clear blue Samantha changed the subject.

"Greta don't forget to make sure that you put in a good word for Tara with your boy Derek. She was just telling me the other day about Derek and how in love she was with him when she was young, and how she wished she could see him again. Why don't you pass Tara's phone number to Derek, so that they can hook up?"

"Well, Tara you got your wish, because you just got the chance to see Derek. But, I don't know about hooking you up with him. It'll be up to him if he wants to date you," Greta said.

"Damn Greta at least try and put in a good word for her. You were already married to a BBA star, let the rest of us have the chance to date the eligible bachelors. Don't be selfish," Samantha said in a sarcastic tone.

Tara decided it was a good time for her to intervene. "Samantha I am cool. When we talked about Derek we were talking about who we considered to be our first loves. It's really not that serious," Tara said.

Greta was pissed and couldn't let Samantha's comment go. "First of all, I'm not selfish. Besides, you didn't even think to ask me if I was interested in Derek because maybe I am. I'm divorced, so maybe I am trying to find an eligible bachelor who I can date. When I lived in LA, Derek and I were acquaintances. Those brothers who worked in the LA's front office always keep their distance from the player's wives and girlfriends, because they don't want or need the drama. I am not married anymore and who knows maybe Derek and I will become friends. When I call him, I'll see what's up. If Derek is interested in Tara, I'll relay her information but you shouldn't assume anything," Greta said.

"Juliette, this is exactly what I have been talking about. These high yellow heifers swear they are all that just because they're damn near white looking with straight, wavy hair. Brothers like Derek and Rayshawn always pick women like her over women like us. Then they find themselves thoroughly disappointed. Women like her think they're too cute to properly hold a brother down, but men like Rayshawn and Derek always look past the chicks like me and Tara," Samantha said.

Juliette closed her eyes and prayed that the situation did not get out of hand.

"Ladies, relax. It's not that big of a deal. Derek might not be interested in either of us so why are we arguing?" Tara interjected.

"I wasn't arguing, I was just stating what appears to be a fact," Samantha said.

Juliette knew right then and there the Anniversary of one of the most horrible days of her life had just taken a turn for the worse.

Chapter 12
Fallin'

Grandville couldn't believe his ears. Rayshawn had come to Oakhill to see him. Grandville had not laid eyes on Rayshawn in three years, and he had little interest in what he had to say, but he did recognize that to refuse to see him could cause him a lot of problems with his jailors. Grandville walked down the old hallways of Oakhill with his Counselor Mr. Bolden while his insides swirled with anxiety. He had spent a lot of time in solitary confinement reminiscing about the good and bad times he and Rayshawn had shared together. Then, out of the clear blue Rayshawn shows up at Oakhill after they had not seen or communicated with each other in the past three years. Grandville had no idea what Rayshawn wanted and couldn't understand why he would show up at the prison on the Anniversary of Jessica's death.

When Grandville walked into the Warden's office he noticed Rayshawn was seated next to an older African American man who Grandville had never seen before. Warden Jenkins was a tall white man in his early sixties, who had blond hair and watery blue eyes and as soon as Grandville entered his office he asked him to sit down. Then he said, "Mr. Stubbs it appears you forgot to inform us that Rayshawn Robinson, starting point guard for the LA's and one of the best point guards that the league has ever seen is your brother in law."

"Sir, my sister and Mr. Robinson are divorced so technically Mr. Robinson is my ex-brother in law."

"Grandville, me and Greta not being together is only temporary. I love your sister, and I'm going to get her to fall in love with me again. I want to introduce you to my Attorney Mr. Williams who represents the Robinson Charity," Rayshawn said.

The man nodded his head in Grandville's direction. Grandville attempted to figure out what was going on but did his best to remain calm and quiet.

The Warden then began to speak, "Mr. Stubbs it seems Mr. Robinson wants to donate money from his charity to have a new state of the art mental health clinic built here at Oakhill. The center will be known as the Jessica Stubbs Behavioral Health Hospital in honor of your deceased daughter."

Grandville was speechless and didn't know how to feel about this news so he kept his mouth shut.

"Mr. Robinson has asked to visit with you for a half an hour. Usually we make all potential visitors engage in a rigorous pre-screening process where we verify their personal information. However, I'm going to waive that requirement as, Mr. Robinson is well known internationally and allow the visit which will occur right here in my office. I usually follow all protocols in respect to visitors, but to have Mr. Robinson seen by the other prisoners will cause more problems than it's worth. Guards are stationed right outside my office door, and you are being monitored by close circuit camera. I have given Mr. Robinson a panic button. Also, you will remain handcuffed and keep your leg shackles on throughout the visit. I have had very little trouble from you since the first day you walked into this facility. I ask you maintain that high standard and continue to remain on your best behavior during this visit. I'm going to take Mr. Williams on a quick tour of our facility, so he can see our current mental health clinic," stated Warden Jenkins.

"Warden Jenkins I assure you, I will be on my best behavior," Grandville replied.

The Warden and Attorney Williams stood up and walked out of the office leaving Grandville and Rayshawn alone.

"So how have they been treating you in here?"

"I'm treated just like the other prisoners are treated. I'm told when to eat, when to shower, when to shit, and when to do just about anything, but all in all I'm okay considering all that has happened."

"Grandville I owe you an apology for not coming to visit you before now. I figured if I came earlier, then it would cause our family additional problems because the paparazzi is always breathing down my throat."

"I totally understand and I'm cool with it, but what I don't understand is why you are here now. What do you want?"

"I wanted to see you so I could tell you man to man, I am sorry for everything. I know that I broke my promise to you and my vows to Greta, but I love you guys and I miss you. I know, I should have been here for you, and I know I let you down. I want you to know that you are my family and I know that you didn't mean to hurt Jessica. Since we can't change what happened and bring Jessica back we can do the next best thing. We can honor her and make sure her name is associated with something good and positive."

"Man I appreciate what you're trying to do for me but I would prefer if you didn't. You don't owe me anything and since you and my sister are divorced you are no longer family so any duty you feel is really unnecessary."

"Divorced or not Greta is still my wife under God's laws and Jessica was still my niece and I loved her too. Therefore, I'm having the clinic built and it will bear her name. I just wanted to come and tell you face to face of my plan. The money will be donated from the Robinson Foundation which Greta helped to grow into a huge charity with millions of dollars in it. I can't change what has happened, but I want you to know I'm trying to become a different man. I also need to talk to you about something really sensitive and ask for your help."

"You better not be here to tell me something crazy like you have HIV and that you might have given it to my sister." Said Grandville.

"No it's nothing like that, but it is still bad. What I have to tell you really doesn't concern Greta but it does concern Juliette but only in a secondary kind of way."

Grandville felt himself becoming stressed, and he attempted to breathe slowly through his nose while exhaling through his mouth to try to stay calm.

"What is it Rayshawn? We don't have much time," Grandville demanded.

"From the moment Greta told me she was divorcing me I went into a deep crazy depression. Grandville, I know I messed up, but despite all that I did to destroy our relationship I did and still do love your sister."

"You screwed your way through half of the women in LA, if that's love I wouldn't want to see how you show hate."

"Grandville let me finish my story, you just said we don't have much time. Without Greta, I was so lost and when my cousin Lovelle invited me to his home outside of Akron to help cheer me up, I couldn't say no. I was lonely and depressed and thought hanging out with him would cheer me up. You've met Lovelle several times when we were younger. He is the only family I have with the exception of my parents, you and Greta and your kids. He is several years younger than me and is engaged in some unsavory business. I don't usually hang out with him, because he can be bad news. After Greta left me, I was lonely even though I was surrounded by a lot of people. I kept thinking Greta would come to realize that despite my mistakes I love her and when she didn't call the divorce off I was devastated.

Lovelle kept in touch with me during that dark period in my life by calling and texting me every day in an attempt to cheer me up. He convinced me to leave LA and come for a visit at his house, so I wouldn't have to be alone on the day the divorce was final. He has a real nice house in Tallmadge right outside of Akron, and it has a huge private backyard. He also threw a party for me. He had this large tent set-up with tables, a bar, a buffet, and he had someone hang a banner which said, "Divorce means the beginning of a new life."

He had a DJ and plenty of alcohol and food. Lovelle invited all these people to the party who I had never seen or met before. He told everybody I was his cousin from the West Coast and my name was Ray Ray. You know that's what my family used to call me when I was young. I didn't shave since it was the off season, and I grew this huge bushy beard, and the people at the party didn't seem to recognize me. For the first time in a long time, I was able to let my hair down and was able to truly be myself. I was having a great time eating, dancing and partying when I saw a redbone who was super bad. She was checking me from across the room. I knew I could be with her without feeling the immense guilt I often felt when dealing with a woman who was not Greta, because I was no longer married and could do what I pleased.

After the party ended the redbone was still there. She and Lovelle took me to one of the spare bedrooms where she rocked me and Lovelle's world. I let her give me a BJ while Lovelle hit it from behind and it was one of the best threesomes I ever had. I find out later this girl is into speed-balling and when under the influence of both heroin and cocaine she is a straight-up freak. I also find out later this girl is not only voluptuous and beautiful but she's also a college graduate.

While she was doing me, I caught a glimpse of myself in the mirror and realized, there is something seriously wrong with me. I know you won't believe me, but I swear I have never put my penis inside another woman's vagina when I was married to Greta. I only let the other women take my Johnson for a spin in their mouths, and I know my actions are still considered cheating. It was like I was possessed, like no matter how hard I tried, I just couldn't say no to the numerous invitations. The morning after the party I woke up in the bed next to the redbone and she called me Rayshawn. She then told me her name is Melinia and she is Juliette's first cousin. She said, she had been to a cookout at your house when I was there and immediately recognized me but assured Lovelle that she wouldn't blow my cover.

I stayed with Lovelle for three days, and Melinia allowed me to experience her oral magic every day. When I returned to LA I immediately sought help for my insatiable need to receive BJs. I have been attending therapy for more than six months, and I have learned that I have a sex addiction which stems from my early adolescence and I am getting help. I find out later that Melinia was only at Lovelle's house because she owes him a lot of money for her habit. She slept with us to pay-off some of her debt and to get more drugs. I recently learned she videotaped our sex sessions, and she's planning to release the tape. Allegedly, she thinks that she can become rich and famous like Kim K if she releases the tape but let's face it, Melinia is not Kim K."

"So what do you want from me?" Grandville asked.

"I want you to talk to Juliette and see if she can convince Melinia to give me the tape and all the copies. I am willing to pay her, and she could use the money to start a new life."

"Rayshawn why do care if she releases the tape? You weren't married when the tape was made so just say it wasn't you."

"Do you remember how badly the sex tape that is rumored to star R Kelly hurt his career? He wasn't married either, and he has always maintained that it wasn't him but people still believed that it was. I have several lucrative endorsements for family orientated products and let's not talk about the morality clause in my contract with the LA's or how badly a tape like this could damage the Robinson Charity Foundation. What a tape like this will cost my reputation if it gets out is more than what it will cost me to pay Melinia. She can use the money to start a new life and get off the junk for good."

"Rayshawn I haven't talked to Juliette personally since the day that Jessica died but I will have Franklin talk to her to see what we can do. Franklin is who I want you to communicate with regarding this matter. You are not to communicate with my wife or my sister and you are never to return to Oakhill to see me ever again. If there is something you want or to need for me to know you send the message through Franklin who will ensure I get it. Is that understood?" Grandville asked.

"Sure, I understand but trust and believe Lovelle and his friends are looking for Melinia too. You know what they will do to her if they find her. Lovelle is very angry Melinia made the tape while at his house, and she stills owes him a lot of money. If he finds her before I do, Melinia might very well become famous but it will not be for the reasons she wants. I can't afford to be associated with any of this, and I know I can always count on you for discretion. Grandville, I also want you to know I purposely planned my visit today, because I know today is the Anniversary of Jessica's death. I have been working with the Robinson Foundation Coordinator, Ms. Walters and the charity's attorney Mr. Williams to ensure the foundation can afford to build the new clinic and still be solvent. I don't want you to think of this day as the day Jessica died, I want you to think of this day as the day Jessica's name will become representative of healing."

"Rayshawn thank you but like I said you don't have to do this."

"I know Grandville but I want too. Do you need anything? Does Juliette or the kids need anything? All you have to do is say the word."

"No Rayshawn, I'm good. I invested well before I got here. So, I have a pretty ample stash of cash and Juliette and the kids are doing well in respect to finances. However, I do want you to do something for me." Grandville responded.

"What is it? All you have to do is ask and it is done."

"I have a friend who's in here with me. I think they are going to release him soon and I want you to give him a job when he gets out of here."

"What is he qualified to do?"

"He was a policeman before he came here, and I think he would be a great addition to your security team."

"Well why is he in here?"

"He killed the man who was sexually abusing his son. He walked in on the abuser while he was making his son perform oral sex and the trauma of witnessing the event made him snap. He's a good guy who probably shouldn't even be here. He has been great to me, and he has been watching my back the whole time that I've been in here. I think he deserves a break." Grandville responded.

"When he gets out let me know, and I'll make sure he has a job."

"Thanks Rayshawn."

"Grandville please give your sister and our family my love and take care of yourself."

"I will and remember what I said about talking to my sister and Juliette," Grandville said.

"I heard you, I will contact Franklin," Rayshawn stated.

Warden Jenkins who was escorted by several guards walked into the office which indicated the end of the visit. Grandville looked at the clock mounted on the wall and noted the Warden ended the visit exactly 30 minutes after it had begun. Rayshawn and his Attorney were led from the office by the guards while Grandville waited for Emerson.

Grandville was then escorted back to his Counselor Mr. Bolden's office by Officer Emerson whose cold demeanor was suddenly thawed.

"Grandville it was a real trip to meet Rayshawn Robinson in person. I had no idea when the Warden told me to take you out of the hole it would result in me meeting him. He is my fourteen year-old son's hero, and I can't wait to tell him I met Rayshawn Robinson in the flesh," Emerson gushed.

When Grandville arrived at Mr. Bolden's office he was escorted into the smaller office and given a chair to sit in directly across from his Counselor who had been waiting for him.

"Well that was awkward. I didn't know that when I woke up this morning I would receive an opportunity to meet the great Rayshawn Robinson. I guess it was a trip having him as a brother in law?" Mr. Bolden asked.

"I have known Rayshawn since we were both young teenagers and to me he is just Rayshawn. I don't have hero worship for him like the rest of the general-public. He has been my friend for many years though we have not spoken to each other in the past three years. I'm just surprised he decided to come to Oakhill today," Grandville replied.

"Grandville how are you feeling? Do you want to talk about the clinic your brother-in-law is going to have built here at Oakhill which will bear your daughter's name?"

"I don't know how to feel about the whole thing. I appreciate what Rayshawn is trying to do for me, but I am not sure I want him to do it. He wants my sister back and building the clinic will get her attention. He tells me, he is going through with the whole thing despite how I feel about it so no matter what, I am going to have to come to terms with it."

"Well how does that make you feel?"

"It makes me feel powerless. I wish I wasn't in this position. I have caused so much pain and I want more than anything to have my life back."

"If there was anything that you could change besides Jessica's death what would it be?"

"I have a bucket list of things I would change starting with spending more time with Juliette and my kids. All I did was work, and I now realize when I was free I neglected them. I threw myself into work, so I didn't have to deal with my memories, but in here all I have is time to reflect on everything which has gone wrong with my life. In hindsight, I had more money than I ever needed or will ever spend. So, working as hard as I did was pointless, and it caused me to not give the time my family deserved. I would also be more honest with Juliette than I have been. There are a lot of things I should have told her about my childhood before we got married."

"Were you abused as a child?"

"Yes."

"Sexually, physically or mentally?"

"I guess that I would say both mentally and sexually."

"How has the abuse affected you?"

"When it was happening I felt powerless. I didn't have any control of what was happening to me. I guess, the feelings are similar to, how I feel about being here at Oakhill. If I didn't do what was asked of me by my perpetrator, I was threatened and I felt as though I had no choice but to perform. The problem was I came to like it, even looked forward to it. My perpetrator had been forcing me into sex for years, but when my mother found out the outcome was different than I thought it would be. She wasn't mad at me but instead she was angry at my perpetrator," Grandville said.

"Maybe if you give this process a chance it will be different then what you expect, kind of like what happened when your mother found out about your abuse. Most of the people I counsel here at Oakhill have been abused in some form or fashion. The difference between the winners and the losers, in my opinion, is some let what happened to them consume them. They brand themselves as perpetual victims. Others use what happened to them to transform their lives and become survivors. The question you have to ask yourself is which do you want to be, a victim or a survivor?" Mr. Bolden asked.

"I want to be a survivor." Grandville replied.

"Grandville, I am going to hold you to those words. I think you need to go back to your cell and get some rest. I don't think it's a good idea for you to go back into isolation. You are going to have to deal with what this day represents, and you might as well start right now. However, the choice is yours. If you really want to go back into solitary confinement, I will have Officer Emerson take you back," Mr. Bolden stated.

"No. I'm tired and if it is okay I really would like to go back to my cell and lie down," Grandville requested.

"Okay I'll have Officer Emerson take you back to your cell," Mr. Bolden agreed.

Chapter 13
Time Will Reveal

When Grandville made it back to his cell he sat on his lumpy little bed and leaned back against the wall. He was still blown away by the fact that Rayshawn had actually come to Oakhill to see him. He mentally processed everything which Rayshawn had told him and decided, he had to put a plan in action. First, he wanted to let Montell know, he had returned from Solitary Confinement. He walked into Montell's cell and found him lying on his bed reading the *Biography of Malcom X,* by Alex Haley.

"Hey man, I just wanted to let you know, I'm back from the hole."

"Good, I'm glad you're back and you got out earlier than planned because being in there can make you crazier then you already are. Do you want to play a game of chess?" Montell asked.

"Sure that would be great, because I have something wild to tell you," Grandville replied.

"What?" Montell inquired.

"You're never going to believe who came to visit me?"

"Grandville I'm confused, because today is not a visit day, and you have not received any visits from anyone other than your Attorneys since you have been at Oakhill.

"I know that's why I was so surprised when Emerson pulled me out of the hole telling me that the Warden wanted to see me. When I arrived at the Warden's office, Rayshawn was there."

"What, you got to be kidding?"

"No man I'm serious."

"Well, what did he want?"

"He wanted to tell me, he was sorry for not visiting and for breaking his promise to me about Greta. He also wanted to let me know that he plans to have his charity build a new mental health clinic here at Oakhill which will be named after Jessica."

"Grandville that's great news."

"I also talked to him about giving you a job when you get out of here, as I suspect the facility will be releasing you soon. You've done everything they've asked of you, and you haven't experienced any mental health symptoms since you've been in here."

"I sure hope so, because I'm anxious about getting my life back. I don't know how to do anything with the exception of protection. I was in the Military before I became a Cop, and since I can no longer be a policeman or get back into the Military, I don't have any idea of how I will make a living when I get out of here?"

"Like I said, Rayshawn is going to give you a job when you get out of here. So, don't worry too much. He owns a Payday loan check cashing center in the city, and he will probably make you a member of their team. It pays decent and the benefits are good."

"Thanks Grandville, I really owe you."

"No you don't. We're friends and friends help each other, and I also need a favor from you." Grandville informed him.

"Whatever it is, consider it done."

"As a Cop I know you had to have worked with someone who is retired and is now a private investigator. I'm going to need to hire someone who is both good at what they do and who is also discreet."

"Yes, I can refer you to someone. When I first got promoted to Detective my Partner was a guy named Oscar McNulty. He is a bi-racial brother whose mother is Black and his father is Irish. Oscar is a good guy whose comes from a long line of Police Officers. When he retired, he started his own private investigation company, besides he's the picture of discretion. He sent me a letter since I've been here and I have his contact info right here," Montell said.

Montell pulled up his mattress and found a folder with his letters in it.

"Here's his number and address, but while I'm writing down his contact information can you let me know what this is about?"

"Rayshawn has found himself in the middle of some bullshit, and I'm going to need to have someone who is removed from the situation to look into for me."

"Okay, here is the number and make sure to use my name and Oscar will cut you a break on the fee."

"Thanks Montell, I will. Now, get the Chess Board set up, so I can quickly spank your behind before I lay down and take a nap," Grandville challenged him.

Later, as Grandville laid on his lumpy little bed, he thought about the issue that Rayshawn had brought to him. He had to find Melinia before Rayshawn's cousin. He didn't want Juliette to have any knowledge of the potential trouble which Melinia was in, because Melinia was Juliette's younger cousin. However, he could always see the freak in her. She even tried to throw-it at him a couple of times. She never came out directly to hit on him with her words, instead she used her body.

Grandville remembered once when Juliette wasn't home, Melinia stopped by unannounced. He was having a beer and watching an Indians game on television when he answered the door. He told her that Juliette wasn't home. She stated, that she would wait for her. After letting Melinia in, he sat down on the couch in the same place where he was seated before she stopped by. Melinia was about 5'6 with a gorgeous body and face. She had on skin tight jean shorts which showed off her big legs and large behind and a short tank top which made her six pack abs and large breasts more noticeable. She tried to walk past where he was seated and rubbed her body up against him, when she could have simply went around to the other side of the couch.

"Excuse me Grandville I didn't mean to run into you." Melinia said with a very sexy undertone.

Grandville scooted his body all the way back on the couch in an attempt to let her get by without her rubbing her big behind against him. He could remember numerous times when she seemed to be trying to push-up on him. Luckily his wife noticed it too and shut Melinia down. When Juliette arrived home and found Melinia waiting for her she let her have it.

"Listen Melinia, we live in a millennium of technology. I better not ever come home and find your behind waiting in my house without me even knowing. I have a cell phone, so make sure you call before you come and don't you bring your fast tail over to my house dressed like you are going to a streetwalker convention," Juliette said very irritated.

"Damn Juliette you don't have to be so crass, and I won't come by again without calling first and there's nothing wrong with my outfit.

"You shouldn't be dressed like that anyway."

"Hell, it's hot outside and everyone hasn't been blessed with central air like you have."

Melinia never showed up unannounced at their home again. But, there had been more than one time in which she rubbed-up against him in a way that let him know, he could hit-it if he wanted to. Grandville did not believe in infidelity, and if he was into cheating, he wouldn't do it with Melinia. He had not seen her in several years, and he had not thought about her until Rayshawn brought her up. He knew Melinia had left home to go to college, and right after she graduated she became addicted to drugs. He had to make sure she was found for everyone's sake.

The next day he was lying in his cell when Officer Emerson came to get him to take him to see Franklin who was in the private visiting room reserved for Attorneys.

"Hey Franklin, "Grandville said.

"What's up Grandville?"

Both men shook each other's hand using their secret fraternity hand shake.

"You're never going to believe who came here yesterday to see me," Grandville stated.

"I have no idea, because you haven't had a visit from anyone but me and Darita since you've been in here," replied Franklin.

"It was Rayshawn."

"Are you for real?"

"As real as a heart attack."

"Well what did he want?"

"He wanted to tell me that his Charity is having a new mental health clinic built here at Oakhill, and he plans to name the clinic after Jessica."

"Grandville, that's awesome." It will go far with the Parole Board when it is time for you to be considered for release."

"Franklin, I'm ambivalent about the whole thing. I'm not sure if I want the new clinic named after Jessica, but Rayshawn says he plans to name the clinic after her no matter what.

"He should, and you shouldn't object either Grandville."

"Honestly, Rayshawn coming to visit me after three years took me by surprise."

"Man, I can imagine. But, it was nice that he came to see you. You need as much support as you can get now that you will be preparing for release soon," Franklin said.

"Yea, I guess. He also apologized for not coming to see me sooner and for what happened with Greta," Grandville said.

"Wow . . . "

"He wants me to talk to Juliette about her cousin Melinia. He has gotten caught up in some shit which involves her." Grandville did not have a pleasant look on his face.

"Oh, my God. Not that little slut." Franklin just shook his head.

"His cousin Lovelle knows her. She actually made a video of her giving Rayshawn a BJ without his knowledge, and now he wants find her and buy it from her," Grandville said

"I told you a long time ago that young girl was serious trouble."

"I don't want Juliette or Greta involved in this in anyway, and I have a few things I need for you to do for me," Grandville said.

"You know I got you. Just tell me what you need," Franklin replied.

"The first thing I need for you to do is to get in touch with this Private Detective that Montell recommended to me.

"Okay, who is he . . ."

"He's a retired Cop and used to be Montell's partner when he first became a Detective and from what Montell said he is also very discreet.

"That could cost a lot of money to hire a Private Detective . . ." Franklin seemed worried.

"He said, that he would give me a discount if we use Montell's name. I also need for you to look through our closed tax files."

"What are you looking for?"

"That's where you will find Mabel Gatlin's tax return and Melinia's birthday and social security number will be on it. Aunt Mabel is Juliette's Aunt. We've been doing her taxes for years. Use the tax return and get the pertinent information to Mr. McNulty, so he can try and locate Melinia." Grandville directed Franklin.

"Okay it'll be done first thing tomorrow morning. What else do you need me to do?"

Grandville pulled a letter out of his waist band and slid it across the table to Franklin.

"I'm going to need for you to deliver this letter to Greta. I need to see her ASAP," Grandville said.

"Okay, consider it done. I will drop the letter off on my way home from here." Franklin agreed.

"I've put all the information for Mr. McNulty on this paper, so don't lose it."

"I won't. Now we need to talk about your case."

"Okay, okay" Grandville said.

"I've spoken to the Oakhill officials and I've just received your yearly Psychiatric Assessment."

"Oh my God, I'm afraid to hear what it says."

"Your therapist and your doctor have reported you're making improvements, and that there's a chance, if you continue to respond favorably to medication and therapy, that you'll be eligible to be released from here in the near future."

"Franklin, I'm not sure I'm ready to face Juliette, the kids and Greta."

"I think it's time for you to reevaluate your strategy of getting out of here."

"That's what I've been trying to do. I even spent time in the hole to remember everything. And, it's scary all of the shit that has happened to me."

"Most people who are ordered to a facility like this spend their time earning their high school diploma or their college degree. Since you have so much education that's really not feasible for you so you need another plan."

"I just don't know what else to do. Montell's been keeping me busy playing chess and listening to me talk things out."

"Grandville, I remember how badly you wanted to be a Law Professor, but life got in the way and you didn't have the time to properly cultivate your dream."

"You're right Franklin, I forgot about that. Wow, I guess it got lost in the hustle."

"In here you have nothing but time on your hands, so you might as well use it for something constructive."

"Okay, I'm listening," Grandville said.

"I think you should ask the Oakhill officials if you could be allowed to teach an English Class while you're in here. Half of the people in Oakhill are here because they don't have the educational foundation for which to build on to become successful in life."

"I could try to do that . . . you know that sounds very interesting."

Grandville, you can help change people's lives by helping these guys receive the gift of the written word. You'd be helping some of these guys understand what they didn't before they came here."

"Yes, that's true . . .

"Maybe even play a role in helping them transform their lives, because they need more than the system is giving them right now."

"Please, we know how much attention is really given to helping these men get an education," Grandville said.

Well, before you flat-out say no just hear me out."

"OK. I am listening."

"I've spoken to our Fraternity's Chapter President along with our chapter members, and we've decided to sponsor your class and pay for all the books and material which each inmate will need."

"I don't know. I hate to put you all out . . ."

Franklin cut him off. "We want to do this, because we need you back. If you can show the prison officials that you are doing something productive with your time, this will go a long way when it's time to talk about you being released."

Grandville's face had lit-up at the plan, because it was one of his long-time dreams to teach and be a law professor. "Okay Franklin you don't have to twist my arm. I think it's a great idea so let's do it," Grandville said all excited about his new project.

"I figured you'd say that, so I've already sent the outline of your course to the officials, and they're going to let us know if the course has been approved. I made a copy for you, so you can tweak it as you see fit," Franklin said.

"Thanks Franklin, you've been a phenomenal friend and partner to me, and I'll never forget how you've held me down since I've been in this place.

"Man, we've been through too much stuff together all these years, and we still have a lot to do. So, I gotta get you the hell out-of-here. But, you know Grandville, you have to want to get out of here too." Franklin looked at him as to ask, are you gonna be crazy or not?"

Grandville didn't respond to the look and said, "I told Rayshawn to get in touch with you if he needed to tell me anything regarding the mess that he's found himself in. I don't want him upsetting Greta or Juliette, and I don't want him to ever comeback to Oakhill."

"Okay, I understand. Is there anything else that you need?" Franklin asked.

"I need you to make sure Greta's name is on my visitor's log, and I need for you to arrange for her to be chauffeured here to see me this coming Monday which is a visit day. Please make all of the arrangements for me," Grandville said. He seemed to be getting a little anxious.

"Okay." Franklin agreed.

"Have you seen Juliette since last month?" Grandville asked.

"No, not since I gave her the money which you told me to deliver to her."

"How about Greta, have you seen her?"

"No, not in a while. I did talk to Juliette for a brief moment yesterday. I wanted to check in since yesterday was the Anniversary of Jessica's death. She said, she was getting ready to go out with Greta and Samantha," Franklin said.

"Good. I'm glad Juliette is going out instead of sitting around all depressed, and I'm glad Greta went with her."

"Juliette seemed to be handling it fairly well. Although I could tell she was a little stressed."

"Why didn't you stop by the house, so you could've seen Samantha and give her some of your chocolate love?" Grandville laughed and teased at Franklin.

"You know, I've told you on countless occasions, that I'm not romantically interested in Samantha. Why, you keep trying to push her on me, man. Don't get me wrong, I do find her to be very physically attractive, but I can already tell it wouldn't work out between us. I'm just not attracted to her like that. She's a nice woman, but I believe our personalities would clash like the Titans at war.

"Aaah come on Franklin, she's not that bad," Grandville said.

"I would have to launch a thunderbolt under that girl's ass to tame her right. I don't have time for that kind of chick."

"I guess you're right. Sometimes she does have a smart mouth." Grandville had to think twice about it.

"I need a ride or die lady who knows how and when to fall back. I want what you have with Juliette and I refuse to settle for less." Franklin wasn't backing down on making his point either.

"You mean what I used to have with Juliette. Right about now, all I have is my memories. Even though she did write to me. I got my first letter from her just a few days ago," Grandville confided in Franklin.

"Grandville that's great. What did the letter say?"

"She told me, that she loves me and misses what we once had. She also said, that she's scared of me and doesn't know if she could be in an intimate relationship with me again. But, she isn't going to divorce me yet, because she's still undecided if we should be together."

"Like I just said, Juliette is your ride or die girl who loves you. If she didn't love you, she would have divorced you when everything first happened, and she'd have a new man in her life by now,"

"Yea Franklin, you got a good point there."

"I mean Juliette is the whole package, she's beautiful and smart and even though she's hurt by all that has happened, she hasn't abandoned you. I think she stills wants to be with you but you're going to have to take it slow," Franklin advised him.

"I agree, she is the whole package. I just feel like I'm stuck in limbo, and I have Juliette and the kids stuck in limbo too." Grandville said shaking his head in disbelief about what had happened to him.

"Given your position it would be natural to feel that way," Franklin agreed.

"Franklin, I would do just about anything to have her back." Grandville sounded like a man determined to change his fate.

"I know you would, but right now the only thing you can do to even get a shot at winning her back is to get better. Don't worry about anything, because I will handle all your business on this end," Franklin promised his friend and partner.

"Thanks Franklin," Grandville said almost with tears in his eyes and voice.

Franklin stood up and pulled Grandville into a bear hug and said, "Grandville, I got your back. You just take care of yourself in here, and I'll take care of things on the outside."

"I will Franklin. I'm following your lead this time. I like your plan, and I will make it work," Grandville said, very humble and with gratitude.

Chapter 14

Gone

Juliette woke up to the smell of fresh brewed coffee and sizzling bacon. It brought her downstairs to the kitchen where she found Greta who had prepared breakfast. This morning was very difficult to wake-up for her. Trying to continue to live like nothing had happened after the death of her child had been stressful. Each passing year, the weeks leading up to the Anniversary of Jessica's death had also really taken a toll on her.

However, the morning after the Anniversary had finally arrived.

"Good morning sleepy head," Greta said with a big smile on her face.

"Good morning," Juliette replied in a groggy voice.

"I figured you might be a little hung over, so I decided to let you sleep in. I made you coffee, toast, bacon and eggs. How are you feeling?"

"I'm a little foggy but I'm okay." Juliette said as she dug her fork into the fluffy cheese eggs and put a bite into her mouth. "Oh my God these eggs are fantastic." Juliette complimented Greta on her cooking.

"Thank you darling. Hey, I was thinking, we could skip Mass and get right over to A Better Tomorrow so we can figure out what's going on with Melinia."

"Okay. It'll only take me a few minutes to get dressed after I take a quick shower. But, are you sure you want to miss Mass?" Juliette asked Greta.

"Yes, I'll go to Confession tonight, and I will ask God to forgive me for my sins which mainly consist of me having un-pure thoughts about Derek and wanting to scratch Samantha's eyeballs out. I'm going to need for the Priest to make me say a couple of Hail Mary's and absolve me of my transgressions." Greta was acting silly, raising her both hands up in the air, bringing them down to the floor and saying, "Hail Mary, Hail Mary . . ."

"You going straight to hell," Juliette said and laughed out loud.

"You know I'm right . . ."

"The whole time Grandville and I were together he never went to Confession. What's it like?" Juliette asked.

"It's like having a spiritual advisor and a therapist all wrapped up into one."

"Really . . ."

"Yes," Greta said and continued. "When you confess your sins you unburden yourself and the Priest uses the scriptures to help you view your actions and thoughts through the context of the bible."

"I was raised a Baptist, and I was always taught that you shouldn't kneel and confess your sins to no man, but instead you confess your sins at the alter directly to God," Juliette said with a questioning look on her face.

"Grandville and I were taught that the Priest is an intermediary for God. Therefore when you confess, in some ways you're talking directly to God through the Priest. For me, confession is a free form of therapy. The Priest is bound by the tenants of Confidentiality and he can't repeat what you tell him. When you talk about your problems you release your burdens and your soul feels much better. The Priest reminds you of your spiritually, and he uses the scriptures within the Bible to remind us of what we have been taught about forgiveness, love and understanding. I know there're a lot of problems within the Catholic Church.

"I know, that's why it's hard for me to get into it," Juliette replied.

"It's a fact, there are some Nuns and Priests who are a part of the Church who have, and still are, molesting our children and doing things they tell us Parishioners not to do. But, if you think about it, there are molesters and abusers in every church. Eddie Long who is the leader of one of the largest Baptist Churches in our Country was even accused of doing a lot of unrighteous things. Hell, some of us even have molesters and abusers in our own families that we may not even know about. We have to remember to do the right thing, because God is still watching us and He is still in control," Greta said with passion and belief.

"Greta, I'm very liberal when it comes down to religion. I believe that all kinds of people will get to go to Heaven, even some people who have committed unimaginable sins, only if they ask the Lord for forgiveness and deliverance. The Lord can wash our sins clean if we ask for forgiveness and open our heart and make a commitment to change and do right by people. One of my biggest beefs with the Baptist religion is, some members of my faith actually believe, if you don't accept Jesus as your personal savior, you'll go to hell. Several religions including, both the Muslims and the Jews reject Christ as the son of God and see him only as a prophet. It's unfathomable to me, because they believe Jesus was a prophet and not literally the son of God that none will get into Heaven. There are people who live in remote villages in the world that have not been touched by modern religion, and I'm sure many of them will go to Heaven. I believe the Lord is all inclusive," Juliette said passionately banging her fist on the table.

"The Bible has stories in it to remind us that we are human and that we will make mistakes. However, with our belief and faith, our sins will be forgiven and over time will be absolved. Hell, look at the Disciples, they were Jesus's crew but several of them were thieves, some were alcoholics and others were considered to be of low moral fabric. Judas who was one of Jesus's disciples, sold him out for a bag a gold. I know people who will sell you out for nothing," Greta was preaching hard.

"Girl, now you know I know," Juliette snapped her fingers loud.

"I saw some of the most craziest things when I lived in LA, and The O'Jays' songs, "*For The Love of Money*" and "*Backstabbers*" were the soundtracks of my life during it all. Oooooh, how I quickly learned everything is not always as it seems," Greta said.

"I know. . . you have to be very careful who you let enter into your "circle of life," Juliette said.

"Juliette, that's why I have so few friends today. I trust very few people. But, you my friend are definitely in my small circle of trust," Greta said and winked at her.

"You know you're my family. We've always been like sisters ever since we met way back when," Juliette replied.

"I trust you, but I don't trust Samantha or Tara. That's why I need to go to Confession. I have to pray and ask the Lord to guide my actions and place me on the correct path, so I don't start acting ugly," Greta laughed.

"It's cool. I have a lot to do today, and I need to come back home to wash clothes and start preparing for the return of my kids anyway."

"Right, the kids come back today. I can't wait to see them."

"My mother will be back with the kids tomorrow, and I want to have a hot meal waiting for all of them. I think I'll make a Pot Roast, Mustard and Turnip Greens and some rice. Hell, I might even make a pan of cornbread. Do you want to come over for dinner tomorrow?" Juliette asked Greta.

"Do you actually think I am going to miss out on a free home cooked meal? You know your Roast and Greens are the bomb. I wouldn't miss the opportunity to eat your home cooked food for the world. Plus, I can't wait to see my nieces and nephews," Greta said.

That teary look came back into Juliette's eyes, "I miss them too. I constantly have to remind myself not to hold onto to them too tightly. After the loss of one child, I'm afraid that something might happen to my other children."

"Girl, don't think like that."

"I know . . . I know the kids are okay when they're with my mother and my sisters. It's just my imagination."

"It's all going to be okay, Juliette. One day you'll look-up and realize the pain inside has subsided."

"I hope you know what you're talking about. Also, Mom called before I went out with you guys yesterday, and she said the kids were having a ball. They had been to the Zoo and the State Fair," Juliette said.

"I am glad they are having fun. Let's take the kids to Fun and Stuff next weekend too," Greta suggested.

"Okay, maybe Sunday after church. I have to go to my book club meeting on Saturday, and I hope you won't mind babysitting while I go? I was going to ask you, because I really don't want to ask my mother to babysit again so soon after she has had the kids for several days."

"I don't mind at all. We'll watch a movie and eat popcorn while you're gone. It'll be fun."

"Cool."

"Let me get up right now. I'm gonna go get dressed, so we can get over to a Better Tomorrow," Greta said.

"Me too."

Greta decided to drive, that way if Melinia hadn't returned to the rooming house Juliette wouldn't be attempting to drive while upset and put herself and others at risk for an accident. When the two ladies arrived at the rooming house Violet was waiting for them.

"Hey Ms. Juliette are you guys hungry? I made a Turkey and we are having turkey sandwiches and watermelon slices for lunch. I'm going to use the leftovers to make Turkey Tetrazzini for dinner."

"Are you hungry?" Violet asked.

"No, we're good. We just ate breakfast a little while ago." Juliette replied.

"Melinia still didn't come home yet," Violet said.

"Okay, I usually wouldn't do this but, because I'm Melinia's cousin I'm going to go into her room. If it was one of the other women here in the house, I wouldn't go into their room without permission unless it was an emergency. I recognize and respect the fact that I'm a landlord and the women who reside here are my tenants, but I got to tell my family something when I let them know Melinia is missing," Juliette said.

"How do you know Melinia is not with your Aunt Mabel? Why don't you give her a call," Greta suggested.

"That's a good idea Greta. I guess I have been so overwhelmed that I haven't been thinking," Juliette responded.

Juliette reached into her purse and pulled out her cell phone and pulled up her Aunt Mabel's number out of her contact list on her phone. The phone rang three times before Aunt Mabel picked up the line.

"Hello Aunt Mabel. How are you?" Juliette asked.

"I'm fine Juliette. I hope you have Melinia with you? I've been trying to reach her for the past two days, but her phone keeps going straight to voicemail. I was going to call you yesterday, but I didn't want to bother you, because I know yesterday was the Anniversary of Jessica's death," Aunt Mabel said worried about Melinia.

"No Melinia isn't with me. I was actually hoping she was with you, because she hasn't been at the rooming house for the past two days and we're starting to get worried."

"Oh my God, do you think Melinia has relapsed?" Aunt Mabel asked Juliette.

"Aunt Mabel I don't know, but I'm going to go to the police station and file a missing person's report on her. Maybe you should start contacting all of the local hospitals to make sure she didn't get in an accident or something," Juliette advised.

"Okay honey but please call me back if you hear anything," Aunt Mabel pleaded.

"Okay and please call me if you learn where Melinia is too. Let's talk soon, and I'm going to let you go," Juliette said.

After Juliette disconnected the call she went to her office and got out her master key set and went directly into Melinia's room. When she opened the door, she noticed the room was both neat and clean. The bed was made up and Melinia's clothes were neatly put away in her small closet. Her attached half bath was orderly and her makeup which was on her small vanity was neatly lined up. Everything looked in place but Juliette decided to further investigate.

She went to the nightstand drawer and pulled it open. She found a stack of old furniture storage bills bundled together and under the bills were several short typed letters.

One letter said, "You better pay what you owe or you will be but a mere memory."

There were several other threatening notes. None were addressed and none were signed and all the letters pretty much said the same things in different ways, that Melinia owed money to an unnamed person, and that she had better pay up or else. Juliette couldn't figure out how Melinia even received the notes. Were they slipped under her door at the rooming house or were they hand delivered to her? The notes were not in envelopes, so Juliette didn't think the notes had been mailed. But, Melinia could have tossed the envelopes and kept the letters.

"Violet can you please go and get me a zip lock bag?" Juliette requested.

"Ok Ms. Juliette," Violet said.

"Juliette you have to take these notes to the police, because they might be clues in helping to find out where Melinia is," Greta said.

"I agree Greta that's why I think we need to put them in a zip lock bag to minimize the damage and to preserve any finger prints that might be on them," Juliette replied.

"Good idea," Greta agreed.

Greta got Juliette to the local Police Station in record time, and Juliette was able to make a missing person's report, because Melinia hadn't been home for more than 48 hours. However, the Officer who took the report was somewhat indifferent to Melinia having been gone missing.

"Your cousin has three old soliciting charges and a couple of misdemeanor drug offenses on her record. She's most likely ran-off somewhere with a John or something. She'll probably be back, but remember she's an adult and can come and go as she pleases," the Officer stated.

"Yes Officer, I understand that she's an adult, but if she was really trying to leave on her own free will wouldn't she have taken some of her clothes or other belongings? And what about these threatening notes I found in her nightstand?" Juliette questioned.

"The notes are evidence, but it doesn't mean something happened to her. We'll start looking for her, but you should go home and contact us immediately if you hear from her," the Officer said.

"Okay Officer. Is there anything else?" Juliette asked.

"We'll be in touch, but you also call us if you find out anything relevant that can help us figure out where she went. We'll call you if we have further questions that can assist us in locating your cousin," the Officer replied.

Greta drove Juliette home and dropped her off with promises to see her the next day. Once Juliette arrived home she got into her SUV and went to the grocery store to buy food for the next week. She came home and cleaned her house from top to bottom including the children's rooms. She also washed and dried several loads of clothes and was in the middle of folding them and putting them away when her cell phone rang.

"Hello Juliette," Tara said.

"T Mor what's going on?" Juliette replied.

"I'm good. What're you doing?" Tara asked.

"Just folding clothes. My mom will be back with the kids tomorrow and I want to have the house in order," Juliette responded.

"Juliette, I know it's late notice, but I was hoping that you would have a drink with me? We could meet at the Applebee's at Willoughby Commons since it's right down the street from your house," Tara said.

"Okay. Is everything all right?" Juliette questioned.

"Yes. I was hoping to get out of the house for a little while, and I'm hungry so I thought it would be fun to hang out."

"Okay, I was just about finished with my chores anyway. So, what time are we talking?"

"I'm walking out right now. I shouldn't be more than a half an hour," Tara replied.

"Alright I'll leave my house in twenty-five minutes and I'll see you there," Juliette said.

Juliette disconnected the call and put away the clothes that she had just folded. Her house was spotless and everything was in place. When she came home she threw the stress of worrying about Melinia and the past Anniversary of Jessica's death into cleaning which resulted in her mopping, vacuuming and dusting her whole house. Now, after spending hours cleaning and washing clothes she was ready for a break. Juliette was happy that Tara had called because hanging out with Tara would offer her a temporary distraction. Also Juliette recognized that this would be the last time that she would be child free for a while and she wanted to take advantage of it.

Exactly thirty-five minutes later Juliette pulled into the parking lot of Applebee's. She noticed Tara's vehicle was already there, and she easily spotted her seated at a small table near the window. After giving Tara a quick hug she sat down and began looking at the menu.

"Are you drinking this evening?" Tara questioned.

"Yes, I am going to have one with dinner but that's my limit. I don't want to get pulled over for drinking and driving." Juliette responded.

"Okay, I will have one too."

After placing their drink and food orders Tara began to talking about their dinner on the Anniversary. "I want to apologize for the debacle that happened last night with Greta. We're going to have to do something about Samantha, because her behavior is really getting out of hand."

"I plan to talk to her the next time we are alone about what happened while we were at dinner. I really don't understand why Samantha has a problem with Greta. She's my-sister-in-law, and I consider her as family, and though I don't expect Samantha to be phony, she could at least try and be cordial for my sake."

Juliette reflected back to several of Samantha's acquaintances who Juliette did not care for. The first was Roman who was a younger guy and had started hanging out with them. He was a member of Grandville's fraternity which was loosely considered to some to be the brother fraternity to their sorority.

Roman's brother was a fireman who was killed while trying to put out a fire that was set by a man who was upset his wife had left him for someone else. The man thought his wife was at her lover's apartment so he set it on fire. Roman's brother was killed when the roof caved in on him as he attempted to fight the blaze.

Samantha had become friendly with Roman when her office prosecuted the arsonist who set fire to the building. Juliette did not care for Roman, because he was stuck on himself. He also had a Rico Suave look which he thought made him God's gift to the female gender. Roman was cheating on his wife with a woman who was also married. Juliette had met Roman years before Samantha did and knew both he and his other woman Jenean casually. Juliette was always polite and cordial, but she made it a point to stay clear of them. She could see that if the two were so bold as to cheat on their spouses so publicly, they were the type of individuals who attracted drama.

Samantha befriended Jenean because Roman asked her to and Samantha considered him like a brother and acquiesced to his request even though she did not agree with him cheating.

Juliette didn't trust them and would make it a point to hang with Samantha when they were around. Not because she enjoyed their company, but more to watch Samantha's back and to make sure that they didn't draw her into the middle of their drama.

Then, there was Millie another one of her and Samantha's Sorority sisters who was initiated with Juliette in College. Juliette's Sorority induction was conducted by the Graduate Chapter Sorors, but some of the Sorors on Juliette's line were taken underground including Millie. This means the undergraduate Sorors hazed the Sorors who were underground before the whole line was taken over by Graduate Chapter who did not allow hazing of any sort. There was controversy on their line and Millie never truly considered Juliette to be her line sister and treated her very unfriendly and unsisterly.

Juliette had also attended high school with Millie and the two had never been friendly with one another. Basically, they didn't speak for many years until Millie started hanging out with Samantha, and Millie learned that Juliette was an Attorney. The way Millie treated Juliette before finding out this information was unconscionable. Juliette didn't care for Millie, because she found her to be overly superficial, but when Samantha befriended Millie, Juliette was always cordial and polite because Millie was Samantha's friend. Over time Juliette got to know Millie better and actually came to somewhat like her though she still found her behavior to be inconsistent.

Lastly, there was Althea, an older woman who Juliette couldn't stand with a passion. Althea also owned a rooming house and was in constant and direct competition with Juliette to obtain, good, paying residents. Althea didn't have a social service program set-up for the tenants who resided in her rooming house. She was only interested in the money which she could obtain from renting her rooms that were so filthy the roaches needed footies. She was an evil, conniving, mean woman who had even started a rumor that Juliette's rooming home had bed bugs in an attempt to prevent her from getting tenants. Samantha and Althea had become friendly because both are avid tennis players. Althea is very, very good at the game and the two play on a Women's Tennis League together and have won money in several amateur women's matches. Samantha knew how much Juliette disliked Althea, but every time Althea was around she made it a point to say, "Juliette say hi to Ms. Althea," and again Juliette would comply just to ensure that Samantha didn't feel uncomfortable.

Tara's loud voice brought Juliette back to the present.

"Hello are you listening to me?" Tara snapped her finger at Juliette.

"Yes, I just zoned out for a minute. What were you saying?"

"I was explaining that Samantha and I were at my house drinking and we started talking about who we considered to be our first loves. I told her about Derek who was my oldest brother's Tim's best friend. At that time in my life I was actively being abused by my older Sister Tina. My mother died giving birth to my youngest Sister Tenia and my father never remarried. Instead he spent all his time chasing and dating other women.

He was never home and spent all his time and money on his women. Tim and Derek would hustle to keep food on our table and the utilities paid. Derek would often give his share of the money he earned from their various illegal ventures to Tim, so he could make sure our needs were met. I'll never forget what a good heart Derek had and probably still has. I was surprised to see him yesterday, but I didn't expect the reaction Samantha had to the whole situation."

"I know the way Samantha acted wasn't cool, but in reality she was looking out for you, because Samantha is very loyal and wants her friends to be happy. It's just the way she went about it was wrong," Juliette remarked.

"All I want to know is what you're going to do about it?" Tara asked.

"I am going to talk to Samantha. What else can I do about it?" Juliette questioned.

"Samantha is your best friend, and it's your job to tell her when she's out of line. Hell, if you can't talk to her, then you can trust and believe that no one else can. Also, given her new public position you need to be able to tell her when she's doing something wrong or if she is out of line. You're the one person Samantha trusts so it really is up to you. It trips me out how you and Samantha's other friends let her get away with saying or doing whatever she wants without consequence," Tara said with an angry undertone in her voice.

"That's not true, and I will talk to her, but like I've told you before, Samantha is very strong willed and doesn't take criticism well. Also, she probably didn't mean any harm. I know she was calling herself looking out for you, but how she treats Greta is really starting to get on my nerves. I love Samantha but I'm starting to develop resentments, because I don't know why she would want to make me feel uncomfortable. She knows how rude she treats Greta makes me very angry and uncomfortable," Juliette said.

"All I know is, I wouldn't let her treat my relatives that way. I mean Greta is your sister-in- law and that makes her family. Even though I can't stand most of the assholes in my family, I'm the only one who can mistreat them." Tara's sarcastic statement was meant for Juliette to stop and take a note of what she needs to do about Samantha.

"Greta has always been very honest and straight to the point. I admire that in her. She's real about who she was and who she is now. She doesn't try and front and admits at times she can be trip. She doesn't care for Samantha, because she doesn't like how Samantha acts towards her, but she doesn't disrespect her or try and mistreat her. She's cordial to her, because she knows Samantha is my best friend and I love her. I don't care if either one of them likes each other, but I do expect them both to be cordial for my sake."

"Well then you better check your girl, because I guarantee you she will continue to disrespect Greta. Speaking of Greta, do you think she's going to call Derek?" Tara sounded disappointed, because she already knew the answer to her question.

"Yes I do. They had an attraction to each other when she lived in LA that they didn't to get to cultivate because she was married. Did you see the way they were looking at each other?" Juliette asked Tara.

"Yes I did and it's cool. I just want you to do something about how Samantha has been acting. I also wanted to tell you about my BFF and how she pissed me off the other day."

"What did she do?"

"Can you believe she said, I wasn't really married to Tabitha's dad right in front of Classy who is a waitress at the Black Badge? She talks too much, and I can't figure out why she would mention something so private about my life in front of another chick that I don't even know like that. I was common law married to Phil, and I have been living with him since I got pregnant with Tabitha fifteen years ago," Tara replied.

Juliette had met Michelle who was Tara's best friend on several occasions and she seemed like a very nice woman.

"Maybe she said it, because she had been drinking and her filter wasn't working. I am sure she didn't make the comment in an attempt to be malicious. Also, Ohio hasn't recognized common law marriage since 1991. So, technically you couldn't have been common law married to Phil. However, I do agree that Michelle shouldn't have said that in front of Classy," Juliette said.

"Well as far as I'm concerned we were married. Phillip told everyone I was his wife and even Tabitha didn't know we were not technically married and she is my daughter," Tara remarked.

"It doesn't matter. Just try and forgive Michelle, because she's a nice woman who seems to genuinely love and care about you," Juliette said.

"Samantha told me the same thing when I told her crazy ass about it. She also told me to tell her go and kick rocks," Tara said, and laughed to herself.

Then, both women squealed with laughter at the inside joke. Years ago Samantha was prosecuting a serial rapist and she put one of his victims on the stand. When Samantha questioned the young lady about what the rapist said to her during the assault, the young lady replied, "He told me that he ought to drag me outside and make me kick rocks." Samantha stated, she was momentarily taken off guard at how nonchalantly the witness had recounted the incident. Samantha said, she had to quickly put her hand in front of her mouth so the victim and the jury wouldn't see her smile because she didn't expect the victim to say that.

Now only a select few were privy to the inside joke and Samantha loved to tell those in her inside circle to go and kick rocks. Samantha never used profanity in the company of the opposite sex, but when she was with her girls, she had a mouth like a sailor. Most would be very surprised that the facade Samantha displayed to the rest of the world was not who she really was. Samantha was multi-layered and that was one of the many reasons Juliette loved her so much. She didn't let everyone get to really know her, and those who were granted an opportunity to see the real her were pleasantly surprised on just how much of a sister girl Samantha actually was.

"That damned Samantha is off the chain. She keeps me in stiches," Juliette laughed hard just thinking about how crazy her girl can be when she lets her guards down.

"I'm going to take you and Samantha's advice, but Michelle is going to know she pissed me off. What are you going to do after you leave here?" Asked Tara.

"I'm going home and have an adult beverage and try to enjoy my last night of peace. I really love my kids but they sure are a noisy bunch."

"Tabitha is at her Dad's house tonight and as you know I am not seeing Maliek anymore, and I'm bored out of my head. Do you mind if I come with to your house and have a drink with you?" Tara asked.

"Sure. Let's pay the bill and you can follow me to the house."

"Okay, I will." Tara stated.

Once at Juliette's house they had more drinks and smoked a small joint which Tara had brought with her. They had a spirited debate on why marijuana should be legalized while Juliette prepped the food that she was making for her Sunday dinner.

"Juliette, I'm telling you, I believe the time has come for the community to decriminalize the use of Marijuana. It is a natural herb which has been grown since the Native Americans inhabited this land. The old boy establishment doesn't want it legalized for fear it would cut into their pharmaceutical sales. Who are they to decide what kind of treatment a person chooses to employ. Marijuana has a medicinal quality which helps many with pain relief. One of my cousins swears that marijuana helped to heal her breast cancer and everyone knows that some of the pharmaceutical drugs on the market are sold for a more then 300 percent profit margin." Tara said, as she takes another puff off of the joint and looks at it.

"Tara, I don't disagree with you but like Samantha said last night Marijuana is considered a gateway drug and there are some who will use it then go on to use harder more dangerous drugs like Heroin and Cocaine."

"The same could be said for the pharmaceutical drugs that the doctors and dentists are prescribing. I have worked with many victims who have become addicted to legal pharmaceutical drugs and then go on to become addicted to street drugs. When a doctor or dentist figures out his patient is addicted the first thing they do is discontinue the prescription. This is what causes many drug addicts to turn to street drugs. I personally know all kind of people who smoke marijuana, and they have never used any other drug. Some marijuana users don't even drink," Tara was very passionate about the lie that marijuana can cause you to get addicted to harder drugs. She just does not believe it's true.

"Like I said, I hear you but I'm concerned about the distributors trying to market their products to kids. There's no reason for marijuana candy, and the only reason anyone would sell it is to get kids to use drugs. I don't have a problem with adults and grown people indulging. But, the studies conclusively prove that it does damage developing brains and there is nothing worse for people experiencing mental health problems. It's proven that marijuana does have medicinal properties, so I believe we should allow the FDA to test it and make it into a pill form. I don't know of any medication that you take by smoking it," Juliette said.

"The worst absolute drug to the human body is alcohol and that's been legal for years. There are thousands of young black men in prison, because they tried to emulate the Kennedys and the Rockefellers who made their fortunes during prohibition by selling alcohol. Instead of selling alcohol these young men sold marijuana, and they have paid with their futures. Legalizing marijuana would allow for these young men to have a chance to start over without the stigma which has been attached to Marijuana," Tara said.

"Tara there are both pros and cons to each side of this argument and even if we agree to disagree it will not make Marijuana use legal."

Juliette and Tara had a good time just talking and debating when Tara said something that Juliette found to be curious.

"Have you read the book for book club?" Tara asked.

"Yes, it was one thing I did to try in order to keep my mind off of the Anniversary and that was read the book. Delores Phillips did her thing with *The Darkest Child*. I loved it. I felt like she did a great job describing how mentally ill the mother was in the book," Juliette commented.

"I'm still reading it but from what I have read so far I would have to agree. You do know that one of our book club members is bi-sexual," Tara tried to whisper even though only she and Juliette were in the room.

"What! I don't believe you. I have never picked that up. Which member?" Juliette questioned and stunned.

"Juliette if the person wanted you to know she would tell you herself."

Juliette let the comment and the conversation end by changing the subject back to the book and at midnight Tara went home. Juliette was curious about what would make Tara say such a thing about one of their book club members but decided to disregard the comment.

The next morning Juliette was up early. She went to the early morning church service at 8am and then got back home to begin preparing her Sunday dinner. Juliette preferred the early service so that she could worship the Lord without having to interact with too many of the other parishioners. She loved her church but didn't feel like she could confide about her husband's mental health issues or the tragic loss of her daughter to her fellow church members or to her Pastor. She went to church so that she could receive the Word and so that she could lay her burdens at the altar. She never shared with others outside of her circle what she had endured as she didn't want her or her family to be judged.

At 2 pm the doorbell rang and when Juliette answered it she found Greta standing at her door.

"Juliette I know you told me to come around 4, but I need to talk to you real quick before the kids get back," Greta said looking at Juliette.

"Greta come on in and have a seat. As a matter of fact you can help me out by stirring this cake batter while I get the baking pans prepped. I'm going to make a chocolate cake for dessert."

"Okay." Greta said as she washed her hands in the kitchen sink and began to stir the batter.

"So, what's up? How was confession last night and what do you need to talk to me about?"

"I didn't go to confession, I called Derek on my way home after I dropped you off, and he invited me to dinner. I accepted his invitation and we had a great time."

"That's great. Where did you guys go to eat?"

"We went to Fridays and after we finished eating we just sat in the restaurant and talked. We were there for so long that Derek gave the Waiter who was serving us a twenty five dollar tip because we hogged the table," Greta stated.

"I'm glad you guys got the chance to hang out and talk." Replied Juliette.

"Me too but I came over early, because I wanted to let you know that when I got home from hanging out with Derek there was a message on my voice mail from Franklin," Greta said.

"Really, what did he say?" Asked Juliette.

"That he left a letter in my mailbox from Grandville. He apparently called while you and I were at the police station," Greta said.

Juliette was both surprised and shocked. Juliette believed Greta when she said, she had not communicated with Grandville since he had been locked up. For him to send a letter meant that he had something important to tell her.

"What did Grandville say in his letter?" Juliette asked.

"His letter chastised me for living in our old house. He's afraid something is going to happen to me in the neighborhood. He also wrote that he needs to see me ASAP. Franklin has made arrangements for me to be taken by Limo Service tomorrow afternoon. I wanted to tell you personally about the letter and to let you know I will be going to Oakhill tomorrow. Is there anything you want me to tell Grandville?" Greta said hoping Juliette would write Grandville a note or letter.

"No. I said what I needed to say to him in my letter. All I ask is that you not tell Grandville about the twins," Juliette Replied.

"Juliette, I am a woman of my word. I give you my word that I won't say anything." Greta said.

"Good, now do me a favor and make this lemonade for me while I finish setting the table. My mother and the kids will be here in less than an hour," Juliette said moving a little faster through the kitchen while Greta just starred at her in disbelief that she did not have anything to say to Grandville. Greta thought, 'Why can't Juliette see this could be the perfect time to talk to her husband again?'

Chapter 15
Back Down Memory Lane

Grandville slipped into Montell's cell to talk to him before visiting time began. Soon, those inmates who had visitors would be gathered together, so they could be escorted to the room where family and friends would be waiting. Grandville had never been to the public visiting room at Oakhill before and he was very nervous for a multitude of different reasons. He was afraid of how Greta would respond to seeing him behind Plexiglas and of how she would react when he gave her the news of who their real father was. He also had to tell her about Rayshawn coming to Oakhill and his plans for building the new clinic. He suspected Greta had a lot of anger towards Rayshawn, and he hoped she hadn't become one of those bitter man hating women who most men tried to stay clear of. In some ways Grandville did not know what to expect from Greta. The only thing he knew in heart for sure is that she would come to the visit even though they had not spoken to each other in three years.

"Grandville I can tell by looking at your face that you're nervous about seeing Greta. Just take a deep breath and relax. Remember, your sister loves you and you're doing the right thing by seeing her," Montell said.

"I'm nervous because I haven't seen or communicated with Greta since right after my mother passed. I feel like I need to offer her some kind of explanation as to how I ended up in here, but there is no explanation that I can give," Grandville responded.

"Grandville just be yourself and tell her the truth. You don't have to try and explain anything. Your sister probably just wants to make sure you're okay. Just seeing you will probably help her more than you know, because she'll be able to see that you are actually physically okay," Montell said trying to help him calm down.

Suddenly Grandville heard the announcement that visiting hours were beginning. Several prison I.D. numbers were called and this indicated who had a visitor. He heard his number which meant he would have to line up to be escorted to the visiting area.

"Okay Montell, I just heard them announce my number, so I'm going to line up, but I'll be back to see you as soon as the visit is over."

"Cool and remember to relax," Montell reminded him.

"Okay."

Grandville walked out of Montell's cell and went to stand in line. One of the guards verified his prison ID number, then all the prisoners whose numbers were called were led to the visiting room. Before the inmates were allowed into the visiting area the guards reiterated the rules, no yelling or screaming or physical contact of any sort would be allowed.

When Grandville entered the visiting area he noticed the visitors were already seated at small stations which were separated by Plexiglas and telephones that were attached to the walls. The guard, in a very authoritative tone directed him to sit at a station which held an anxious Greta. She looked beautiful and had her long hair pulled into a ponytail. Greta had been through a lot in the past three years, but she looked as though she hadn't aged one day. However, he did notice small worry lines at the corner of her eyes. Grandville sat down and picked up the phone and Greta did the same.

"Hello Greta. Thanks for coming up to Oakhill on such short notice. Did Franklin arrange for a driver to pick you up and bring you here?" Grandville asked.

"Yes, he hired a real nice young guy who owns a small limo service. Thanks for having Franklin arrange to pick me up, but I could have managed to get here on my own," Greta said into the attached phone.

"I know you could have, but I really didn't want you to have to drive yourself, and I didn't want you on the facility's bus. How have you been doing?" Grandville questioned.

"I've been doing my best, all things considered," Greta replied.

"I know I should have written to you and contacted you before now, but I just didn't know what to say in a letter, so I didn't write," Grandville said trying not to sound like he was making an excuse for not writing her.

"Grandville it is okay. I didn't write to you either, but I'm here now. I know there has to be a specific reason why you asked Franklin to arrange for me to come up here today. I wasn't home when he dropped off your letter, because I was with Juliette at the police station. Franklin left a message on my voice mail about your letter being in my mailbox and about me coming up here today."

"Why was Juliette at the police station, is everything all right? Did something happen to one of the boys?" Grandville asked with concern in his voice.

"Juliette and the children are fine. Her cousin Melinia has been living in Juliette's rooming house for the past few months, and she hasn't been home in several days and we are a little worried. The police think she may be doing drugs again and maybe she's with a John holed up in a hotel somewhere. They more or less said, she will probably be back soon. Juliette found some threatening notes in her room which indicated Melinia owes someone money, and they want her to pay up. We are just praying nothing horrible has happened to her," Greta said.

"Damn, I wish there was something I could do. I know Juliette is worried to death, she's always been crazy about Melinia. Did Juliette show the police the notes?"

"Yes, but they said just because Melinia received the notes does not mean someone did something to her," Greta replied.

"The whole thing sounds crazy. When was the last time anyone has seen Melinia?" Asked Grandville.

"Last week. Someone at the rooming house overheard her on the phone, and it sounded like she was saying she would pay what she owed soon. We don't know what Melinia was in to, just that she is gone. I'm sure you didn't have me come all the way here to Oakhill to talk about Melinia?" Greta asked.

"No, I wanted to talk to you about you living in our old house. The neighborhood is in bad shape and you shouldn't be living there by yourself." Grandville chastised.

"I know the neighborhood isn't the best, but many of the people who lived on our street when we were growing up still live there. I have not had one problem since I have come home because some of our old neighbors keep a close eye on me and the house. Responded Greta.

"But aren't you worried that someone is going to recognize the fact that you used to be married to Rayshawn and try and rob you or something?"

"Grandville, most of the people in our old neighborhood are good people, and they're very protective of me and will make sure that nothing happens to me. Remember it's not where you live, but how you live that makes all the difference. The people who live on our street are just trying to survive. Do you remember Cindy who lived two houses from us? I don't think you could ever forget her because she had the biggest crush on you."

"Of course I remember her. We grew up with her."

Well, her mother passed away a few months after Mommy did and Cindy inherited her house and decided to move into it rather than sell it. Cindy has three strong, young, adult sons who also live with her and apparently everyone in the neighborhood knows them and are scared to death of them. Curt, who's Cindy's oldest son, got into trouble a few years back for assault, and I paid his bond and hired him a great criminal attorney who was able to convince a judge to find him not guilty. Curt has passed the word in the neighborhood that if anyone even looks at me the wrong way there'll be hell to pay" Greta said.

"What? I had no idea you did that for Cindy. You should've called me I would have given you a referral. You always did have a beautiful heart and that's why I am so afraid something is going to happen to you while you're living in the old neighborhood," Grandville said.

"I had Willie Garrison who went to high school with us represent Curt. I didn't want to bother you, because I knew you were busy and Willie really needed the money. He and Rayshawn have kept in touch over all of these years, and that's how I knew how to get in contact with him.

Rayshawn mentioned Willie's youngest daughter had Leukemia, and I wanted to help him out so I sent him the case. Also, you don't have to worry about me because nothing is going to happen to me in the neighborhood. It really didn't make sense for me to go and get another spot since I have to finish packing up Mommy's house, so I can put it on the market. I figured, once I sold the house I would give all the money from the sale to Juliette. Though, I'm going to have to lie and tell her, Mommy wanted the kids to have the money in order to get her to take it. You know how stubborn Juliette can be," Greta stated.

"Yes I do. How does Juliette seem to be doing? Does she need more money, because I can arrange for Franklin to give her more?" Grandville asked.

"She says, she's doing fine financially, and she refuses to take any of the money that I offer. She said, that you are still sending her money through Franklin, and that her business is making a profit, and she and the kids are fine."

"Great . . ."

"Grandville you don't have to worry, because I'm all over it for you. I'm constantly at the house with Juliette trying to fill the void that you left when you were sent here to Oakhill. I want you to know Juliette is still in love with you, but confused about her feelings toward you."

"I love her and the kids too. I wish there was something I could do to ease their pain. Greta, I want to thank you for helping Juliette while I've been in here," Grandville said to his twin sister.

"Grandville you don't have to thank me. I love Juliette and the kids. It's not a problem, but there is something that you can do for me. You can get better and come home and show Juliette that despite what happened, you are a better man then you were before all of this, Greta said.

"Greta, my therapist tells me that in order for me to get better, I'm going to have to deal with some traumatic events from my past. I asked you to come here, because I need to tell you right before Mommy passed away she told me who our real father was."

"Before you say anything I want you to know, I found some of Gina's old things in the attic at the house last week. When Gina died, Ms. Forrester boxed up her belongings and had them sent to Mommy's house. It doesn't appear as though Mommy ever went through any of the boxes. She just put all of her things in the attic. Last week I was up there trying to clear it out when I came across Gina's old diary. I read it and in Gina's words I learned more or less that our uncle Greg was also our father. Also, I know you were present when Aunt Genevieve killed herself. Gina saw you hiding at the top of the steps when everything went down," Greta remarked.

"Did you tell Juliette?" Grandville asked anxiously.

"No of course not. I would never do something like that. I remember the promise we made to each other when we were kids. We promised to always be true to each other and to never tell someone else something bad about the other twin. I would never tell Juliette something so personal about you. I feel like you should be the one to tell her when and if you decide to. What I want to know is why you never told me that you saw Aunt Genevive kill herself?"

"Mommy told me not to tell anyone, not even you. I fainted after seeing what Aunt Genevieve did, and Mommy found me passed out at the top of the steps and put me back in my bed. We were only five years old when it happened, and I was traumatized from seeing something so horrible. There was no reason for you to have been traumatized too by me telling you about it, so I understand why Mommy didn't want you to know. This is the very first time I have ever spoken about this to anyone besides Mommy, and we never talked about it. She just told me not to tell anyone what I saw, not even you, and if anyone asks to tell them I was in my room asleep when Aunt Genevive came over."

"That's simply madness, and I just wish you would have told me about all of what was happening to you Grandville. That's crazy."

What else was in the diary?" Grandville asked his sister hoping there would be something about Gina's baby.

"Gina put a lot in there, but most of the diary was about you and how much she loved you. She wished the two of you were not related, because she wanted to marry you. She put in there how she would hold you down and perform oral sex on you. I had no idea Gina was doing that to you. She sexually abused you, and to find out that she was our half-sister and not just our cousin is even deeper. Grandville, I'm so sorry me and Mommy never noticed what Gina was doing to you. I had no idea until I read Gina's diary. We should have seen what was going on and we didn't." Greta said as a tear started running down her right cheek.

"What else is in the diary?" Grandville asked.

"Gina seemed to stop writing the diary after she went to Ms. Forester's to live. The passages that are in the diary are not dated and the whole diary is sporadic and all over the place."

"Mommy knew about what happened between me and Gina, because she caught us having sex in my room." Grandville felt so ashamed all over again. However, this time there was a sigh of release as he spoke the words from his mouth.

"What? That wasn't in the diary."

"I wonder why she didn't tell that story."

"I feel like I'm in an episode of the Twilight Zone. How did I miss all of this, and why didn't you or Mommy ever tell me? I can't believe you would leave me in the dark all of this time." Greta said. She was very upset at Grandville for hiding all of this deep and personal stuff from her all of their lives especially since they are twins.

"I was ashamed. Why would I want to tell you something like that?" Grandville questioned her.

"Wait, is that why Gina went to live with Ms. Forrester in the first place?"

"Didn't Gina write about why she went to live with Ms. Forrester in her diary?" Grandville asked.

"No, the passages in the diary are not dated, and she didn't go into much detail about all that she was doing to you."

"Well, she did a lot more than she's telling in her diary. She ruined my life. That's what she should have written about." He was fighting back the tears and pain he endured as a kid, and Greta could tell he was starting to cry. So, she changed the topic to Gina's abuse.

"In the diary Gina also goes into great detail about how Uncle Greg forced her to perform oral sex on him and how Aunt Genevive found about it, because she came home early one day from work and caught them. Gina was sent to her room but she could still hear her parent's argument."

"What, oh my God. That's where she learned all of that stuff about sex at a young age."

"According to the diary, Aunt Genevive called Uncle Greg an incestuous pedophile. She told him she was going to take Gina and go and stay with Mommy.

Allegedly, Uncle Greg said, "good that way Gina will be living with her brother and sister." That's when Gina heard a loud pop and her Mother came to her room and told her to come with her and made her go with her to our house."

"Now, it all makes sense why Aunt Genevive was so mad at your mother. I meant our Mother."

"In the diary Gina wrote how that comment had to mean Uncle Greg was also our Father. When Gina's Mother found out about Uncle Greg and Mommy, it made her go off like a character in a Snapped TV Show. I didn't know what to believe after I read Gina's diary. But, after careful thought I came to the same conclusion. We both know Aunt Genevive was always a little off. We may have been young when she passed away, but I can still remember her," Greta said.

"Greta, I'm sorry I didn't tell you Uncle Greg was our biological father right after Mommy's funeral. Mommy explained to me right before she passed on that she and Uncle Greg were together just one time. It happened when they were trying to console each other when Aunt Genevive was in the psychiatric ward. Mommy said she never told Uncle Greg or anyone else who our father was. So, everyone assumed her ex-boyfriend was our father."

"Wow . . ."

"Mother didn't know how Aunt Genevive found out," Greta said.

"Wow . . . I am sooo sorry for not telling you."

"Grandville you don't owe me an apology. Me knowing all of this information sooner rather than later doesn't add or subtract anything from my life. I owe you an apology for not being there for you and to help you deal with all of this." Greta had her head hung down and was trying to hide the fact that she was in tears, so the Guards wouldn't come over harassing them.

"Greta, there's nothing you could have done that would have changed what happened to me, Mother, Gina or Aunt Genevive. Please don't leave here beating yourself up for not seeing what Gina was doing to me.

Greta was trying so hard not to break down, because she could now understand what had happened in Grandville's life was very traumatic.

"When Mommy found out what was happening she did protect me by having Gina go and live with Ms. Forester. I had put what Gina did to me out of my mind for years. But, when Mommy told me that Uncle Greg was our biological father, I realized Gina was not just our cousin but also our sister. Then, Mommy died, and it was like all the thoughts of watching Aunt Genevive kill herself and remembering Gina's touch came back to me. I felt like the walls were closing in on me and I just couldn't take the pressure." Grandville said feeling anguish throughout his entire body again.

"Grandville, I understand and you don't have to explain anything to me, because you don't owe me an explanation but you do owe Juliette one. In your letters to her, have you ever tried to explain the pressure you were under?" Greta questioned him.

"No, because then I would have to tell her about Gina, and I have never told anyone about what she did to me. Besides Mommy, you are the first person who I have ever talked to about this."

"You should have told somebody and not just hold it all in. You have to release bad stuff that happens to you in your life."

"When Juliette asked me who I lost my virginity to I lied. I told her, I lost my virginity to a girl who went to our school. I couldn't tell her, the first orgasm I ever experienced was at the hands of our older cousin who I find out later is really my sister." He replied with a bit of sarcasm in his voice.

"Grandville, Juliette loves you. If you tell her the truth it might help her to understand," Greta urged her brother.

"Greta, I don't know how to tell her any of this. I love her so much. I feel like I tricked her into being with me, because I didn't tell her the truth in the first place. When Mommy died I began hearing voices in my head that nobody else could hear, and I started drinking in an attempt to drown them out. I can never tell her on the day Jessica died that I was drunk and out of my mind to the point I thought that Jessica was Gina," Grandville said desperately hoping he could find a way to tell the true story to his wife about the death of their daughter.

"Grandville, telling Juliette the truth will help explain how you came to be in this position. Juliette would understand, because she loves you and knows that you would never hurt Jessica or the other children intentionally. I know you love Juliette, and as your twin I'm here to tell you that if you are for real with Juliette there is a good chance she'll take you back," Greta said trying to convince her brother to stop hiding behind the truth.

"I'll think about it Greta. But, right now I'm here at Oakhill trying to work through my issues, and I'm just not ready for her to know yet," Grandville said.

"Like I said, you don't have to worry about me telling Juliette, because that's something that should come from you. But, I believe you should tell her sooner, rather than later."

"I could never tell her this by letter. This is something I would need to tell her in person. What do you think the odds are that I will get Juliette to come here to Oakhill?" Grandville asked his sister knowing she would be able to bait Juliette for him.

"I think the odds are definitely in your favor. You got me here."

"Thank you Greta. Now, I want to know how you have been doing since you and Rayshawn's breakup?"

"I've been doing fine, because in reality Rayshawn and I were over a long time before we physically split up."

"When was the last time you saw or spoken to Rayshawn?"

"Last year at our divorce hearing. There's no reason for us to talk. We don't have any children together and he got the house in the settlement. I didn't want it. I had decided I wanted to come home to Cleveland so I could help Juliette, and because I needed to do something about Mommy's house. It was nice that Cindy kept a close watch on Mommy's house for me until I could move back to Cleveland permanently. Why are you asking me about

Rayshawn? I know he was one of your best friends, but I know you can understand why I exited stage left."

"Greta, I love Rayshawn like a brother but you are my sister and my loyalty is to you. If divorcing Rayshawn is what you needed to do in order to be happy, then I support you. I just wanted you to know Rayshawn came here to Oakhill to see me."

"What!?" Greta exclaimed.

Finally the guard gave Greta and Grandville a withering look.

Greta looked at the guard and smiled. "Please forgive me Officer. I momentarily forgot the rules. It won't happen again," Greta said all polite and innocent.

The older black guard almost melted at the sight of Greta's smile. He nodded and turned his body away from them signaling the two could continue with their conversation.

"When was he here?" Greta questioned.

"He came last week on the Anniversary of Jessica's death. He wanted to let me know that his charity is going to have a new clinic built here at Oakhill which will be named after Jessica," Grandville replied.

"That was my idea and the next big project that I wanted the Robinson Charity to work on. I guess Rayshawn found out about what I wanted to do from the charity staff and decided to move forward on it."

"I rather Rayshawn not build the clinic, but he told me that despite what I want, he is building the clinic anyway," Grandville said.

"I think the Robinson Charity should build the clinic and name it after Jessica. Having a clinic named after Jessica is a tribute to her and makes her death less senseless. Her name will be associated with healing and that's a good thing and at least Rayshawn has enough respect to move forward with my idea. If the Robinson Charity was not moving forward with my concept, then I had planned to raise the money to try and get it done myself." Greta said.

"I'm glad you guys want to help, but have you ever thought about the pressure I might feel when the clinic is opened? That I'll have to go to a clinic named after my deceased daughter who I killed?" Grandville wanted her to wrap her head around his personal thoughts about the project, because he needed help in trying to agree with the whole idea of a clinic named for his daughter.

"Grandville the clinic will not be opened for at least two years, and it's our hope you will be home by then. Also, everybody knows what you did to Jessica was nothing more than a horrible accident. We forgive you for that, but none of it matters if you don't forgive yourself," Greta responded.

"I've been trying to forgive myself, but it's just not working for me Greta. I can't get over the pain I've caused my family, my wife, my children and you. Sometimes when I close my eyes at night I can still see the look of horror on Jessica's face." Grandville said as he lowered his face in his hands and holding his head, so the loud cry and tears could not be seen by the guard.

"Grandville, have you been to church since you have been here at Oakhill?" Greta asked him as she touched the Plexiglas like she was wiping his tears. But, he wiped his face on the sleeve of his shirt.

"No." Grandville replied through his sobbing.

"Then, maybe you should go, so you can be reminded that the Lord will forgive you no matter what you have done. He knows your heart just like I do. I know you didn't mean to hurt Jessica, but you have to pray and ask the Lord to deliver you from the guilt that you feel. You have to talk to the Priest or the minister and your therapist and tell them the truth about what happened to you, so they can help you come to terms with your trauma. You also have to tell Juliette the truth. You don't have to be ashamed of what Gina did to you, because you were a child and it was not your fault."

"Thank you for being so understanding Greta. When Rayshawn was here he told me, he still loves you, and he plans to try and get you back. He apologized to me for not doing right by you."

"I don't doubt Rayshawn loves me, but for me it is too little too late. I'm done with Rayshawn, and there's nothing he can do to convince me to go back to him. I hope he understands and respects my wishes. I've forgiven him for disrespecting our marriage vows. But, I will never forget what he did to me nor how he treated me while we were married and for those reasons our relationship is over." Greta responded, and Grandville could hear the bitterness and hurt in her voice.

"Greta if you can't forget Rayshawn's cheating what makes you think Juliette will forget the fact that because of me one of our children is dead?" Grandville questioned her reasoning on this issue.

"Juliette knows what happened was an accident and that you weren't purposely trying to hurt Jessica. Every time Rayshawn let another woman touch him in a sexual way he purposefully, intentionally, and willfully desecrated our covenant. I think you can understand there is a huge difference between our situations. I spend a lot of time with Juliette and she still loves you. If you tell her the truth about what happened to you she will understand how all the trauma you experienced as a child and Mom's dying affected your actions. The other day she mentioned to me that she knows something happened in our childhood that traumatized us," Greta said.

"What do you mean when you say us? Did Gina touch you too?" Grandville questioned.

"No, but Uncle Greg did?" Greta replied.

"What? Oh my God, why didn't you tell me?" Grandville asked in an exasperated whisper.

"Because Uncle Greg died a couple of days after he made me perform oral sex on him. He told me, if I told anyone he would kill you and Mommy. He showed me a gun and I believed him.

"What the f - - -."

"We were five years old and in the kindergarten the one and only time that it happened. One day when we were at school I became sick, because I ate something at lunch that upset my stomach. My Teacher sent me to the Nurse who tried to call Mommy who was working a double. Aunt Genevive was also at work so Uncle Greg came to pick me up. Remember, Uncle Greg was an Accountant and he made his own hours. When I got to Aunt Genevive's house Uncle Greg took me into Gina's room and told me that we were going to play a game called lick the chocolate. Uncle Greg then put chocolate on his privates and then put it in my mouth. I cried like a baby during and after he made me perform oral sex on him. Uncle Greg told me to stop crying, and then he gave me ten dollars and some candy. He then showed me the gun. He told me that if I ever told anyone about the game we played he would kill you and Mommy.

That night when I said my prayers I asked God to make Uncle Greg disappear and never come back, and a few days later Aunt Genevive killed him and then herself. I never told anyone except Father McNeal about what Uncle Greg did to me. I was afraid if Mommy found out she would be mad at me. Father McNeal explained to me, I was a child and I didn't do anything wrong and that God could and would heal me. He helped me to understand it was not my fault Uncle Greg and Aunt Genevive were dead. He gave me scriptures to read and with his help and the help of the Lord, I was delivered from the shame I felt. I believe what Uncle Greg did to me is the reason I was not able to please Rayshawn. I refused to even discuss oral sex, let alone perform it because it would flash me back to how Uncle Greg hurt me. Grandville, you and I our survivors, not victims and it's time you remember that," Greta said.

"Greta, I'm sorry. I had no idea Uncle Greg did that to you, but Mommy confided in me right before she died about what he did to Gina. Now to find out, not only was Uncle Greg our father, but he apparently knew who he was to us is difficult to digest," Grandville stated.

"Grandville, you don't have a thing to be sorry about. Uncle Greg was responsible for planting the seed that gave you, Gina, and me life; but his actions hurt us all. He was obviously a very sick man," Greta responded.

"Greta, you're right. I don't know what to say. It's obvious he was mentally deranged. Something really bad must have happened to him as a child," Grandville replied in total disbelief of his family's tragic story.

"Say you'll tell Juliette the truth, and you will go to church and pray. Say you'll allow the Lord to pick you up and carry you over the threshold of this pain and that you'll ask him to help you. Say you'll have faith that he can and will heal you. Say you'll pray for Uncle Greg, Gina, Aunt Genevive and your Mother's souls. Say you'll get your Bible out and read Psalms 139 verse 16, where David prayed to the Lord and said, "You saw me before I was born. Every day of my life was recorded in your book. Every moment was laid out before a single day had passed." The Lord has a plan for you and this situation. For all you know, the reason you had to experience this pain is because the Lord wants your situation to be a catalyst to help others. There are so many children who have and are being abused. When we bury what happened and never talk about it eats us alive from the inside out until eventually we break down and die. I have met so many people who've been abused sexually as children, and I think this is so outrageous. We are not the only ones who had our innocence stripped away by a relative who is supposed to love and care for us. Talking about it helps, because when we talk about what happened to us we release the feelings of shame which could have imprisoned us," Greta stated so passionately.

"My therapist wants me to join a support group here at Oakhill, and I was resistant to the idea but I will now think more about it. Also, I want you to know. I'm sorry about what Uncle Greg did to you and that I wasn't there to protect you. I want you to know, I respect what you are saying, but in some ways you have not taken your own advice Greta."

"What do you mean?" She asked.

"You never told Rayshawn about what happened to you and why you have an aversion to oral sex. The Bible also says that a marital bed is infallible. I have come to learn this means, that a husband and wife are allowed to do anything they want to for one another sexually. This is permissible as long as they are doing it with each other. According to God's law, a marital bed has no rules. Rayshawn shared with me, that he has a sex addiction in respect to oral sex, and he is getting help for his problem. If you had told him the truth about why you hate it so much, then maybe Rayshawn would have understood and maybe your marriage would have been saved. I know you don't want to be with Rayshawn anymore, and I understand but you can't tell me to be honest in my marriage when you weren't honest in yours."

"Grandville I have never thought about what role I played in the failure of my marriage until just now. Rayshawn cheated on me so much that I blamed our breakup on his infidelities. I never took any responsibility for not even attempting to try and please Rayshawn. I will think about what you said, and I may at some point decide to talk to him and explain my side of the story. This will help both of us have closure but too much has happened for me to go back. However, what I told you about Juliette still stands. She loves you and you love her so please don't be as dumb as Rayshawn and I have been. Learn from our mistakes, find God and let him lead and guide you. He is inside of you waiting for you to ask him to help you. Remember what we have been taught in respect to our faith and fall on your knees in prayer," Greta said as the room began to be filled with the time over warning signal.

One of the guard's loud raspy voice invaded the twins' ears over a loud speaker, "Visiting hours are now over. You have approximately two minutes before visitors will be escorted to the exit."

The twins looked at each other saying goodbye with their eyes before Greta stood up to be led away from Oakhill. Grandville remained seated while he waited for directives from the prison guards. Once he was back in his cell he sat on his lumpy little bed and reflected back to his visit with Greta. He realized though, he and Greta had shared their mother's womb for nine months and in essence were together even before they were born, neither knew the other as well as they initially thought they did. He wondered how each of them would have been different if they had confided in each other about the abuse each of them had endured when they were younger. Maybe they could have helped each other instead of silently suffering alone.

Grandville reflected back to the conversation with Greta concerning Melinia. He sure hoped her disappearance didn't have anything to do with Rayshawn or his cousin, and that Melinia ran off with a John like the Police theorized. Grandville had his fingers crossed Franklin had hired the private detective like he had asked him to, and they could find out where Melinia was before it was too late.

Chapter 16
Find My Way

Juliette sat on her sun porch watching the leaves fall from the trees and onto the green grass. She was reflecting on the recent changes which had occurred in her life. It had been three months since the third Anniversary of Jessica's death, and her world had taken further twists and turns which she hadn't foreseen. First, Melinia had not yet returned to the rooming house and had been missing for three months. Secondly, her long lasting friendship with Samantha had come to an ugly, abrupt end.

Juliette's mind wandered back to the events that caused her and Samantha to stop speaking to one another. The two friends had not seen or spoken to each other for over two weeks after the Anniversary. That's when Samantha sent her a text message asking her to get a babysitter and to meet her out. There had been a time when Juliette did not know how to send or receive a text message. Samantha taught her how to text, because they were both so busy it was the easiest way for the two ladies to stay in touch. Also, Samantha could not talk on her cell phone while she was in Court but could text. When Samantha first showed Juliette how to text it was before smart phones, and Juliette had become quite proficient at typing out the messages using the number pad on her flip phone.

As Juliette and Samantha's friendship grew so did technology, but despite new advances Juliette refused to get an account on Facebook or to engage in Twitter preferring to talk to people face to face or by telephone. Samantha and Grandville dragged her kicking and screaming into the twenty first century's technology era, pressuring her to get a smart phone with all the bells and whistles. Samantha's reasoning for encouraging Juliette to use Facebook and Twitter was, because she felt Social Media could help Juliette with advertising A Better Tomorrow. Juliette refused to engage, because she felt Social Media was one of the means for the Government and others to track her and her business.

Juliette also thought, it was outrageous for people to send every thought and to give a play by play account of every activity that they engaged into Cyberspace for the world to see, and she didn't want any part of the Fad. Also, Juliette knew a lot of people and didn't want to be inundated with Friend requests which she wouldn't have time to answer. She already didn't have enough time to do everything she needed to get accomplished in a day, and she didn't want to add any new tasks to her daily schedule. However, Juliette was on Linkedin.com as the professional site was viewed by many in the helping professionals, and Juliette found the site to be of assistance when she needed a new tenant for her rooming house.

After texting back and forth, the Supper Club known as "Under" was where Juliette and Samantha decided to meet. The owners came up with the name for their club, because their patrons had to go down steps or take an elevator from the street to gain entrance into the club. The place was huge and lavish and quite unexpected when you considered the fact the club was literally under the street. Under was Black owned and both she and Samantha were very well acquainted with the owners and both tried to frequent the club whenever they were meeting out. Juliette was feeling stress and pressure, because Melinia had already been missing for more than two weeks. It was like she had just vanished without a trace, and meeting Samantha out was just the distraction Juliette needed to get her mind off of the whole situation.

The Police had looked everywhere for Melinia, but the last time that she had been seen by anyone was when Violet last saw her at the rooming house. There were very few theories as to what could have happened to Melinia. The police told Juliette and her family, they had been unable to locate her and maybe she ran off with a John to start a new life. Melinia didn't have a smart phone and the throw away phone that she had been using wasn't traceable. She also didn't have any credit cards or bank cards so the police couldn't use them to attempt to track her movements. Juliette was afraid Melinia was hurt or even dead, because Juliette didn't believe

Melinia would leave for more than a few days without letting her family know where she was. Melinia had been strung out before and even when she was deep in the throes of her addiction, she had always let her family know where she was.

Samantha had been in trial on a controversial child rape case and not had much time to hang out. She had decided not to attend Book Club, because she had to work on preparing for the trial. As a result Juliette had not seen her since they went out to dinner on the Anniversary of Jessica's death. As the County DA, Samantha, rarely tried cases anymore and most were assigned to one of the junior prosecutors. But some cases carried so much media attention Samantha felt that it was prudent for her to handle them personally. Samantha was waiting for a Jury to deliver a verdict on one such case. Lawrence Willard had only been released from Lucasville prison for nine months before he was arrested for the rape of his live in girlfriend's six year old daughter.

Mr. Willard's family are very prominent in the Cleveland area. Willard had gone to prison for allegedly killing a young sixteen year old girl when he was eighteen. Willard maintained her death was accidental and occurred when the two were engaged in rough sex. Willard now twenty-eight years of age was maintaining that Samantha's office and his girlfriend's ex-husband who is a Cleveland Police Detective are trying to frame him. There was a Dateline episode being taped of the trial, and Samantha was under a lot of pressure to get a guilty verdict. After two weeks of testimony the Jury was finally deliberating Willard's fate and Samantha wanted to meet for a drink to blow off some steam.

When Juliette arrived at Under Samantha was already seated at the bar waiting for her. After saying hello and giving Samantha a hug, Juliette took a seat next to her BFF at the bar.

"Juliette, I ordered you a Vodka and Cranberry. Do you want me to order you a light beer to chase your drink before I close my tab?" Samantha asked.

"Yes, thank you. I got the next round." Juliette told her.

Samantha called the bartender over and proceeded to order her drinks, then she turned her attention back to Juliette.

"I haven't been eating and sleeping because of this Willard trial, and I'm waiting for the Jury to deliver a verdict. I can't believe they're still out. They've been out for two days, and I just can't figure out what's taking so long. That Bastard Willard is a child rapist and the child's mother is an idiot. Can you believe she actually called me and asked me not to prosecute her piece of shit boyfriend? This retarded woman cares more about her boyfriend then she does her own child, unbelievable," Samantha said.

"Some women are so desperate for a man they'll do anything to keep him, even sacrifice their own children." Juliette couldn't help but flash back in her mind about her own situation.

"Tell me about it."

"You look very nice Samantha. Your lavender tank matches the lavender stripes in your suit perfectly and will show up well on TV."

"You know that I don't like seeing myself on TV, so I never watch the news or any of the other shows that feature me if I know I'll be on. Thanks for the compliment though. I got this tank at Victoria Secret. I love shopping there. You look good too. So what's up, how've you been Juliette?"

"Not so good, my cousin Melinia has been missing since right before the Anniversary?"

"You know Melinia is probably holed up somewhere getting high with a guy who has a lot of product. You know how your cousin rolls. I'm sure Melinia is okay."

"Samantha I know Melinia has done a lot of dirt while trying to feed her addiction, but she's never disappeared for two weeks and not let someone in our family know she's okay."

"You know what they say, there is a first time for everything, so never say never. Melinia has always been a little wild, and she may have relapsed and is afraid to face all of you. People who have addiction issues often feel great guilt after they relapse and many become extremely depressed. Melinia is most likely okay, but just afraid to come home. When Melinia returns I'm going to tell her to go and kick rocks for putting you and your family through this kind of drama. I'm also going to tell Greta the very same thing. Did you see how she acted on the Anniversary? Her behavior was flipping unbelievable. Why does she have to be so selfish? Why wouldn't she give Tara the opportunity to go out with that fine man? Damn, she already had Rayshawn Robinson why not let another one of us get a chance?" Juliette could tell Samantha was irritated.

"Honestly Samantha I think you were way out of line when you said those things to Greta. First, Derek didn't even recognize Tara until she made it known to him who she was. Second, Greta and Derek have an attraction to each other that began before Greta came back home to Cleveland."

"Screw that witch Greta. I've made it very clear that I can't fucking stand her. Derek didn't recognize Tara, but when he realized who she was he was nice."

"Samantha, Derek was looking at Greta like she was a piece of chicken and he was a chicken hawk. He was polite to Tara, but he was into Greta who is my sister-in-law and that makes her family to me. She's a huge help to me with the kids and this is like the fourth time I'm asking you to be nice. I really would appreciate if you would try and get along with her. Can't you try and be nice for my sake?"

"No. I don't like that witch, and I have been tolerant for your sake," Samantha replied.

"It doesn't really seem like you're being very tolerant. I'm nice to your friends, even the ones that I really don't care for, including that no good Althea who you know I can't stand and I have a legitimate reason. She's tried to do all kinds of things to me including trying to destroy my business. Greta has never done anything to you." Juliette was getting upset with Samantha because she was acting very arrogant.

"First of all, she did something to my girl Donna. Rayshawn was dating her, and he dropped her for Greta. Trust and believe witches like her can't be trusted."

"Are you aware that Rayshawn and Greta had been together since high school? Which would have made your girl Donna the other woman not the other way around."

"I don't care. I don't like her and I'm not going to be phony. I would prefer not to be in her company, and if I'm around her she's going to get the cold shoulder from me. If it's that serious then maybe you and I shouldn't be friends anymore. If we stop being friends I wouldn't be out there spreading your business in the streets," Samantha said.

Juliette could not believe her ears. Samantha's words had hit her right in her heart. She couldn't believe Samantha was willing to throw away their twelve year relationship just because she asked her to get along with Greta. Juliette remembered all the times she was cordial to Samantha's friends that she couldn't stand. But, she endured them because she didn't want Samantha to be uncomfortable. Juliette was angry, but before she could respond to Samantha's hurtful words Samantha's cell phone began to ring. Samantha answered her phone and learned the Willard Jury was on its way back into the court room with a verdict.

"Listen Juliette the Willard Jury is coming back in. I have to go, but I will catch up with you at Tara's get together next week," Samantha hastily replied, as she turned around to get out of her seat, got up and walk away from the table.

Before Juliette could respond she was gone, leaving her to sit and ponder Samantha's hurtful words. On the drive back to her house Juliette silently fumed with anger, because she was hurt that Samantha found it so easy to throw away their friendship. In some ways Juliette felt used. She had always been a great friend to Samantha and even defended her when she thought she was wrong against the many people who disliked Samantha. Ever since Samantha had won her race and become the County's District Attorney, she had come across like she was drunk with her own power. It dawned on Juliette, Samantha was losing the respect she used to have for her and appeared to be taking her friendship and loyalty for granted. At home she sat in her office in complete darkness thinking about Samantha's hurtful words.

This was not the first time in their twelve year friendship that she and Samantha had had a disagreement. There had been several arguments in the past and Samantha would stay away for a couple of days, and then she'd return like nothing had happened and all was forgotten. However, Juliette reflected on the fact that the disagreements between them seem to be happening more frequently. and not just with her. The more Juliette pondered on Samantha's conversation the madder she became. Juliette decided to release her anger by completing the assignment for her therapist by writing a letter to Samantha. Reaching for her laptop she typed in her password and then logged onto her internet account. After checking her email she pulled up her Word application and began composing her letter.

Once she finished her letter to Samantha, she read her words over and noted that she was angrier then she first thought. She remembered all the times in the most recent past where she silently wondered in the back of her mind if Samantha's loyalty to her was as strong as hers was for Samantha. Samantha would catch an attitude for the slightest infraction and her friends, in particular Juliette, would scramble to make her feel secure. Samantha's behavior had become more erratic after she won her race, and Juliette attributed her behavior to the pressures of public life. Juliette both loved and admired Samantha. However, while she read her written words, she contemplated if she and Samantha's relationship was headed for a collision course.

Juliette was a woman who tried to avoid arguments in particular with Samantha, because she recognized behind Samantha's tough exterior was a very fragile woman who was easily wounded by those she loved. However despite this, Juliette realized conflict was a part of all relationships, romantic or otherwise. Her words in written form were strong, and Juliette was glad that Samantha would never receive her letter. If Samantha ever read her written words, she would probably refuse to speak to Juliette again. Instead of Samantha attempting to understand Juliette's feelings and how her words and recent actions had made her feel, Samantha, would walk away from their longtime friendship. Juliette re-read the letter a second time, and then decided to leave the letter on her laptop while she contemplated if she would give the letter to her therapist to complete her assignment.

After Juliette wrote her letter to Samantha, she remembered she forgot to check her postbox. When she did retrieve her mail, she noticed there were several envelopes. After she sorted the letters from the bills, so she could write checks to pay them later. She saw another letter from Grandville, and she was anxious to see what he had to say.

Grandville had been writing to her for the entire two and half plus years he had been at Oakhill. His letters always began with an apology for what he had done to Jessica and a hand written plea begging for her forgiveness. In the beginning she would read the letters and weep but over time she didn't have as many tears left for which to cry. The letters also detailed Grandville's life at Oakhill and asked for her to advise him in writing of how she and the children were doing.

For almost three years Juliette ignored Grandville's requests that she respond to his many letters. However, after she began working with Emily, she gained enough strength to finally respond to Grandville's request. Her letter to him was honest, true and intense. In it she told him how much she loved him. She also explained, how even after he had committed a desecrating act to their daughter, she could not bring herself to divorce him and walk away from what they once had. With the passage of time her heart had softened, and she almost believed if Grandville was fully rehabilitated they could be together once again.

What Greta had said before was true, Grandville had spoiled her. She didn't want anyone else but him, because despite what he did, deep in her heart she was still in love with him. Juliette had witnessed what some of her friends were enduring with their men, and she didn't want any part of the dating scene. At her age she found that many of the older Black single men were single, because they had some issue which prevented them from finding a mate. Many were weak and looking for a woman to take care of them financially while they tried to be Casanova Brown to as many women who would have them. Some were hooked on drugs, others were abusive, and some were even bi-sexual.

In her experience, many of the new millennium single brothers were Metrosexual. She found many spent a lot of their time and money trying to look as good as a woman. Some was going as far as getting facials and their nails done on a weekly basis. She liked those brothers who were white collar men with blue collar hands, which meant she liked a professional man who knew his way around a toolbox and wasn't afraid to get dirty. She had found exactly what she was looking for in a mate with Grandville, and she wasn't anxious to get out to meet someone new. She could honestly say before Jessica's death, Grandville treated her like a Queen. To Juliette having a man was liking owning a dog, once you get them trained to do the tricks you like, you are not anxious to get a new dog. Because training both dogs and men can be a hard, difficult process. She knew to most, she was throwing away the best years of her life waiting for a man who most likely would never be the man she fell in love with but Juliette didn't care. She wasn't going to walk away from Grandville for good. He was everything she wanted in a man, but she had to be one hundred percent positive Grandville would never be the same man again and that what they had couldn't be rehabilitated.

The newest letter from Grandville was brief but to the point. He had been keeping himself busy by teaching an English class to the other inmates. In his letter he went into detail regarding the course curriculum. He assigned *Animal Farm* by George Orwell as the first book which he wanted his new class to read. The book could be understood by third graders, and it was easy for almost all of his students to comprehend.

Grandville decided, he would use the book to help his students understand the Russian Revolution. Juliette was ecstatic for

Grandville, because she knew he had always wanted to teach. Though Grandville always thought he would one day be a Law Professor, teaching English to the other inmates was a worthy cause in Juliette's view. It was a great way for him to give back and to do something constructive with his time at Oakhill.

In his letter Grandville also wrote that he was being allowed the opportunity to have an Extended Family Visit with her. Due to the fact Grandville's three year anniversary for being at Oakhill was coming up, and he had not been in any trouble for more than a year. The visit was also commonly referred to as a conjugal visit, and she and Grandville would be allowed to touch each other without the eyes of the guards and officials at Oakhill on them. Juliette could not believe Grandville's written words. There was an opportunity for her to feel his touch once again. On one hand she missed him and the way he made love to her, but on the other hand she knew if she went to the Family Extended Visit there would be no turning back. If she allowed him to enter her once again she would be committing to him and to their future. Juliette didn't know yet if she was ready to commit to being a part of Grandville's future although she understood and recognized she was an integral part of his past.

As Juliette gazed out the window into the October day, she realized it had been approximately three months since the Anniversary. It was also ten weeks since she had her fight with Samantha which was ironically the same day she had received Grandville's request for her to come to Oakhill for his congenial visit. Summer had turned to fall and soon, fall would become winter and Juliette had to advise the authorities at Oakhill if she planned to go through with the contact visit. The deadline for giving the authorities at Oakhill her answer was looming and Juliette was still undecided as to what she was going to do. Grandville made it clear in his subsequent letters to her that she would have to contact the Oakhill Administrator very soon if she planned to go through with it. If she said yes, the Administrator would need to do a thorough background check on her. Further, she would be subject to the same searches as Grandville if she decided to consent to the visit.

Juliette sat on her sun porch contemplating her decision. The mere thought of Grandville and what he used to do to her body made her insides quiver, but she knew with Grandville it was all or nothing. If she came to the visit and made love to him, then she would be in essence telling Grandville that she was all in, but she didn't know if she could make that commitment. Juliette loved Grandville but she also loved her children. She had to ensure Grandville was not a danger to her and her children before she could agree to a possible reconciliation.

Juliette felt resentful that she couldn't talk to Samantha about her situation and the newest dilemma that she now found herself in with respect to Grandville. Samantha had cut off all contact with her when the letter Juliette composed for her therapist was inadvertently emailed to Samantha. Juliette kept all correspondence which she sent and received from Samantha by computer in a special file on her desk top. Juliette did this just in case Samantha deleted a message she might one day need.

When Samantha's father was ill, Samantha did not have a lot of time to talk to her friends by telephone about what was going on with her father's hospitalization. So, she would email updates on what the doctors were saying in respect to her father's health to her friends. Juliette had a feeling Samantha would one day need the emails, so she had Grandville put the special file on her computer. After Samantha's father passed away Samantha was able to sue her father's doctor for negligence. Juliette was the only one out of Samantha's friends who had a copy of every email which Samantha had sent regarding what the doctors had told her they were doing in respect to her father's treatment. The emails were evidence Samantha's attorney was able to use to help establish a negligence case and the doctor and hospital settled with Samantha and her family for an undisclosed amount.

Juliette thought she was putting the letter in her Samantha e-mail file, but instead she sent a copy of the letter to Samantha's e-mail address by mistake. Once Juliette realized her mistake, she didn't have any other choice but to live with the words she had put in the content of the letter. She had written the letter in a moment of extreme anger, but that didn't matter anymore now that Samantha had read it. Juliette couldn't bring herself to explain to Samantha the letter she wrote was never meant for Samantha's eyes but instead was an assignment for her therapist. No one with the exception of Greta and her mother was aware she was even seeing a therapist and Juliette was anxious to keep it that way. It was no one's business except hers and some would be judgmental of the fact that she sought out professional help.

Juliette found some African Americans were very leery about receiving mental health treatment or seeing someone to talk about their problems. Some black folks have been taught that to lay on a couch and to talk about your problems is a means for the establishment to get into your business. Some of her close friends and associates would think she was weak for seeking out help. Juliette felt it was healthy, and in her best interest to get assistance but she didn't want to broadcast this fact to the world. Samantha had always liked Grandville and encouraged Juliette to search her heart for forgiveness, but Juliette had no idea of what she would think about Juliette engaging in a congenial visit with Grandville.

Samantha and most of the other members of her book club were in between relationships. However, that didn't stop them from criticizing other females regarding their choices in respect to their men. Tara for instances was always making disparaging remarks about her best friend Michelle for staying with a man who she felt was worthless. Tara wanted her friend to follow in her footsteps and leave her man but her friend refused. Her friend had five children by her husband and he was sick. The words that would come out of Tara's mouth regarding her friend's marriage were vile and Tara would self-righteously call her friend a fool. Juliette came to soon understand that Tara had used her own common law husband to get out of her father's house and away from the abuse she was experiencing at the hands of her older Sister. Now that Tara was established and older she no longer needed or wanted her husband who was more than ten years her senior, so she dropped him like a bad habit. Tara often claimed her husband was cheating on her, but Juliette and several others knew the truth of the matter was that Tara was also cheating but unlike her husband she had never been caught.

Juliette had made the fateful mistake of confiding in Tara about how angry she was with Samantha and it had proved to be a big mistake. Now in hindsight Juliette felt in her heart that Tara may have been jealous of the friendship Juliette and Samantha had once enjoyed, because she had done everything possible to discourage the two friends from a reconciliation. Once Samantha received a copy of Juliette's email letter, she waited two weeks and then responded to Juliette's e-mail letter with one of her very own that she entitled The Decision.

Samantha's letter to Juliette was mean and venomous. It advised Juliette that Samantha no longer considered her as a friend. Juliette was broken hearted for the loss of her friendship with Samantha. She tried to apologize for some of what she had put in the letter, but Samantha was unwilling to forgive her words that were written at a time when Juliette was very, very angry. Juliette forgave the words Samantha had put in her Decision response e-mail letter, because she loved Samantha like a sister. However, Samantha refused to forgive Juliette and even went so far as to tell her that she would never again be welcomed at her home. Samantha also advised that she no longer trusted Juliette. And just like that, she and Samantha's twelve year friendship evaporated into thin air and Juliette had no choice but to part ways with one of her oldest and dearest friends.

In the past three months all of her so called friends who used to run with both she and Samantha had deserted her. Now, Juliette had few people that she could trust outside of Emily who she could talk to about Grandville's request. She couldn't talk to Greta, because she felt Greta would be biased and encourage Juliette to go and be with Grandville. Tara who Juliette had once really liked and admired proved to be a true hater. Juliette knew in her heart that she played a major role in her and Samantha's estrangement. Tara was very calculating and Juliette suspected Tara wanted to replace her as Samantha's best friend, so she could receive the perks that she perceived Juliette had received because she was friends with

Samantha. What Tara didn't seem to realize is that most people treated Juliette well because of her own merits. Juliette even suspected that Tara was even trying to convince Samantha to engage in Lesbian activity.

Juliette didn't really think Samantha was bi-sexual but she did find Tara to be suspect. Tara had learned to use her body to be manipulative and to get what she wanted. Also, Juliette remembered when Tara mentioned that someone in their book club was bisexual, maybe she was referring to herself. In Juliette's view Tara was tri-sexual, the kind of chick that would try anything if she could gain something from it. Juliette wouldn't be surprised to find that Tara was trying to turn Samantha out, because she thought she would receive extra benefit from being a close friend of the County District Attorney.

Juliette did admire the fact that Samantha was unwilling to put up with bullshit just to say that she had a man. When Samantha was in a relationship she went all out trying to show her man that she cared. She wasn't cheap and spent both money and time. Juliette did not think it was wrong for Samantha to expect the same treatment and to drop those guys who wouldn't reciprocate. Juliette saw first-hand what her single friends were experiencing trying to find and keep quality men of color. It was a rat race and she watched how so many women cut each other fighting over men who were not worthy and she was not anxious to enter that race.

Immediately after her and Samantha's estrangement, Juliette made the grave mistake of disclosing to Tara about the letter she wrote to Samantha and some of the contents. Once Tara learned of the situation, she also advised Juliette to stand her ground with Samantha because according to Tara, Samantha needed to know and understand that she shouldn't mistreat her friends. Juliette's suspicions regarding Tara were further solidified when Greta interrupted her thoughts with a phone call revealing what a no good back stabber Tara was.

Juliette was just about to put the twins to bed when Greta called her upset. Without a hello, Greta said, "I told you that some women can't be trusted."

"Greta what are you talking about?" Juliette questioned her.

"I'm talking about our so called friend Tara. She invited Derek over to see her brother Tim who she claimed was in town. When Derek got there he found out Tara had made the whole thing up, and she was dressed in lingerie looking like an overweight Vanity 6 wannabe. She tried to throw it at Derek, but he refused to catch it. He called me as soon as he ran out of her house to spill the beans on what she tried to pull. See what I mean Juliette about how some women can be? I was honest with Tara and told her about how Rayshawn's infidelities hurt me. Derek has won serious cool points with me by telling me what went down. Rayshawn probably would have took what Tara was offering, and then she would still be trying to smile in my face while she was sexing my man behind my back." Greta said pissed-off.

Before Juliette could respond to Greta's comment her other line rang.

"Greta hold on a second, my other line is ringing," Juliette said.

She clicked over and picked up her other line, "Hello."

"Juliette, thank god your home. This is Tara."

"Tara, what's up?" Juliette asked.

"I need to talk to you. Something terrible just happened and I need to talk someone about it." Tara said.

"What's wrong?" Juliette questioned.

"Well, Derek just left my house and I think we had a misunderstanding?" Tara replied.

"What happened?" Juliette asked.

"My brother Tim was supposed to come into town tonight. I thought it would be a great surprise for Tim if he got the chance to hang-out with Derek. So, I called Derek at work yesterday and asked him to stop by, but I found out earlier today that Tim had to cancel his trip. I left a message on Derek's voicemail at work but apparently he didn't get it and he came to my house anyway. I was expecting my new beau to come thru so I was dressed inappropriately. I felt bad that Derek had come all the way across town for nothing, so I offered him some of the food that I had prepared for dinner. I am afraid that Derek may have thought I was trying to hit on him," Tara said.

"Okay, I understand but listen, I'm going to call you back in a few minutes, because I have my Mom on the other line," Juliette told her.

"Okay but please call me back," Tara said.

"I will," Juliette replied.

Juliette clicked over to her other line where Greta was patiently waiting. "That was Tara, she is upset, because she doesn't want Derek to think that she was hitting on him. According to her she left him a message at work telling him that her brother Tim cancelled his trip. She claims that she was waiting for one of her dates when Derek got to her house and that he may have gotten the wrong idea," Juliette conveyed.

"Bullshit, he didn't get the wrong idea. He knows when someone is hitting on him. Tara has been trying to act like me dating Derek doesn't bother her but it does. She put it out there to see if Derek would bite and when he didn't she had to come up with a story," Greta said.

"It doesn't matter. Derek is not interested in Tara because he is in to you," Juliette said.

"We are taking it slow and I have not made love to him yet. We are not in a committed relationship, and I don't know if I'm ready to trust anyone after what I went through with Rayshawn. That still doesn't excuse what the skank tried to pull," Greta said.

Juliette was thinking the exact same thing. She couldn't understand why Tara thought it was okay to contact Derek without going through Greta. Granted, Tara knew Derek as a kid, but she hadn't interacted with him in years. Also, Tara did know that Greta and Derek were dating and to call him without informing Greta was in some ways sneaky and underhanded.

Juliette decided it was probably best for her to cut off communication with Tara and she wanted to kick her own behind. From the very beginning she had serious reservations about Tara, but she pushed them aside because Samantha and her friend Toya liked Tara so much. Now, because she didn't trust her own instinct, she and Samantha's friendship was destroyed and Greta's new relationship with Derek had been put at risk due to Tara's toxic behavior.

"I'm about to get off the phone. I have to put the twins to bed and then I'm going to call Tara back. I know what she says will be bullshit, but I still want to hear how she will try and spin the story. Derek let you know the truth and what was up with Tara. You're right when you said, him telling you exactly what went down says a lot about his character. Get some rest and I'll call you in the AM," Juliette said.

"Okay" Greta replied.

After Juliette hung up she went and put the twins to bed and then read some poems from Mia Angelo to her sons. She wanted her boys to understand poetry and found that reading to them and having them read to her increased their vocabulary and comprehension. As soon as she finished tucking the boys into bed Jabari stopped her as she was leaving the room.

"Mom, when can we see Daddy? When will he get to come home? I miss him." Jabari was kind of whining as he talked to his mom, and this made her think about Grandville's request.

"Your Daddy is out of the Country for his job. He can't come home right now but I know for a fact that he misses you too," Juliette said giving him a big hug.

"We haven't seen him in so long. Do you think he forgot about us?" Jabari asked innocently.

"No, your father writes me letters all the time, and he asks me to tell you how much he misses you and loves you," Juliette told her son.

"Well, why hasn't he called me? My friend Billy's dad travels all over the world but he still calls," Jabari questioned.

"Because where your father is there are no phones. But guess what? I am going to see your father very soon. How about tomorrow you start writing him a letter that I will give to him when I see him," Juliette stated.

"Okay Mom." Jabari innocently replied.

Juliette kissed her sons and then went to the living room couch to sit down and try to pull together her thoughts. There had been too many moments where her sons almost begged to see their father and Juliette still couldn't bring herself to tell them exactly where their dad was. It occurred to her that she had been trying to be family to Samantha and Tara when in reality she had a duty to her own family. Juliette realized she owed Grandville and her kids more than she had been giving them. It was time to for her stop living in limbo and make plans regarding both her and her children's future. She decided at that very moment that she was going to attend the Extended Family visit with Grandville. However, she had not yet decided if she would allow him to touch her. At the visit she would look into his eyes and determine for herself if Grandville was truly healing. At the end of her visit she would then make the decision if she was going to stay with Grandville or if she would move on.

Juliette knew that no matter what decision she made in respect to her and Grandville's personal relationship, she still had to make plans on what she was going to do about her kids. Luckily, her sons were clueless as to what their father did to Jessica and where he was because of it. Her sons were getting older and sooner or later she would have to explain. Her sons still talked about Jessica and the hardest day of her life was when she had to bury her only daughter while her young sons watched.

The boys understood that Jessica was gone home to be with the Lord, but they were unaware that Jessica was dead because of Grandville's actions. Juliette did not know how her sons would feel about their father once they learned the truth. Juliette decided that she would contact Oakhill the very next morning and accept the invitation to participate in the Extended Family visit program so they could begin her background check.

Chapter 17
Always In My Head

Grandville laid in his lumpy little bed and again thanked God which was something he had not done in a long time. It had been two months since he had made his hand written plea to Juliette asking her to come to Oakhill to engage in an extended family visit with him. He didn't really think she would consent to the visit, because it took her almost three years to answer his numerous letters. For two months he had been telling himself, no news was good news, and that she had not flat out said no. Then, he did something he had not done since Jessica died, he prayed. He got on his knees in his small cell and talked to God. He told him that he had already taken so much from him, his mind, his daughter, his freedom, his family and his career. He asked God, or more like begged him to allow him to receive an opportunity to see the only person who mattered to him other than his sons, his sister, Franklin and Montell. On his knees he told God that he wanted more than anything to see his beloved Juliette.

Life had changed drastically for him at Oakhill since he now had something to do which was worthwhile besides playing chess with some of his time. He was now teaching English to some of the other inmates at Oakhill, and he had to admit that he was enjoying it. It didn't take long for the Warden and the Oakhill officials to green light the project and before he knew it, he had 30 inmates in his class. His Chapter Fraternity brothers had come through with the books for everyone in his class and the superiors of Oakhill did not have to put any money into the project.

Now, three days out of the week at 1:30 pm he taught the other inmates English and about the Russian Revolution at the same time. *Animal Farm* by George Orwell was proving to be a great choice for his student's first assigned book, because the words in the book were small and easy to understand. Also, many of the inmates could relate their experience of being incarcerated with how the animal characters in the book felt about being forced to work for the farmer. Grandville found most of the inmates in his class were working towards achieving their GED high school equivalency and his teachings was preparing many to pass the exam. Grandville was surprised so many inmates had signed up for his class. He was more shocked when he discovered that Big Joe had also enrolled and more surprised that he was a model student.

He had been teaching for two months on the day he glimpsed a small ray of sunshine. He was lying on his lumpy little bed when Emerson came to his cell and informed him that he was being summoned to his Counselor Mr. Bolden's office. Grandville thought Mr. Bolden wanted to talk to him about the schedule for the support group which he finally consented to join, but he was blown away when he learned the real reason why he was called to Mr. Bolden's office.

After he arrived and was seated and after they made insignificant small talk Mr. Bolden delivered the news.

"Well Grandville, as you know you have been here at Oakhill for almost three years. In that time you've only had one altercation which was more than one year ago. As such you are eligible for a Family Extended Visit with a close relative. The Extended Family Visit is a new pilot program we are trying out here at Oakhill. It allows those inmates who have not been in any altercations or trouble for at least one year the opportunity to spend the weekend with a loved one. I understand that you wrote your wife and asked her to attend the visit?" Mr. Bolden asked.

"Yes, I did but that was almost two months ago. She didn't respond to my letter which probably means she isn't going to come," Grandville replied.

"Well Grandville the reason I requested to see you is to inform you that your wife has consented to the Extended Family Visit. She contacted Oakhill this morning and your visit has been scheduled for three weeks from today," Mr. Bolden stated.

Grandville was in a state of shock, and he put his hands over his face and closed his eyes shut, silently thanking the Lord for granting his prayer. He was speechless and Greta's words rang in his ears. He had gotten down on his knees and begged the Lord to grant him his prayer and the Lord had heard him. His beloved Juliette was coming to him, he would gaze upon her beautiful face once again.

"Grandville, I want you to know I'm very pleased with your progress so far. You're doing something productive with your time by teaching your English class and you are not experiencing symptoms as often. You are signed up to begin your support group too, and I really believe if you continue on this course you will have made enough progress to be released from Oakhill," Mr. Bolden informed him.

Grandville was ecstatic. He wanted more than anything to again be a part of society and to have the opportunity to reclaim his place in his family. However, Grandville was suddenly filled with fear and anxiety at the thought of actually being free again, and he remembered the old saying, be careful for what you wish for because you just might get it.

He had not had sex with his wife since the day before he had committed his heinous crime and he was suddenly afraid that he would not be able to perform. His nature would rise whenever he thought about Juliette, but he didn't know if she would allow him to touch her once she came for the visit. If she didn't want to make love to him during the visit he would definitely understand. He wanted them to be one once again but he also wanted to talk to her. He had missed her voice and her laugh and he was anxious to hear them once more.

Franklin had brought him his family portrait which he had kept on his desk in his tax office shortly after he came to Oakhill. It was the only picture he had of her and when he closed his eyes he could remember how she used to look. He wanted to see how she looked now. He wondered if she had lost or gained weight or if her appearance had changed, but even if she looked different he wouldn't care because his attraction for her was much deeper then skin. Mr. Bolden's voice brought him back to the present.

"Grandville, I know you've not seen or spoken to your wife since you have been at Oakhill. When she does come to the visit it would be a good time to talk to her about her plans for the future. If you are released will she allow you to return home? You also need to find out about your sons. Will she allow you to see them, and if she decides that she won't allow it how will this affect your mental health? I think you need to start thinking about how you are going to react if your wife has decided to move on without you." Mr. Bolden was very stern, because he did not want Grandville to get hurt and fall back into a relapse if Juliette did not respond in a positive way.

Grandville knew in the heart of hearts that what Mr. Bolden said was true. He had spent so much time caged like an animal, that he rarely thought about tomorrow and instead focused his thoughts on making it day by day. Thinking about tomorrow required hope and Grandville only had a small amount to spare. He had pinned what little hope he had on Juliette. In his mind what they shared could not be broken, and he imagined coming home to his Juliette who would be waiting with open arms when in reality the likelihood was that Juliette was done with him. Her letter gave him a glimmer of hope but what Mr. Bolden said was true. He had to prepare for the fact that he might have to be without Juliette and his sons when he was released.

He knew that once he was released from Oakhill he would immediately have a job. He didn't need to ever practice law again, and he would still make a good living. Before he came to Oakhill he surrendered his law license and getting reinstated back into the Ohio Bar would be an expensive, lengthy process. Luckily he still had a huge chunk of money put up and he could also live on the interest the money generated if he had too. He and Franklin's tax business made so much money it was unbelievable, and Grandville didn't need a law license to prepare taxes. However, he had always assumed when he was released he would go home to his beloved Juliette and though he gave it lip service, he had never thought seriously about being released. He knew what he did was terrible and though, he hadn't meant to hurt Jessica, he assumed the authorities would make him pay for his crime with his freedom for years to come. Now, Mr. Bolden was offering him something he had not had in a long while, anticipation for his future.

As soon as he was returned to his cell Grandville sought out Montell to tell him about Juliette coming for the Family Extended Visit. When he walked into Montell's cell he was sitting on his bed with his face in his hands.

"Hey Montell. What's going on are you okay?" Grandville asked.

Montell looked up and Grandville noticed tears in his eyes.

"Man, I'm better then okay, I'm fantastic. Grandville, I just got word that they are releasing me. I'm going home." Montell was so happy he couldn't stop crying while he was talking.

"Montell that's great news. I'm so proud of you. Franklin will be here to see me tomorrow and I'll have him to get in touch with Rayshawn ASAP, so you can start working as soon as you get out of here," Grandville said.

"Thanks Grandville, I sure appreciate it." Montell said looking up at him still teary eyed.

"No problem, I came to tell you Juliette contacted the prison, and she's coming for the Family Extended Visit," Grandville stated.

"Grandville that's great news. Hopefully you and Juliette can reconnect and put what happened behind you."

"Montell, I'm going to pray about it, because I'm beginning to learn that prayer works."

"You got that right. I have been praying since I got here. The Lord has finally answered my prayers and is allowing me to get my freedom back. Grandville I'll never forget all the things you've done for me. If you need anything, all you have to do is let me know and it's done," Montell said.

"Montell, I'm straight. I only need one thing from you when you're in the outside world." Grandville responded.

"Whatever it is you need, you know I got you." Montell declared.

"I know that you're not a snitch, but I need for you to keep your eyes on Rayshawn for me. He is caught up in some shit involving Juliette's first cousin, Melinia who is currently missing. Franklin got in touch with your friend McNaulty and he nor the Police have been able to figure out what happened to Melinia. It's like she just vanished and she's been missing for more than three months. Rayshawn has a cousin who knows Melinia pretty well and he may be behind her disappearance. If you do hear something which might help us figure out where Melinia is please do me a favor and let Franklin know," Grandville requested.

"Grandville consider it done. I will keep an eye out, and if you need me to do anything else get word to me through Franklin," Montell said.

"I will."

"So when are you being released?"

"In a month. When are you and Juliette having your Extended Family Visit?"

"In three weeks. My counselor is suggesting I talk to Juliette about her plan for the future when she comes up here. He says I'm making great progress, and if I continue on this course I too will be released. I haven't seen or spoken to Juliette in more than three years, and I'm surprised she consented to the visit. I'm a little nervous, because I don't know what to expect. Maybe she wants to ask me for a divorce," Grandville said wondering what the outcome of Juliette's visit would be.

"Grandville don't start thinking the worst. If Juliette wanted a divorce she could have already done it while you've been here at Oakhill. You know better than anyone that Juliette doesn't need your permission to divorce you. You know she could have prepared the paperwork herself. She might have just needed time to digest all that has happened. This is your chance to apologize in person for what happened to Jessica," Montell advised him.

"I know in my mind you're right, but my heart tells me she's the only woman for me. If I get out of here and she doesn't want me, I don't know how it will affect me," Grandville confided in his friend.

"If Juliette doesn't want to be with you anymore, then there's nothing more you can do with the exception of accepting her wishes. If you love someone then let them go, if they love you they will return. You can't hold onto Juliette if she doesn't want you anymore. All you can do is understand and respect what she wants and move on. You're a good looking, intelligent, professional guy. Even Big Joe wanted you," Montell teased.

"Don't f - - - ing go there with me."

Grandville and Montell both chuckled and Montell continued, "No, really what I'm trying to say is, if Juliette has decided to move on in time you will meet someone else who you can love and who will also love you back in return. You have given up years of your life and you shouldn't lose any more time trying to make things like they were. Was is no more, so you have to focus on now and your future," Montell said trying to help his friend get it through his head that his life maybe much different then he wants it to be.

"Damn, you're right. I'm just overwhelmed right now. So, I'm going to go in my cell and lay my head down for a minute," Grandville said seeming kind of depressed.

"Okay, but after dinner I want to play chess. We will only have so many more times where I can spank you with the board," Montell laughed again.

"Okay, but I don't know about the spanking part." Grandville tried to respond in a positive way, but he was not feeling playing chess or anything else. He just wanted to figure out how to make Juliette want to forgive him and take him back.

Grandville went back to his small cell and laid on his lumpy little bed and reflected on his conversation with Montell. What he said was right. He had lost so much time, and it was time for him to pull himself out of the despair he'd been feeling for so long. He wanted Juliette back, but if she decided that she didn't want to be with him he had to understand her decision. He also wanted a relationship with his sons. Though Jabari was not his biological son, Grandville had been raising him as his own since Jabari was three and in his heart Jabari was his biological child. Grandville realized he might lose Juliette, but he could not bear to lose his sons Jabari and Jonah also. They were the only kids he had left and the likelihood of him having more children were slim to none. He had already lost Jessica and maybe even Juliette so he couldn't lose his sons too. The only way he would be allowed access to his sons was to convince Juliette they would be safe with him and he wouldn't hurt them. Grandville understood that Juliette might not trust him with their sons given all that has happened.

Grandville also realized he had to tell Juliette the truth about his problems. He had to show her that he's a different man despite all that has happened just like Greta had advised. In three weeks he would see her again and he was both excited and petrified at the same time. His life was changing for the better and despite obstacles being placed in his path he could almost taste his freedom. He just had to come to terms with the fact that he might gain his freedom but lose his family. Grandville closed his eyes and prayed to the Lord again thanking him for answering his prayer. He also prayed that the Lord placed forgiveness into Juliette's heart and allow him an opportunity to try and make up for what he had taken from her.

The next day Grandville laid in his lumpy little bed and felt happy, which was an emotion that he rarely felt anymore. Franklin was due to arrive at Oakhill right after he finished teaching his class, and he couldn't wait to tell him that Juliette was coming to the Extended Visit. He had given his class a writing assignment and right after breakfast he planned to go to the library, so he could finish grading their papers as a means to keep his mind occupied and to stay busy. Many of the inmates in his class had remedial reading and writing skills and Grandville felt that giving them an opportunity to write was the best way to help them increase their skills.

At his monthly visit with Franklin, Grandville planned to ask him to go back to his chapter fraternity brothers to see if they could spring for pocket dictionaries for everyone in his class. At Oakhill there were few modern conveniences like computers. Grandville felt that having pocket dictionaries would allow his students to spell better and to learn the definitions of words. The inmates at Oakhill didn't have access to smartphones and there were few dictionaries in the library for them to utilize. Grandville planned to give his students weekly spelling tests using some of the easier words from the *Animal Farm* book, and he wanted them to have access to a means to really understand the words.

After a breakfast of sausage, gravy and biscuits which looked and tasted like garbage, Grandville went to the library. It only took an hour and a half for him to finish grading the tests. Then Grandville turned his thoughts to the support group which he would start right after his visit with Juliette. He knew in order to truly get better he would need to talk about the sexual abuse that had occurred to him. He had to admit he felt better after he had told Greta the truth about what happened to him.

However, Greta was his sister and telling her was not the same as telling a room full of men about how his female cousin forced him into sex. He knew many of them would consider him lucky because many of his fellow inmates have been sexually abused by men. He knew the other inmates would tell him how lucky he was for having a willing older female who voluntarily taught him about sex, but what had occurred still hurt him in more ways than one. However, the emotional damage and trauma of being forced to have sex with his cousin did not manifest itself into tragedy until Grandville learned that his cousin was also his half-sister. Also, he was still harboring the secret that a child had resulted from his and Gina's relationship.

The day he found out that he and Gina had a son was also the day his mother died. Grandville had not been the same after learning of his no named son's existence. He wondered constantly about his first born son and in his head he had a lot of unspoken questions. Did the child look like he and Greta or did he look like Gina? Was he happy? Did he get good, loving adoptive parents or was he living with adoptive parents from hell? His son was now a young adult and as such would he attempt to find him one day? The most difficult question was if his son was deformed mentally or physically due to his and Gina's blood being so close?

He knew in his heart he had to tell Juliette the whole, horrible truth when he saw her in three weeks. There was a remote chance the child would one day look for him and Grandville wanted Juliette to hear the truth from his lips. He understood once he told her the truth she might decide that too much had happened for them to ever get back together. He wanted just one more night with her where he could show her with his body what she meant to him. Then, he would walk away from her if she decided she could not be with him. That part he knew he had to do and what Montell said was right. If he ever loved Juliette, then he had to be prepared to let her go. He wanted her to be happy, and if being with him made her unhappy he would have to let go, as difficult as it might be.

After lunch Grandville taught his class where he continued to be amazed at how bright many of his students were even despite their lack of formal education. He started each of his classes with a discussion on the chapters which the class had been assigned to read, and he encouraged all of the men to participate in the verbal discussion. When class was over he went back to his cell to wait for Franklin. It wasn't long before Emerson came to escort him to the private visit room.

After exchanging their fraternity handshake Franklin and Grandville sat down to begin their visit.

"Grandville how have you been?" Franklin asked.

"Believe it or not Franklin I'm doing great. Juliette just sent word to the prison that she's coming to the extended family visit. I'm going to get to spend three days with her," Grandville replied.

"Grandville that's great. I was already aware that you would be visiting with Juliette. I did the application on your behalf, so that you could participate in the program. Your counselor Mr. Bolden called me as soon as Juliette contacted Oakhill. Mr. Bolden seems to think you are making great progress and you may be ready for release soon. Our corporation recently acquired a small four suite apartment building located in Euclid. I have some workers renovating the building as we speak. You will be able to live in one of the units when you leave here because you have to have a spot to stay when you get out of here. I know you hope to go home when you are released from Oakhill but you have to be prepared for Juliette to be against the idea. If you move in the building you would be close to A Better Tomorrow and you'll still be relatively close to you and Juliette's house. When you see Juliette at the extended visit I think you ought to let her know that when you are released you have somewhere else to go besides home with her. We can also talk Greta into taking one of the units and the two of you can keep an eye on each other. Also, you can talk Juliette into allowing you to date her again, so that you can help her remember why she fell in love with you in the first place. The last thing you want to do is to make her feel pressured," Franklin advised Grandville.

"Franklin thanks for thinking ahead about my living arrangements. It seems the plans for my release are moving very quickly. I really didn't believe the authorities would ever consider letting me out of here. I guess I really hadn't made a plan and I am grateful I have you to help me," Grandville said.

"Grandville you're my best friend, and I know if the shoe were on the other foot you would do the same for me," Franklin replied.

"In a heartbeat but thanks anyway. Also, I just found out that Montell is being released. I need for you to catch up with Rayshawn and let him know that Montell needs to start the job that we discussed immediately," Grandville said.

"No problem. How do I get in touch with Rayshawn?" Franklin asked.

"You can always reach Rayshawn through his agent Zach Jordan. Zach went to undergrad at Ohio State with Rayshawn and is one of his closest friends."

"I know Zach, he went to law school with me. I didn't realize he was Rayshawn's agent," Franklin said.

"Yeah, Zach doesn't like all the attention so on paper his firm represents Rayshawn except Rayshawn is the firm's only client. Zach handles all of Rayshawn's legal needs and those legal issues he doesn't want to personally handle, he farms out to other Attorneys who have been personally vetted by Zach. When you call his secretary say you represent Panther and she'll make an immediate appointment with you. Make sure that you make an appointment to meet with Zack in the Cleveland office because he has two offices, one in Cleveland and another small office in Los Angeles which he uses when he's in California with Rayshawn," Grandville explained to Franklin.

"When is Montell being released?"

"He's getting out in a month. When he's released, I want you to give him two thousand dollars. It's not a lot but it well help him make a modest start."

"Grandville you're a good man who is very good to your friends. You'll be blessed for how you look out for your people."

"Montell is a good man, and he has been watching my back since I got to Oakhill. He has provided me with hundreds of hours of company and distraction. It's difficult to explain how slow times passes here at Oakhill. It's kind of like watching paint dry," Grandville chuckled.

"Candidly, I really don't want to know. I'm just glad Montell and you became friends and you had someone watching your back. Who will look out for you now?" Franklin asked.

"Honestly, I don't anticipate any trouble. Now, that I've been teaching the English class, I've gotten to know some of the other inmates. Before the class I didn't even bother trying to get to know anyone besides Montell. Luckily several of the guys from my class are very protective and they call me Teach. No one even glances the wrong way at me," Grandville responded.

"That's great. Do you need anything?" Franklin asked.

"Yes, do you think you could go back to the Chapter Frat and see if they would spring for pocket dictionaries for my class? Having a pocket dictionary will help my class with spelling and comprehension."

"No problem and if I can't get the brothers to purchase the dictionaries, then I'll have our non-profit get them. We could use the write off. I have to come back this way in a few weeks to attend a seminar. I'll bring them then with me."

"Cool. Has there been any developments with Melinia?" Grandville asked.

"Not one. It's like she just vanished. McNaulty has Rayshawn's cousin's house bugged, and it appears he has nothing to do with her disappearance. Hell, Rayshawn's cousin seems extremely pissed he also can't find her, and he has a whole posse out looking for her. I don't know, maybe Melinia knew she had people after her and purposely disappeared," Franklin said.

"How is Juliette holding up?" Grandville asked.

"I guess she's okay. I haven't talked to her, but I have talked to Greta who told me Juliette and her family have passed out flyers and are simply trying to get the word out that Melinia has gone missing. Juliette's family has held several fundraisers and are now offering a twenty-five hundred dollar reward to anyone who provides clues to Melinia's whereabouts," Franklin told Grandville.

"Franklin, I'm going to need you to get twenty-five hundred dollars from my safety deposit box and match the reward money. Make sure we remain anonymous when you reach out to Juliette and her family."

"No problem but I really want to caution you. You have spent close to ten thousands on this Melinia endeavor when you add up McNaulty's fee and adding to the reward. I really think you should rethink the idea of contributing to the reward money. If Melinia is hiding she'll surface when she is ready to reveal her whereabouts. You have a responsibility to Juliette and your kids and you can't afford to continue to throw money at this situation," Franklin advised

"You know you are absolutely right. That's why I want you to get my money back from Rayshawn when you talk to him about Montell and the job. Tell him we hired someone to try and locate Melinia, and we need to be reimbursed for our costs. Believe me when I say it, there will be no problem with Rayshawn reimbursing us immediately. Once Rayshawn gives you my money back, I want you to donate the twenty-five hundred dollars to Melinia's fund for me and put the rest back into the slush account," Grandville directed Franklin.

"Consider it done. Do you need me to do anything else?"

"Just for you to continue to pray for me." Grandville said.

"I do that anyway.

"Thank you for being a loyal friend."

"See you soon," Franklin said.

"Okay Franklin, take care." Grandville said and they hugged each other goodbye.

"You too," Franklin replied.

Chapter 18

Bag Lady

Juliette drove down 71 South with the heat blasting in her rented loaded Ford Focus and her stomach in knots. The early November sun was shining but there was no warmth coming from the rays. She was on her way to the extended family visit with Grandville and she was a nervous wreck. The visit was being held at the Homewood Suites which was located around the corner from Oakhill. Juliette was both excited and afraid at the same time. Since she had made the decision to visit Grandville her life had been moving forward at top speed. Melinia had been missing for almost four months and Juliette had been spending all of her free time trying to help the rest of her family locate her.

As a result Juliette spent very little time thinking about her upcoming visit with Grandville, but instead focused her available free time on trying to locate her cousin. Before she knew it, she was on her way to Dayton Ohio where Oakhill was located. She had left her sons with her mother and her daughters with Greta and she was now travelling on a road to an uncertain fate. Could she handle the new Grandville? When she actually spent time with him would she still be in love with the man he is now? These were the questions that swirled inside her brain.

Driving down the highway she watched the trees and shrubs change in color from dark greens to various colors of brown and red. She reflected back to her secret, the burden of which was eating her from inside out. Even during her last therapy session with Emily, Juliette could not bring herself to utter the truth. Emily had graciously saw her for two hours the day before to help make sure she was emotionally prepared to spend time with Grandville. From the moment Juliette sat down with Emily she knew she was making the correct choice in attending the Extended Family Visit.

"Juliette I'm really proud of you for agreeing to attend the visit with Grandville. I hope you know this is a huge step in your recovery."

"Thanks Emily, because of you I now feel ready to take control of my life. The kids and I have been living in limbo for far too long."

"You haven't seen or spoken to Grandville in more than three years. What do you expect to accomplish from the visit?" Emily asked.

"I guess I expect to decide if I'm going to stay with Grandville and fulfill my wedding vows or if I am going to divorce Grandville and walk away from him for good. Then, there is the matter of the children, I got to start telling them something in particular Jabari and Jonah, they are older and have been asking to see Grandville." Juliette replied.

"Make sure to put your listening ear on and try and be open minded when you see Grandville. Also remember to make your decision based on how you feel and not based on what others think you should do. People are quick to pass judgment when most don't know what they would do if placed in your same situation," Emily advised Juliette.

"Thanks for telling me that Emily, because right about now many of my so called friends have abandoned me due to me and Samantha's estrangement. Samantha and I have not made up, and it looks like our friendship is lost forever. I really thought the sisterhood we shared with each other would last a lifetime. I'm hurt that she could discard me and twelve years of loyalty like I was nothing. The silver lining in this situation is that Samantha and I are no longer friends. I don't have to try and explain to her why I'm attending this visit with Grandville. I know if we were still friends she would be trying to talk me out of attending."

"Juliette, I know you really miss Samantha, but you will still need to make your decision around visiting Grandville based on what's good for you and your family and not based on what Samantha and your other friends might think. You and Samantha were very close so maybe you should reach out to her and apologize."

"I tried that and she sent me a text saying she and I were no longer friends. She even told me that I would never again be welcomed at her house. Despite the way she has treated me, when I heard Samantha had to be hospitalized, I sent her a beautiful card and wrote a message to her in it. I told her that, even though she was mad at me I still loved her. I was very upset and worried when I found out she was sick enough to be hospitalized. In the twelve years we were friends she never had to stay overnight in the hospital. She sent me back a thank you card on her office letterhead and signed it District Attorney Truck instead of Samantha. In all of her cards to me she has always included a short personal message and in this card there was nothing. That hurt me and I finally got it, she doesn't want to be my friend anymore. I've given Samantha way too much of my energy when I really should be focusing my time on Grandville and my kids. Frankly, I'm glad that I don't have to deal with Samantha's negativity regarding this whole thing." Juliette blew out a big sigh of relief which actually felt like a weight rolled off of her chest.

"Juliette, you do realize one day you and Samantha will make up and you will have to tell her of your choice to spend intimate time with the man who took your daughter's life?" Emily asked her.

"I don't know about us making up, but I am prepared to stand by my choice to engage in the visit despite the outcome and what Samantha or anyone else may think. At the end of the visit I will either walk away from Grandville and prepare myself to start a new life or stay with him, again ready to start anew," Juliette replied.

Emily and Juliette talked about strategies which she could employ to keep herself calm while spending time with Grandville. They also talked about how she would explain to her children all that had transpired and when their session ended she went home and finished packing, took a long bath, then went to bed.

Now, Juliette was on her way to an unexpected fate. She didn't know how she would feel once she left the visit. However, she had resigned herself to know that at the end of the visit she and Grandville would begin making plans for their future or she would be making plans to divorce Grandville and move on with her life.

Juliette thought back to the comments that she made to Emily about Samantha. She was hurt because she really and truly believed Samantha was her best friend. She also thought Samantha was the one person she could say anything to and still receive her unconditional love. So, Juliette just couldn't believe that her written letter was so bad Samantha would refuse to offer her forgiveness.

It occurred to Juliette, she was doing the very same thing to Grandville that Samantha had done to her, because she was not really attempting to forgive Grandville for his actions on that fateful day. Juliette often said she had forgiven him, but in reality it was just lip service. She was on her way to see him, but in order to consider a future with Grandville she had to truly forgive him and accept the fact that what happened to Jessica was a horrible accident. Juliette wondered if she could. Grandville was very sick on the day he hurt Jessica and up until the day of the tragic event which separated their family he had treated Jessica like a little princess.

She had found herself sometimes getting jealous, because when she told Jessica to do something she would often run crying to her father who would hug and kiss her and bribe her to behave. Juliette was a serious disciplinarian and it upset her when her children were disobedient. Even on the day of her death Jessica refused to follow directions and her disobedience contributed to her death.

Juliette reflected back to the worst day of her life. It was a beautiful sunny Saturday and she and the kids had gotten up and gone shopping. Jabari was eight and the twins were four. Juliette wanted to get the kids out of the house because Grandville was acting strange. The night before he had made love to her like a man possessed and no matter how many times they made love the fire that burned within him would not be extinguished.

When she got into the bed to go sleep she was surprised that he wanted to make love. She had been using a diaphragm for birth control, but they had not been intimate in weeks. Her body immediately responded to his touch and she didn't want to break their connection to go and put it in. After their marathon lovemaking session Juliette was exhausted. Her body was tired and sore but the afterglow of the pleasure he brought her made her nerves tingle. She closed her eyes and experienced some of the best sleep of her life.

The next day when she woke up Grandville was acting strangely. He appeared to be talking to himself and he seemed more hyper than usual. This was not the first time she had caught him talking to himself. She had confronted him about the behavior a few days before, and he explained he was under a lot of stress. He said, he was not talking to himself but instead going over language for a Brief which he had to write for the Partners at his Law Firm. His explanation was feasible, but Juliette noticed that since his mother's death Grandville had not been quite right. He still went to work every day and he still performed his fatherly and husbandly responsibilities with the exception of making love to her twice a week. She understood he was depressed about losing his mother, so she did what she thought a good wife should do, she gave him his space.

On the fateful day of the incident she and the kids had just returned from the Mall where Juliette had purchased each of the kids a new outfit. She told Jabari to take the twins to their rooms so they could all take a nap and her pretty little feisty daughter told her no, she didn't want a nap. Juliette explained to Jessica, if she did not do as she was told then she would take her new outfit back to the Mall and she would also spank her. Juliette left the children in their bedrooms and set off towards the back of the house in search of Grandville. She spotted Grandville in the backyard from the family room window and she noticed he was using their chain saw to cut the hedges. She couldn't understand why Grandville was using a chain saw instead of the hedge clippers. She needed to use the bathroom before going out to question Grandville about using the chain saw, so she decided to use her half bathroom located at the bottom of her kitchen steps.

She was on the toilet relieving herself when she heard a blood curdling scream, the sound of which still haunts her. She couldn't get off the toilet fast enough, because she knew something was terribly wrong. She ran towards the back of the house where she heard the scream originate from and as she ran into the backyard she saw Jessica lying in a pool of her own blood. Grandville was kneeling beside her with the chain saw in his hand.

Grandville was crying and talking to himself. "Look what you made me do! Why did you make me hurt her?"

Juliette jumped into crisis mode and took off at top speed towards her house. Once inside she grabbed her cordless phone and called 911.

"What is your emergency?" Asked the 911 operator.

"Please get someone here quick. My four year old daughter has been injured in a chain saw accident. We are in the backyard." Juliette replied hastily.

Juliette didn't even wait for the 911 operator to ask her questions. She dropped the phone and ran into the bathroom and grabbed several towels, and then ran at top speed towards where her injured baby was lying. Grandville was hysterically crying and holding a bleeding Jessica when she returned.

"Baby wake up for daddy, please wake up. I love you and I'm so sorry, I didn't mean to hurt you," Grandville pleaded.

Juliette applied pressure with the towels to the gaping hole in Jessica's neck and prayed for a miracle. Soon the ambulance arrived along with the police who raced into the backyard to help but by the time they made it to them, Jessica was gone. Once the EMT's announced that Jessica had passed away Juliette crumpled to the ground crying. The ambulance workers picked up Jessica's bleeding body and placed her on the gurney and put her in the ambulance while the police began to question Grandville who was inconsolable and out of his mind.

"Mr. Stubbs, tell us what happened?" Asked the officers.

"I killed her, they made me," Grandville was tearful and making loud whaling noises.

"Mr. Stubbs there is no one else here. Who made you kill your daughter?" The police questioned him.

Grandville started to whisper to himself as tears streamed down his face. The police looked at each other realizing they were dealing with a mental health emergency. They handcuffed him and led him to the police car.

One of the police officers who was an older white gentleman helped Juliette off the grass and led her towards the house.

"Mrs. Stubbs, is there anyone you want me to call who can come and be with you? I am going to have to take you down to the station so you can make a statement about what happened here," the officer inquired.

"My sons are asleep upstairs. I need to call my mother so she can come over and stay with the kids and I also need to call my best friend" Juliette said.

Juliette made her calls while in a state of shock. She kept seeing her beautiful daughter in a pool of blood and closed her eyes to try and erase the images from her head. It took everything she had in her not to break down, but she had to try and remain calm and in control for the sake of her sons. Juliette called her mother and calmly told her there had been an emergency and she needed her to get to her house ASAP. She then called Samantha and quickly explained what happened. Once Samantha heard the news she began weeping.

"Juliette, it's going to be okay. I can't believe that this has happened," Samantha said between sobs.

Samantha was always an Attorney and even though she was distraught she put her thinking cap on.

"Listen Juliette simply tell the police what you saw and only answer the questions they ask. I will get one of my colleagues who works out in Lake County to meet you at the station. She should beat you to the station but don't answer any questions until she gets there," Samantha advised her.

Juliette and the policeman whose name was Officer Harris didn't have to wait long for her mother to arrive because she made it to her house in twenty minutes. Officer Harris explained the situation to her mother who broke down in tears. Juliette was able to calm her mother down and explained the boys were napping. She asked her mother to contact Franklin and advise him of what had occurred. She also asked her Mom not to say anything to the kids about what happened to Jessica until she returned and she also advised her not watch the news.

Samantha sent her friend and colleague Darita Dorrow to Juliette's rescue, and she was at the station waiting when she arrived. After she gave the Police both a written and verbal statement regarding what she had seen and heard, she was released. Darita explained to Juliette that Grandville had been taken directly to the hospital and was undergoing psychiatric treatment. She also advised Juliette, she would be following her home so she could fend off the news reporters. When Juliette arrived back at her home she found several TV cameras parked in front of her house. Darita gave a beautiful statement advising, Jessica's death was an unfortunate accident and the police were investigating. Darita asked the reporters and the general public to give Juliette and her family privacy during this unfortunate time. Once Darita gave her statement, the news reporters packed up their equipment and quickly exited Juliette's property.

Juliette would never forget how Samantha held her down when she really needed a friend. She sent her Darita who to this day was still close to Juliette. Darita made it clear that she would not charge her for her legal service, because any friend of Samantha's was a friend of Darita's. Darita told her that Samantha talked about her all the time and that she was sad that they had met due to tragic circumstances. Darita and Samantha helped her to be strong when she needed support. Samantha spent hours on the phone with her, because Samantha decided not to attend any of Grandville's hearings with Juliette. Samantha had political aspirations and felt it was not a good idea to attend the trial. Despite this, Samantha was a good friend and made her get out of the house and engage in activities so she was not isolating.

Darita's legal advice during that time in her life was invaluable, and it was Darita who assembled the legal team which made Grandville's deal that resulted in him voluntarily choosing to go to Oakhill. Sadly, Darita and Samantha stopped speaking to each other a year after Jessica's death. There was nothing Juliette could do but stay out of their fight and try and support each one individually. The last time they saw each other Juliette did not tell Darita about her and Samantha's estrangement. When they were together neither woman brought up Samantha's name.

Together she and her mother explained to her sons that Jessica had gone to be with the Lord. Thankfully the boys did not see or hear what had happened to Jessica. However, now they were older, Juliette was afraid they would start asking her for the details as to what exactly happened. Juliette realized it was time for her to tell them the whole truth as difficult as it might be. Then, there were the twins who were a little over two years old. What Juliette could not bear to tell anyone is that she slept with Franklin three days after the incident and not three weeks after the incident like she had told Emily.

When she looked at Janae all she could see was Grandville as she had his hazel brown eyes and his coloring. Jolene on the other hand was the spitting image of Franklin, she had his eyes and nose and a deep chocolate brown complexion and wavy hair. Luckily Juliette was the only person who had seemed to notice the physical similarities between her daughter and Franklin. Juliette felt it was due to the fact, she and Franklin mostly interacted with each other by phone. They chose to avoid each other since that one and only time they were intimate.

The last time she had seen Grandville was at his Preliminary hearing which was held three days after Jessica died. Everyone assumed she didn't attend the rest of Grandville's hearings, because she was angry at him for taking Jessica's life when the real reason was she couldn't bear to look at Grandville after her betrayal. Then, she learned she was pregnant and five months along. She thought she was missing her period due to being stressed out. Juliette had blamed her weight gain on the fact she was eating everything that wasn't nailed down due to being depressed. It took Samantha to make her think back and realize there was a possibility she was pregnant.

She and Samantha decided to meet for dinner and Juliette had eaten almost all the bread in the bread basket, because Samantha stayed away from Carbs as a general rule. Out of the clear blue Samantha remarked, "Juliette I'm not trying to be funny but I don't know if you have noticed but you have put on a lot of weight. Girl, you're starting to look like one of the Weather Girls. The only time I've ever seen you put on this kind of weight is when you're pregnant," Samantha had said.

The realization of Samantha's comment hit her like a ton of bricks and Juliette thought back to the last time she had her period. She then realized it was before Grandville and the incident. Juliette immediately busted out into tears and Samantha picked her up and wiped away her tears and assured Juliette everything would be all right. Samantha helped to pull her together and was with her when she took the home pregnancy test which indicated she was with child.

When Juliette went to the doctor, he confirmed Juliette was five months pregnant with twins as the doctor could hear both babies' heartbeats. Juliette was unsure if Grandville or Franklin was the father of her twins, and she was too far along in her pregnancy to consider abortion. For Juliette abortion wasn't a viable option. Despite how many months she was in her pregnancy, she had already lost one child and now she was being given two more and she considered her unborn children as gifts from God. Once Juliette learned she was pregnant, she prayed daily for a daughter. She couldn't believe it when the ultrasound revealed, she was having two daughters.

When the babies were born and she saw them she suspected her twin daughters were fathered by two different men. She had not had her daughters tested but she knew the truth in her heart. So far no one seemed to notice, but once Grandville met the girls she was positive he would see what everyone else had been blind too.

In order for her to move forward with Grandville she would need to tell him the truth. She didn't know if it would set him back in his quest to achieve his sanity. She could only hope and pray once Grandville learned she had given birth to twin girls, and that there was a possibility one maybe fathered by his best friend, that he would accept the girls despite everything. Juliette knew only time would tell the tale.

Chapter 19

Confessions

After three weeks of anticipation the day Grandville would see his beloved Juliette had finally arrived. Grandville lay in his lumpy little bed and again sent up a silent prayer to the man up above, that all he had planned and hoped for the visit would actually transpire. Grandville thought back to the conversation which he had with Emerson two weeks prior.

Emerson was escorting him to teach his class when Grandville approached him.

"Officer Emerson, how is your son?" Grandville asked.

"He is good. His birthday is coming up in three weeks and he'll be turning fifteen," Officer Emerson replied.

"What are you going to get him for his birthday?" Grandville asked him.

"I don't know, I haven't thought that far ahead," Officer Emerson responded.

"I got the perfect idea for a gift," Grandville offered.

"Really, what do you suggest?" Officer Emerson asked him in curiosity.

"How about an autographed basketball from Rayshawn Robinson? Didn't you tell me that your son was his number one fan?" Grandville reminded him.

"Okay Stubbs I'll play along with you on this one. What'll I need to do in order to get an autographed ball from Rayshawn Robinson for my son?" Officer Emerson inquired.

"Not a whole lot. Listen, you know my wife is coming for the Extended Family Visit. I want to have a pre-Thanksgiving Dinner with her, and I was hoping you could assist me with getting the food for it. I'll give you the money to purchase a small turkey and all the fixings. I will even give you some of the food I prepare. If you do me this solid, I will ensure that you receive an autographed ball signed by Rayshawn Robinson for your boy for his birthday," Grandville promised hoping he would go along with his request.

"What's the catch?" Officer Emerson asked.

"I want you to get a bottle of wine for my wife and sparkling cider for me. I shouldn't be drinking on the medication I'm on, but I want to have a toast with my wife, and I want her to have real wine when we do it," Grandville replied.

"I don't know Stubbs. Oakhill had pretty strict rules about alcohol, and I could lose my job if anyone found out," stated Officer Emerson.

"You have been around me for three years and despite my being in here I think you can see my character. If anyone found out about this I would be in trouble too. I'm trying to get out of here and any infraction could derail my efforts. I'm willing to take the risk, because I want a romantic evening with my wife where we can make believe for just a moment that I wasn't in here. If you help me make this happen you'll be well compensated. What I'm going to have delivered to you is a gift that you couldn't buy, and a fifteen year old son who'll look at you like you're his hero for getting him something his friends would die for." Since Grandville had Office Emerson engaged in his plan he pushed a hard sales pitch.

"Okay Stubbs I'll do this for you, but I'm telling you right now if you burn me you'll pay. Even if Oakhill fires me I have plenty of friends who work at Oakhill who'll make sure your life is a living hell. What they'll do to you will make what the other prisoners can do to you child's play," Officer Emerson said with a matter-of-fact look on his face.

"Officer Emerson, I'm a man of my word, now let's talk about what I want you to purchase for dinner."

A few days later Franklin made a surprise visit to Oakhill to bring him the pocket dictionaries. He had decided to use their non-profit to purchase the dictionaries to ensure he got them to Grandville in a timely fashion, because he knew if he went through their Fraternity it could take months. Franklin had to attend a Continuing Legal Education seminar on Tax Preparation and the seminar was being held in Columbus, and he realized by driving another hour he could kill two birds with one stone. Franklin contacted the Oakhill administration before leaving Cleveland to go to Columbus and had received permission to bring the dictionaries directly to Grandville. Franklin only stayed at Oakhill a few minutes, but before he left Grandville had arranged for him to open a small account at a local store close to where Oakhill and the Homewood suites was located so that Emerson could purchase the food. Franklin had already set-up an appointment to meet with Rayshawn the following week, so Grandville also arranged for Franklin to have Rayshawn autograph a ball for Emerson's boy and an autographed jersey as a surprise to Emerson for putting his neck on the line for Grandville.

Now, Grandville lay in his lumpy little bed knowing that for at least three days and two nights, he would leave his bed and the institution that had imprisoned his body for almost the last three years. He was excited and nervous all at the same time. He had not seen the moon or the stars since he had been at Oakhill except through wires and bars, and he couldn't wait to view them unrestricted with Juliette, even if it was through a window.

He was anxious about the first of two special dinners, the first of which he had planned for that very evening. If all went according to plan, Emerson had already purchased the food, and he could began the meal almost immediately after arriving at the Homewood Suites. While he cooked he would talk to Juliette and tell her his story from beginning to end. He would hold nothing back and at the end of the visit Juliette would decide if she was in or out in respect to their marriage and no matter what she decided Grandville would accept her decision.

He and Montell had talked extensively the day before as they kept their minds occupied by playing hours of chess. Both realized their time together was coming to an end, and they wanted to enjoy each other's company as much as possible before Montell was released. While they played chess they talked about their futures.

"You know Grandville I really want to thank you for hooking me up with a job. I talked to my wife and she actually seems excited about me coming home, and she was ecstatic when I told her I had a job. I got a good feeling it's going to work out between us. I've decided, I'm going to give her a pass on anything she did while I was locked up in here," Montell said quietly knowing somethings had already happened on the outside.

"What, you think she was with someone else while you were in here?" Grandville asked.

"Man, I know she was with someone else. While I was in here and to be honest I'm not mad at her. I've been here for almost five years, and it would be unfair for me to believe that a woman as beautiful as my Maria wouldn't have many suitors. It would also be selfish for me to want her to be miserable because I am. I hope whoever occupied her time treated her well and showed her a good time. I just hope she was smart about whatever she was doing and didn't get herself tangled up in something she can't get out of. I know in my heart Maria loves me, but I hope whoever she was doing didn't take the only thing I hope to always have and that is her heart," Montell replied.

Now Grandville lay in his lumpy little bed contemplating Montell's words. He had never thought about Juliette being with someone else while he was at Oakhill and that was naive on his part. Juliette was a beautiful woman and Grandville had always felt grateful she had chosen him out of the many who actively pursued her. Any man who had half a brain in their body would feel the same way. He had to emotionally prepare himself for the fact that Juliette had been seeing someone else while he had been incarcerated at Oakhill. He had decided, if she had been with someone else then like Montell; He didn't want details, he simply wanted to know if they could be together even if it meant starting all over.

It wasn't long before Emerson came and retrieved him from his cell to transport him to the Homewood Suites where Juliette would be coming to meet them.

"Okay Stubbs, today is your lucky day. You're going to spend time with your Lady Love and all the preparations have been made," Officer Emerson said.

"Thanks Officer Emerson. There will be a package arriving to you soon from a very special person," Grandville told him.

"Great, now let's get this party started," Officer Emerson laughed.

After signing all the necessary paperwork, Emerson, Grandville and two guards who Grandville had never seen before set out in one of the unmarked prison vans in route to the hotel. The suite where the visit would take place was only utilized by Oakhill specifically for the extended visit program. As such, it could not be rented by the general public. The windows had locks on them and the room had security features which were designed to ensure that if a prisoner tried to escape or become violent he or she would be quickly contained and detained.

Once they were in the suite, Emerson introduced the other two guards as Officer Billups and Officer Tatum, and then the Officers checked the rooms in the suite for contraband. It was explained that two guards would stay in the bedroom directly across from the bedroom he and Juliette would share. Also, there would always be one guard stationed right outside of the door which led into the rooms. The guard's bedroom door would remain open at all times, but Juliette and Grandville would be allowed some privacy and could close the door to their bedroom.

As soon as Grandville arrived he turned on the television and started prepping the food that he was preparing to cook for the first meal he would share with his wife in more than three years. He had just put some water on the stove so that he could have some tea and was seasoning the baked potatoes which he was making for dinner when there was a knock at the door indicating Juliette had arrived. Grandville took a deep breath and waited for Emerson to open the door.

Juliette entered the hotel room looking just as beautiful and radiant as she did on the first day he met her. Just seeing her after three years made his heart skip a beat. He walked over to her, taking her in with his eyes.

"Juliette, may I hug you?" Grandville asked.

"Yes, you may," Juliette replied.

Grandville pulled Juliette into his body for a hug and his body immediately responded to her touch, and he stepped back so that she wouldn't feel just how happy he was to see her.

"Juliette it's great to see you. Thanks so much for agreeing to come here to meet me for the visit. I'm just making some tea. Would you like a cup?" Grandville asked her in a soft polite voice.

"Yes, that would be fine, but if it's okay I would like to freshen up. It was a long trip," she said.

"Sure, that's fine. The bathroom is located inside the bedroom, right over there."

Juliette made her way into the attached bedroom carrying her overnight bag with her and Grandville went to the stove where he had water on the stove that he was boiling for the tea. He took the pot off the stove, and put the tea bags into the water, and then he covered the pot so it could steep the tea. He then took a deep breath and sat down at the table and waited for Juliette to return.

It didn't take long for Juliette to come into the kitchen area of the small suite. Grandville stood up and pulled the chair out so she could sit across from him. He then got up and got two tea cups out of the cupboard. After cleaning the cups he poured the tea and took her cup over to the table.

"Do you want sugar and lemon?"

"Yes, please," Juliette responded.

Grandville retrieved some sugar packets from the counter and some lemon wedges out of the refrigerator. He placed all the items on the table and then went and got his tea. The air around them was strained and Grandville struggled with his words.

"How was the trip?" Grandville asked.

"Long but the traffic was okay, and I was able to make good time."

"So how have you been doing Juliette?"

"I've been doing as well as I can considering all that has happened."

"Juliette, the first thing I want to say to you is that I'm sorry about everything. I know that I screwed up, and I will do anything to make it right."

"Grandville, make me understand what happened that day?" Juliette inquired.

"I will if you would just indulge me. I need to tell you so much, but I don't want to get ahead of myself," Grandville responded.

"Okay, that's fine but before I leave Dayton to return to Cleveland I need to know what happened on that day," Juliette replied.

"Okay but before we get into it, please tell me how are the boys?" Grandville inquired.

"They're fine."

Juliette reached into her purse and pulled out a letter from Jabari and a picture that Jonah had drawn for his dad.

"I told the boys I was coming to see you today, and they asked me to give these to you."

As Grandville unfolded the letter and the picture of what he could only assume was their house. He blinked his eyes so that he would not break down in tears.

"Tell Jonah I will hang his picture, and I will write Jabari a letter if you will allow it?" Grandville said.

"Yes, I will allow it," Juliette replied.

"Thanks Juliette. I want you to know that I've thought of you and my children daily since I've been at Oakhill. You guys are the reason I've made it this far. When the accident happened I was out of my mind, but I want you to know that I loved Jessica, and that I would have never intentionally hurt her. There are several things I need to tell you which I should have disclosed before we got married," Grandville stated.

"Like what? I hope you are not about to tell me something off the wall like you're bi-sexual or that you were on drugs," Juliette sarcastically replied.

"What? It's nothing like that," Grandville said.

"Hey I'm sorry but I'm a little on edge. I am confused, because I don't understand how we could go from being on top of the world to the very bottom in one day," Juliette stated.

"I've had nothing but time to think since I've been at Oakhill and hopefully before you leave here I will be able to make you understand what was going on in my head. Greta came to see me a few months back and she told me Melinia is missing. Have you guys made any progress in locating her?"

"No, we were able to raise twenty-five hundred dollars as a reward for any information leading to her whereabouts and a few weeks ago an anonymous donor gave another twenty-five hundred dollars to add to the reward. Hopefully, someone has some information that they will consider telling to the authorities in order to receive the reward money," Juliette said shrugging her shoulders.

"I sure hope so. I know Melinia having gone missing has been stressful on you and your family. Has Samantha been able to use her office to get additional clues as to where Samantha could be?"

"Samantha and I had a really bad falling out and we are not friends anymore."

"What? You and Samantha have been the best of friends since well before I met you. What happened?"

"It isn't important."

"Well when did you guys stop speaking?"

"A few months ago. Right after the Anniversary of Jessica's death."

"I'm really sorry to hear that. I know how much you loved Samantha."

"I still do love Samantha and wish her nothing but the best. Now let's change the subject. I am starving, do you have something that I can munch on?" Juliette asked.

"Yes, I got you some veggies and dip." Grandville went to the refrigerator and pulled out a small tray with cut vegetables and dip in the middle.

"Juliette please help yourself. We also have bottled water, ginger ale, cranberry juice and orange juice. Would you like something else to drink," Grandville offered.

"Yes, could I please have some water?"

Grandville went back into the refrigerator and got out a bottled water and took it back to the small table.

"Juliette I'm going to prepare us a great meal, and I honestly think my food might rival Chef Rico," Grandville boasted.

"Really? I'm looking forward to it." Juliette replied.

Grandville knew he couldn't put off explaining his story for too much longer, so he decided to dive right in at the beginning.

"While you eat your vegetables and dip I want to share something with you," Grandville quietly stated.

"What?" Juliette asked.

"I want to tell you about my first bad memory. I recently did an exercise which was a part of my therapy that required me to remember my first bad memory. I believe it contributed to everything that has happened," Grandville replied.

"I thought you didn't remember your childhood?" Juliette inquired.

"I lied when I said that. What I should have said was there were events that happened to me that were too traumatic to recount so I buried them."

"What happened?" Juliette asked.

"When I was five my Aunt Genevive shot herself in the head in front of my mother, my cousin Gina and me. She didn't even know that I was there, because I was hiding at the top of the stairs when everything happened. I was so traumatized after I saw my Aunt take her own life that I fainted. When my mother found me, she made me promise not to tell anyone what I witnessed. So, I never told a soul. My Aunt Genevive had already killed my Uncle Greg before coming over to our house and taking her own life in front of us."

"Grandville, oh my God. That's horrible and I'm so sorry you went through that. Did you ever get counseling or therapy to help you deal with what you saw?" Juliette gently questioned.

"No, and I never spoke of what I saw to anyone. On the night my Mom passed away we talked about what my Aunt did to Uncle Greg and herself for the first time since it happened. Greta didn't even know that I was there when Aunt Genevive killed herself until she visited me at Oakhill," Grandville shared with her.

"Did you ever find out what upset your Aunt so badly that she committed murder and then suicide?" Juliette asked him.

"Yes, but I didn't find out until the evening my Mom died. I don't want to get ahead of myself. There is a beginning, middle and ending to my story and I'm still at the beginning. Juliette I know a lot has happened, but I'm asking you to be patient with me. The story that I need to tell you is painful and difficult, and I've never told the complete story to anyone. I love you, and I hope you still have enough love and respect for me to allow me to share my story at my pace. I want to stop for a moment and start getting dinner prepared. I'm going to make lobster tails, steak, salad and potatoes. I have had a lot of extra time on my hands, and I've been watching some of the cooking shows on the food network. The food at Oakhill is terrible and I want more than anything to eat a home cooked meal with you," Grandville stated.

"Okay Grandville. Do you want me to help?" Juliette asked him.

"No, I just want you to keep me company. I'm going to make some food for the guards also. Officer Emerson has been fair to me and I want him to know that I really appreciate it," Grandville replied.

"Okay, Chef Grandville let's see what you have," Juliette teased and smiled at him.

Grandville pulled the steaks out of the refrigerator where he had been marinating them.

Grandville did his best impression of Julia Childs. "First you start with top pieces of meat. Fillet Mignon is always a great choice. Then, you marinade the meat in special seasoning in a glass dish or plastic zip lock bag in the refrigerator for at least 45 minutes."

Juliette laughed at Grandville's attempt at a imitating a female British accent. While Grandville heated the oven they made small talk.

"So, Juliette I understand that A Better Tomorrow is doing well?"

"Yes, we are at full capacity with the exception of Melinia's room, and I am going to hold her room until she's found" Juliette responded.

"Do you have any idea of what could have happened to Melinia?" Grandville asked.

"No. She just disappeared. I don't know if she left on her own and is somewhere hiding or if someone kidnapped her and is holding her against her will or if she's dead," replied Juliette.

"This whole situation is tough. Do you think maybe Melinia relapsed and left with some guy with a lot of product and is afraid to come home?" Grandville asked.

"That's exactly what Samantha said right before we fell out, but honestly I don't think Melinia would ever do something like that. She has always contacted one of us to let us know she was okay when she is on a binge, and she's never been missing for more than three days. This time Melinia has been gone for more than three months and I'm scared. I'm afraid someone is holding Melinia, or she may have even been sold into the Human Sex Trade. Ohio is one of the primary states this is happening in due to the accessibility to numerous highways that can take you in several different directions headed out of the State."

"Well don't give up hope and right about now, no news is good news. Hopefully Melinia will be found safe and sound," Grandville said.

"I sure hope so, but I'm really afraid Melinia is dead. I keep trying to think positive, but I know Melinia would never do something like just leave and not call. Melinia is my Aunt Mabel's only daughter and Melinia is very close to her. She wouldn't have her worried like this. If Melinia hasn't called it's because she can't and I firmly believe that," Juliette stated very passionately.

While Grandville listened to Juliette talk he arranged the steaks that were ready to be broiled. He had heated the oven to the required temperature and was now ready to cook the Filet Mignon steaks. He had five of the best cut of steaks money could buy. The trick was in the marinade and Grandville hoped the Steaks would be tender enough to be cut with a butter knife, as steak knives were considered contraband and not allowed in the suite. Grandville and Juliette both got quiet and Grandville recalled his purpose.

"Juliette, I remember one time where we played truth or double dare. I asked you to tell me about your first sexual experience. I remember you told me, you lost your virginity on your prom night when you were a senior in high school to your boyfriend who was also your date. When you asked me about who I lost my virginity too I told you about my tenth grade girlfriend Nadine. Nadine really was my girlfriend, but I didn't have my first sexual experience with her."

"Well, who did you lose your virginity to?" Juliette asked.

"My cousin Gina. When I was ten and she was seventeen."

Chapter 20

Touch Me Tease Me

Juliette couldn't believe her ears. Grandville had just revealed to her that he had been a victim of incest and sexual abuse. She had no idea that when she came to Oakhill she would receive this kind of news. She tried her best to not appear overly shocked even though she was. Grandville never let on that he had any problems with his childhood. Although, she did think it was strange when he claimed he didn't remember a lot of it. She had never met his cousin Gina. All she knew about her was that she and her parents had died before Juliette met Grandville, and Gina was raised with Grandville and Greta.

Now, she was learning the reason Gina had grown up without her parents was because her mother had killed her father and then herself. Grandville, Greta, and Mother Stubbs always said that Jessica bore an uncanny resemblance to Gina. However, in Juliette's eyes Jessica looked like both she and Grandville. She had Juliette's deep dark mahogany complexion and long hair, Juliette had no idea where Jessica got her deep dimples, but she had Grandville's eye shape and his nose.

Juliette didn't really have a way to process the information Grandville had just delivered. She did have questions, but she didn't want to overwhelm him. Despite the fact they had been a part for more than three years Grandville could still read her face.

"Juliette, I can look at your face and see that you have questions. Go ahead and ask me what you want to know." Grandville prodded her, because he wanted to be as open and honest as possible.

"Did Mother Stubbs know about what happened to you?" Juliette questioned.

"No, not at first. You see what I failed to mention was that Gina forced me into sex acts from the time I was ten until I was sixteen. I know there are plenty of people who believe boys can't be sexually abused by women, and the older woman is doing the boy a favor by teaching him about sex but I didn't want to do it.

When I said no, Gina threatened me. When it first started she would hold me down and force my penis into her mouth. She told me if I told anyone the authorities would make her leave and my mom would lose us because she wouldn't have a babysitter. My mom was very dependent on her job and worked the night shift so she could be with us during the day. She was always under the impression we were asleep at night. What she didn't realize was Gina would wake me up many nights. My brain and mouth said no, but my body said yes. I couldn't stop myself from responding to her touch, and I was always in constant turmoil and conflict. I knew what Gina was doing to me was wrong, but I was afraid if I told my mother, she would be angry with me or Gina's threats would come true. I was afraid Greta and I would be removed from my mother and put into foster care, maybe even separated from each other. Then, Gina started making me have intercourse with her. She would threaten me and told me if I told anyone she would say that I raped her." Grandville confessed, and as he talked he could feel the turmoil which he had gone through with Gina all over again. However, since he was finally telling Juliette about his past, he begun to release some of the pressure and pain of hiding his life story from her all of these years.

The timer Grandville had on the stove began to buzz indicating the steaks were ready to be removed. Grandville had precooked the potatoes in the microwave and only needed to put them in the oven for a few minutes along with the lobster tails which he planned to broil. Grandville also had salad which came from a bag that he planned to serve with dinner. He put the salad in a bowl and took a container with cut up strawberries and chopped nuts and put them in the bowl with the salad mix. He then took out a strawberry vinaigrette salad dressing and tossed the salad with it. The small suite started to smell delicious from the food cooking. Juliette's stomach did somersaults. She was starving, but she didn't know how much she would be able to eat.

Juliette could not believe Grandville had endured so much and that she had been clueless to his plight. She now understood why he was so adamant about her having her own business. He really wanted her to be home with their kids. She also realized he only talked about getting her a Nanny to indulge her. In hindsight she remembered he also didn't seem to want anyone but his or her mother babysitting their children. Juliette had always assumed this was due to the fact that as a father he was overprotective, but she was now learning his paranoia stemmed from much more.

Juliette watched in disbelief as Grandville calmly moved around the small kitchen preparing the food like what he had just told her was no big deal.

"The food is almost ready, and I was hoping you would help me set the table," Grandville asked her.

"Sure that's cool," Juliette replied.

"I put the plates on the counter. The guards are going to eat in their bedroom, and you and I will eat at the table."

"Okay."

Before she knew it their plates with steaming hot food was on the table. Grandville had arranged for two battery operated candles to be placed in the center of the small table. He gave the guards their plates and silverware. Then, he dimmed the lights before he sat down.

"Juliette, before we eat I would like to bless the food," Grandville asked.

"Okay," Juliette replied.

"Dear Lord thank you for giving me an opportunity to share a meal with Juliette. Thank you for this food that will provide nourishment to our bodies and please bless the hands of the cook who prepared this meal and those who will consume it. Amen."

Grandville said, lifted his head up from prayer and noticed Juliette was looking at him with amazement in her eyes. He could feel and tell she was still in love with him. Now, he had to finish telling her the rest of his life's story.

"Thanks for the blessing and the food. It smells delicious." Juliette said realizing why she loved Grandville so much.

"I sure hope you like it," Grandville chuckled.

Juliette used her butter knife and cut into the steak and put it in her mouth. The meat was tender, juicy and filled with flavor and almost melted on her tongue.

"Oh my god Grandville this steak is fantastic. I can't believe how tender it is."

Juliette then took a piece of her lobster tail and put it in the draw butter Grandville had placed next to her plate and then put it in her mouth.

"Grandville it seems as though you were right, your cooking is giving Chef Rico a run for his money," Juliette praised her husband.

"Thank you Juliette. Maybe when I leave Oakhill I can work in a restaurant using my new found culinary skills, because it'll be years before I can practice law again, if ever. I want you to know my Counselor feels I'm going to be released soon. I love you, but I understand a lot has happened. I want you to know that I respect you and your space. When I'm released from Oakhill I'm going to move into an apartment in one of the corporation's residential buildings that's not too far from the rooming house. It's a new property Franklin just acquired on behalf of our business. I want more than anything for us to be together, but when I get out of Oakhill, I know you'll need time. It will also take time for me to prove to you that I'm not a danger to you or our sons. All I ask is that you allow me to see my boys when I get home." Grandville was so humble in his request, because he didn't want anything to stop him from sharing time with his children.

Juliette was taken off guard because she didn't expect Grandville to steer the conversation towards his release and seeing their sons. She didn't know how to feel, disappointed or relieved, about Grandville's decision not to move back into their home. She also felt conflicted about him seeing their sons though she knew it had to be done.

"Grandville, I'm glad you brought up Jabari and Jonah. I want you to know the boys don't know you are at Oakhill. They do know Jessica has passed on, and there was an accident but they do not know the specifics," Juliette shared.

"Where do the boys think I am?" Grandville asked.

"They think you're out of the Country for your job. The boys are getting older and asking a lot of questions. I don't know what to tell them when I don't understand myself."

"If you prefer we can wait until I'm released, and I will tell them what happened. I can also write a letter to them explaining about the accident. Juliette, I need for you to know I didn't even realize you and the kids had come home from the Mall on the day of the accident."

"Well why did you tell the police they made you do it?" She asked.

"Because I was delusional, and I was hearing voices in my head."

"Grandville I still don't understand."

"Juliette, I've been diagnosed with Bipolar Disorder, and I know you do understand my diagnosis. You're a Licensed Independent Social Worker. I know you learned about my disease in your Master's program and you've worked with lots of people who suffer from the disease. I know some of the kids you have worked with and some of the women who live at a Better Tomorrow suffer with the same disorder. The doctors said, I developed psychotic features from the trauma of my Mother's death, and from what happened to Jessica and without medication I can become delusional.

I didn't know I was suffering with Bipolar Disorder and the professionals say it appears that I experienced a late onset of the disease. Now, in hindsight I realized that I have been suffering with symptoms of Bipolar Disorder for years. Mr. Bolden who is my Counselor has explained to me that it is not normal to sleep for only three hours a night. Getting the appropriate amount of rest and sleep is key to my recovery."

"I didn't realize you were getting such little sleep."

"That's because I hid it from you and you sleep like a log," Grandville teased.

Juliette and Grandville ate in silence for a while and Juliette silently marveled over how good the food was which Grandville had prepared. She surprised herself and ate everything on her plate. Juliette did understand Bipolar Disorder. She had been told by both Greta and Franklin that Grandville suffered with the disease, but she couldn't believe that she had married a guy who had it. She had been in denial about this fact for a long time. In her opinion Grandville had never exhibited signs of a mental illness until after his mother died. In some ways she was disappointed in herself for not recognizing that he had the symptoms. She had to admit, Grandville was always kind of hyper, but he was so quiet most people didn't even notice.

However, she never saw signs of him being depressed until his mother passed, and his moods did not appear to cycle which is one of the major symptoms of the illness.

"Grandville the food was delicious thank you." Juliette said.

"You're welcome. Juliette, I want you to know, I regret not cooking for you more when I was home and able. I promise once I'm released from Oakhill and come home, I'll make you dinner, breakfast and lunch if you will allow me. All I did was work, and I now realize in some ways I neglected you and the kids. I want you to know that I'm sorry." Grandville said apologetically.

"Grandville, I've never felt the children or I were neglected. You were always a great provider and protector. I miss you, but I'm not going to lie. I don't know if I can feel safe with you again, and I don't know if I can trust you with the boys," Juliette stated.

"That's understandable and all I'm asking is for you to give me an opportunity to show you, that you can trust me with you and our sons," Grandville was trying to make sure he did not push her too hard for an answer right now, because this wasn't the time or the place to get Juliette upset with him.

"All I can say right now is, I'm willing to keep an open mind," Juliette said.

"That's all I can ask. Thank you. So how is Greta?" Grandville asked quickly changing the conversation to a lighter topic.

"She's doing well. She's been spending a lot of time with me and the kids."

"That's great. Did she mention to you Rayshawn came to see me on the Anniversary of Jessica's death? His Charity is planning to build a new mental health hospital which will be named after Jessica?"

"No. Greta has not talked to me about her visit with you and has actually been very closed mouth about it. I really didn't want to talk about it and Greta didn't bring it up. At the time Greta visited with you I was undecided as to if I would see you again. But, I have since decided the children and I need closure and that is why I came to this visit.

Greta did tell me on the night of the last anniversary of Jessica's death it was her idea to have a new mental health hospital built and to have it named after Jessica. She said, she left Rayshawn before she could have the Charity pitch the idea to Oakhill, and she was going to raise the money to have it built herself. I don't know if Greta told you, but she gave a four year scholarship in Jessica's name to a student from your high school. The winning student had to write an essay, and I got to judge all the entries and to pick the winner," Juliette replied.

"No, she didn't mention it. What did the winner have to write about in order to win the scholarship?"

"The winner's name is Jamila Stevens, and her essay is about living with a parent who has Bipolar Disorder. I brought you a copy of her essay so you can read it later," Juliette said.

"Juliette I'm going to be honest. I'm not happy with the new clinic being named after Jessica. It's hard enough for me to live with the fact that my actions killed my daughter. I'm not anxious to walk into a clinic that's named after our daughter who died due to my hands," Grandville said almost in tears.

"Grandville it's an honor for the new clinic to be named after our daughter. Jessica is now at home with the Lord, but with her name on the clinic she'll never be forgotten. I would like to see someone else benefit from our pain. I believe this is one of the ways that will help us overcome what happened. It helps to bring me peace knowing Jessica's death will bring healing to someone even if it's only in a secondary kind of way.

Think about it, because of what happened to Jessica a deserving student will get to go to college. Also, when the clinic is opened a lot of people will receive the help they need and it will be attached to her name. I appreciate the fact that Rayshawn and his Charity are willing to spend their money this away." Juliette wanted Grandville to realize what a great honor this would be for Jessica's name sake. She was very passionate and positive about the clinic being built and how it could help people just like Grandville.

"I appreciate what Rayshawn is trying to do also, but I know he's doing it to get Greta's attention. He's hurt that she divorced him and he wants her back." Grandville stated.

"I'm pretty sure Greta would never entertain the idea of getting back with Rayshawn. She's pretty bitter about all of Rayshawn's infidelities. Also, she has a new beau named Derek and she seems to be into him."

"Greta never mentioned she had a new boyfriend."

"She's only been dating him for a few months and actually reconnected with him around the time she came up to Oakhill to visit you."

"What do you mean when you say reconnect?"

"She knew him when they both lived in LA, but their relationship was strictly platonic due to the fact she was married," Juliette explained.

"What's his name?" Grandville asked.

"Derek Dolan. He used to work for the LA's Front Office, but he now works for the Cleveland Avaliers' Front Office. Neither he nor Greta knew the other was from Cleveland. Samantha took Greta and me out to dinner on the last Anniversary of Jessica's death, and we ran into him at Shooters," Juliette explained.

"Well, do you like him?" Grandville was curious to know what Juliette thought about the guy.

"He seems like a nice enough fellow."

Both Juliette and Grandville chuckled as Juliette's impression of Margie from the movie *Fargo*.

"No but for real, he seems like a nice guy, and he's treating Greta well. She's just leery of relationships after all that has happened with Rayshawn. So, she and Derek have decided to take it slow."

"Good, I hate to see Greta hurt again."

"I don't want to see her hurt either."

Their conversation was interrupted when Emerson came out of the Guards room with all the guards used dishes and utensils.

"Stubbs the food was awesome. Thanks so much for sharing it with me and the other Guards," Officer Emerson said.

"No problem. I'm glad you guys enjoyed it. I personally thought it was a lot better than the food at Oakhill. Actually, it's the first decent meal I've had since coming to Oakhill," Grandville said.

"Listen Stubbs, Tatum and I are going to do the dishes. You and your Lady Love should go into your room and watch a movie or something," Emerson offered.

"Officer Emerson, I really appreciate the offer but you and Officer Tatum don't need to worry about it I will do it," Grandville replied.

"No we insist. The food was fantastic and we also appreciate receiving a home cooked meal. Usually when we have to work this detail we eat fast food for breakfast, lunch and dinner," Officer Emerson said.

"Tell Officer Tatum I appreciate you all doing the dishes for me." Grandville was so grateful for having security officers who were nice people too.

Grandville stood up and pulled Juliette's chair back and took her hand and led her into the bedroom. Juliette was a nervous wreck. She looked at the queen bed and thought about sitting on it. She didn't want to give Grandville the idea that she was ready to be intimate with him, because she was still unsure if she should commit to Grandville. She walked over to the chair which was in the corner of the room and sat down.

Grandville also appeared nervous and sat on the floor next to her.

"Do you want to watch a movie like Officer Emerson suggested?" Grandville asked.

"No, not right now, maybe later," Juliette replied.

"Okay, let's continue our conversation from earlier," Grandville suggested.

"Ok. You left off at the part where Gina was forcing you to have sex with her. I asked you if your mother knew and you said not at first. That meant she must have found out?" Juliette questioned.

"Yes, she caught me and Gina having sex one night when she was supposed to be at work,"

"Well what happened?" Juliette asked.

"My mother was very upset about the whole thing, but when she found out what had been happening to me she swore me to secrecy. She told me not to tell Greta or anyone else what Gina had been doing to me. She then made Gina move out of our house and in with one of her friends from church. As a result, I rarely saw Gina again after we were caught. I finished high school and then went off to college. When I left home, I buried the memories of what happened to me. I resented the fact that Gina had control over me and my body, and I hated myself for having sexual feelings for her. I pushed down my resentment and worked like a slave to keep my mind occupied and to forget about my memories. Then, Gina passed away shortly after I came back to Cleveland and there was no reason for me to think about her.

In hindsight I think the failed relationships I have experienced in the past were in part due to my abuse issues. When I was in college I had an episode where I was hospitalized. The doctors said I was suffering from exhaustion. I rested and I was okay, but it didn't take long before I fell back into my old routine, staying up most of the night and burning the candle from both ends. I had managed to make it through, but I wasn't living, just existing. Then, I met you and fell in love for the very first time in my life, and you didn't try to control me and you always gave me my space. I refused to screw up the best thing that ever happened to me, so I made the conscious choice to not tell you this information before we were married. I was selfish and I was wrong. All I can say is, I'm sorry and ask for your forgiveness and understanding," Grandville confessed.

Tears threatened to fall from Juliette's eyes. She had no idea that Grandville was dealing with the internal pain came from years of past sexual abuse and from the trauma of watching his aunt take her life. She felt like a terrible wife for not sensing how hurt and damaged her husband was. Grandville looked up at Juliette and saw her unshed tears and stood up. He grabbed her hand and pulled her into a standing position and used his thumb to individually wipe both of her eyes.

"Juliette, please don't cry. I don't want you to feel sorry for me. I'm telling you this because I want you to understand what led up to my mind snapping and the accident. I don't want you shedding tears for my past. I'm coming to terms with what happened, and I'm ready to focus on my future. I want you to be a part of my future Juliette, but I understand if you decide you don't want to be. I only ask that you allow me to see my boys, allow me to spend time with them. I also ask you give me one more night where you allow me to make love to you just one more time. I brought protection, but I want to assure you that I have not touched anyone but you or allowed anyone but you to touch me since the day we met," Grandville stated.

Juliette was momentarily taken off guard and did not know how to respond. Before she could say anything Grandville pulled her face into his and kissed her slowly, but with such passion and intensity she felt her knees go weak. When he finally broke their kiss she was left panting, her body wanting him to touch her all over.

She couldn't help herself when she said, "Grandville please touch me." Her reasoning had been abandoned and all she wanted to do was make love to him.

"Juliette I want you also, but when we make love again it will be because you want me for more than for one night or a weekend. I want you to want me for a lifetime, but I don't want to rush. I want you to be absolutely sure when we do make love. Let's take Officer Emerson's suggestion and watch a movie. I haven't had an opportunity to see anything good at while at Oakhill, so let's flip through the channels and see what is on," Grandville suggested to her.

Grandville gently pushed Juliette onto the bed and used the remote control to turn on the television. He gave her the remote, stood up and removed her shoes, and then sat on the bed next to her placing her feet into his lap and began massaging her feet. Juliette immediately began to relax as she channel surfed.

"Have you seen Flight with Denzel Washington?" Juliette asked.

"No," Grandville replied.

"Good I haven't either. Look it's just coming on." Juliette said.

Juliette propped herself up onto the pillows which were spawn around the queen bed and settled into watching the movie.

Chapter 21
Love's In Need of Love Today

Grandville gazed at Juliette while she watched the movie and tried to calm the fire that quietly burned within him. He could not believe how he had controlled himself when he wanted nothing more than to throw Juliette on the bed and make slow, long, passionate love to her. He rubbed her feet and wondered to himself if he would be able to control himself throughout the night. He wanted her badly, and he had to shift his body so she wouldn't realize just how much.

However, he meant what he said. If she decided she didn't want to be with him again, he would force himself to live with her decision, but before she left him he planned to give her a night she would never, ever forget. His plan was to make her a pre-thanksgiving dinner with all the trimmings. He had a small turkey and a small ham. He had collard greens that came in a bag, stuffing from a box, and cranberry sauce from a can. It would be a decent meal, but nothing like the Thanksgiving dinners he and Juliette shared before he came to Oakhill. He would do his best to create an atmosphere of cheer before delivering the most dreadful part of his story.

"Grandville are you even watching the movie?" Juliette asked.

"No, because I am too busy watching you. I think you are beautiful and I missed you so much. I want to sear your image into my brain. I'm sorry if I'm making you nervous by staring at you."

"It's okay, you're not making me nervous. I missed you too Grandville, but I want you to know I'm scared." Juliette confided in him about her true feelings.

"What are you scared of?" Grandville already knew the answer, but he wanted to hear her say it.

"I'm scared because I love you so much, and I would have trusted you with my life or any one of our children's lives before Jessica's accident. Now, I'm afraid to put my trust in you again," Juliette honestly replied.

"Juliette I'm asking you to give me the opportunity to show you, that you can trust me again. Let me prove to you that I won't hurt you or our children," Grandville pleaded with her.

"I want to and I'm trying to keep an open mind, but how do I know you won't become ill again?" Juliette asked.

"You don't know and to be honest neither do I. I can't promise that I'll never get sick again. I've come to learn that what I have will never go away, but I now realize what to do when I'm having symptoms. I'm also on medications and it helps to control my illness. I'm putting everything out in the open. This is so that I can reduce the stress of keeping the kind of secrets which I have been harboring from you," Grandville replied.

"Grandville, I know there is more to the story so go on and tell me," Juliette advised.

"Did Greta tell you that she found Gina's diary?" Grandville asked.

"No. I had no idea. When did she find it?"

"She found it a couple of days before the anniversary of Jessica's death. She realized my Mother didn't even know it existed. My Mother had never read it, and when Greta read it she learned what Gina did to me. According to her, Gina put it all in her diary. Greta encouraged me to ask you to come to Oakhill, so that I could tell you the truth about everything."

Juliette looked like a light bulb had come on in her head. "Greta came over a day before the anniversary of Jessica's death and told me there was more to your story. She encouraged me to reach out to you. What was in the diary?" Juliette questioned him.

"I haven't ever seen it. But according to Greta all kinds of things from Gina's perspective. I didn't even know Gina kept a diary until Greta told me about it. She found it when she was cleaning the attic trying to get everything out of the Mom's house so she can put it on the market. My mother wanted the kids to have the money from the sale of her house. She told me right before she died. So, when Greta sells the house please accept the money she's going to give you. Do whatever has to be done for the boys and for the house."

"Okay and I want you to know, I appreciate how you have been holding us down financially while you have been here at Oakhill. What I don't understand is how you have been able to give me so much money when you haven't been working?"

"Juliette I have another secret I've been keeping from you."

"Damn Grandville am I on a frigging reality show? How many more secrets do you have?" Juliette angrily questioned him.

"Let's just say, my life is more complicated than it would appear at first blush," Grandville replied.

"Okay Grandville out with it. Go ahead and tell me something crazy like you're the head of some drug cartel or you robbed a bank," Juliette said with a sarcastic tone and look on her face.

"Why would I have to be engaged in an illegal activity to make money? Damn girl, I thought you were better than that?"

"Grandville I'm sorry. I wasn't trying to imply that you have to be criminal to make money, but if you were me what would you think? I'm only saying that I feel like I'm in an episode from *Tales of the Crypt*. Hell everything that has happened since Jessica death has been crazy."

"I know it feels that way, but I actually invested very, very well and as a result I made a lot of money in the market. I made my windfall when we first start dating. I should have told you the truth about my net worth before we were married. At that time I still had serious trust issues that I'm now understanding are related to my abuse. Despite my problems, I want you to know I trust you more than any other person with the exception of Greta."

"Grandville, I'm glad you told me the truth about how you have been able to afford to send me money because I didn't know what to believe. I would have married you despite how much you were worth because I love you, and it's not because of your earning potential. All I ever wanted was to be happy, and I was until the day the Jessica died. I am just hurt you didn't feel that you could trust me enough to share some of your secrets," Juliette stated.

"Juliette it had nothing to do with you. I do trust you, and that's why I'm telling you all of this now. I was afraid you wouldn't want to be with me if you knew my horrid past. Also, I don't want you to be my Counselor, Therapist or Social Worker. I just want you to be my wife and my best friend like you were before. I wasn't fair and this I know, but one good thing is that you nor the boys will ever have to worry about money again in life, and for me as a man this fact is very important. If we continue to live the same lifestyle like we are now, we are set for life."

"Grandville I don't understand. How were you able to keep the fact that you're loaded away from me?"

"I have the money in a Trust and I never touch the principal only the interest. The company that manages the Trust would send the statements to my mother's house."

"It doesn't matter. A Better Tomorrow is turning a good profit, and I'm making a lot of extra money on my accident cases. I also started doing Involuntary Commitment hearings for Lake County."

"That's great, but I want you to know that no matter what, I will always support you, financially, mentally and physically.

"You've done a great job of that as a husband, so I know you will continue despite what I say." Juliette just shook her head.

"How do you like working on the Involuntary Commitment cases?" Grandville asked.

"It is okay. So many of the people I'm attempting to have the court hold for further observation are out of their minds. When they're sick and a danger to themselves and others, they should be put into the hospital so that they can receive the care that's necessary to help them become contributing members of society."

"My friend Montell was put at Oakhill and held even though he is one of the sanest people I know."

"Well he must have done something to make the authorities put him in Oakhill."

"He killed his son's Karate Instructor after walking in on his son's sexual assault," Grandville explained.

"That's a horrible story," Juliette replied.

"Yeah the clinicians at Oakhill said Montell experienced what is known as a Brief Psychotic Disorder, but he has not suffered one solitary symptom of mental illness since being brought here to Oakhill. Yet, he has lost four years of his life by being institutionalized. To add to it, he killed his son's perpetrator right in front of his son Monty. Now, he's been experiencing mental health problems since he watched his dad kill his instructor. Montell can't even help Monty because he's here at Oakhill," Grandville elaborated on the situation.

"Grandville I know you would have to agree the authorities owe society a certain measure of protection. We can't allow people who are psychotic to just be running around killing people. Many of the people I'm fighting to have the court hold for further treatment could become contributing members of our society if they receive the correct intervention. What happened to your friend's son was terrible, but that still didn't give your friend the right to take a life. I understand your friend's mind snapped, and because it was determined by the authorities he was insane at the time of his crime. He was sent to Oakhill to receive the help he needs," Juliette replied.

"You may be right, but I want you to know Oakhill is not Club Med. It's a maximum security institution. It has all the same dangers of any facility where you have violent, marginal people.

Montell was a Police Officer before coming to Oakhill and what he did in my opinion was protect his son and society. I know how it feels to have your innocence stripped away by someone who is supposed to care for you and what Montell did was make sure the bastard didn't have the opportunity to hurt another innocent child," Grandville passionately stated.

"No what Montell did was become Judge and Jury. Maybe this Karate Instructor had a brain tumor or some other disease which made him commit his crime? I understand Montell was sick, and this is why he took a man's life. I actually understand why he did it, but that does not mean what he did was right. Thou shall not kill is one of the Ten Commandments," Juliette said.

"All I'm saying is there are some people who can understand why Montell's mind snapped. I'm honest enough to admit if I was faced with the same set of circumstances, that I would have done the very same thing. Hell you have told me on more then one occasions about how your clients are all screwed up because they were sexually abused. I'm sure you can understand why I wasn't all that anxious to share the news of what happened to me with anyone. All I'm conceding is, if I walked in on some pervert sexually abusing one of our kids I wouldn't be responsible for my actions," Grandville passionately declared.

Juliette became quiet choosing not to continue the conversation and tried to focus on the movie. Soon both she and Grandville were enthralled in the plot of the movie. Denzel did a great job bringing to light a brilliant dysfunctional Airline Pilot with serious addiction issues. After the movie ended Grandville and Juliette quietly discussed the movie and Denzel movies in general.

"Denzel Washington did a fantastic job in this movie. I loved it but of course *Malcom X* was my movie. I always felt Denzel and Spike Lee were cheated when they didn't get an Oscar for it," Juliette said.

"You're right, but my favorite Denzel movie was *Training Day*. Anyone who has seen the movie has to admit Denzel did a great job. He almost always plays good guys, and when he played a bad guy he was very convincing. He has shown that he has range in his acting skills. I felt he deserved the Oscar he received," Grandville said.

"At least they got it one hundred percent right when they gave Denzel his best supporting Oscar for *Glory*," Juliette remarked.

"You're so right," replied Grandville.

Juliette found her eyes were heavy. She was suddenly exhausted and she just could not keep her eyes open and she promptly fell asleep.

Grandville gazed upon her sleeping frame and then pulled her body into his. He was very tired, but he wanted to savor every moment of his time with Juliette. He was afraid to fall asleep for fear of losing time with her. Juliette snuggled her body into his and before he knew it, he too had fallen into a deep peaceful slumber.

Grandville woke up at exactly six-thirty AM which was the time the lights came on at Oakhill. He gently untangled his body from Juliette who looked like a sleeping angel and kissed her on her forehead. He wanted to surprise her with breakfast in bed. He quietly went into the bathroom to wash up and then he headed into the kitchen to begin breakfast.

After he said good morning to Officer Tatum who was sitting outside the door to his room, he made coffee and soon the small suite smelled of eggs, cheese grits and bacon. He topped the meal off with biscuits from a bag. The small suite came with all of the basic cooking utensils needed to make a home cooked meal and Grandville cleaned the kitchen as he cooked. It didn't take long for Officer Emerson to make his way to the small kitchen.

"Stubbs it smells delicious in here. I know your Lady Love has to be very pleased with your culinary skills. Hell if I wasn't already married, I might be tempted to ask you for your hand," Officer Emerson teased.

"My Juliette appears to be pleased with the food, but I am the one who is ecstatic. I hate the food at Oakhill, it's almost not even edible. I'm glad you and the other guards like my food because I made you guys breakfast," Grandville stated.

"Thanks Stubbs we really appreciate it but you didn't have too. Trying to feed five grown people has to be costing you a mint. How about you allow me and the other Guards to get you and your Lady Love's lunch?" Officer Emerson offered.

"I really appreciate it but we may not have room for lunch. I plan to make a pre-thanksgiving meal, and I have more than enough for you and the other guards. I planned to serve dinner at 7:00 pm," Grandville told him so they could be prepared for dinner.

"Stubbs you're spoiling us. Thanks a lot," Emerson said.

"Actually I should be thanking you. I really appreciate you picking up the food for me."

"Not a problem. Don't forget we have a deal," Officer Emerson reminded Grandville.

"We most certainly do. Your son's package will be at Oakhill when we return. When is your son's birthday?"

"Next week." Officer Emerson replied.

"Good, he will be very pleased with his presents."

Grandville put the food on all the plates and prepared a serving tray with Juice, Coffee and Juliette's breakfast.

"Officer Emerson please let the other guards know their breakfast is ready. I'm going to take this tray to Juliette."

"No problem," Officer Emerson replied.

Grandville quietly opened the door and closed it behind him. He put the tray on the dresser and peered down at Juliette who slept peacefully.

He got back in the bed with her and gently pulled her into his embrace and kissed her on her cheek.

"Hey there Sleeping Beauty. I brought you breakfast." Grandville whispered softly into her ear.

Juliette open up her eyes and looked up at him. Even half asleep with her hair all over her head she looked beautiful to him. He couldn't help himself when he brought his lips down on her hers and lightly kissed her.

Juliette pushed him away and then said, "Grandville I haven't brushed my teeth yet and I'm certain that I have morning breath."

"Your breath taste fine to me." Grandville got off the bed and went to the dresser to get the food so he could give it to Juliette.

"Oh my God Grandville, if you keep feeding me like this I am going to weigh a ton. Then you're not going to want me anymore," Juliette said.

"Juliette I will always want you. Even if you are fat, toothless, blind and deaf. No matter what, you'll always be my girl and I love you," Grandville replied.

"Thanks Grandville and the food does smell delicious, but I don't know how much of it I will be able to eat. I'm still full from last night's meal."

"Eat as much or as little as you want. I don't plan to prepare lunch, but I do plan to prepare a special dinner for you tonight. We're going to eat at around 7pm. So, if you don't eat all your food I'll put it up for you, and you can have it later if you start to get hungry."

"Thanks Grandville," Juliette gratefully replied.

Grandville got up out of the bed and brought the tray to Juliette, and she immediately reached for the coffee and took a healthy sip.

"I see you still love your coffee first thing in the AM."

"Yes, and I see that you still remember how I take my coffee."

"How could I possibly ever forget? It's ingrained in my memory. One teaspoon of creamer and two teaspoons of sugar. It's the only thing that I would consistently make for you."

"Since you've been here at Oakhill I've been making my own coffee, and it sure tastes better when someone else is making it for you."

"Juliette if you give me a second chance I promise when I come home from Oakhill you will never have to make your own coffee again. You don't have to teach me how to make it, because I already know the way that you like it."

"Thanks Grandville I'll keep your proposal under review."

Juliette tasted the grits and the biscuit which was filled with both grape Jelly and butter and again marveled at how good the food was.

"So when was the last time you've seen Franklin?" Grandville asked.

Juliette was momentarily thrown off guard at the mention of Franklin.

"Not in a while. I've spoken to him by phone though. He called me on the anniversary of Jessica's death, but we both have been busy. How about you?" Juliette asked.

"Franklin still comes to see me once a month, sometimes he even comes twice a month. He works closely with Darita and relays everything about what my legal team is doing on my case to me. I can honestly say there's a chance I might be released from Oakhill in the not so distant future, but I'm afraid to get my hopes up too high."

"I can understand,"

"I was once told you are a blessed man when you have one or two true friends in a lifetime. With the exception of you, Franklin has been that friend for me. I don't know if I can ever repay him for all that he has done for me while I have been here at Oakhill. There are so many people who'll abandon you when you are at your worst and could really use a friend. Even Rayshawn who is my oldest friend and was my brother in law has only recently reached out to me after three years. Franklin has been true and has been my right hand man since before I came to Oakhill."

Juliette suddenly lost what little appetite that she had.

"You know what Grandville, I'm going to take you up on the offer to have you put up my breakfast. I'm not hungry but I will probably get hungry later. I'm going to get up and take a shower and pull myself together. I fell asleep in my clothes and I'm sure that I'm a wrinkled mess."

"You always look great to me. But, you go ahead and get yourself together. I'm going to go into the kitchen and start working on prepping and preparing our special meal." Grandville gave her a thumbs up.

And Juliette replied, "Okay," picked up her overnight case and walked towards the bathroom.

Chapter 22

Is It a Crime?

Juliette stood under the spray of water in the shower and attempted to gather her thoughts. The visit was going well, and she had to admit to herself that she was still in love with Grandville and the man he appeared to have become. She was impressed he had managed so well even after all he had endured. She actually understood why he hadn't shared the details of his past with her sooner. She believed him when he said, he had not shared his whole story with anyone else, and by telling her the awful details he was showing her how much he actually trusted her. She just wished he had believed in her sooner. Juliette knew in her heart even if she had been aware of Grandville's past she would have still married him. What she was having trouble understanding is what made Grandville snap to the point where he had become psychotic. She also believed Grandville when he said, hurting Jessica was an accident, and the stress of losing his mother could have awakened his dormant Bipolar Disorder. The fact that Grandville's aunt had been hospitalized several times for her mental health issues indicated that Grandville's family had a predisposition for the disease.

She wanted the reconciliation he was offering, but after hearing Grandville's feelings about Franklin she knew to tell Grandville about what happened between the two of them would be a very bad idea. Grandville had already admitted he had trust issues and despite what happened between she and Franklin, Franklin had proven himself to be a great friend to Grandville and for that she was grateful. Franklin had been a friend to Grandville when he really needed one. To tell Grandville of their illicit encounter would reinforce his reasons for not trusting, and that was the last thing she wanted to do. However, she still had to find a way to tell him about the babies which she delivered while he had been locked up. She didn't know if the news would set him back or if it would help him to become more determined in his recovery. All she knew was that she was running out of time and that she had to make some decisions before she left Oakhill the next day to go home.

After her shower Juliette put lotion on her body and got dressed. She looked into the mirror and chastised herself for almost begging Grandville to make love to her. She admired and respected Grandville for being man enough to turn down her offer when so many men would have taken what she was willing to freely give. She didn't know how much she missed Grandville's touch until he kissed her, and then she couldn't control herself. She was glad Grandville explained the parameters of what he wanted from her in a way which left little room for misunderstanding. She was either all in or she was out. Juliette decided to stop running from fate, because in her heart she knew that she wanted to be with Grandville but the particulars still needed to be worked out.

Juliette took one last look at herself and noted, she looked and felt rested. She had to admit to herself that she had experienced some of the best sleep in her life while lying in Grandville's arms. It was almost like when they were dating again. She was reminded of some of the reasons why she fell in love with him almost from the beginning. Despite all that had happened Grandville was still thoughtful and always placed what she wanted above all else and she appreciated that in him. Before he came to Oakhill he didn't really cook anything except breakfast for her, but he did take her to great restaurants and always spent quality time with her when he wasn't working. His new found culinary skills was an added treat, and Juliette was enjoying the meals which he was preparing for her.

She regretted losing her appetite, because the breakfast he had prepared for her tasted delicious. However, when Grandville talked about how much Franklin had done for him she felt dirty and underhanded, and she couldn't force herself to take another bite. She loved Grandville, and he loved her. She knew she couldn't be with him until she forgave herself for her one and only transgression. She also had to tell Grandville that she forgave him for his role in the accident which took their daughter's life. Juliette went out into the small suite and found Grandville in the kitchen cooking.

"It sure smells good in here."

"Thanks. We are going to have a special dinner tonight."

"Are you sure you're not trying to make me fat?" Juliette asked joking with Grandville.

"I'm positive. Honestly the food at Oakhill is terrible, and I just want to spend time with you doing something I dreamed of doing for more than three years."

"What's that?"

"Eating a meal that actually tastes good and hopefully making love to you," Grandville replied.

Juliette blushed and tried to steer the conversation to a place where she could explain about the twins.

"Grandville, what are you making for dinner?"

"I want you to know, I miss you and the boys, but I miss you most during the holidays. You know Thanksgiving has always been my favorite holiday, because when I was with you and our kids I had my own family. I've realized while I have been at Oakhill just how much I used to take for granted. I'm making a pre-Thanksgiving meal for the two of us. I just put the turkey in the oven, and I'm going to prepare the rest of the meal while we talk."

"Okay, and I want to thank you for fixing me all this food. I'm not going to want to ever cook again."

"Juliette, I know you have been working hard taking care of A Better Tomorrow, the house and the kids. You deserve to have somebody take care of you. Please forgive me for not being home to do that for you."

"Grandville I do forgive you."

"Are you afraid of me?" Grandville asked.

"No. But, honestly I'm a little apprehensive of what you might do if you're under stress."

"Juliette, I can understand what you're saying, but honestly a lot of my stress resulted from me trying to keep my past secret from you. I don't want there to be any more secrets between us no matter what you decide. I also want us to make love to each other tonight. I know you wanted us to be together last night, but I want to know before we are together where we stand in our relationship. Sex could cloud our decision making ability, and I want you to be 100 percent sure on what you are getting into or giving up before we re-consummate our relationship."

"I understand and I'm sorry that I threw myself at you last night. Thank you for being a gentleman and the voice of reason," Juliette responded.

"Juliette, I don't know how much more control I'll be able to exhibit. I've dreamed of touching you, kissing you and making love to you on a daily base. Sometimes I even dream of you when I'm awake. I feel like I'm in a dream right now. You coming here and spending time with me has made me one of the happiest men on earth."

"Grandville, I missed you too, and I'm glad that I came to this visit."

"I've been thinking about Melinia's going missing, and I wanted to run something by you."

"Okay what?"

"I think you should go back to the treatment facility that Melinia initially went through. I believe she may have other friends and supports outside of your family and a Better Tomorrow. You should also go to some of the Narcotics Anonymous and Heroin Anonymous meetings close to where the treatment center is and show Melinia's picture and try and see if anyone there has seen her. Your cousin probably had at least one friend that she made while she was getting help."

"I hadn't thought to do that."

"I believe that Melinia may have had a Sponsor, but that you and your family may not be aware of who the person might be. The individual may not even know Melinia is missing. I remember once when we were dating you told me a story about one of your clients who had become addicted to Crack and you were able to get her into rehab where she got help. However, at some point she started dating her Sponsor. If I recall you and the other staff thought her Sponsor was a female, because the dude's name was Tracy, and he spent time talking to your client by phone. Maybe Melinia talked on the phone to her Sponsor more then she actually saw him or her." Grandville suggested.

"I had not even thought about it quite that way. As soon as I get home I'll follow up on your leads."

"Good. Hopefully Melinia will be found soon.

"I hope so too, because I'm really worried about her."

By the way, you look great. Can I get you something to drink like water or tea?" Grandville asked Juliette.

"No, I'm fine. Tell me, how you are enjoying teaching your English class?"

"Actually, I'm enjoying it very much. Many of the guys in my class are not stupid. They just were never given an educational foundation to build upon. Franklin was able to drop-off pocket dictionaries to me last week and now each one of my students has one. I'm hopeful the dictionaries will give the men the means and the ability to understand words and there meanings. Once this happens a new world might open-up for them that will help them pass their time at Oakhill. Their horizons could be expanded through books and poetry which could inspire and educate them. You know what they say, better late than never. It would really help the guys in my class if they could learn to read and write better. Also, some of my students might decide to write or journal as a way of escaping the reality of being behind bars."

"I think it's commendable that you're spending your time this way," Juliette said.

"My teaching the class was actually Franklin's idea. Once he presented it to me, I decided to give it a try. I've come to realize, I'm truly enjoying myself. Right now my class is reading *Animal Farm*, and the guys seem to understand that the book is a metaphor for the Russian Revolution. Some of the guys in the class only have a fifth grade reading comprehension, but are now beginning to understand the Russian Revolution. Teaching the class has given me something else to do besides playing chess with Montell, who is going to be released next week." Grandville sounded and looked very disappointed. Although he was super ecstatic for his friend.

"I'm glad you are doing something productive with your time. But, how are you feeling about Montell being released?" Juliette questioned.

"I'm more than happy for him. He's paid his debt to society, and I hope he's given an opportunity to show the world that he's rehabilitated. Honestly, I feel Montell should not have been placed in Oakhill or any other institution because all he did was defend his son." Grandville replied.

"Grandville yesterday you revealed to me that your Mom caught you and Gina in a sexual act. You had also been raped both mentally and physically by your Cousin who was much older then you. Would it have been okay for your Mom to have killed Gina when she saw what was happening? For me there is no way to condone murder except in the case of self-defense. You and I both know what your friend did was not self-defense or even defense of others. He was a Police Officer and could have arrested his son's perpetrator on the spot or called the authorities." Juliette passionately stated.

"Juliette, I understand your point but to me the situations are totally different. Gina was a teenager when she started abusing me. When my Mom caught us, I was sixteen and Gina was twenty three. Gina was also my Mother's niece and despite what she did to me my Mother still loved her. She knew something had to have happened to Gina to make her touch me in an inappropriate way. Montell saw a grown ass man with his penis in his young teenage son's mouth. All I'm saying is the average individual would have snapped and killed their child's perpetrator or at least seriously injured them if they walked in on that scene. Montell doesn't even remember killing him, because he was so traumatized from what he witnessed. I'm not saying that I condone murder, but what I am saying is, there are times when murder is justified. One of the worst parts of being in here is knowing that I'm not there to protect you and my young son's from the monsters who are lurking. I don't know what I might do if something happens to you or my boys while I'm in here."

"Grandville, we are keeping a close eye on the kids so you don't have to worry. I talk to the boys about good touches and bad ones and I monitor who's around them. The only new person who's been around the boys is my former friend Tara's daughter, Tabitha. The kids and I haven't seen Tabitha or Tara since Samantha, and I had our falling out."

"How old is Tabitha?

"Tabitha is sixteen. She has only babysat for me a few times when I needed to run errands."

"Okay, I know you're doing a great job teaching the kids to be careful, but just remember almost everyone who has been sexually abused had a perpetrator they knew before they were abused." Grandville stated.

"I'm aware of this and I'm being as careful as possible."

"Juliette, I'm not trying to criticize you. I'm both thankful and grateful you're taking care of the boys. I want you to know, I know you've had offers from several men who wanted to take care of you while I've been away. I hope if you're involved with someone else, he understands I would never hold anything you did while I was at Oakhill against you. I hope whoever he is understands, I love you and I will not give you up without a fight."

"Grandville, I'm not presently involved with anyone but my husband, don't forget I'm a married woman."

"The question is do you want to stay married to me? Give me the chance to prove to you that you didn't make a mistake when you chose me."

"Grandville, I want to reconcile, but you have to understand I want to take it slow. I think it's a good idea you're getting your own place when you are released as I want us to take our time to re-acclimate to one another. Also, before you move back in with us I want us to engage in family counseling."

"Juliette, I will consent to almost anything if it means I'll have a chance to get my family back."

The kitchen timer went off causing Juliette to jump.

"It's time for me to baste the Turkey. Sorry the timer startled you. It's going to go off a few times while I cook our meal. I want it to be perfect, because tomorrow night it's back to Oakhill's and the horrible food that they serve." Grandville complained and sighed at the same time while shaking his head in disbelief the food at Oakhill could be so bad.

"Does Oakhill allow you to receive food, because if they do when I get home I'll make you something and send it to you?"

"I don't know, and I appreciate your offer but I'm good. I want to remember our time together, and I want to have your home cooking to look forward to. It'll motivate me to work harder to get out of Oakhill. The only thing I really want you to do for me when you go back home is to write to me. It's so lonely at Oakhill, and when I receive letters from you I feel connected to you and my sons. You don't know how happy I was when I received your letter right before the Anniversary of Jessica's death. Juliette, I was about to give up on you and us, but Montell told me every single day you would come through for me and that you would eventually write to me. Then, when my counselor told me you were actually coming for the extended visit I was beyond happy. Now, you are here, and I'm barely able to control myself."

"Grandville I've dreamed of you too. We were so happy, and I want us to be that way again. I do love you, and I want us to be together but there are a few things I need to tell you."

"Do I get to ask if you are about to tell me something crazy?" Grandville questioned her and it seemed to be sarcastic, but it wasn't.

"If me giving birth to twin girls is crazy then yes, I guess what I'm about to tell you is something crazy." Juliette looked him dead in the eyes to see what his reaction and expression would be.

Chapter 23

Between the Sheets

Grandville felt like he was hearing things. Maybe they were having a communication issue, but he could have sworn he heard her say she had given birth to twin girls.

"Pardon me? Would you please repeat what you just said?" Grandville asked Juliette looking horribly confused.

"Grandville, I said while you've been incarcerated at Oakhill, I gave birth to another set of twins." Juliette repeated herself and said it a little louder.

"I don't understand?"

"Grandville, what is confusing about the fact that while you have been locked up I had another set of twins?" Juliette asked.

"How old are the twins?"

"They are close to two and a half years old."

"Are they mine?"

"Yes, Grandville you are the girl's father."

Grandville was in a state of shock. He sat down at the small table and attempted to digest the news. When he found out Juliette was coming to the visit, never in a million years did he think she would tell him that while he had been at Oakhill they had more kids. Kids who he had not yet seen. Girls who needed the protection of their father.

"Do you have a picture of them?"

"Yes, when I go back into the bedroom I'll get it for you. The girls' names are Janae and Jolene. They keep me pretty busy."

"Does Greta know about the girls?"

"Yes, but I made her promise to never to tell you about them. I basically advised her, if she told you then I would stop her from seeing me and all of the children. I've been afraid for you to find out, but I must admit I feel better now that I've told you about the girls."

"Why didn't you want me to know about our daughters?"

"I needed to determine for myself that you learning this news would not set you back in your recovery. Grandville I love you, but I love our kids more. It's my job to protect them, and I want you to have a relationship with them, but not if you're going to hurt them. Up until this moment I felt you not knowing about the girls was for the best." Juliette confessed to him in a brave and matter-of-fact manner.

"Does Franklin know?"

"No. I have barely seen him since the accident. The one time he did see me with the twins I lied and said I was babysitting for one of my cousins."

"Juliette I'm speechless. I can't believe you've given birth to two more daughters while I've been here at Oakhill."

"I'm only telling you about the girls now, because I want the reconciliation you're offering. However, I want you to understand I'll need to ensure you're not a danger to our kids."

"Juliette, I promise that I'll never hurt you or our children. I'm begging for a chance to show you I'm the man for you, and that I can be a good father to our kids."

Before Juliette could respond the timer went off again indicating it was time to baste the Turkey, and she again jumped because her nerves were on edge.

"Juliette, I need to baste the Turkey again. I'm sorry the buzzer keeps startling you." Grandville said.

"It's not a problem."

Once Grandville finished basting the Turkey he sat down and pulled Juliette's hands into his.

"Juliette, thank you for telling me about my daughters. I can't wait to meet them. I want to apologize again for all you've gone through since the accident. How did you get through the birth of two more kids without me there to help you?" Grandville questioned.

"My mother and my whole family helped and are still coming through for me. Even Samantha, who doesn't particularly like kids helped. Greta also has been invaluable to me since she moved back to Cleveland. Plus, the boys are older and also pitch in. Greta is keeping the twins this weekend and my mom has the boys." Juliette said.

"Do you need anything?" Grandville asked still in a state of shock from hearing the news about his two daughters

"Yes, I need for you to get better so you can help me raise our children. I'm going to be completely honest, I've been overwhelmed. First your mother died, then there was the accident resulting in the loss of Jessica and without warning and out of nowhere you were gone sent here to Oakhill. To top it all off, while I was trying to come to grips with what happened to Jessica, I found out I was pregnant with another set of twins. It's taken me this long to get myself together and face my future. The children and I can't continue to live in a state of limbo."

"I definitely understand. I want to be there for you. Knowing you'll allow me to show you and our children despite what happened, we are a family. I want you to know that means a lot to me. You can set-up family counseling, and I'll happily engage in it as soon as I'm released from Oakhill."

Again the timer went off, but this time Juliette did not jump. She had anticipated the timer would buzz again and was waiting for its signal. Grandville calmly went to the stove and again basted the turkey. After he put the Turkey back into the oven he sat down across from Juliette at the small table.

"Juliette, tell me about our daughters."

"The girls are your average rambunctious two and a half year old kids. They are healthy and they love to run and play. Janae is the only one of our kids who has you and Greta's hazel colored eyes. People often assume Greta is her mother and Jolene favors me more. Let me get you a picture."

Juliette got up and went into the bedroom where her purse was and retrieved photographs of all four of the children. She returned back to the table where she had left Grandville sitting and passed him the photos. He looked at the picture as tears streamed from his eyes.

"The girls are beautiful, and I can't get over how big our sons have become. When I've thought of our sons, I couldn't help but remember how they looked more than three years ago."

"Yes the children are forever changing. I see them every day and they change from hour to hour to me. You can keep the pictures, there're for you. I was hesitant and didn't know if I was going to give them to you when I came yesterday."

"I totally understand, and I want to thank you for trusting me enough to share this information. I want you to know, I'll do whatever I need to do to get out of Oakhill, so I can be there to support you and our family."

"Grandville like I told you yesterday, I do trust you and I'll help you as long as you remember to never shut me out. I understand why you didn't tell me about your childhood and all the horrible things which happened to you. But, I need to be sure you won't keep secrets from me ever again. To me, you are more than just my husband, you were always my best friend. You and Samantha, were the closest people to me with the exception of my family. I need to know what I'm doing to give you all the impression that you can't talk to me?"

"Juliette I can't speak for Samantha, but you didn't do anything wrong when it came to me. It was shame and fear that prevented me from being honest with you. My past is a train wreck, and I was afraid you wouldn't want me if you knew the truth. I also didn't want counseling. I felt you would have pressed me to get it if you knew all the details. I just wanted to forget about everything that happened and I put my focus on being a good husband, father, brother, son and friend. We have some time before the food will be ready. I found some board games, and I thought we could play Monopoly while I finish cooking the food. Are you up to it?"

"Sure, that's a great idea. I'll set up the board. Where is it?"

Grandville reached under the table and got the game. He passed it to Juliette who immediately began setting up the board on the coffee table in the small front room which made up the suite. Juliette and Grandville used to play Monopoly often when they were dating. Both, often joked about how the game could imitate real life. In the game just like in life, you could land on Community Chest and end up in jail or owing some tax which you didn't know you would have to pay or you could end up with a fortune which you didn't anticipate receiving. The game was unpredictable just like real life.

"Since you set the game up you can be the banker, and I'll even let you roll the dice first." Grandville said to Juliette.

"Ok that's cool.

Grandville decided to be the iron and Juliette picked the dog to represent themselves on the Board.

Juliette set the properties up and passed out the money. After each had moved their pieces around the Board they started to buy property. Grandville bought every property which he landed on but Juliette employed a different strategy. She only purchased those properties that paid well if Grandville landed on them. Soon they were laughing and having a great time.

"Come on Juliette let me get the Pacific. I have the other two properties and I'll have a Monopoly if you let me buy it from you."

"No way. I'm no fool. If I land on it when you have a Monopoly I'll have to pay you even more for rent. However, I will consider selling it to you if you let me get Park Place." Juliette countered the deal.

"No way Park Place is absolutely not for sale. You already have the Board Walk, and if I give you Park Place you'll have a Monopoly. If I land on one of your properties you'll bankrupt me." Grandville reasoned with her.

"That's exactly what I'm trying to do, isn't that the object of the game?" Juliette was straighten-up her money and properties and then sat back into the couch.

"Yes, but I'm not going to make it easy for you, and I'm not going to hand you my demise. You know Juliette all jokes aside, this is the first time in more than three years I've played any game other than Chess. I'm having a great time, but I'm going to have to excuse myself so I can go and check on the food. It's getting close to being done, and I wanted us to sit down to eat at about seven. How does that sound?"

"It sounds great. It smells wonderful in here. I can't wait to taste the food. I can't get over how good all the food you've prepared tastes."

"I can't believe it either. I think, I memorized at least a hundred recipes from watching the cooking shows on the food network channels. I imagined cooking for you and the food tasting delicious. I'm glad my dream is actually coming true." Grandville said.

"Me too." Juliette concurred.

Grandville walked into the small kitchenette and basted the Turkey. He then took out the stuffing which he had mixed and laid in a pan to bake and stuck it in the oven. He pulled out the store brought greens that he had put in a pot earlier. He spiced up the greens with chopped onions, seasonings and put the pot on the stove to heat. He pulled out the ham which he had basted with a brown sugar pineapple glaze and put aluminum foil on it so he could prepare to heat the meat.

When he walked back into the living room Juliette was waiting. "It's smelling like Thanksgiving around here."

"I know it's not Thanksgiving but let's make believe it is." He laughed.

"I love it."

"Hey, you weren't in here cheating were you?" Grandville asked playfully.

"No, and be reminded I don't need to cheat to beat you in a game of Monopoly. You're about to go down soon and very soon." Juliette laughed and couldn't stop.

The two began the game again and Juliette's strategy was working. Grandville made the grave mistake of landing on Juliette's high-end properties where she had a Monopoly. Juliette was taking all of Grandville's money little by little. Grandville was forced to sell Juliette the Park Place property which she wanted, because he was virtually out of money. Selling the property to her was the only way he could stay in the game. Juliette landed on his low end properties often. She had to pay him several times. Then, Grandville landed on her Boardwalk which she had hotels on and it was a rap. Grandville was bankrupt and could not stay in the game.

"Go ahead and say it. I'm the Queen of Monopoly." Teased Juliette.

"Your victory was luck. When I come home I'm going to want a rematch."

"Whatever. When you come home I'm going to again spank you with the Monopoly Board. We'll also let the boys play. I play with them all the time and they are quite the Monopoly players." Juliette said.

"The food will be ready very soon. I'm going to go ahead and set the table." Grandville pointed in the direction of the dining area.

"Do you need any help?" Juliette asked.

"No, I'm cool. You can go ahead and wash up for dinner and I'll get the food on the table."

Juliette went back into the bathroom and washed her hands. She looked at her watch and noted it was already 6:50 pm. She couldn't believe how quickly time was passing. Tomorrow this time she would be home with the kids reminiscing about the time she'd spent with Grandville. She took a breath and anticipated the night to come. Her nerve ends tingled with the mere thought that she and Grandville would be making love again. She almost couldn't wait, but she didn't want to rush as she was enjoying the build-up to that magic moment. However, Juliette was still puzzled, because deep in her gut she felt that Grandville had one last serious confession to make. She hoped whatever it was didn't make her change her mind about giving her heart and body to him again.

When Juliette returned back to the small kitchenette, the table was set and a beautiful battery operated Candelabra sat in the middle of the table. Grandville had put the food on their plates and sat them on the table along with plastic wine glasses. The Guards also had plates which were piled high with Grandville's delicious foods. Soon it was just Grandville, Juliette and Officer Emerson alone in the small kitchenette.

"Stubbs this food smells delicious let me do the honors of pouring you and your Lady Love a drink. I believe a toast is in order." Emerson took control of pouring the drinks just to make sure no mistakes were made with the real wine.

Thanks Officer Emerson." Grandville replied.

"No problem."

Officer Emerson poured wine into Juliette's glass and Sparkling Grape Juice into Grandville's.

"I propose a toast. To yesterdays, todays and tomorrows. May the Lord keep you and bless you." Officer Emerson said, and they all touched the tips of their glasses.

"Thanks Officer Emerson." Grandville was very grateful to have Office Emerson as a supporter during his time with Juliette.

"I'm going to take my leave and enjoy this meal. I'll be in the front room. I'll be back in a few minutes to refill your glasses." Officer Emerson said as he picked up his plate.

"We appreciate it." Grandville said.

Officer Emerson walked out of the small kitchen leaving Juliette and Grandville alone.

Grandville held up his glass. "I want to also make a toast. To us and our children. Thanks for having Thanksgiving with me." Grandville told his wife.

Juliette sipped her Chardonnay wine. It was excellent, sweet but not too sweet. She put her glass down and took a bite of her Turkey which was smothered in gravy. The food was again delicious and the mood was reminiscent of the many Thanksgivings which she and Grandville had shared together.

"I hope you like the wine. I have Grape Juice, because as you know me consuming alcohol is against the Oakhill's rules. Also, I don't want to drink while I'm on the medications that I'm taking to control my Bipolar Disorder." Grandville wanted to be open and fill Juliette in on the details of the dinner.

"That's good. Drinking alcohol is the last thing you to want to do while taking the meds. The interaction of the two could cause the meds to stop working." Juliette informed him.

"My doctor told me the very same thing. I have pretty much come to grips with the fact that I can't ever drink alcohol again. It's easy while I'm here at Oakhill, but I know it'll be harder when I come home." Grandville told her.

"I agree, but you never did drink much when you were at home." Juliette looked at him with a puzzled look on her face.

"Juliette on the day of the accident I was drunk out of my mind." Grandville confessed.

"What? I had no idea."

"That's because I hid my drinking from you. This last part of my story is the hardest for me to tell. Absolutely no one knows what I'm about to share with you." Grandville said quietly with a shameful undertone in his voice.

Juliette was suddenly very nervous, because she knew in her heart whatever Grandville was about to say would be life changing. She continued eating to comply with Grandville's request to allow him the opportunity to tell his story at his pace. Grandville took a large sip of his grape juice at the same time that Officer Emerson came back into the room.

"Stubbs it looks like I came in at the right time. Looks like you and your Lady Love need a refill," Officer Emerson stated.

"Thanks Officer Emerson," Grandville replied.

Officer Emerson poured more wine into Juliette's glass and then poured more Grape Juice for Grandville.

"Stubbs, this food is great."

"Thank you sir. I'm glad you enjoyed it."

"I'm going to return back to the front room. I'll also do the dishes so when you and your Lady Love have finished your meals you should retire to your room. The other Guards have already swept it and is cleared it for your return. I have to do one more pat down on both of you and then I'll leave you be." Officer Emerson was a very kind person. Grandville could also tell he didn't like being a hard ass, but it's his job to be one if he has to.

"No problem Officer Emerson," Grandville replied.

Grandville stood up and Officer Emerson patted him down using standard procedure. When he was finished with Grandville, he then went around to where Juliette was seated. Juliette stood up and he repeated the procedure on her in a cold, detached and mythological way. He then walked into the front room leaving Grandville and Juliette alone again.

"Juliette, thanks for agreeing to come to this visit. I know it's difficult to be treated like a criminal when you've done nothing wrong."

"Honestly Grandville it's not a problem. I don't mind at all. If it's allowing me the opportunity to spend time with you without having to visit with you behind bars or Plexiglas." Juliette responded.

"I wish you didn't have to see me at my worst, but I have always felt you loved me for me and not for the superficial facade that I portrayed to the outside world."

"That's because I do love you for you. Haven't I always tried to show you that?"

"Yes, you have always shown me, but my insecurities had nothing to do with you. I always felt incomplete, because my Mom refused to tell me or Greta who our biological father was. Sometimes I silently wondered if she knew who our Dad was, and right before my mother passed she revealed to me my father's identity." Grandville confessed.

"Well, who is he? If you want we can look for him?"

"We wouldn't be able to find him, because he's dead. I know exactly where he is buried." Grandville replied.

"Well, what did Mother Stubbs tell you?" Juliette questioned as her curiosity peaked.

"She said, my Uncle Greg was Greta and my father." Grandville spoke slowly as he released the words from his mouth.

Juliette almost held her breath, but took another sip of her wine in an attempt to not let Grandville see the shock in her body.

Grandville continued on, "My Mom said, she and Uncle Greg were only together once when my Aunt Genevive was in the psychiatric hospital suffering with Depression. On my Mom's death bed is when I found out my cousin Gina wasn't just my cousin, she was also my sister. I was sick from the thought. From the moment I learned this news I haven't been right, mentally or spiritually."

It all started to come together and Juliette was beginning to gain some understanding as to why Grandville's mind had snapped. She calmly listened to him explain about how his mother waited to right before she died to tell him the dreadful news of who his biological father was. Juliette couldn't understand why Mother Stubbs would not take the information to her grave when Grandville interrupted her thoughts.

"My mother also told me something else that still has me messed up. If you don't mind, I would like to take Officer Emerson's advice and finish the rest of this story in our room. Is that okay with you?" Grandville asked.

"Sure, that's fine." Juliette replied.

Grandville took Juliette's hand and led her to the bedroom. He closed the door, then took his shoes off, laid down on the bed and closed his eyes. Juliette decided to follow his lead and also got into the bed. Silence engulfed the room when Grandville suddenly began speaking again in a quiet monotone voice.

"My mother also told me that Gina and I conceived a son together. The child was put up for adoption. Mom told me about the child, because she was afraid he would one day look for me. She was afraid the shock of learning the news from someone that I didn't even know existed would send me over the edge. It seems that learning the news from someone I knew is what propelled me over an emotional cliff. I can honestly say, telling you all of this makes me feel like a huge weight has been lifted off of me." Grandville said emotionally and almost in tears again.

"Does Greta know about you and Gina's son?" Juliette asked him.

Tears streamed down Grandville's face as he continued talking. "No. I haven't told anyone about the child. I have been left to wonder if me and Gina's son was born deformed due to our blood line being so close. I've been praying the child got a good life. I've been fearful of how I'll react if he ever one day finds me." Grandville confided in her.

Juliette rolled over and looked Grandville directly in his eyes.

"Grandville none of this is your fault. Yes, you should've been honest with me from the very beginning, but I don't begrudge you for not telling me. I'm just sad you've been carrying this heavy burden all alone. I'm your wife, but like I said before, I'm also your friend. I want you to know I'm here for you, and we'll get through this together," Juliette said.

Grandville was moved by the sincerity in Juliette's words. He could barely control himself when he reached out and grabbed her into a strong embrace while gently pulling her body on top of his. He then kissed her hard on her lips with a passion which consumed them both. They couldn't get their clothes off fast enough before they slipped under the covers and back into each other's arms.

Grandville and Juliette became one once again, and the heat they shared threatened to almost burn a hole in the mattress. Juliette had to put a pillow over her mouth to try and muffle her cries of ecstasy as Grandville explored her body with his tongue. His kisses and his touch was reminiscent of home for Juliette, and she eagerly reciprocated her love. In between making love they talked to each other about their future together. It was decided Juliette would reach out to Mr. Bolden, Grandville's Oakhill therapist to see if it was possible to begin family therapy while Grandville was still at Oakhill.

They also decided Grandville would write a letter to their sons and explain about the accident which took Jessica's life and the role Grandville played in it. The intimacy they experienced reinforced Juliette's love for Grandville and vice-versa. Soon it was morning and neither had slept all night. At exactly 6:30 am Grandville rolled out of the bed.

"Where are you going?" Juliette asked.

"Going to make you breakfast," Grandville answered.

"No, I don't want food for breakfast. I want you, now get back into this bed with me baby. I'm freezing, and I need you to warm me up." Juliette said in a sexy tone.

Grandville got back in the bed and pulled Juliette's body close to him and then kissed her softly. He looked into her eyes then said, "I'm going to miss you, but I'm going to work hard so I can come home to you and my kids. Promise me you'll wait for me my love," Grandville eagerly pleaded with her.

"I've been waiting Grandville, and I'll wait longer but only if you are serious about doing the work so you will not hurt us or yourself." Juliette was wrapped up in her husband's strong arms, touching his body with her finger tips and wanting so bad for things to be normal again.

"Juliette, I'll do the work. Telling you about my past is part of what I needed to do in order to truly deal with my problems. I love you and being with you this weekend just reinforced how much. I meant what I said before, if there was or is someone else, he better know that I'll fight for you and my family. I don't care what you have done in the past while I was at Oakhill. Honestly, I don't want to know but from this day forward you belong to me and only me. When I get home I want us to renew our vows, but until then I want you to promise me if there is someone else you'll kick him to the curb," Grandville reiterated looking down at her while his eyes scanned her face, eyes and body.

"Grandville, I'm not currently involved with anyone but you, and I want you to remember that we belong to each other." Juliette reminded him that their love and their friendship was deeper than any of life's problems.

"It's something that I will never forget baby. Never will I let anything get between our love, and that's a promise." Grandville passionately whispered to her and kissed her on the forehead.

"You better not," Juliette said and kissed him on his lips.

Chapter 24

Controversy

Juliette drove down Interstate 70 on her way home from her weekend with Grandville, and she was still on a high from the time they has spent together. She was thankful she and Grandville were given a weekend where they could become reacquainted and be reminded of the love they still shared. She had to stop herself from bursting out into tears when it was time for the visit to end. She and Grandville were saying their goodbyes when Officer Emerson did something that made her tears dry up.

"Stubbs, I have a little surprise for you," Officer Emerson said.

"What is it?" Asked Grandville with a curiosity in his voice.

"I found one of my old Polaroid cameras and it still has film it. I can't allow your Lady Love to use her phone to take a picture or video of you, because it's against Department of Correction policy, but I can use my polaroid camera to take a picture of the two of you which you each could take with you," replied Officer Emerson.

"Thanks so much Officer Emerson we would greatly appreciate it," Grandville stated.

Now, Juliette had a new picture of Grandville, and she could gaze upon his handsome face and reminisce about the time they spent together. One of the conditions of her visit was she had to agree to give the guards her phone. As a result she was virtually unreachable during her weekend with Grandville. As Juliette raced down the highway towards Cleveland, she charged her phone because the phone's battery had died. She had forgot to turn it off when she gave it to begin returning calls. She could only hope and pray nothing crazy happened while she had been with Grandville. It had been years since she had gone off the grid for a weekend, but she had to admit it felt good to not to have to focus on anything or anyone else besides Grandville. It also felt good to have Grandville cater to her with his fantastic culinary skills. She would have to work out for an extra half hour a day for the next week to try and burn off all the calories she consumed during their weekend together.

She then reflected back on her weekend with Grandville. Juliette had to acknowledge to herself, she loved him even more now that he had told her the truth about his past. Grandville had more skeletons than she had ever imaged. Like Greta had advised several months prior, he had secrets. However, his problems were issues which Juliette felt she could deal with now that she knew what they were. Now, she had some idea of what was going on in Grandville's head. He had always been so quiet and though they talked often before he went to Oakhill, she was clueless to the stress he had been internalizing for years.

Her body was still tingling and the memory of his touch was still a clear vision in her mind. She was trying to commit everything he did to her body in her brain to keep her until he returned home.

Grandville had provided her with a possible lead in respect to her cousin's disappearance and made her look at Melinia's situation from a different point of view. Until Grandville brought it up, she had never thought to try and locate Melinia's Drug Rehabilitation facility or attempt to locate people who may have known and helped Melinia prior to her coming to her rooming house. She planned to follow up on the leads as soon as she made it back home to Cleveland.

Juliette also decided, as soon as she returned to home, she would take Greta and her children out to dinner. She planned to call Greta while on the road when her cell phone battery was recharged. She didn't plan to eat while at dinner. She was still full from all the food she consumed with Grandville, but she knew that Greta and the kids would appreciate going out. While she was at dinner she would begin the painful conversation with her sons about where their father had been for more than three years. However, she was committed to the promise which she had made to Grandville. She was going to do her part to help get their family back on track and she would wait for him just like she told him.

She wanted her family to be open about Grandville's condition. She also knew the conversation had to begin with her older children in order to accomplish this goal. She didn't want to be a parent who never dealt with the White Elephant who was sitting in the middle of the room. In her heart, she knew she should have dealt with this subject a long time ago. However, Juliette decided she would make up for lost time as there was no time like the present, and she wanted to begin to explain to the kids sooner, rather than later.

Juliette reflected back to Grandville's story about who his biological father was, and she thought about the parallels to her own life. Mother Stubbs got pregnant after sleeping with her brother-in-law one time. She didn't have an affair with him she just had one indiscretion which was still causing her family pain all these many years later. Juliette didn't know if she would ever reveal her one indiscretion to Grandville. She didn't want to be deceitful to anyone, but telling Grandville would cause everyone involved pain and they had all suffered so much. She wanted her family to begin healing, and she didn't want to do anything which could potentially destroy the peace she had found.

Juliette felt selfish for not revealing her suspicions to Franklin about the possibility that he could be the father of one of her daughters. In some ways she also felt like she was protecting him too. He was Grandville's best friend, and she didn't want him or Grandville to feel conflict in their relationship due to her. In many ways she could relate to how Mother Stubbs must have felt when she found out that she was pregnant. Even though their circumstances were different there were many similarities. Mother Stubbs could never reveal to her sister that she had slept with her husband and Juliette could not reveal to Grandville about what happened between she and Franklin. Both had excellent reasons for keeping their secrets but for Grandville, Mother Stubbs secret resulted into something tragic in his life. She could only hope her secret would not one day wreak havoc on her family.

Juliette had driven for about forty-five minutes when she decided to stop at a rest area so she could use the ladies room and boot her phone up. After she used the rest room she turned her phone on where she noted that she had received 20 missed calls over the course of the weekend. Juliette was becoming anxious and concerned that something had happened to one of her kids as she attempted to search her history to see who had tried to contact her. The number was coming up as anonymous and Juliette looked to see if she had received any messages. She noted that she did have three messages and put the phone to her ear to see who had called. All three messages were from Samantha.

"Juliette this is Samantha, I know we haven't spoken in a long time but I really need to talk to you. Would you please call me as soon as you receive this message at 330-214-3545?"

Juliette was perplexed, she hadn't heard from Samantha in months. She also didn't understand why Samantha's phone number was coming up as anonymous and the number she left was not the number Juliette knew which meant Samantha had changed her number. Juliette was suddenly afraid and sent up a silent prayer that nothing happened to one of Samantha's relatives. The other two messages basically said the same thing as the first message, asking Juliette to call her. Samantha had left a message every day that she was with Grandville.

Juliette sat in her car and decided to call Samantha back before getting back on the road. She was afraid if Samantha would tell her something really bad her driving might be impaired. She held her breath and dialed the number which Samantha had left on her voice mail.

The phone rang three times before Samantha picked up the call.

"Hello," Samantha said.

"Hello Samantha, its Juliette returning your call." Juliette said into her phone.

"Juliette thanks for calling me back. I was hoping you were free, because I want to take you to dinner. I really need to talk to you," Samantha quickly replied.

Juliette was momentarily taken off guard. Samantha had not spoken to her in months, and now she was talking to her as though she was no longer angry. Juliette was happy but curious as to what was going on.

"I'm out of town, but I'm on my way back home now. I won't arrive in Cleveland until approximately 5:30 this evening depending on traffic," Juliette said.

"That's cool. When I see you, you can tell me all about your trip. I know we haven't spoken in a long time and that's my fault but I really need to see you. The sooner we can meet the better. I'll clear my evening to be available for us to sit down to talk," Samantha said.

Even though Samantha was trying to disguise it, Juliette could hear the urgency in Samantha's voice and knew whatever was going on was important.

"Ok, I'll make arrangements for the kids, and I'll meet you at Under at 6:30 pm. I don't know what kind of traffic I'm going to run into, but I'll be there . . . though I might be a little late." Juliette hesitated a little.

"No problem player. I want you to know, I missed you and I can't wait to see you," Samantha replied.

"I missed you too, and I'll see you in a little while." Juliette said and then disconnected the call.

Juliette was cautiously happy about seeing her best friend again, because she wanted to repair their relationship. Together, they had many years of friendship and though Juliette had been angry with Samantha, she really loved her like a sister.

However, Juliette was a little worried about Samantha's request to see her immediately which indicated that whatever she needed to tell her was of the utmost importance.

Juliette decided to call Greta and ask her to pick-up her sons from her Mother's house, and if she would keep all the kids until she made it home from her dinner with Samantha. She needed to start making arrangements if she was going to meet Samantha at Under. Juliette dialed Greta's cell phone number. Greta answered the phone after two rings.

"Hello," Greta said.

"Hello Greta how are the twins? Juliette asked.

"They're fine and we are having a great weekend. Derek took us to the movies and the mall. He wants to end our weekend by taking me and the girls to dinner. I know you miss your kids, but will you let me have the girls this evening?" Greta requested.

"Actually, I was calling you to ask if you could keep them longer so this works out perfectly. I was also hoping that you could pick up the boys and take them too," Juliette responded.

"No problem the more the merrier. Is everything okay?" Greta inquired.

"Everything is fine. I will be on the road for a few more hours, and as soon as I arrive in Cleveland I'm meeting Samantha at Under," Juliette explained.

"I thought you guys were not speaking? Greta questioned.

"I thought we weren't either, but Samantha left me several messages while I was away, and I just talked to her. She says she needs to see me right away, and I can tell whatever she needs to talk to me about is important," Juliette replied.

"Hopefully she will be apologizing to you for the way she's treated you. I want you to know I don't have anything against Samantha. I just didn't like how she had been treating me and I'm not feeling Tara either. That stunt she tried to pull with Derek proves she's scandalous and cannot be trusted.

"I know . . . I know Greta you're right."

"You and Samantha were very close. You guys have been friends for years, so I'm hoping your meeting is the first step in repairing your relationship," Greta said.

"I do too. I really love Samantha, and our falling out was partially my fault. I was mean and venomous in the letter that I wrote. I know, I hurt Samantha. I'm a woman, and I'm prepared to apologize for my role in our fight," Juliette said.

"That's why I love you so much. You have and will always be real. When you're wrong you take responsibility for your actions. I wish more people were like you."

"Thanks Greta. It's important for me to keep it real, because life is way too short," Juliette humbly replied.

"So, how was your trip?" Greta asked.

"It was good. I'll tell you all the details as soon as I get home."

"If I'm going to pick up the boys I'd better get going. Derek will be here in a few minutes to pick us up for dinner," Greta said.

"Why don't you wait until he gets there before you pick up the boys? Take my Volvo SUV, because it has more room and the twins car seats are already in it. You still have the spare keys that I gave you? Juliette asked.

"Yes, I still have them. Okay, that's a good idea. I'll take the SUV." Greta joked.

"Good, I need to call my Mom and let her know you're on your way to pick up the boys, so she can have them ready. Please make sure they have everything they brought with them. The kids are always forgetting their belongings and pressing me to go out of my way to pick up whatever they have left."

"Okay. Well, I better get off the phone so I can be ready when Derek arrives."

"Alright. I'll see you later on this evening. I'll text you as soon as I arrive in Cleveland to let you know I made it back into town." Juliette said, and then she disconnected the call.

After calling her Mother to let her know Greta was on her way to pick-up the boys. Juliette called Violet to ensure everything was running smoothly at A Better Tomorrow. Juliette drove down the highway and focused her mind back to Grandville and their reconciliation. Juliette was happy that she had finally made a decision in respect to her relationship with Grandville. However, she was unsure if she was ready to share the plans her and Grandville had made with anyone else besides Greta and her immediate family. Juliette decided to play it by ear in respect to others.

Greta and her Mom thought she had attended a Sorority Convention. It was perfect timing, because the convention was held at the same time as her visit with Grandville. Only Emily her therapist and the Oakhill Prison Officials were aware she had actually been with Grandville. But, she did plan to tell her Mom and Greta where she had really been when she got home.

Juliette headed towards 71 North after exiting Interstate 70 towards Cleveland. She decided to stop at another rest area, so she could again use the ladies room and quickly stretch her legs. Drinking bottled water during her drive resulted in a need to constantly relieve herself. When she exited her rented Ford Focus she noted a Black Honda Accord with tinted windows pull up next to her. Juliette glanced at the vehicle and quickly walked towards the ladies room as it was frigidly cold out.

When she returned to her rented vehicle she saw a huge dent on the driver's side of her white rented vehicle. She also noted black paint specs mixed into the white paint. The black Honda had also had white on the passengers' door. Juliette quickly realized whoever had gotten out of the passenger side of the black Honda had hit the driver side door of her rented Focus with such force it had dented it. Juliette was furious. She had rented the vehicle for her trip to visit Grandville mainly to prevent putting extra miles on her SUV. She had very few miles on her vehicle, because she did not use her SUV when she took road trips. Also, A Better Tomorrow was relatively close to her home, and as a result she did not have to drive far, which resulted in less miles being put on her vehicle.

Juliette took out a pen and paper and wrote down the license plate number of the Honda and used her cell phone camera to take pictures and video of both vehicles and waited for the driver of the vehicle to return. She didn't want to have to file a claim with her insurance company, because she had declined to purchase the rental company's insurance. She was sitting in her rented vehicle with the heat blasting when she spied the driver of the Honda approach. The driver was a tall dark African American man with curly hair and a strong jaw line. His companion was a short, very light skinned African American woman who looked like she had been soliciting in Downtown Cleveland. As the woman approached the car she pulled her skirt down and attempted to fix her clothes. Juliette got out of her car as the couple got to the Honda doors.

"Excuse me." Juliette said to the unknown man and woman.

The man looked Juliette up and down and then smiled and said in a suggestive tone. "Yes, can I help you with something?"

"It appears when you all got of your vehicle you accidently hit my car and dented it," Juliette explained.

"That's crazy. How do I know your car didn't have the dent in it when you pulled into this rest area?" The man sarcastically questioned.

"This is a rental car, and I assure you there wasn't a dent in this door until you parked next to me. Look you can see the paint from your door on my car. Also the paint from the rental is on your door." Juliette irritated that the man would even suggest she was lying about the incident.

The man walked around to where Juliette was standing and looked at the door, and then he glanced at his companion and gave her a withering look. The woman suddenly seemed afraid.

"Get your ass into the car." The man said to his companion who scurried into the car with light quickness.

"I still don't know if this car had a dent in it when we arrived. At any rate I'm not taking responsibility for the damage. I did nothing to your car. Now, my escort who I barely know may have done it by accident when she got out of the car, but I didn't see her do it. I'm late for another engagement. So, how about I provide you with her information. You can contact her later to make arrangements to pay for the damage," the man said.

"Excuse me but that's not going to work. I need to exchange information with both you and your lady friend. I don't know you, and I'm not trying to get stuck having to pay for this dent," Juliette stated.

"Well, unfortunately you will have no other choice, but to take my word for it. Like I said before, I'm late for another appointment. Now, if you have a pen and paper I suggest you write down this information." The man said with an attitude.

Juliette was incensed as she struggled to maintain control. "I don't have a pen or paper. But, you do what you think you have to do, and I will do what I have to do," Juliette said.

"What's that supposed to mean?" The man questioned.

"If you don't want to exchange information then you are leaving me no other choice but to call the authorities," Juliette stated very angry about the whole incident.

"Do what you have to do." The man stated and then walked around to the driver's side of his vehicle, open the door and sped off.

Juliette was furious. She pulled out her cell phone and contacted the State Highway Patrol. She had to wait more than forty-five minutes before two Officers from the State Highway Patrol arrived. Juliette showed them the video which she made and the pictures that she took. She also advised the Officers of what the Unknown man had said to her. The Officers took all the information and gave her a report number. As a result of having to wait for the Officers to arrive Juliette was way off of her schedule. She was also potentially being faced with having to make a claim with her insurance company which was a five-hundred dollar deductible.

Juliette was more than one hour late for her meeting with Samantha. When she finally arrived at Under, she was furious with the Unknown Man and his companion for costing her time and potential money. As she walked into the club she saw Samantha at a small table next to a wall. After greeting the owners of the club she made her way to the table where Samantha was seated.

"Hello Samantha I'm sorry for being late, but you wouldn't believe what I've just been through trying to get here," Juliette told her.

"It's not a problem. I'm just glad you came. I was starting to get worried you would stand me up," Samantha chuckled a little.

"I would never do anything like that. I know we have not spoken in a while, but I'm still a woman of my word," Juliette said.

"I knew you would come that's why I'm still here," Samantha said.

"You are not going to believe what happened to me on my way back home to Cleveland."

"What happened?" Samantha asked

"I stopped at a rest area to use the ladies room, and when I came out there was a huge dent in my driver's side door. It was apparent the car parked right next to me dented my car when the passenger got out, because the driver apparently parked too close to my car. I waited for the driver and his female passenger to come out of the rest room. When they returned the driver told me, he was not taking responsibility for the damage to my vehicle. Do you know this idiot refused to give me his or his passenger's information? That's why I'm late getting here to you. I had to wait for The State Highway Patrol to make a police report," Juliette said.

"Are you for real?" Samantha asked.

"As real as a heart attack. Now, I'm going to have to pay a five-hundred dollar deductible in order to get the dent fixed," Juliette explained.

"That's messed up. Also, I know how much you love your Volvo SUV, and it's a bummer that this fool and his bimbo damaged it, "Samantha said.

"The only good thing about this whole situation is that I was not driving the SUV. I rented a Ford Focus. You know how much I hate putting extra miles on my Volvo. I took video and pictures of both my rental and of his car, and I got his license plate number. The State Highway Patrol said, they would send their report to the State Prosecutors office. The guy could be charged with leaving the scene of an accident. However, since there was not technically an accident, and there are no witnesses the Prosecutor might decline to charge the guy," Juliette explained.

"That's a damn shame. People kill me. His actions damage your property, and he has the audacity to not give up his information so that he can attempt to rectify the situation. I'm really sorry you're going through this. Is there anything I can do?" Samantha asked.

"No but I really appreciate you asking."

"Juliette I asked to meet with you this evening for two reasons. The first is, I want to apologize to you for how I treated you. I was wrong. I know that, and I don't really have an excuse for my behavior. I had someone else in my ear, and I let that someone get in my head. You were right to stand up for Greta, because she is your family. You also were right to expect me to treat her with respect, because she is with you just like you said in your letter."

"Samantha, I also owe you an apology. My letter was mean, and it was never my intent to hurt you."

"I know Juliette. It's okay, because I probably deserved it considering how I acted. I want you to know although I acted ugly, I thought of you almost every day. There were so many times I almost picked-up the phone to call you, but I was afraid of how you would respond."

"It's okay. You're here now, and we're going to put all that happened behind us," Juliette said.

"I also needed to see you for another reason. I want you to understand that what I'm about to convey to you is very sensitive, and as such I'm going to need to swear you to secrecy, "Samantha explained.

"I totally understand. Whatever it is sounds really serious," Juliette said.

"It's serious. That's why I called you from a throw away cell phone to set-up this meeting, because I'm not supposed to tell anyone what I'm about to tell you. If anyone traces my phones they'll not know our meeting was prearranged. As far as anyone is concerned we just ran into each other at Under and reconnected," Samantha stated.

Juliette was suddenly very nervous, because she knew whatever Samantha was about to say was very serious.

"As the County Prosecutor my Office sometimes has to work with the FBI when they are investigating Federal Crimes which might be occurring here in Northeast Ohio. A couple of days ago two FBI Agents met with me and my cybercrimes unit about a crime which they believe is happening here in Cleveland. I'm about to show you something, but I'm going to ask that you give absolutely no indication of what you are watching. I'm going to warn you up front that what you are about to see will disturb you so put your game face on," Samantha said.

Juliette felt her heart racing, and she calmed her breathing in an attempt to brace for whatever Samantha was about to show her. Samantha reached into her purse and pulled out a small portable DVD player. She discretely passed the device to Juliette.

"Watch the video, it is short and remember what I said." Samantha directed her in a stern manner.

Juliette took the machine and pushed play and had to do everything in her power not to scream when she saw the video was of Melinia and an unknown man whose face was not visible. Melinia was high out of her mind as she performed various sex acts on the man. The man's face suddenly became visible and Juliette realized that she recognized the man. His curly hair and strong jaw line was unmistakable, the man was the driver of the black Honda which dented her rental. Juliette could only stomach a few minutes of the video before she closed the DVD player and quickly passed it back to Samantha.

"Juliette, I know you and your family are worried about Melinia and this is why I felt that it was important for me to show you this video. I want you to know according to the FBI, this video was made about three weeks ago. From what we can gather Melinia is very much alive but being held as part of a Human Sex Trafficking Ring. The women in the ring are all addicted to Heroin and their captors are using Heroin to control them and to get them to perform the sex acts. We have come to learn that many of the sex traffickers are former and current drug dealers who have learned that selling women is better financially for them. The women are their property, and they can sell their captives over and over again and in essence turning them into modern day slaves. The leaders of these rings keep the women high and feed them fast food for every meal which is cheap. The women are addicted, so they will do whatever they have to do to make sure they get their fix. It's a terrible cycle and unfortunately your cousin is seriously caught up in it," Samantha explained.

"Samantha I'm about ninety percent positive the guy in the video is the guy who was driving the Honda that just damaged my rental," Juliette said.

"Are you sure?" Samantha asked.

"Yes, relatively sure unless the guy has a twin," Juliette replied.

"Okay, give me the license plate number, and I'll have my office run the plates and try and locate this guy. We don't know if the guy in the video is a John or one of the people holding your cousin and the other women. We hope he may be able to give us some valuable information on where the women are being held. All we know for sure is someone is broadcasting freak shows across the internet and the FBI agents are relatively sure the videos are being broadcast from somewhere in our area," Samantha said.

"Samantha I want to thank you for sharing this information with me. I've been under such stress, because I was afraid Melinia was dead. I feel much better knowing there's a strong possibility that she's alive, but she's still seriously at risk. Whoever is holding her or one of the Johns who she is forced to have sex with could kill her or she could overdose," Juliette stated.

"You are right which is why we're trying to find Melinia and the other women as soon as possible. We have to be extra careful, because if Melinia's captors find out we are close to maybe finding them, they'll just move their operation to another city," Samantha explained.

"I totally understand, and I'll not tell anyone about what you have shared with me," Juliette said.

"I trust you Juliette even though I know I said that I didn't. I was just angry with you because my feelings were hurt. I read your letter and I wondered if that's how you really feel about me."

"Samantha, I was very angry also. All I wanted was for you to hear where I was coming from. I'm sorry about the whole thing, and I should not have let myself get that angry. I should have tried to talk to you way before it got out of hand. I just don't like to argue with you. You are my girl and I don't like to see you upset, but how we both handled the situation was wrong," Juliette said.

"I couldn't agree with you more so let's make a promise here and now that we will talk to each other no matter what it is when we are upset about something," Samantha said.

"I promise to never let things get out of hand again." Juliette assured Samantha.

"I promise too. You're my best friend and you should be with me. I've finally achieved one of my professional goals and to have you out of my life was hell and only pride stopped me from reaching out to you. I'm sorry your cousin is missing. I should've been right here next to you helping you to make it through this.

"It's okay Samantha. You have so much on your plate as it is."

"But, I promise I will be here now and in the future. I also promise to make things right with Greta. Like you said in your letter, I had no right to treat her the way I did. I'm not going to lie to you, I have never really cared for her. I also know several people who don't care for her including that scandalous witch Tara. I found out that Tara is a really jealous person, and that may have influenced her intense dislike for Greta. I also have to admit I let her get in my head when it came to Greta," Samantha said.

Juliette shook her head and thought about Tara who had proved to be an extremely dirty witch. Juliette remembered when Tara called Greta and asked her to have dinner with her and Greta went as requested. According to Greta, Tara spent the whole dinner encouraging Greta to stand up to Samantha for being rude to her. Juliette realized from the moment Tara saw Derek she had a master plan to try and get him. Tara would say and do anything to accomplish her goal. Juliette was also curious as to what made Samantha see Tara for what she really was. However, the drive, the stress of the day, finding out Melinia was being held against her will, and the one alcoholic drink which she had consumed was really getting to her and she was suddenly exhausted. Samantha who had not seen Juliette in a long time could still read her like a book.

"Juliette, I know you're exhausted after your trip, and the news I just laid on you regarding your cousin has to be overwhelming. We have plenty of time to catch up. I want you to go home and get some rest. I'll call you in a few days so you can come over for dinner. Then, we can really talk, and I can thank you for forgiving me," Samantha said with sincerity.

"Samantha I love you like a sister, you don't have to thank me. You know for a fact that me and my sisters are always getting into it. But, we always come through for each other when it's necessary. Just like you came through for me with this information about my cousin. I want you to know I really appreciate it too. I recognize you took a big risk sharing this information with me, and I promise you I will tell no one. I'm just happy Melinia is alive, because I have been thinking the worst," Juliette said.

"I know you've been worried that's why I knew that despite our argument I had to tell you. Whoever is running the ring that's holding Melinia has a computer genius on their payroll. Whoever he is has made it very difficult for us to find them. He or she is using a sophisticated scrambling device, and it's making their actual location almost impossible to track. Melinia and the rest of the young ladies could be anywhere in Northeast Ohio. All we know for sure is that the ring appears to be operating here in our area.

"Wow . . . people are really crazy and selfish to hurt women like that and men too," Juliette said.

"Enough about Melinia, I want you to go home now and get some rest. I'll take care of the bill and James who is one of the Security personnel here at Under and a Cleveland police officer is going to walk you to your car. I'll call you in a few days. Maybe I'll have more info on Melinia that I can share with you when you come to my house for dinner." Samantha said as she stood up and hugged Juliette.

"Thank you Samantha."

"No thanks is necessary. I will see you soon."

"Ok." Juliette replied.

Chapter 25

Olivia

(Lost and Turned Out)

Grandville lay in his lumpy little bed and reflected back to his time with Juliette and smiled. He was grateful his visit with Juliette had went according to his plans. His fantasy regarding Juliette forgiving him and allowing him to make love to her again had become part of his reality. He felt like bricks had been lifted out of his soul since he had unburdened himself of his many secrets.

Juliette had responded more favorably then he could have ever imagined to his truth. He felt foolish for keeping the information about his past from her for so long. He couldn't wait until he could see Montell, so he could tell him about how great his visit had went with Juliette. But, he had to wait until after he was cleared to return back to the general population before he could see any of the inmates at Oakhill. While he was waiting for the facility to complete his process Officer Emerson slipped into his cell to talk to him.

"Stubbs I want you to know I just learned my supervisor accepted a package for me which was delivered to Oakhill while we were away at the extended family visit. I opened the package, and I almost didn't believe my eyes. The package contained a signed Rayshawn Robinson Jersey and a basketball which is autographed by Rayshawn Robinson and several members of the LA's. Both are worth a fortunate and my son is going to be the happiest teenager on earth. I'm going to buy a glass case where he can display his ball and Jersey. I want to thank you for coming through above and beyond our original deal," Officer Emerson said.

"No Officer Emerson, I thank you for helping me to pull off the best weekend of my life and certainly the highlight of my time here at Oakhill. I didn't realize the magnitude of how much I missed my wife until I spent time with her. What you did by picking up the food for me helped to make our time together even more special."

"I'm glad you and your Lady Love had a great time. I just wanted to stop by and thank you, because I'm going to be off for a couple of days. I also want to let you know you're now cleared to go back into the general population," Officer Emerson stated.

"Thanks Officer Emerson and please enjoy your time off," Grandville said.

"I will and I want you to try and stay out of trouble." Officer Emerson replied as he left Grandville's cell.

Grandville got off of his lumpy little bed and immediately searched out Montell who was in his cell sitting on his bed.

"Montell, I'm back." Grandville high-fived him.

"I know and I have been waiting for you. Did you have a great time?" Montell asked.

"I think my time with Juliette was the best time I've ever experienced in my life," Grandville replied.

"Do you want to play a game of chess and tell me about it?" Montell inquired.

"You bet I do. Be prepared to get crushed by my kingdom," Grandville teased.

"I've heard that before. Set the board up and tell your kingdom to get ready to take the beat down I'm about to deliver to you all," Montell teased back.

Grandville looked around Montell's cell while Montell set the chess board-up and noted that the cell was almost bare as Montell was clearing out his sparse belongings to prepare for his release.

"Montell how does it feel to know, in approximately one week you will be walking out of Oakhill?" Grandville questioned him.

"It feels damned good, but the only problem I'm having is, I'm going to truly miss one of my best friends. A man who I'm going to be leaving in here," Montell said.

"Now who might that be, Big Joe? Grandville teased.

"Go ahead with that, you know I'm referring to you. You're my Dogg and it's going to be hard not talking to you every day like I have for more than the past three years," Montell said.

"All jokes aside, it's going to be hard for me too. Making friends with you is what has made Oakhill bearable for me. The only silver lining to all of this is, I plan to walk out of those doors someday soon and reclaim what has been taken from me when I got sick.

"I know man . . . damn . . . we both will be out soon." Montell was trying to encourage Grandville.

"When I get out of here, I promise I'll have your number on speed dial. We'll talk everyday just like we have been since I came to Oakhill. I'll also meet you once a week to continue to beat your behind in Chess," Grandville joked.

"Whatever. I want you to know, I'll be praying for both you and your family," Montell said.

"Thanks Montell. I am going to need all the prayers I can get. While at the visit I was able to apologize in person to Juliette for what happened with Jessica, and I feel like a weight has been lifted off of me. However, what is most important is that she has forgiven me. She and I plan to renew our wedding vows as soon as I'm released from Oakhill.

"I'm so happy for you Grandville. I told you man . . ."

"In our short time together I feel like we definitely reconnected. I'm going to work very hard to get out of here. I have to get back to her and my freedom.

"She'll be there waiting for you. They say that men shouldn't pray or cry, but I was praying so hard for you my brother that everything would work out for you and Juliette."

"Thank you so much, because I was so worried about how things would turn out with the visit," Grandville confessed.

"I know . . ."

"I start my support group tomorrow. It's my hope, like you once said, listening to everyone's horror stories will help me to put my own story into perspective," Grandville honestly confided in his friend.

"I'm proud of you Grandville, and I believe you have grown since you've come here to Oakhill. Everything which happened has to be part of the Lord's divine plan. I believe we were destined to meet, but I just wish it was not under these circumstances.

"Tell me about it," Grandville said.

"I know we met once before we both came here to Oakhill, but we wouldn't have gotten to know each other as well if we were not incarcerated here together. Maybe, we would not have even known each other at all. Especially if we hadn't been sent here and ended up in cells next door to each other. After all, at first glance we have absolutely nothing in common," Montell said.

"I have never looked at it quite that way before, and I would have to agree with you. Greta also told me she believed that me coming to Oakhill was part of the Lord's plan.

"See, I'm not the only one who knew there was a divine intervention," Montell laughed.

Guess what? You're never going to believe what Juliette told me while at the visit, Grandville said.

"No, I will never guess so go ahead and tell me," Montell replied.

"I'm once again the father of twins, this last time I made two girls. They are almost three years old, and I didn't even know they existed until Juliette told me," Grandville said.

"Man that's crazy. What're their names?" Montell asked.

"Jolene and Janae. I have a picture of them in my cell and Janae looks just like me and even has my eye color. I'm in amazement that Juliette gave birth to two more healthy kids under the circumstance she endured. I just wish I had been there to help her now that she has four kids and a Better Tomorrow to run she needs me home in my right state of mind," Grandville stated.

"Good, I'm glad you've come to realize just how much Juliette and your family needs you. You've already missed almost three years of your daughter's lives so you definitely have to work hard to get out of here," Montell stated.

"You're so right. I've decided to stop feeling sorry for myself. I'm now coming to terms with the fact that I have a mental health disease. My Counselor told me, twenty-five percent of the population suffers with a mental health problem. I'm starting to accept the fact that I'm now an official member of that group. I feel grateful that Juliette has forgiven me and is willing to give me a second chance to prove to her that though I might have changed, I'm still the man she fell in love with," Grandville quietly replied.

"I can definitely relate. I can also honestly say that though I'm happy about getting out of Oakhill I'm also scared to death," Montell stated.

"What are you afraid of?" Grandville asked him.

"Man, I'm afraid of having another episode with my Brief Psychotic Disorder. I've never had that happen to me before or since but who's to say it won't happen again." Montell admitted questioning himself and wondering if he could control himself if he was to break down again.

"Montell you just have to trust yourself. You became sick because of what you saw happening to Monty. The odds of something like that happening again are very low." Grandville told him point blank it was the incident which caused his breakdown.

"I'm afraid, though I have no intentions of ever losing control again, the fact is I could. I don't ever want to hurt Monty or my Maria."

"You won't. Just do what the doctors have told you and you should be just fine. Also, you have to forgive yourself for what has already happened. That's what you told me, and that's what I'm really working on myself. We can't do anything about what has already happened. "

"I know, but just thinking about it is scary to me."

"A great man once told me that we can only change our present and our future but not our past," Grandville said.

"What great man said that?"

"You my friend are the great man behind that particular quote, and I really believe you should take your own advice."

"Thanks Grandville, but seriously the closer I get to my release date the more nervous I'm becoming."

"I think that's normal. Things have changed since we have come here to Oakhill, but you'll adapt like you adapted when you were brought here. Just try to go with the flow and use what you don't know to bond with Monty. Ask him to give you a tutorial on how to use your cell phone and the computer."

"That's a great idea," Montell said.

"Tomorrow I start my Survivors Support Group. Right after my group I'm going to meet with Franklin. Hopefully, he'll have news on when you can start your job," Grandville stated.

"I sure hope I can start right away. One of the conditions of my release is that I have to get a job immediately. I'll also have to work with a mental health counselor and a psychiatrist as well as meet with my providers every two weeks. They'll have to assess my progress and ensure my mental health is in check. I also have to report once a month to my Parole Officer where I'll be given random drug and alcohol tests. It's my understanding my Parole Officer and my mental health providers are part of a special team who works with individuals that are transitioning from Oakhill and other mental health facilities and prisons." Montell wanted to explain his plans to Grandville which also helped him to get a grip on the follow-up schedule he would have to work through on the outside of Oakhill.

"Cool once you're released, you'll begin convincing everyone on your team that you're fine and what happened with Monty's Karate Instructor was an isolated incident." Grandville added to the conversation to ensure Montell wasn't beating himself up too bad again.

Later after Montell beat him in chess, Grandville lay in his lumpy little bed and reflected on the past few days. He was beyond happy that he was again a father but what Montell said was right, while he was at Oakhill he was missing a large part of his daughters' lives. He wanted them to know him and to develop a bond which only daughters can have with their fathers. The Lord designed it so the first man who would take care of a woman is her father. This is where a young lady is supposed to learn how a man should treat her, and also where she learns the man's role is to protect and provide for her and their family. He wanted so much to teach and guide all of his children, because he wanted them to grow up with the one thing which he never had, a father. Grandville knew he could not teach his children anything as long as he resided at Oakhill.

The next morning after another almost inedible breakfast of watery grits and mystery meat patties, he was the first person at the Survivors Support Group that Mr. Bolden had scheduled him to attend. He sat down and watched in amazement at the large number of inmates who completely filled up the medium sized room. The biggest shocker for him was when Big Joe walked into the room and took one of the chairs which was closer to the front of the room. Grandville purposely sat in the back of the room and attempted to make himself invisible. The support group leader soon took his seat in the very front of the room and Grandville sat patiently and waited for him to begin.

"Welcome everyone my name is Mr. Grange, and I'm the Facilitator of the Oakhill Survivor support group. The group runs for twelve weeks and once you have completed this program you will have the option to attend a second twelve week advanced Survivors support group. We're going to begin, but before we do so let's go over the ground rules which we expect every participant to abide by.

First, what is said in this room stays in this room. There is a confidentiality statement that every participant has signed in order to be a member of this group. If we find out any member has breached this agreement, he will immediately be removed from the group. He will also face punishment from the Oakhill Administration. Secondly, absolutely no profanity will be allowed and there will be absolutely no yelling or fighting. This is a safe environment where those who have experienced abuse can talk about their trauma openly and without judgement.

Now, we're going to do introductions, and today I will tell the group my story. Then starting next week, one participant of this group will tell the rest of us his story. Everyone who is a member of this survivor group will have their name placed in this brown paper bag. Every week at the end of the meeting, a name will be chosen from this bag and the named individual will tell his story to the group at the next meeting. If the rules as outlined are not acceptable to you, now is the time for you to get up and leave. As an inmate here at Oakhill you have very little control over your choices or your person. However, being a member of this group is one area where you do have a small measure of control. If you don't want to be a member of this group or do the work which will help you heal, get up and leave now." Mr. Grange was adamant about setting the rules for the group, and everybody could tell he was very serious about the men wanting to be a part of the group and to talk about their personal stories.

"When you talk about your problems it helps you with both forms of communication which are intrapersonal (dealing with your-self internally) and interpersonal (dealing with others externally outside of yourself).

Everyone in the room remained quiet and no one got up to leave.

"Good, now that we have that out of the way, please start introducing yourself starting with the first gentleman seated to my right," Mr. Grange said pointing to a tall, brown skinned, and very handsome, young man who also looked like he should not be in the room. Grandville had seen him many times while at Oakhill, and he was always very quiet and reserved.

After all the inmates introduced themselves, Mr. Grange began telling his story.

"Abusers exist in all genders, races, religions and in every socio-economic status. Some-times abusers are members of our families, co-workers, friends, acquaintances and even strangers. I was assaulted by several of my co-workers who I believed were my friends. I was a proud member of the United States Marines when I was gang raped by five members of my Company. I had just re-enlisted and had been deployed to Iraq when I was attacked in the shower by individuals who were supposed to be my Brothers in arms and who had taken a vow to protect me against the enemy. I'm not Gay and though this fact is irrelevant, I tried to make sense of why this happened to me.

I did not report the assault because I was embarrassed. Also, because I was fearful of what my fellow soldiers would think about me. I was afraid my peers would think that I was gay, and I was also afraid that if the rest of my company found out what happened to me I would be assaulted again. My self-esteem plummeted while I contemplated if my attackers saw something in me that I didn't see in myself. They made me feel weak and vulnerable and to make matters worse I had to see the men who raped me every day, and they behaved like what they did to me was no big deal.

The stress of my ordeal caused me to suffer an emotional breakdown. I couldn't sleep, I lost my appetite and found absolutely no joy in living. I was seriously considering suicide and my superiors were concerned about my performance. I was a very good solider and overnight I stopped caring. I was sent home to Toledo, Ohio to get some rest. I was only supposed to be home for three weeks when my mind snapped.

My parents could tell when I came home something was wrong, but they attributed my behavior to my having viewed the horrors of the war. At the time I couldn't tell them or anyone what had happened to me. One day while I was at home I went to the Mall where I saw a guy who looked like one of the Marines who had assaulted me. I thought he was following me, because when I went into one of the jewelry stores he seemed to be right behind me. In my mind this Marine was sent from my Company to ensure I didn't tell anyone what he and his friends had done to me.

I waited until the guy came out of the mall and was on his way to his car in the parking lot and then I attacked him. I punched him in his jaw without provocation or warning. The guy fought me back and in the midst of our physical altercation I body slammed him and he hit his head on the cement and died. The Police were called and I was arrested for Involuntary Manslaughter.

It was at this point that I suffered a complete nervous breakdown to the point where I was unresponsive and almost comatose. I was sent to the State Psychiatric Hospital where the Psychiatrists and Mental Health clinicians did their best to restore me to competency. Like many of you, I came here to Oakhill voluntarily and of my own volition. I could have attempted to be found Not Guilty by Reason of Insanity. There was a strong chance I would have won my case, but when I learned who I killed I could barely live with myself.

Charles Desaul was at the Mall looking for a wedding ring for his pregnant girlfriend when he had the unlucky experience of running into me. He had just graduated from college and had recently enlisted in the Marines where after basic training he would have been an Officer. I was distraught and realized that my actions had destroyed a whole family of innocent people's lives.

I made a deal with the Prosecutors and was sent here to Oakhill where the Psychiatrists and my Clinical team helped me to understand the stages of grief and how trauma played a role in my underlying mental state. I walked out of Oakhill three years ago, but I volunteer my time to facilitate this Survivor Group. I'm now able to tell my story without shame or stigma. While I was at Oakhill, I learned valuable information which helped to make me the man I am today.

There were more than fourteen-thousand men who were sexually assaulted while enlisted in the Military in 2012. My goal is to help Survivors understand that what happened to them was not their fault. This group will help you learn and understand the Phases of Trauma Recovery. We'll start with the first phase of Trauma Recovery known as Safety and Stabilization. This stage is very important and will include helping you all understand the emotional and overwhelming stress associated with trauma. It's like a bottle of soda which has been shaken, and when the top is opened it explodes all over the place with no care of who it hits.

In order to be considered for this group you had to be recommended by your Oakhill Counselor, and it's been assumed you have done the preliminary work to handle the stress of reliving your trauma. It's my hope by the time you've finished this process each and every one of you will be able to also tell your story without fear or shame, and that you will have gained an understanding of how trauma has played a role in your underlying mental health. Now, I'm going to ask the gentleman to my left to pull the name of the next Survivor who will tell his story at our next meeting," Mr. Grange said.

Mr. Grange shook the brown paper bag which held the names of all the participants of the Survivor group. Then, looked at Oliver who was an inmate at Oakhill and who was sitting to Mr. Grange's immediate left. Oliver reached his hand into the bag and pulled out a folded piece of paper and then handed it to Mr. Grange.

"The individual who will present his story at our next meeting is Joseph Jacobs," Mr. Grange announced.

Grandville glanced at Big Joe who seemed to be in shock that he would be the first inmate at the group to tell his story. The support group meeting soon ended and Grandville rushed back to his cell to await word that Franklin had arrived for their visit.

It wasn't long before one of the Officers came to his cell to retrieve him and escorted him to the Attorney's Visiting Room.

As soon as Grandville arrived at the visiting room Franklin took one look at him and knew his visit with Juliette went well.

"How was your visit with Juliette? Judging by the smile on your face, I would say it was a huge success," Franklin smiled.

"Thanks for asking Franklin. The visit was great, and I want to thank you for arranging it for me. Juliette has helped me to see I need to do everything necessary to get out of Oakhill, so I can help her with raising our children and being a good husband. I also want to thank you for arranging for Officer Emerson to receive his package. I'm also assuming you were able to speak to Rayshawn, because Montell is being released from Oakhill next week. I really want to make sure he can start working as soon as he gets out of here," Grandville stated.

"Yes, I was able to sit down and talk to Rayshawn in private, and he had a stack of autographed balls and jerseys in his office. He gave me one of each. You were right when you said, he would reimburse you with interest for what you've spent on trying to locate Melinia. He actually had Zach to send you a cashier's check in the amount of fifty-thousand dollars. I was tripping on how much he sent. So, when I received the check, I called Zach who advised me Rayshawn wanted to ensure your efforts in respect to trying to locate Melinia would not cause you financial stress. So, he paid you for what you have already spent and gave you an advance for future fees. He also said, tell you if there is any money left after we've found Melinia to keep it as a tip. I put the funds from the check in your safety deposit box, and I want to get your okay to pay McNaulty before I did anything else. He called me the other day and asked me to come to his office," Franklin said.

"He asked you to come into his office to talk to you about the bill?" Grandville questioned.

"Not exactly. He actually got a lead on Melinia and wanted to show me what he found."

"Well what did he find?" Grandville questioned impatiently.

"Looks like Melinia is alive and she is all over the web," Franklin replied.

"Franklin what does that mean? Connect the dots for me," Grandville said.

"Melinia is performing freak shows that can only be accessed on the internet. It doesn't look like she's performing by choice. She's out of her mind high and she looks scared. You can hear someone in the background directing her to do the various sex acts. McNaulty is a very good Detective. He used the social security number we provided him and was able to access the Ohio BMV where he got an old driver's license for Melinia. He took a copy of her driver's license picture and scanned it into a software program that analyzes internet video and pictures. He was able to use the program to locate Melinia on the Freakshow website. The bad news is though we know what Melinia is doing we have no idea where Melinia is. Whoever is holding her has scrambled their internet signal and McNaulty has no idea where she is being held. She may not even be in Ohio," Franklin advised.

"Oh my God. Juliette was right about Melinia being held against her will. She was adamant that she would not just leave and not tell someone in their family where she was," Grandville commented wondering what they could do to find out where she is being held.

"McNaulty says, he doesn't think Lovelle has anything to do with Melinia's disappearance. Lovelle is still looking for Melinia, and he has all his hired hands scouring the streets trying to find her because she allegedly owes him money. We have to decide what's the next steps that we want McNaulty to take. He wants to know if you want him to contact the police, so that he can share what he's found and make sure that the police are also looking for Melinia too," Franklin said.

"We really need to be careful. I don't want Juliette or Greta to know how involved we've been in our efforts to locate Melinia. Also, according to Juliette she and her family are working with the police already. The police probably already know what Melinia is being forced to do. During our extended family visit I promised Juliette to never keep secrets from her. I don't want to blow our reconciliation. Please ask McNaulty to stand down for now and to continue to monitor the website that Melinia is doing the Freakshow from. Maybe he will pick up a clue as to where she's being held by watching the site," Grandville instructed him.

"I heard you when you said, you and Juliette reconciled. I want you to know I'm thrilled for the both of you."

"Thanks Franklin, and I want you to know, I owe it all to you. I won't ever forget all that you've done for me."

"Grandville you're my best friend and you don't have to thank me. How did Officer Emerson like his kid's gift?" Franklin asked.

"He was more than pleased. He says, he is going to buy some glass cases so his son can display his Jersey and Ball."

"So, how did your meals turn out?" Franklin questioned.

"They turned out perfect. Thanks again for ordering the food for me so Officer Emerson could pick it up and deliver it to the hotel. Juliette and the Guards seemed to really enjoy the food. We had a pre-Thanksgiving dinner which was one of the highlight of my time with her. While we were together she told me something that blew my mind." Grandville said

"What did she tell you?" Franklin asked.

"She told me that she gave birth to twin girls while I've been locked up. Their names are Jenae and Jolene, and they are close to turning three years old. She showed me a picture and Janae looks just like me and even has my eye color. She didn't want me to know about the girls until she was sure I was getting better given all that has happened," Grandville stated.

"That's crazy. How did I miss the fact that Juliette had two more kids?" Franklin questioned.

"Juliette said, she purposely stayed away from you. She kept the girls a secret from you, because she didn't want me to find out. She also swore Greta to secrecy and told her that she wouldn't allow her to see the kids if she told you or I about the girls.

"What . . .!

"Honestly, I'm not even mad about it. I'm just glad she came to the visit and told me to my face about my daughters. I have to work harder to get out of here because now that I know she has four kids to take care of, I need to be there to help her." Franklin could hear it in Grandville's words that he was determined to find a way out of Oakhill. But Franklin was also taken a back about the news of the twins. He was sitting there trying to figure out in his mind if she had gotten pregnant during the time they were intimate with each other. He had to play it off and not let Grandville see the nervousness which was rocking through his entire body.

"Well, I've spoken to Darita and the rest of your legal team, and we're going to petition the court and ask for your immediate release. Your psychiatrist wrote a letter on your behalf stating, he believes you have made enough progress to be released. Your records were also reviewed by a second psychiatrist who also concurs with this assessment. You have responded favorably to treatments, and you've even given back to the institution by teaching your English class. It's time for us to put the steps into motion so you can come home," Franklin explained.

Grandville was in shock. He didn't want to get his hopes up too high so he did his best to control his emotions. Franklin could see how the news was affecting Grandville, and he decided to change the subject.

"While I was with Rayshawn we talked about Montell's new job. He wants him to work as the maintenance man in his check cashing center. He'll have to do light cleaning like sweeping and mopping, but he wants him to operate in an undercover security manner without the title. He likes the fact Montell used to be a cop. Rayshawn feels him being there will provide his other employees with another measure of security. He will pay Montell forty-thousand dollars a year plus family health and dental benefits. He wants Montell to call Zack as soon as he's released, and he will provide him with his start date." Franklin said.

"Franklin that's great news. Montell's going to be relieved. He's a little worried about how things are going to be once he's released from Oakhill. He's also anxious about the idea of being a free man again.

"It must be hard after being locked down for so long. Then, all of a sudden you're free, it's a big adjustment, and it's shouldn't be taken lightly. That's good he's thinking about a plan to stay free."

"I want to ease some of his worries. Please get twenty-five hundred from my safety deposit box and ensure that he receives it as soon as he is released. I'm going to let him know to call you as soon as gets home from Oakhill so you can give him Zach's information and the money." Grandville said.

"No problem. Do you need me to do anything else?" Franklin asked.

"No, I'm great. All I need from you is for you to continue to pray for me, because I've come to learn your prayers are working." Grandville looked at Franklin and laughed out loud. He was thinking about all the things his friend had prayed for him and done to help him.

"Like I told you before, I do that anyway. You take care Grandville," Franklin said. But, he couldn't wait to walk out of that place so he could decide his next move. He had to decide if he would confront Juliette about having twins and if they were his.

"You be sure to do the same Franklin my friend," Grandville replied.

Chapter 26
Tha Crossroads

J uliette stared at Grandville's picture and sighed. It was time for her to tell their sons the truth about where their father had been for more than three years and she was both nervous and apprehensive. It was best to start mending her family back together again no matter how thick the questions may get. She knew it was necessary for her to be honest, but she was still hesitant to begin the process with the kids. She had been home from her visit with Grandville for over two weeks. Within that time Grandville had already written the boys a letter which she had planned to read to them when she sat down to explain to them what happened to Jessica.

In the past two weeks she kept putting off having the conversation about where their father was because, she had been wrapping her head around the fact that Melinia was not dead and racking her brain on how she could find her.

She put on a good positive face for her family and convinced them to keep hope alive. She could not tell her family what she learned about Melinia, because she had been sworn to secrecy. However, she could keep them motivated to continue to search for her.

She and Samantha had dinner at Samantha's house just like Samantha promised where it was just the two of them. They took the time to have a true heart to heart about their falling out and they made a pact for their future. They decided to allow very few people into their small circle. Both women were positive that influences from other people helped to contribute to their argument and vowed to never allow it to happen again. Samantha also shared with Juliette that the Prosecutors Office nor the Police had any idea where Melinia was being held. Also, the man who was in the video with Melinia was like a ghost and the police nor the FBI had any idea of who he was. When Samantha ran the license plate of the Honda which was involved in denting Juliette's rented Ford Focus, she learned the Honda had been reported stolen. This meant attempting to figure out who was driving it when Juliette's rented car was dented was almost impossible.

Samantha sent Officers to interview the owner of the car who reported his twenty-year old son had taken the vehicle to the roller skating rink and when he came out the vehicle was gone. The car had been reported stolen in Willoughby which was very close to where Juliette lived. However, Juliette's rented car had been dented over a hundred miles away from Northeast Ohio. Samantha and her colleagues had no idea what to make of it. The car could have been on its way to a chop shop because the rest stop is the last place where the car was seen.

Once the Highway Patrol ran the tags they too learned the vehicle was stolen and put out an All Points Bulletin for the vehicle but it was like the car had just vanished. Also, Samantha could not be sure the man who was driving the car that dented Juliette's rented vehicle was the actual guy in the sex video with Melinia. Juliette's description of the man was all she had to go on as the rest stop video cameras were broken.

Juliette was so consumed with trying to locate Melinia that she had not followed through on her promise to Grandville. She was supposed to start repairing their family with one of the biggest steps being to explain to their sons about the accident which took Jessica's life and Grandville's freedom. She also had not scheduled the family counseling sessions with Grandville's Prison Counselor Mr. Bolden which was another task on her to do list. She felt like she needed to talk to her sons before she scheduled the family session.

Juliette realized that she had wasted enough time putting off the task and finally made plans to tell her sons the awful story about what happened to Jessica. She swallowed her apprehension and gathered her sons to take them bowling. Greta had taken the twins to the Children's Museum and while she and her sons spent quality time is when she planned to tell her boys the story of what happened to Jessica. When she came out of her bedroom her sons were down stairs waiting, excited about spending time with her without their demanding sisters.

"Mom are you ready to go?" Jabari called out to his Mom.

"You boys can go on ahead and get into the car." Juliette said trying to get the words in her mind straight.

In the car on the way to bowling alley Juliette started the conversation. "Jabari, do you remember when I told you that I was going to be seeing your father?" Juliette asked.

"Yes Mom. I remember.' Jabari responded.

"Well, I want you to know I saw him. He asked me to tell you that he loves and misses you both," Juliette said.

"Well, did he say when he's going to come home?" Jonah innocently asked.

"Hopefully he's going to be coming home in a few months. Are you guys hungry?" Juliette asked.

"I want Pizza," Jonah responded.

"How about you Jabari do you want pizza too? Juliette asked.

"Yes, that would be great. Can we have Sausage and Pepperoni?" Jabari asked.

"Sure. We can have whatever you want," Juliette responded.

Once they arrived at the bowling alley Juliette busied herself with getting bowling shoes and ordering the pizza. They had bowled two exciting games where Jabari beat both she and Jonah.

"Jabari you are quite the bowler. How did you learn how to bowl so well?" Juliette asked.

"I play it on my video game all the time. I guess that's how I got so good at it," Jabari told his Mom.

Soon, their pizza was ready and Juliette felt it was the perfect time to begin the conversation which she's been avoiding for years.

After putting several slices of pizza on each boy's plate. Juliette took a deep breath and asked, "Do you guys ever think about Jessica?"

"I think about her all the time, but I know she's in heaven with Mother Stubbs and my biological dad. Maybe my biological dad and Mother Stubbs were lonely and wanted Jessica to keep them company." Jabari reasoned in his own fantasy.

"How about you Jonah. Do you ever think about Jessica?" Juliette inquired.

"Yes Mom but then I get sad. Jessica was here and then she was gone like on one of my video games," Jonah replied in his little voice.

"I miss Jessica also and I'm sorry I haven't talked about Jessica as much as I should. I miss her so much I guess it's been very hard for me to talk to you guys about how she died," Juliette began.

"I know how she died," Jabari said.

"How did she die?" Juliette asked.

"Dad hurt her with the chain saw. It was an accident and he didn't mean to hurt her," Jabari replied.

Juliette was in shock. She had no idea that Jabari had details about how Jessica died and was curious as to how he knew.

"Who told you?" Juliette questioned.

"No one. I saw what happened from the back window in the hallway. You told me to put Jessica in her room, and you told us all to take a nap but Jessica didn't want too. After I put her in her room I decided to go and check on her but she was gone. I looked out the window and saw Jessica go behind Daddy as he was cutting the hedges. He didn't see Jessica and when he turned around the chain saw hit her in the neck. I got in the bed and acted like I was asleep, because I didn't want to get into trouble for not going to bed like you told us too," Jabari said.

"Jabari why didn't you tell me that you saw what happened?' Jessica gently inquired.

"I don't know. You didn't seem like you wanted to talk about Jessica or Dad and you seemed so sad. I just want you to be happy. I'm glad I have two more little sisters, but I miss Jessica and Dad," Jabari said.

Jonah was quietly listening to the conversation, and he had not said one word.

"Jonah did you know about this?" Juliette asked.

"No Mom, this is the first time that I heard what happened. I just know that I woke up from my nap and Jessica and Dad were both gone," Jonah replied.

"I owe you both an apology for not talking to you before now about what happened. Your father was so upset from the accident that his mind became sick. He is not out of the country like I told you, because he is actually in a mental health prison trying to get help for his problems. Your father loves you guys and he misses you both very much. He wrote a letter to me and he asked me to read it to his sons. Jabari your Dad really loved your letter, and he told me that he plans to hang-up your picture Jonah. I will read the letter that he wrote to you all tonight when we get home," Juliette said.

"I was afraid that Dad forgot about us," Jabari said and wiped his eyes with the back of his hand.

Juliette felt terrible. Jabari had saw the whole accident. She was afraid he may have suffered trauma issues from witnessing something so horrible though he didn't appear to be showing any signs or symptoms. Juliette felt the best course of action was to ensure that she allowed Jabari an opportunity to talk about what he saw and how he felt as a result of the whole situation. She made a mental note to call Emily the first thing in the morning to pick her brain on how she should respond to the fact that Jabari saw the whole accident.

Juliette found it ironic that while she had been trying to protect her sons from learning how Jessica died, Jabari had been trying to protect her by not revealing the fact that he had witnessed the whole incident. Juliette realized she had to work on communication within her family. She had to make Grandville and her children understand they could tell her anything without repercussion.

After they finished eating their pizza they bowled one last game and headed home. Once in the house Juliette lit the fire place in her family room and had the boys wash up and change into their pajamas. It was early December and the Lake Erie snow and wind machine was in full force. Cleveland was predicted to get six inches of snow and the temperature was supposed to fall to below zero. Juliette hoped Greta made it home with the girls before the weather took a turn for the worse. She was starting to get a little worried, because The Children's Museum closed at 7 and it was approximately 9. Juliette wanted Greta to know she trusted her with her kids, and that's why she fought against the urge to call her to make sure they were alright.

Juliette got Grandville's letter and gathered her sons around her.

"Your father mailed this letter to me a few days ago, and he ask me to read it to you guys. He wants you to know that he loves you both and he hopes to be home soon," Juliette said.

Juliette unfolded the letter and read Grandville's written words to her sons in a strong steady voice.

"My dearest sons, I hope you know how much I miss and love you both. I'm sorry that I have been gone for so long. As you now know, I haven't been out of the country like your mother told you. I've been in a mental health prison trying to recover from the loss of your sister Jessica. It causes me pain to have to tell you that your sister is dead because of me. I want you both to know that I didn't mean to hurt your sister and what happened was an accident. I was cutting the hedges when Jessica came up behind me. I didn't know you all had returned from the Mall and when I turned around the chain saw hit her in the neck. I haven't been right mentally since the accident but I am working on my problems.

I want you boys to know that with the exception of your mother and your little sisters and my sister Greta you are the most important people on the planet to me. I need for both of you to help your mother and be the men of the house until I return home to you. I don't want the two of you to be afraid of me when I come home, and I'm going to show you that I won't ever intentionally hurt you, but I understand if you're angry at me for what happened. All I ask is that you guys remember to always do the right thing and to continue to get good grades in school. Remember to do what your mother tells you to do, and I'll be home as soon as I can and lastly know that I love you."

Juliette swallowed to stop the tears which were threatening to fall from her eyes as she folded Grandville's letter up and put it back in the envelope.

Jabari and Jonah were very quiet after she read the letter. She realized it was important for her to process Grandville's written words with her sons.

"So, Jabari do you have any questions about your dad's letter that you want to ask?" Juliette inquired.

"Yes, does dad being in a mental health prison mean that he's crazy?" Jabari asked.

Juliette knew the way in which she responded to this question would forever shape how her young sons felt about their father and his illness.

"Your father had a breakdown. His mother had just died, and he was under a lot of pressure at work. The accident broke his mind, kind of in the same way your friend Trevon broke his leg. Once a body part has been broken all you can do is reset it and give the injury time to heal. When your mind has been broken you have to rest it in hopes that it will heal. That's what your dad has been doing, he has been resting his mind. Hopefully, when he comes home he'll be able to live with the fact that there was an accident and the fact that Jessica has passed on due to it.

Jonah who had said very little since learning that his father was responsible for Jessica's death suddenly said, "Mom, I don't think that daddy is crazy. What happened was an accident and no matter how much I miss Jessica I know that daddy didn't mean to hurt her. I hope daddy is getting the rest he needs and he comes home soon.

"I do too baby. Now, I want you young men to get some rest. I don't know about you guys, but I'm tired from rolling that heavy bowling ball," Juliette replied.

"I'm tired also mom but it's too early to go to bed. Can Jonah and I watch television for a while?" Jabari asked.

"Sure, you guys can watch television. What do you guys want to see?" Juliette inquired.

"Can we watch the *Raven* show?" Jabari asked.

"Sure you can." Juliette said and turned the television on. She had taped several episodes of the now cancelled show through her HD Cable system Raven Simone had become a huge childhood star when she had played the role as the grandchild on the Cosby Show Kids. In the *Raven* show, she was a psychic teenager who always seemed to find herself in comedic trouble. The show was cute and funny and her sons seemed to really enjoy it.

Juliette had just walked out of Jabari's bedroom where she had left her sons watching television when the doorbell rang. Juliette rushed to the door to find Greta with her daughters.

"It's freezing out here," Greta complained shivering as Juliette opened the door and took one of her sleeping twins out of Derek's arms and into the house.

"I'm so glad you guys made it home safely. I was beginning to get a little worried. We're about to get some nasty weather," Juliette said.

"I'm sorry Juliette, I should've called." Greta said as she held firm to one of her sleeping daughters.

"Derek, please take your shoes off and have a seat while I help Juliette put the girls to bed. I will be ready to go in a few minutes," Greta said.

"Okay." Derek replied as he removed his shoes and coat and walked into the house towards the family room.

Juliette who was always a gracious host said, "Derek the bar is over there in the corner. There is some Jack Daniels, Vodka and Wine. There is also some juice and soft drinks in the refrigerator. Please help yourself."

"Thanks, can I make you ladies a drink? It is no fun to drink alone," Derek asked.

"Sure, I'll have Vodka and Cranberry," Juliette replied.

"I'm going to have Jack and Coke," Greta responded.

Derek got up and headed towards the kitchen while Greta and Juliette each carried a sleeping child down the hallway to the twins bedroom.

As Greta started to remove Janae's clothes, she whispered, "Juliette, thanks for letting me borrow your children. Derek and I had a great time. People always think the twins are me and Derek's. After we went to the museum, we took the girls to a McDonalds that has an inside playground. The girls have tired themselves out and I'm sorry I brought them back to you sleep."

"Are you kidding me? You don't need to be sorry. It's you that I should be thanking. Now, that the girls are asleep I can have an adult beverage with you and Derek before you leave." Juliette sighed and blew out a big breath of air.

Juliette and Greta got the girls into their pajamas and Greta helped her wash the girls' hands and faces without waking them up. Juliette decided she would give them a bath in the morning.

"Where are the boys?" Greta inquired.

In Jabari's room watching television. We're exhausted from rolling those heavy bowling balls. Soon the two of them will also be asleep and then I can really chill," Juliette said.

The women went into the family room where Derek was waiting with their drinks. Juliette turned on the television and discovered a Chicago Bulls game was on and she knew Derek, like most men, would soon be into watching the game.

Greta took her drink and then said, "Juliette let me run something by you," as she walked out of the family room towards the front of the house where the living room was located. Greta sat down on the couch with her drink.

"I need to talk to you," Greta said.

"About what? Have you decided to finally put an end to your self-imposed celibacy? I hope you don't expect me to try and talk you out of it," Juliette joked.

"Yes, tonight is the night where I'm going to finally allow Derek to make love to me and I don't want you to talk me out of it. I'm actually looking forward to it," Greta confided in her.

"I'm so happy for both of you. Just relax and have fun," Juliette advised.

"I've never let anyone but Rayshawn touch me in an intimate way. I'm a little nervous but I'm excited at the same time. We went together and got tested, so we're both positive that we don't have any sexually transmitted diseases. We've also been dating for months, and he has more than passed the probationary period which Steve Harvey recommends in his book and television show and honestly my hormones are going crazy. Despite what Rayshawn thought, I actually do enjoy making love. I have to trust my partner and Rayshawn had destroyed my trust. I also have to feel secure that whoever I'm with won't abuse my gift for me to truly enjoy myself. I feel like Derek has shown me through all these months that he's down for me."

"I definitely agree," Juliette replied.

"Actually Derek and I consummating our relationship is not why I needed to talk to you." Greta said.

"Okay, what's up?"

"I need you to hear me out and don't ask any questions until I'm done and please don't get mad at me."

"Greta, what did you do?" Juliette questioned.

"I appreciate you sharing with me that Melinia is alive. I decided to take action to help you find her, and I think I got us a lead which may get us closer to finding her," Greta shared.

Juliette was so excited she almost jumped off the couch, but did her best to remain calm and cautious. She was a little nervous, because she had made a promise to Samantha not to disclose to anyone about Melinia's circumstance. However, ever since she had learned the news, she had been feeling like the walls had been closing in on her.

Juliette was afraid Melinia would be killed before they could find her, and she needed to talk to someone besides Samantha about what she learned about Melinia. Juliette told Greta, because she knew she could trust her. She had also sworn her to secrecy not to tell anyone else. She could only hope Greta wouldn't do anything to put Juliette's trust in her into jeopardy.

"I found out Melinia was a resident of the Collins Treatment facility before coming to live at a Better Tomorrow," Greta said.

The Collins Treatment facility was a Drug Rehabilitation Center which specialized in working with the female population. The facility offered a trauma centered approach to treatment which helped each woman to pinpoint the source of their emotional pain and the cause of the women's addiction. The facility accepted women with drug and alcohol problems from all walks of life, but the waiting list was very long and it took some months to become a patient of the program. Juliette silently wondered what Melinia did to get accepted into the program so quickly despite the waiting list.

"How did you find out what rehab Melinia was in? My Aunt didn't even know where she went to rehab, and despite my rule that all tenants prove in writing they had attended rehab before moving into a Better Tomorrow, Melinia nor my Aunt never told me where she went?" Juliette asked.

"This is where I need for you not to get mad. I hired a hacker and he broke into the computer system of every Rehab center within a fifty mile radius of Cleveland. The young man just finished college and is computer wizard. I just created a small company to help me with my fundraising efforts, and I hired him as my first employee. His name is Lonnie Lexington, and he looks like a super model and the quite opposite of what you would think a hacker would look like. He had put an ad in the Cleveland Post and I answered it. I had him sign a confidentiality agreement, and he gave me his word that this will never come back to you. He is going to be worth every dime I'm investing in him, because he's very good at what he does. My company is going to need IT support, so I figured I could kill two birds with one stone," Greta said.

Juliette took a large gulp of her drink and tried to stop the questions which were swirling around in her head.

"I went to the Collins facility and talked to some of the residents who are allowed to leave the program to go to work. I learned that once a resident is in the last phase of the program, the residents can receive passes to leave the facility. Many of them go to the Healing Baptist Ministry to attend outside Narcotics Anonymous Meetings. I found out when the meetings starts and ends and the church is only a couple of doors down from the McDonalds that we took the girls to this evening.

This evening I went to the Church right when the meeting was ending and I met a young lady who knew Melinia. I hope you don't mind, but I left the girls with Derek but it was only for a few minutes. They were having so much fun playing it didn't make sense to try and make them leave to go with me. I showed the missing flyer to all the people coming out of the meeting and explained we were trying to locate Melinia. I also promised to give two hundred dollars to anyone who could give me any information as to who Melinia used to hang out with when she used to attend NA meetings at the Church. One of the participants of the group admitted to knowing Melinia. Her name is Michelle, and she has agreed to speak to us tomorrow evening at Denny's which is located up the street from the church where the meeting is held," Greta said.

Juliette was suddenly hopeful and optimistic the woman would be able to offer valuable information which would get them closer to finding Melinia.

"Did you know your brother suggested I figure out where Melinia attended Narcotics Anonymous to see who she hung out with?

"Really . . ."

"I had no idea on how I could get that information. It seems the plan you've employed to figure out what group she attended is brilliant. Thank you so much." Juliette praised Greta.

"You know what they say, great minds think alike, and if Grandville was home he would have already found Melinia by now.

"I'm sure he would have, because he's a smart man."

"Derek says, he can hang out at your house tomorrow evening so you and I can meet with Michelle. If you want I can talk with her alone. Don't worry I did not tell Derek anything about what's going on," Greta said.

"No, it's cool. I don't mind Derek staying at the house with the kids. Jabari does a great job with his brother and sisters so Derek won't have to do very much."

"This way we can dig a little deeper."

"Okay, we've spent enough time talking about Melinia tonight. It's time for you to go and spend some quality time with your man." Juliette said as she stood up with her drink and headed towards the family room where Derek was patiently watching the game.

During half-time the trio laughed and talked about the twins' antics at the Children's Museum, and they were finishing their second drink when Greta suddenly stood up.

"Well, Soror it's getting late. Thanks again for letting us take the girls out. We really enjoyed them and thanks for the drinks. We're going to get out of here. I'll call you tomorrow morning so we can coordinate what we're going to do tomorrow evening," Greta said as they walked out the door and into the cold snowy night.

Later while lying in bed, Juliette closed her eyes and thought about Greta's plan. She hoped and prayed the woman Greta had met at Melinia's former NA meeting could tell them something that would help them locate Melinia.

Then, Juliette's mind reflected back to the conversation with her young sons. She still could not believe the fact that Jabari had witnessed the accident which took Jessica's life. She could only hope and pray that Jabari didn't at some point start to exhibit problems due to suffering from post-traumatic stress. She also hoped once Grandville learned that Jabari saw the whole incident, this would not set him back in his quest to recover from his illness. Juliette decided to wait until Grandville came home from Oakhill before advising him of what Jabari had seen. Juliette could only pray that Grandville would not let this new revelation regress his progress.

Chapter 27
Hard to Say I'm Sorry

Grandville lay in his lumpy little bed with the scratchy wool cover pulled up to his neck. He was freezing, because the temperature had dropped below zero. Oakhill's policy was to never turn the heat up past sixty degrees. Life at Oakhill was lonely for him since Montell no longer resided in the cell next to his. It has been six weeks since Montell walked out of Oakhill a free man. The holidays had come and gone and Grandville was thankful he had reconciled with his beloved Juliette. However, he was still suffering from sadness due to Montell's leaving. Grandville reflected his mind back to the day of Montell's release.

On the Monday after Thanksgiving, Montell finally achieved his goal of being emancipated from confinement at Oakhill. Grandville was happy for Montell, but sad that he would no longer have him to provide a distraction from the mundane repetition which made up the very essence of Oakhill. Grandville was doing his best to remain upbeat and was trying his hardest to wear a happy face when he really wanted to go into his cell and break down in tears and begin mourning the loss of his friend's presence. Montell could tell Grandville was happy for him but sad about him leaving. Montell sat him down and said, "I'm going to be walking out of here in a less than one hour and there is only one thing I have left to do."

"What?" Grandville inquired.

"I have to say my farewell to you because as far as I'm concerned this is not goodbye. I also want to give you this." Montell said as he reached under his bed and gave Grandville his chess set.

"I want you to know I'm not giving you my chess set, because you already have the one I got for you when you first came to

Oakhill. What I'm asking is that you hold it for me and return it back to me when you are released." Montell said.

Grandville looked at the chess set with tears in his eyes. The pieces to the set had been personally carved by Montell himself in a ceramics class which Montell took when he first arrived at Oakhill and the set was his pride and joy.

"No man I can't. I know how important this set it is to you. You should take it home and give it to Monty," Grandville said.

"Like I said before I'm not giving it to you. I want you to bring it back to me as soon as you are released. Then I'll give it to Monty. This set will be the one that we play our first game on when you get out of here."

"Okay, I'll hold it for you, but I have no idea how much longer I'll be in here. It might be a long while before I can bring it to you."

"Grandville, you can't be negative and you have to believe that you'll be released in the near future. You have to remember your goals and do everything in your power to achieve them," Montell reminded him.

"I'll try and remember what you're saying, and please don't forget to take your own advice," Grandville said and winked at him.

"I'll apply my own advice this I promise you," Montell said.

"You better, because you have a big world out there waiting for you."

"I want to reiterate that sooner than later you'll be released too, but you have to do the work to get out of here too."

"Oh, I know what I have to do to see my family again."

"I want you to know though I won't be here with you in person, I will be with you in spirit. I'll also be checking in with Franklin, and if you need anything from me send word and it is done." Montell spoke to his friend with a sincere heart and wishing they could both walk out of Oakhill together.

It was now the middle of January and Grandville had spent another Christmas and New Year's locked behind bars. This year was better than the previous years due to his reconciliation with Juliette. For the very first time since his arrival at Oakhill he actually had felt somewhat in the holiday spirit. This was due in part to the many letters, gifts and cards that he received from Juliette and his kids and even Greta had sent him several presents. He also had his memories of his weekend with Juliette to help occupy his mind. He had joined an arts and craft class at Oakhill and was able to make beautiful handmade gifts for his family including a Christmas ornament which the whole family could enjoy.

He was also enjoying his new IPod which Juliette had sent to him as one of his many Christmas gifts. The IPod was loaded with all of his favorite songs. He now was listening to music from some of his favorite artists like Stevie Wonder and Pharrell William's of N.E.R.D. and it helped him to reminisce and pass the time. Also, he didn't have to worry about his new belongings being stolen by his fellow inmates, because the other prisoners treated him with the upmost respect and kept their distance. This was mostly due to the fact that one of the leaders of one of the Gangs was in his English class, and he had put the word out that Grandville was untouchable. Now, that Montell was gone from Oakhill, Grandville was cordial to the other inmates but kept to himself.

Franklin had been to visit with him several times during the holiday season. He had reported that Montell started his new job as a maintenance man at Rayshawn's check cashing center one week after being released from Oakhill. Grandville had arranged for Franklin to deliver a card to Montell with a gift card for fifteen-hundred dollars and five hundred dollars in cash inserted in it. Grandville had written a short note in the card thanking Montell for his years of friendship and for loaning him his Chess set. Grandville was very thankful Montell had given him his chess set as it indicated how much Montell trusted him. Now, he had two chess sets in his possession. However, he had no one to play with, because he didn't know if any of the other inmates at Oakhill indulged in the game.

In the card, Grandville also advised Montell to use some of the money to open up a checking account as a means to start to repair his credit. Franklin told Grandville that Montell was moved by the card, and the fact he had been given a little money for which to help his wife pay a few bills. This gift had helped him to get on his feet again. Franklin said, it also made Montell break down in tears. Grandville was happy that Montell was doing well. Since he was now a praying man again, he asked the Lord to allow Montell to acclimate well to being home. He also prayed that Montell was repairing his relationship with both his son and his wife.

Grandville was doing his best to keep busy and was now teaching two English classes at Oakhill. When his class ended for the semester his students made it very clear on their course evaluation forms which was given to Oakhill's administration that they enjoyed his class. He had been told by his Counselor that his students were getting along better in the facility and they attributed their good behavior, in part to his class. The administration thought the program had been a success and decided to assume the cost of the classes. Grandville was even being paid a small stipend for agreeing to teach two classes instead of one. His second class was a continuation of his first class, and Grandville decided to develop the course curriculum along the way. Now, four days a week he spent his time teaching English to his fellow intimates from 10:00am to 12 noon.

For his second class Grandville introduce his class to the *Diary of Anne Frank*. He picked this book for numerous reasons. The first being that the book was very easy to read and to understand because Anne Frank was a young teenager when she wrote the book. The second reason is that he could also teach his class about the Holocaust while also teaching them about Anne Frank's story. Lastly, the book is written in diary form. It was Grandville's hope that some of his students would be inspired to journal or keep a diary after reading Anne Frank's account of her life. Grandville really believed this could help his fellow inmates with passing their time at Oakhill.

On the first day he taught his second English class Grandville was again surprised to see Big Joe who was always early for each of his classes. After the beating which he inflicted on Big Joe, he was surprised Big Joe would be a part of any class he taught. Joe was actually reasonably intelligent and was much smarter then he initially appeared. Since Grandville had started to attend the Survivors Group, he also understood Big Joe much better.

Grandville, would never forget Big Joe's testimony at the Survivors Group where he was made to tell his story of how he was abused to the rest of the group.

Big Joe's voice was loud and strong as relayed to the other members of the group about how his Uncle sexually abused him. He told the members of the group about the first time his Uncle performed oral sex on him, and how his Uncle talked Big Joe into sodomizing him. Big Joe said, he was conflicted on how he felt. He didn't like what his Uncle was doing to him, but he did like how his Uncle made him feel. Joe was angry and rebellious as a result of what was happening to him. He started getting in trouble for fighting and stealing. When he was 14 years old, he was sent to a Dentation Home and was repeatedly sexually assaulted by the older, bigger, teenage inmates. Big Joe confided to the group that most of his sexual experiences have been with men. He could only enjoy sex with other males and the every attempt he made to be with a woman ended in failure.

Joe told the group that he wanted kids and a family but due to his sexual desire for men, his fantasy of getting married and having a child would likely never be his reality. Big Joe confided that he had started drinking as a way to deal with his problems and the voices that were constantly chattering in his head.

Joe said, the voices told him how unworthy and worthless he was, and he ended up at Oakhill after he beat-up his girlfriend when she made fun of him when he couldn't perform sexually. Joe broke down in tears as he recounted his story. Grandville felt sorry for him, but was also irritated as he couldn't understand how Big Joe could rape innocent inmates when he had been raped and sexually abused by family members and strangers from the time he was young.

One of the other inmates decided to verbalize Grandville's thoughts.

Big Joe had just ended his testimony when Mr. Grange said, "thank you Joe for being courageous enough to be the first member of our group to share your experiences. How do you feel now that you have told your story?"

"I feel like a weight has been lifted off of me. I've been holding that pain inside for a very long time. It feels good to finally tell the truth about what happened to me. Joe confided to Mr. Grange and the group.

Anthony who was a member of the group and had been an inmate at Oakhill for the past few years couldn't help himself and decided to interject.

"Mr. Grange, it's not my intent to break the rules, but I was wondering if I could ask Joe a question about his story?"

"Yes, you may but Joe doesn't have to answer if he doesn't want too," Mr. Grange replied.

Anthony turned and looked directly at Joe and then passionately said, "Joe after everything you been through why do you rape innocent inmates? You even tried to get me, and if it wasn't for Montell you would have done it. You even tried to assault Teach but he beat you up twice."

Joe dropped his head then looked up at Anthony and said, "You're right. I guess I'm physically attracted to men who have naturally wavy hair. My Uncle had naturally wavy hair like you and Teach. I guess in some ways I'm still trying to punish him through others for what he did to me. All I can say is, I'm sorry. I won't ever try and hurt you again." Joe meant what he said, because he felt the healing from releasing his secrets to the group. He was also feeling better since he spoke the words from his mouth about what had happened to him as a kid. Releasing the pain he had been holding in for so long made Big Joe realize the things he had done to the other inmates was very shameful.

Big Joe ended his story by telling the members of the group that he felt like a deviant, and he joined the group in part, to try and control himself from sexually assaulting people. Big Joe's story was sad but compelling and when Grandville heard it, he was reminded in part of his own story. Both he and Big Joe were violated by people who was supposed to love and protect them. However for Joe, he had become what he claimed he hated, a rapist who preyed upon the vulnerable and the weak. Grandville had to admit that Joe attending the Survivors group was a first step to hopefully helping him to understand, though he was hurt by the actions of others, his pain did not give him the right to victimize innocent individuals.

Grandville had been a member of the Survivors group for almost two months where he had heard many of his fellow inmates account their sexual abuse when the inevitable happened. His name was pulled as the next individual to tell his story. Grandville was nervous about talking about what happened to him in front of the rest of the group and had spent several nights losing sleep and worrying about what to say to explain his story and just how much of it to tell.

The next morning after a breakfast of burnt bacon and burnt toast, he went to the library to grade the spelling tests his classes had taken the day before. Grandville knew his students were anxious to receive their grades after they took a test or exam, and he worked hard to get their work back to them as quickly as possible. Also, planning the course curriculum, grading his classes, tests, exams and papers was a way to keep his mind busy and off of the added loneliness he felt as a result of Montell no longer being a prisoner at Oakhill.

He had his head buried in his student's spelling tests when he felt someone staring at him. He looked up and saw Big Joe looking at him from across the room. Before Grandville could look away Big Joe pushed his seat back and headed towards the table. Grandville picked up a heavy hardback Dictionary which he had on the table next to him just in case Big Joe wanted to start an altercation.

Big Joe hesitantly walked up to the table and said, "Teach, do you have a minute?"

"Sure, have a seat," Grandville replied.

Joe pulled out the chair opposite to Grandville and sat down.

"Teach, I want to personally apologize to you for trying to assault you in the shower. I've been working a twelve step program to help me with my alcoholism, and one of the steps of the program is to make amends to everyone that I have wronged. I know what I tried to do to you was foul, and I want you to know I'm sorry," Joe said.

Grandville was shocked and surprised by Joe's seemingly sincere apology. However, he kept his grip on the dictionary just in case Joe tried to catch him off guard in order to attack him again. It seemed awkward talking with him, because this was the first time Joe had initiated any type of conversation with him since he had beat him up in the shower. Though Joe had been in his first class and was now in his second class, Joe only spoke to Grandville when Grandville asked him a direct question in class.

"I also wanted to talk to you about something else," Joe quietly stated.

"Ok, but you know I'm grading your spelling tests right now, and I plan to pass them back to you tomorrow in class."

"No, that's not what I wanted to talk to you about." Joe wanted to see if Grandville would be open to talking with him in spite of what he had done to him in the past.

"Okay, then what's up?" Grandville questioned.

"I know you used to play Chess with Montell, and now that he's no longer here at Oakhill I was wondering if you would consent to playing with me. I know you don't feel comfortable with me around you. I really don't blame you, but we can play right here in the library out in the open," Joe replied.

"I want to make it perfectly clear to you, I'm not interested in you in a romantic way. I'm married to a beautiful woman, and I'm not into sex with men. If you want to play Chess with me as a means to try and get me to sleep with you, I'm here to tell you that you are wasting your time." Grandville was forcibly letting Joe know if he was playing some kind of cat and mouse game, he wasn't falling into his trap.

"I know you are not interested in having an intimate relationship with me, and after the last beating you inflicted on me I'm no longer sexually interested in you. I just don't know anybody else here at Oakhill who knows how to play Chess. When I was younger, I was very good at the game. I thought, if I started practicing again I could become good once again. I understand if you're apprehensive about playing with me, no worries. I'm hoping you will seriously think about it, because it could also help me get my mind off of my problems."

Grandville was looking deep into Big Joes' eyes as he talked about playing Chess, and realized he was sincere.

"Okay . . ."

"We could meet once a week right here where there are a lot of people. I give you my word I won't ever try and hurt you again," Joe said hoping Grandville would approve.

"Okay, Joe meet me here tomorrow at 2:00 after lunch. I want you to know I'm not going to take it easy on you just because you haven't played in a while," Grandville said.

"I give you my word if I lose I will take my beat down like a man. Actually, I'm pretty sure you'll win, but that will only be because I haven't played in a long while," Joe smiled.

"Okay whatever. I'll see you here tomorrow afternoon," Grandville replied.

Joe stood up and then said, "Okay Teach I'll let you get back to grading the tests. See you tomorrow."

The next day Grandville arrived at the library at 1:45 with his chess set. He set the board up and waited for Joe. He was tired, because he had slept poorly the night before. He kept going over what he was going to say to the members of his Survivors Group about what happened between he and Gina. He didn't know how much of his story to share with the Group. He had heard his fellow inmate's stories and was shocked to learn, there were so many other men who had shared the experience of being violated and forced into sex against their wills. Several of the members recounted their experiences of how they were forced to lose their innocence far before they should have, because of someone else's lust or control issues. Just like Grandville suspected some of the men had been assaulted by men where others had been assaulted by women and the abusers ranged from babysitters, relatives and family friends.

Grandville was due to tell his story to his Survivor's at the next meeting but the Group was not due to meet for more than a week. He wanted to talk to Joe about how he handled the experience of telling his story to the Survivors Group, but he didn't know how friendly he wanted to be with Joe. He also didn't know if he could actually trust that Joe hadn't come up with the idea of playing Chess with him as a means to get him to drop his guard so he could attempt to try and assault him again. At exactly 2:00 pm Joe walked into the library and took a seat across from Grandville.

"Hey Teach. Thanks for agreeing to play with me," Joe said.

"No problem. Since you haven't played in a while I'm going to let you go first," Grandville replied.

Joe went into his pocket and pulled out a Chess piece which was shaped like a King and put it in on the side of the Board.

"This is my lucky charm." Joe said.

He then immediately moved the pawn right in front of his Queen and patiently waited for Grandville to make a move.

Grandville was reviewing the board and Joe's move when Joe started a conversation like they were the best of friends.

"Teach, I can't wait to hear your testimony in our Survivor's Group. Hearing what some of the other inmates have endured in their lives has given me a new perspective on mine. I really did have a crappy childhood, but so did a lot of the guys who are here. I can't wait to hear your story. Are you nervous?" Joe inquired.

"As Hell," Grandville replied.

"I can relate. I was nervous also and I had the added pressure of having to go first

"Well, how did you decide what to say?"

"I decided to just speak from my heart. I didn't put too much thought into what I was going to say," Joe replied.

"Well, I've been obsessing about what to say," Grandville said.

"My advice is, you shouldn't be obsessing. You're the only person who knows your story, so tell it the way you want it to be told," Joe said.

Grandville and Joe were silent for a while as they played the game. It was not long before Grandville had Joe in Checkmate and Joe had to concede defeat.

"You're a very good Chess player, and I really think I could learn to play better if I continue to play with you. Hopefully, you will allow me the opportunity for a rematch," Joe said.

"Okay, no problem but only under one condition." Grandville replied.

"Okay, teach what's the condition?" Joe questioned.

"After I speak at the Survivors Group I'm not going to want to talk about my testimony, so please don't ask me any questions about it," Grandville replied.

"I give you my word, I won't ask you anything if you just agree to play with me again," Joe responded.

"Okay, meet me here at the same time next Monday."

"Thanks Teach. See you on Monday," Joe replied, pushed his chair back and headed toward the Library's exit sign.

Chapter 28

Clocks

Juliette sat across from Emily advising her of the recent occurrences in her life. Melinia was still missing, and Juliette and her family were doing their best not to give up hope. Juliette told her she was feeling much better about her situation with Grandville, but was also feeling added stress due to Melinia's plight. It had been more than two months since she and Greta had met with a woman named Michelle. She had claimed that when Melinia was in rehab the two had attended NA together.

Michelle had very light skin and a significant acne issues and very bad teeth as a result of her sustained Crystal Methamphetamine use. She said, she was 26 years old but to Juliette she looked like she was 36. Her long hair was pulled into a ponytail, and you could tell she might have been a decent looking girl if not been for her journey with the illicit substance. Juliette and Greta met Michelle at Denny's restaurant and watched her consume a meal like she had never seen food before.

In between gulps of food Michelle told them that when she first arrived at rehab, Melinia was in the last phase of the program and as a result received more privileges then she herself did. However, both were allowed to attend an outside Narcotics Anonymous meetings and Michelle reported that she did notice sometimes Melinia would sit with another resident named Mona when they attended the outside NA meetings. According to Michelle, there was a woman who Michelle did not know who used to come to the meetings and was very friendly with Melinia, and she would sit with Melinia and Mona. According to Michelle, the mystery woman stopped coming to the NA meeting when Melinia and Mona left rehab. Michelle said, the mystery woman and Melinia acted like they knew each other before Melina came to rehab. Some of the residents of the rehab had their friends come to the NA meeting as a means to see them without the Rehab Administration being aware.

After meeting with Michelle, Juliette and Greta had more questions about where Melinia could possibly be then answers, and they still were no closer to finding her.

This was two months before and Juliette had become more anxious about Melinia's fate. At one time Melinia's nude and sexual images had been all over the internet, but recently Melinia had not been on the World Wide Web. The FBI and the local sex crimes Detectives didn't know what to make of it. They didn't know if Melinia had been taken out of circulation, because her captors realized the authorities were close to finding her or if it meant Melinia was dead and forever silenced. Juliette and her family celebrated Christmas and started a New Year without knowing if Melinia was dead or alive.

To make matters worse, Juliette was never able to share with her family what she discovered about Melinia being a possible victim of Human Trafficking. To her family, Melinia was most likely dead but everyone tried to keep up a brave face. In the past week Aunt Mable, Melinia's mother, had received an unsigned post card from the Bahamas Islands. Aunt Mable was convinced the post card had been sent to her from Melinia. She insisted the Post Card was written in handwriting which was identical to Melinia's. All the post card contained was a series of numbers. Juliette nor her family could figure out what the numbers meant. The card did not have a return address, and it was not signed. There was a question as to if the card had been sent to Aunt Mabel by accident. Juliette was now attempting to explain to Emily about how she felt about the whole situation.

"Emily, I don't know what to believe. I'm afraid to try and keep hope alive for my family, because if we find out Melinia is dead it will devastate them further. However, if Melinia is alive I want her to know we are looking for her." Emily could tell Juliette was trying to make sense of what had occurred.

"You're faced with a very difficult situation, but I think you should think positive and not negative. There's still a good chance Melinia is alive, and you have more evidence then the rest of your family. At least three months ago she was alive. Remember she had been missing for three months when you found out she was alive and not dead. Maybe your Aunt is right, maybe the post card is from Melinia and she is trying to let you all know she is still here," Emily said.

"I sure hope you're right. I've been so focused on Melina gone missing that I haven't thought much about Grandville's situation. I got an email from Darita advising me that she and Grandville's legal team have filed a motion for Grandville's release. Darita believes there's a good chance Oakhill is going to recommend he be released," Juliette said.

"Juliette that's wonderful. How do you feel about this news?" Emily asked her.

"I'm hopeful, but I'm still also just a little apprehensive. During my visit with Grandville I realized that I'm still in love with him. I'm also happy we will be able to be intimate together on a regular basis, but I must admit I really don't know what to expect. When I visited with Grandville he told me, when he is released from Oakhill he would be moving into an apartment in one of the buildings he and Franklin's corporation owns. I don't know how to transition Grandville back into our lives," Juliette admitted.

"I would suggest you allow for a natural transition. I also think Grandville moving into his own place is a good idea. It'll give the two of you time to ease back into everything," Emily replied.

"I'm afraid to get my hopes too high about the possibility of Grandville coming home, because if his motion is denied I will be crushed."

"It is understandable. Have you told anyone else about the possibility of Grandville's release?"

"No. I'm going to tell Greta soon, but I'm still trying to process the news myself."

"You are going to have to prepare your sons."

"I think its best I wait until I know for sure he's coming home before I say anything to the boys."

"I think that's wise. How does Jabari seem to be doing?"

"He actually seems to be okay. It's still difficult for me to fathom that Jabari saw the whole accident. So, far he hasn't exhibited any negative signs from witnessing Jessica's death."

"Do you plan to tell Grandville that Jabari witnessed the accident?"

"Yes, I do plan to tell him, because I don't want to keep secrets from him but I think it's best for me to wait until he comes home."

"How do you think he will take the news?"

"I don't know. It's my hope he'll take the news well. Jabari actually corroborates Grandville's version of the events of that horrible day. It helps to bring me some peace to know Jessica's death was not actually purposeful and Grandville really didn't mean to hurt Jessica. I'm better able to deal with Jessica's death knowing it really was an accident and not because Grandville was psychotic."

"Do you plan to set up family counseling?"

"I do plan to do that but we decided to wait until Grandville got home. I called my insurance company and they gave me a list of names of Family Counselors covered under my medical plan. I brought the list with me in hopes you might know one of the people on the list and could give me a recommendation."

"No problem, let me see who they recommended." Emily said as she took the list from Juliette's outstretched hand. Emily reviewed the information and then said, "I actually know everyone your insurance company has referred. I think they are all great Counselors, but I think the best Family Counselor on this list is Hunter and Associates. They are very skilled at what they do. I also want to give you a referral to the National Alliance for the Mentally Ill's Family to Family program. NAMI is an organization for friends and family members of individuals suffering with Mental Illness. They do a great job of helping to advocate for individuals who are suffering with mental health disease. It's an organization I believe you should familiarize yourself with. NAMI's Family to Family program is an eight week program which helps family members better understand mental health diseases. It's an awesome program and one I highly recommend that you take.

"Okay, as soon as I find out when and if Grandville is being released I'll set up an appointment."

"Great. How are things between you and Samantha?" Emily questioned.

"Things are great. I'm going to have dinner with her as soon as I leave here."

"That's good. Did you tell her about your visit with Grandville?

"Yes, and she has been very supportive. I simply told her I was still in love with Grandville, and I was going to do everything in my power to make it work. I told her, I visited with Grandville but I did not go into specifics. She told me that she was my friend and as such, she's okay with any and all decisions that I make in respect to Grandville. She doesn't really bring Grandville up, and when I told her about the visit she really just listened and she asked very few questions."

"Excellent. You are doing great and I don't think I will need to see you again until next month. You have the assignment of setting up an appointment with Hunter and Associates. You will probably want to meet with them to see if they are a good fit to provide your family with Counseling when Grandville is released. However, if you decide they're not a good fit, give me a call and I'll recommend someone else. You should also get in touch with the local NAMI Office to get the schedule for the Family to Family Group in your area, and you should probably start going as soon as a new group begins. You will want to start learning about what you can do to create a conducive home atmosphere that's good for Grandville's mental health as soon possible," Emily suggested.

"Thanks Emily. I'm feeling better about my relationship with Grandville. I attribute this to the fact that I've been working with you, now I'm able to move forward in my marriage. Thank you so much for all of your help," Juliette said.

"I've enjoyed working with you too Juliette, and I feel that you've made great progress. It won't be long before you won't need my services anymore," Emily said.

"I know, but I still have more work to do."

"That you do. I will see you next month." Emily replied.

After leaving Emily's office Juliette headed downtown to Legacy which was another Black owned restaurant that the two ladies enjoyed frequenting. Legacy was one of the oldest restaurants in Cleveland Ohio and was known for its Catfish which is served with the bone in the middle and its eclectic clientele. It was one of the few places in the City of Cleveland where the Pimps, Prostitutes, Players and Politicians comingled while enjoying the restaurant's delicious foods.

After parking her car Juliette headed into the restaurant where she ran right into Georgio the owner of the restaurant.

"Hey Juliette, it's so good to see you. You sure are looking good." Georgio said as he pulled Juliette into a friendly embrace.

"I see you and Samantha are still as thick as thieves. Your crazy Soror is in the back waiting for you, let me take you to her." Georgio stated as he led Juliette towards the back where Samantha was patiently waiting at a small table.

"Juliette I am buying you and your crazy Soror your first round. Are you ladies having your usual?" Georgio questioned.

"Yes that would be great." Juliette said.

"Okay your server will be over shortly with your drinks and to take your dinner orders. You ladies have a great night and Samantha you better stay out of trouble or I am going to be forced to prosecute you," Georgio teased laughing.

"Not if I prosecute you first," Samantha teased back.

After Georgio left Samantha stood up and gave Juliette a quick hug and then said, "Hey Juliette it's good to see you. How are you?"

"I'm good. How are you?" Juliette questioned.

"Excellent now that I'm getting ready to have dinner with my BFF," Samantha replied.

"Thanks, I feel the same way and I am also starving. I have been fantasizing about this catfish all day."

"Where are the kids?" Samantha asked.

"With Greta. She took them to the Science Museum." Juliette replied.

"That's nice. There are a whole lot of Aunts and Uncles who don't do half as much as Greta seems to do for your kids. I think that's cool how Greta helps you out with the kids," Samantha commented.

"Like I told you before, she's invaluable to me. My mother is getting older and has her own life. She works so hard that I don't want to burn her out. If my sisters were in town they would help me but they are not here. My brothers and their wives help some but Greta can always be counted on to help me with the kids. Anyway she and Derek are hanging strong, and they use my kids to have a make believe family together. I have a feeling Derek is going to propose to Greta soon, and the two of them will start working on making their own addition to our large family," Juliette playfully stated.

"I'm happy Greta and Derek have found happiness together. I again want to say, I'm sorry about how I acted when we first met Derek."

"It's not a problem. As far as I'm concerned it's in the past."

"Thank you again for forgiving me. I want to let you know that I really appreciate it," Samantha said.

"No, I want to thank you. Now enough about that," Juliette replied.

"I also want you to know we think that the individuals who're holding Melinia have decided to take a little vacation. Melinia and the other women we believe is being held have not been spotted on the Internet for the past two months. We figured out what is still posted on the website is old footage," Samantha said.

"You know I meant to call you and let you know my Aunt received a strange post card. There was no return address but the card was addressed to her. The post mark on the post card indicated it was mailed from the Island of the Grand Bahamas," Juliette stated.

"Well what did the postcard say?"

"It didn't say anything. The only thing that was written on the back of the card was a bunch of numbers that don't mean anything to us. The post card wasn't even addressed to my Aunt. It just had her address on it, but it did not have who the card was supposed to go to. I can't even be sure if the post card was meant for my Aunt. Juliette replied.

"Juliette, this is important information and I'm glad that you told me. Remember there are no such things as coincidences. You can best believe the post card means something, and it might even be a clue as to where Melinia and the other women are being held. I'm going to need you to get a copy of the back of the card, and get it to me ASAP so I can have my team to look into it," Samantha directed.

"Okay Samantha, I'll call my Aunt as soon as I leave here. If she's home I'll swing by and take a picture of the card with my cell phone and then email it to you," Juliette replied.

"I know you and your family have been consumed with Melinia's situation but what else has been happening in your world?" Samantha asked.

"Well, I just recently received an email from Darita advising me that Grandville's legal team has filed a motion for him to be released. It could take up to three months before there's a ruling made by the Judge, but according to Darita's email, Grandville's Clinical Team at Oakhill believe he's no longer a danger to himself or society."

"Oh my God that's great. Grandville might get to come home soon."

"I'm happy, but I'm still a little nervous. I don't want to get my hopes up too high, because I'll be crushed if the motion is denied. That along with what's going on with Melinia is a lot to have on my plate."

"You've been carrying a large load for a long time. I'm here as your best friend to help you with the heavy lifting. Is there anything you need? If so all you have to do is let me know," Samantha said.

"No, I'm good. You're giving me what I need, support. You may not know it, but you just listening means an awful lot to me. It also feels good to just hang out sometimes, and as much as I love my kids going out with you gives me something adult to look forward too," Juliette confided in her friend.

"I'm glad because as your BFF that's one of my jobs." Samantha gave Juliette a thumbs-up and smiled at her.

After Samantha and Juliette had dinner, Juliette got into her SUV and headed towards Aunt Mabel's house. As she enjoyed the drive, she thought about the great time she and Samantha had just experienced. The food was excellent and they talked and reminisced about days of old as they enjoyed their delicious meals. Samantha had a meeting for one of the Boards which she serves on early the next morning so they couldn't stay out too late. She had to get to her Aunt's house and then back home to the kids.

When Juliette walked out of Legacy she was so full that she could still taste her Catfish, Macaroni and Cheese and Collard greens, and she was feeling sluggish from consuming the heavy meal.

She and her family had the kind of relationship where they each could drop in on one another without calling, and Juliette was pretty certain that Aunt Mabel would be home.   She had always been someone who stuck close to her house. With Melinia missing Aunt Mabel went out even less, because she wanted to be home just in case Melinia called or returned.

Aunt Mabel resides in Cleveland Heights which is located in one of the inner ring suburbs of Cleveland, and is located about fifteen minutes away from Downtown Cleveland. It wasn't long before Juliette was parking her car in front of Aunt Mabel's large house. She could see by the illumination of the living room reflected through Aunt Mabel's large picture window that she was home. She pulled into the driveway and walked up to the front door and rang the doorbell. It wasn't long before Aunt Mabel came to the door.

"Hello Juliette what a surprise.   Come on in," Aunt Mabel welcomed her.

Juliette followed Aunt Mabel into her large house and closed and locked the door behind her. She then gave her Aunt a big hug and a kiss on the cheek and sat down on the couch in the living room.

"Juliette, I just finished eating some left over bake chicken, Lima beans and mashed potatoes I made for dinner yesterday. Would you like for me to make you a plate?" Aunt Mabel asked.

"No thank you Aunt Mabel, I just got finished eating myself and I'm still full," Juliette replied.

"Would you like something to drink? I have bottle water, Cola and Ginger ale?" Aunt Mabel offered.

"You know I think I'll have a bottle water."

"Help yourself the water is in the refrigerator."

Juliette went into Aunt Mabel's immaculate kitchen and marveled at the updated layout and modern design. Aunt Mabel had her kitchen remodeled five years before, and it contained all the bells and whistles a top of the line kitchen would have. Included in the new kitchen was granite countertops, a sub-zero refrigerator and freezer and a double oven with a six plate cooktop.

Juliette's kitchen was nice but Aunt Mabel's kitchen was spectacular. Juliette quickly got her bottled water and returned back to the living room where Aunt Mabel was still seated.

"Aunt Mabel, Samantha and I went to dinner downtown at Legacy and I decided to take Cedar Hill instead of the freeway to go home. My sister-in-law Greta has my kids, and it's a nice night so I decided to take the scenic route to get home. I was close by and decided to stop by," Juliette explained.

"I just got back not too long ago. I went to church and met with my prayer group. The weather had been so awfully cold that we have not been able to meet in person, so we have just been meeting by conference call. I'm so glad the weather is finally breaking. It feels good to get out of the house for a while, because I really don't go anywhere with the exception of church," Aunt Mabel said.

"I'm glad you got out to get some fresh air. I don't want you to be isolating too much because it is unhealthy," Juliette replied.

"I'm trying not to spend so much time alone. I don't know quite what to do, because I want to be here when Melinia returns. Suppose she comes home, and I'm not here. Suppose she calls, and I'm not here to pick up the phone? It could be her only chance to use the phone, and I wouldn't want to miss her call."

"If you're not here when Melinia comes home she'll wait for you, and if she calls she'll leave a message. You can't become a prisoner in your own house because Melinia is missing."

"You sound just like your mother," Aunt Mabel replied.

"Speaking of my Mom, she mentioned to me that you received a postcard the other day, and you think it's from Melinia?" Juliette questioned.

"Yes, I did receive a post card. Do you want to see it?" Aunt Mabel asked.

"Sure if it won't be too much trouble," Juliette replied.

"Let me go and get it." Aunt Mabel said as she headed up the stairs that were located right off the living room to where her bedroom was located.

It wasn't long before Aunt Mabel returned back to the Living Room where Juliette was seated. Aunt Mabel gave her the post card, and Juliette examined it. She noted on the front of the post card there were palm trees and a beautiful sunset with the caption, "Wish You Were Here," and on the back of the card there were a series of random numbers. The card contained nothing more than the sequence of numbers. The card was handwritten and Juliette had to admit the writing did look a lot like Melinia's distinct penmanship.

"Aunt Mabel, I'm going to take a picture of this card with my phone," Juliette told her.

"Okay." Aunt Mabel said as she passed Juliette the Post Card.

Juliette put the card on Aunt Mabel's coffee table and used her cell phone to snap pictures and to take video. She then put her phone up and focused her attention on Aunt Mabel.

"Thanks Aunt Mabel for letting me see the card. I'm going to study it and try to see if I can make sense out of the numbers. I agree the penmanship does look like Melinia's, but it doesn't mean she sent this card. It could have been mailed to you by accident, because it is not addressed to you," Juliette said.

"Juliette in my heart I believe Melinia sent the postcard. I don't know what the numbers mean, but I believe Melinia is trying to get word to us," Aunt Mabel replied.

"I'm going to study the picture of the postcard, and maybe I can decipher what the numbers could possibly mean."

"Thank you Juliette for at least trying. It's been so hard for me to have my child missing and not knowing if she is dead or alive. In my heart I believe Melinia is alive, and I refuse to believe she is dead. I pray daily for peace, but I don't think I will have peace ever again until Melinia is found and we find out what happened to her."

"Aunt Mabel, I too believe in my heart Melinia is still alive. Keep praying and stay positive and everything will be okay. Greta will be at my house with my children in a few minutes so I better get going."

Juliette gave Aunt Mable a long hug before walking to the front door and letting herself out.

On her way home Juliette thought long and hard about the conversation she had with her Aunt. There was something about the numbers on the postcard which seemed familiar to her. As soon as she got home and got the kids situated, she planned to email the pictures of the postcard to Samantha. Maybe the two of them could figure out if the card was really from Melinia and what the numbers meant.

Chapter 29

People Make the World Go Around

It had been approximately two weeks since Grandville stood before the members of his Survivors Group and shared his story about how his cousin sexually abused him during his childhood. In a strong steady voice he recounted what he had spent most of his adult life trying so desperately to forget.

He told the other members about when Gina started touching him and the lust he used to feel for her. He explained to the group about how her touch affected his young body and about the guilt he felt for having sex with his cousin. He attempted to verbalize to the group about the internal torment he felt during that time, because he both enjoyed and hated what his cousin was doing to him. Then, how his mother's discovery of their illicit relationship put an end to the sexual and mental abuse.

He concluded his testimony by telling the group about how he accidentally killed his daughter, and about how the sexual abuse perpetrated by his cousin contributed to his breakdown.

Grandville did not tell the group about the revelation that Gina was also his half-sister and the fact that they conceived a child together. Grandville decided the advice he received from Joe and Franklin was sound. The group didn't know his story and Grandville strongly felt certain parts of what occurred was not meant to be shared with others outside of his immediate family and very close friends.

He had to admit after giving his testimony to his Survivors Group he felt lighter and unburdened. It actually felt like he dropped all the baggage which had been weighing him down, and he realized that he had made a big deal over nothing.

The day before he spoke to his Survivors Group he met with Franklin. He decided that before he barred his soul within the group he wanted to tell Franklin about all that led up to the tragedy of his daughter's death. He didn't want everyone else to know about some of the most painful and intimate times in his life without first telling his best friend.

As soon as Franklin and Grandville sat down in the private visiting room Grandville began.

"Grandville, how have you been?" Franklin inquired.

"Honestly I have been stressed," Grandville candidly replied.

"What are you stressed about? Is it something I can help with?" Franklin asked.

"Actually, I do need your help. Tomorrow I'm going to stand up before the members of my Survivors group and talk about abuse that occurred to me in my past. I'm a nervous wreck, and I don't want anyone else to know certain aspects about my life which I haven't yet shared with you yet. You're my best friend and right now I just need for you to listen," Grandville asked him very humbly.

"Okay, no problem," Franklin replied.

When Grandville had finished the uncensored version of what had occurred between he and Gina there were tears streaming down Franklin's face. "Damn man, I didn't know you were going through so much. No wonder you became sick. The average person wouldn't have been able to endure half of what you have been through before suffering a mental breakdown. Does Juliette know about the child that you had with Gina?" Franklin asked.

"Yes, I told her everything at the extended visit," Grandville said.

"Grandville, I know you're apprehensive about telling your story to your Survivors Group, but I actually believe your testimony will both touch and help others in your group. I know you're nervous, but just tell them what happened the same way you told me. Omit those pieces you don't want to share and keep it moving. Remember, no one knows your story the way that you do," Franklin advised him.

"Thanks Franklin. It's do or die time and talking to the group about my abuse is one of the requirements of me being a member of the group. Enough discussion about my past, tell me how have you been?" Grandville asked.

"I'm doing well in particular since I received word from Darita that the decision regarding your release is due to come down sometime in the next two weeks."

I'm afraid to get my hopes up, because I want so badly to be released from Oakhill, and if my motion is denied I will be devastated." Grandville stated.

"I know, but Darita and the rest of the members of your legal team are very hopeful. Grandville, I have a very good feeling so try not to worry too much. The building that our corporation purchased has been completely renovated and your new spot is absolutely beautiful. I spared no expense, and I even had the contractors put wood floors in both you and Greta's unit."

"Thanks Franklin. I'm blessed to have you as my best friend. I know that I can always count on you to hold me down and for that I am grateful."

"Grandville, I've always felt exactly the same way about you. Even when we were pledging into our fraternity you never let me fall. You were always there to catch me, and if I were here at Oakhill I know you would do the same for me.

Have you talked to Greta about her moving into our new building, because it's ready and she can move in right now?" Franklin questioned Grandville.

"No, because I can guarantee you that Greta will not even consider the idea unless I present it to her in a certain kind of way. I have to wait until I know I'm being released and then pitch the idea. I'll have to tell her, that her moving into the building and living next door to me is a condition of my release."

"I totally understand but like I said earlier, I have a really good feeling about you getting out of here."

"How is the search going in respect to Melinia?" Grandville inquired.

"Very slowly. At one time Melinia's images were all over the internet, but in the past two months there have been no new images of Melinia that have emerged. McNaulty doesn't know what this means. It could mean Melinia's captors took her deep underground, because they know the authorities are looking for her, or they could have killed her or she might have overdosed, because we both know Melinia is in love with Heroin. When she was all over the internet we at least knew she was alive. Now, we don't know what's going on."

"Have you talked to Montell?" Grandville asked.

"Yes, and he wanted me to let you know that he is doing very well. Two individuals posing as customers came into the checking cashing center and attempted to rob it. The two assailants quickly knocked out the Security Guard and was about to try and get behind the security door with the Guard's gun when your boy Montell sprang into action. He was able to use the mop that he was pushing as a weapon and took out both men with light quickness. Rayshawn gave him a large reward for putting his life at risk. Montell asked me to tell you not to worry too much, and that he also has a good feeling about your release."

That was two weeks ago and Grandville was barely holding it together. He was in the library trying to concentrate on grading both of his classes' final projects, but his mind kept straying back to his potential release. He wanted so badly to have hope, but he kept thinking about his reaction if the Oakhill authorities denied his motion.

In the past two weeks he had to will himself to believe that no matter what decision the Oakhill officials and the courts made, he was going to be alright. He shook his head and attempted to focus on the task of grading his classes' final project. He had asked his more advanced class to write a mock diary as their class assignment, and he had to admit he was very impressed with Joe's project. Joe's mock diary was compelling and told the story of his youth complete with dates and times. Grandville did not know if the contents were fact or fiction. If they were fact, Joe had experienced a dismal childhood filled with horrible poverty and abuse. It amazed Grandville as to just how bright Joe was. It was a real shame his talents had gone unrecognized for so long. He was looking at Joe's mock diary when he heard Joe's now familiar voice.

"Teach, do you have a minute?" Joe asked.

"Sure, what's up," Grandville responded.

"I was hoping you had a few minutes to play an impromptu game with me. I know we usually play on Monday's and Wednesday, but I really want to play right now if you are available," Joe asked him not knowing what he would say.

"Yes, I can take a break from grading these papers, but I don't have my board with me," Grandville replied.

"That's okay Teach, I recently acquired my own board." Joe said as he walked over to the table he had been sitting at and brought back a box with a chess set in it.

"I recently saved enough money to buy my own set at the Commissary. I don't have any family members to put money on my books here at Oakhill, because my family has long since abandoned me, because they consider me as a menace to society. Everything that I have, I had to work very hard to get. I guess that is one reason why I have spent most of my life acting like a thug. If I don't come across like I will seriously hurt people the other inmates will try and take what little I've accumulated. I've been working in the laundry room for months just to save enough money to afford this set," Joe confided in Grandville.

"Okay go ahead and set up the Ivory."

Grandville decided to use the time that he was spending with Joe to ask him about his mock diary.

"Joe, I just finished reading your class project, and I must admit I'm very impressed with your work."

"Thanks Teach. I put much time into it. As you know we have nothing but time here at Oakhill. When I was kid I was constantly being moved around. My mother could barely keep a roof over our heads and we were always being evicted. I loved school, but I never got to go to the same school for very long. Luckily, every community has a public library, and I often checked-out books. I tried to teach myself reading, writing and math in an attempt to keep up some educational skills in my life," Joe advised.

"I wanted to ask you something about what you wrote," Grandville stated.

"Ok let's make a deal. I'll answer any question about my class project if you agree to answer a question from me about your Survivors Group testimony," Joe negotiated.

"I thought we agreed that I wouldn't be speaking to you about my testimony," Grandville said.

"I know we had an agreement, but I think it's only fair you answer a question for me, if you want me to answer a question for you. Also, I wanted to tell you that your testimony really touched me. I realized when I heard you speak at the Survivors Group that we're more alike than we are different. You're educated and very well spoken, but despite your camouflage we have been through almost identical situations. You know how it feels to be betrayed by someone who's supposed to love you and protect you." Joe said, and Grandville could feel the emotion and compassion Joe was feeling as he spoke with him.

"Okay, Joe you convinced me. I have to admit I agree with your reasoning. What do you want to know?" Grandville asked him.

"Are you pissed with your family for not recognizing what was happening to you and stopping it?" Joe was still very bitter and angry with his Mother for not protecting and helping him when he was a little boy.

"No, because when my mother found out about what me and Gina were doing she did stop it. By that time I lusted for Gina so strongly my Mother finding out was the only thing that could deter my behavior. Gina often told me that I liked what she was doing to me and in some ways she was correct. It took me coming here to Oakhill and participating in the Survivor's group for me to come to terms with it and admit it to myself."

"Thank you for answering my question."

"No problem."

"I've been so angry with my family that it has caused us to be estranged for many years. The Uncle who abused me was my Mother's oldest brother, and my Mother thought the sun rose and set in him. I could never tell her what her brother was doing to me, because she couldn't get past her hero worship for him to even see the truth. Since I've been at Oakhill, I've been thinking about reaching out to my mother and my siblings. I don't want to hurt my Mother, but I want her to know why I turned out like this." Grandville had never really seen Joe like this before. He was pouring his heart out and the pain was wedged so deep inside of him that tears were rolling down his cheeks. Grandville reached in his inner pocket and handed him his handkerchief to wipe his face.

"Okay, Joe now it's my turn. Are the contents of your diary fact or fiction?" Grandville questioned.

"The contents of my mock diary are in fact true." He said through his remaining tears and gathering his emotions, and at the same time wondering why Grandville had asked him that question. "I can remember every event that occurred in my life and what exact day of the week it occurred on as though it happened yesterday," Joe replied.

"You can't possibly remember every day of your life," Grandville replied

"Honestly Teach I really can, I have some uncanny weird gift." Joe replied.

"Okay, what were you doing on June 12, 2004?" Grandville asked.

"June 12, 2004 was a Saturday. I got up early that morning and went to the gym and lifted weights for two hours. For lunch I had a burger and a protein shake. I took a nap, because I had a date with a young lady named Sharon. I picked her up at exactly 7pm to go to dinner and a movie. The date didn't go very well. After I dropped her off at home, I ended up at a sleazy adult book joint where only gay guys seem to go which is located out in the middle of nowhere," Joe said.

Grandville got up and went over to one of the only computers at Oakhill and searched Google and learned that June 12, 2004 was in fact a Saturday. He also searched Google and learned that Joe's ability to remember almost every day of his life was called Hyperthymesia. He walked back to the table he had left Joe at and sat back down.

"That is absolutely amazing. You have an extraordinary gift which could be making you a lot of money. If you can learn how to market yourself in the right way, you can cash in on it," Grandville complimented Joe on his talents.

"What do you mean?" Joe asked.

"You could be doing your own stand-up show. Even if you were to entertain people by letting them ask you questions about a certain date. Just the mere fact you can recall what day of the week a certain date in the past fell on is amazing, and you can get paid on that fact alone," Grandville replied.

"Do you really think so?" Joe asked.

"Yes, I really do," Grandville replied.

Before Grandville could utter another word Officer Emerson was standing in front of the table.

"Grandville, I'm sorry to interrupt your game, but your Counselor has requested to see you ASAP," Officer Emerson said.

"Okay," Grandville responded to him.

He then turned his attention back to Joe and said, "Joe because I have to leave before we've completed the game, and there's still a slight possibility you could win this game, I will forfeit and let you count this one as a win," Grandville said.

"Thanks Teach, because to date I haven't yet beat you. I appreciate the gesture, but I don't want to win by default. I want to actually spank you with the ivory," Joe laughed out loud at Grandville.

"Now that you have your own board you might just get there. Keep practicing," Grandville encouraged him and walked away.

It wasn't long before Officer Emerson was delivering him to Mr. Bolden's Office. On the walk there Officer Emerson actually treated Grandville like a human being instead of a prisoner, and he talked to him like he was one of his personal friends when they were alone. Emerson was also one of the guards who was stationed in Grandville's class. Grandville often watched Emerson's face while he taught his classes, and he noted that Emerson appeared to be really into the content Grandville was teaching. He could see him struggling to pay attention to the Security in the classroom while soaking up the material associated with the *Diary of Anne Frank.*

"Grandville, I want to again thank you for hooking me up with my son's birthday presents. You were right, he looks at me like a god since he received his gifts. He has his ball and jersey in a display case in his bedroom. It's the first thing he sees when he wakes up in the morning and the last thing he sees before going to bed at night," Officer Emerson gushed.

"No problem. I'm glad he's enjoying them."

"I've been listening when you are teaching the inmates in your class about Anne Frank's diary. It's made me want to learn more about the Holocaust," Emerson said.

"I'm glad, because being knowledgeable about the subject is the only thing we can do to ensure that the Holocaust doesn't ever occur again. The Holocaust and World War 2 were horrible events which left a stain on the world. It's probably the second most terrible event to happen to Europe and the USA since Slavery," Grandville replied.

Once he was seated across from Mr. Bolden he took one look at his face and knew in his heart that things were truly going to be okay.

"Grandville, I have great news. Your motion has been granted. You're going to be released from Oakhill in approximately one month," Mr. Bolden stated.

Grandville put his face in his hands and savored the news. He had waited so long to be told he would be offered the opportunity to walk out of Oakhill and back into his life where he would be surrounded by his family and friends.

"Mr. Bolden are you sure?" Grandville asked.

"I'm one-hundred percent positive. So, I suggest you start getting your affairs in order here at Oakhill, because in approximately one month from today, you will leave here. You'll be sent directly from Oakhill to a pre-release center, but you'll only be there for two weeks. Then, you'll be allowed to move to your own private residence," Mr. Bolden advised him.

"Mr. Bolden I want to thank you. You're the main reason why I'm going to be allowed to leave Oakhill. I want you to know I'll never forget all that you have done for me," Grandville looked at Mr. Bolden and spoke with sincerity from the bottom of his heart.

"Grandville, I appreciate the kind words, but I really did very little. You did the work and your clinical team here at Oakhill believes you'll be successful. Don't let us down, continue to work the Recovery Program we have set up to help you deal with your mental health issues, including taking your medications so that you can get your life back. It's my hope that I never see you at Oakhill ever again," Mr. Bolden said smiling at Grandville.

"Mr. Bolden, I promise once I leave Oakhill, you'll never ever see me at Oakhill or any other facility ever again." Grandville promised.

"Good, because you can best believe, I will hold you to that promise," Mr. Bolden stated in a matter-of-fact tone.

Chapter 30
Let's Get Married

 It had been two weeks since Juliette had visited with her Aunt Mabel and used her phone to take pictures of the post card that her Aunt believed that Melinia had sent. Juliette had been racking her brain but she could not make heads or tails of what the numbers on the card could possibly mean. True to her word she immediately emailed the picture of the post card to Samantha who had in turn forwarded a copy of the card to the FBI team and the Sex Crimes Detectives who were working on locating Melinia and the other young ladies that they believed were with her. Samantha and her team had not been able to decipher the sequences of numbers on the card either. Further, there was no definitive proof that the post card was even from Melinia.

Juliette had been super busy with running A Better Tomorrow and attempting to keep her mind off of Grandville's pending motion. She dreamed of Grandville's touch daily and privately hoped he would be released from Oakhill very soon. She had finally sat down with Greta and explained to her Grandville's legal team had filed a motion for his release, and as a result there was a chance he would be coming home. She hugged Greta as they both cried tears of anticipation and joy. Juliette was on pins and needles as she was aware the decision regarding Grandville's release could come down at any given moment.

Juliette was very nervous about Grandville's potential release. After her visit with him, she felt pretty certain he was better. She realized he was not a threat to himself, their children or her, but in the back of her mind she was also worried he would get sick again. She couldn't help but wonder how she would handle it if he came home and had another psychotic episode. She knew that Grandville was now a different man, but despite his changes she loved him. Every night she got on her knees and prayed daily for the courage she would need to remain married to him despite his diagnosis and the potential for problems.

Juliette desperately wanted to fulfill her wedding vows and the commitment she made to him. She knew, she would walk away from him if there was any indication he would hurt her or another one of her kids by accident or otherwise. She prayed for the strength to stay committed to the vows she made to both Grandville and God. She also asked the lord to spare her family from further turmoil and heartbreak.

When Juliette was alone she spent almost all of her time thinking about Grandville and praying for his release. She decided to get her thoughts off Grandville by completing some paperwork for A Better Tomorrow in her home office. She had a new resident who had recently aged out of Foster Care and Juliette felt that with correct intervention the young lady could go very far. She was very bright, but had experienced a series of bad breaks in life which resulted in her ending up in the system.

Juliette turned on an 90's hip hop CD which she had brought from DJ Emory and sat down at her computer. She lost herself in the music while she worked, and before she knew it the CD had ended and the room was silent until she heard her cell phone ringing. Juliette rushed to pick up the call.

"Hello," Juliette breathlessly stated.

"Juliette, are you at home?" Greta questioned.

"Yes, I'm here." Juliette responded.

"I called the home phone but I got no answer."

"I had the music blasting while I was doing some paper work, and I guess I didn't hear the phone."

"I know you're busy, but I need to see you right now. I'm standing at your front door," Greta replied.

"Okay, I'm on my way downstairs to let you in."

When Juliette got to the door she found Greta with tears in her eyes.

"Greta what's wrong? Tell me what happened, why are you crying?" Juliette questioned.

"Juliette, you are not going to believe it."

"I probably won't believe it so just tell me."

Greta put her left hand up, so Juliette could see the three and one half carat princess cut diamond which rested on her ring finger.

"Oh my God, that's one big diamond. Wait a minute are you telling me Derek popped the question?" Juliette loudly inquired.

"He did and I'm in a state of shock," Greta whaled crying and laughing at the same time.

"I just told Samantha a couple of weeks ago I thought Derek was going to propose to you. I'm so glad I was right. Come on in, let's go on out to the sun porch and have a glass of champagne. I would say, a toast is in order. I want a play by play of how Derek popped the question."

Juliette went into the dining room and grabbed a bottle of champagne which she had owned since right before Xmas. She was given the bottle as a gift from the Cleveland Rooming House Association where she is a member. The Association's main goal is to advocate and lobby for housing policies which are favorable to those who owned rooming homes. She used her membership as a means to keep up with all that was occurring in the market.

It was early April and Juliette had spent New Year's Eve with Greta, Derek and her kids at her house. The family watched Dick Clark's New Year's Eve special which was now hosted by Ryan Secrest as they all anxiously waited for a new year to be ushered in. Greta had brought a bottle of Martini and Rossi's Champagne and had also gotten the kids sparkling grape juice to go with the small meal which Juliette had prepared. They ate and toasted to a New Year while Juliette silently prayed this was the year that Grandville came home. It was now mid-April and Juliette had not opened the bottle of champagne which she had received from the rooming house association. Now, she felt like this was the perfect occasion which warranted opening up the bottle.

After grabbing two champagne Flutes and a bucket of ice Juliette made her way to the sunporch. Greta was sitting on the love seat waiting for her. Juliette put the champagne into the bucket of ice and sat down on the glider which was directly across from Greta. It was a beautiful spring afternoon and the temperature was in the early seventies with a light southerly breeze.

"While we wait for the champagne to chill, I want to hear the whole story. Start from the very beginning," Juliette requested.

"Where are the kids?" Greta asked.

"They went with my Mother to Columbus to see my sisters. They left yesterday and they will be home later on today," Juliette replied.

"They didn't have school today?" Greta questioned.

"No, it's the first day of their Spring Break. It just so happens that my sister's kids are out of school at the same time."

"I can't wait until Jabari sees my ring. He just asked me last week if I thought Derek and I would get married. I told him we might if Derek asked me. I think Derek overheard us," Greta excitedly stated.

"The whole thing is excellent. The kids and I just want you to be happy."

"I'm happy, happier than I've been in a long time. It's something about Derek that makes me feel as though he can be trusted. His patience and easy spirit has made me fall in love with him."

"I know, and I can tell."

"I've already been thinking about what kind of wedding I want."

"Nice."

"I've decided, I want a small intimate affair. When Rayshawn and I were married it was a large, flashy affair. This time I only want you, the kids, your family and a few very close friends in attendance. I want fifty people at most and I don't want a long engagement. I want Derek and I to start working on giving your kids some more little cousins to play with. I'm am older and I don't have much time to wait before having my own children,"

"I'm glad you're happy, but you probably want to slow down and savor this moment. Tell me exactly how he proposed?" Juliette asked her.

"Well, we made plans to spend Saturday evening at his apartment, so I could spend the night and then spend Sunday together. On Saturday evening I went to his apartment and he surprised me with a beautiful dinner by candlelight."

"What did he make you? Juliette asked.

"He made, steak, lobster tails, baked potatoes and asparagus. He had candles lit all around his apartment which added to the atmosphere. It was very romantic. He lives in the Penthouse Suite of a building located right on Lake Erie. You can see all of Downtown Cleveland from his patio and picture windows,"

"I wasn't aware Derek lived in the Penthouse," Juliette replied.

"Don't worry you'll get to see his spot in the very near future, because I think we're going to have our engagement party in the building's party room. I'm going to need your advice on the decorating and catering.

When I married Rayshawn I had an army of wedding planners. This time I'm going to do all the planning myself."

"Okay that sounds great but get back to the proposal," Juliette said.

"After dinner we just chilled watching movies. On Sunday morning we got up and went to my Church for Sunday Mass. After Church we decided to go to Brunch at Hyde Park next door to Tower Center. They have a fabulous brunch, and I decided to have the chicken and waffles. When my meal came and the Waiter took the cover off of my food, the ring was sitting square on top of the waffle. Before my brain could comprehend what actually was happening Derek got down on his knee in front of everyone in the restaurant and asked me for my hand." Greta was gushing with a bright light glowing around her entire face and head.

"Oh my God, how romantic. I say, now is the time for us to have a toast to you and Derek and your pending matrimony." Juliette said as she popped opened the now chilled bottle of champagne which was on ice waiting for Greta's story to be finished.

Juliette poured the bubbly liquid into the flutes. Then, she gave one flute to Greta and took the other one and said, "I propose a toast to my girl Greta and her new Fiancé Derek. May God bless the two of you."

"Thank you Juliette," Greta said still beaming.

"Let's just hope Grandville's motion is granted, so he can attend the wedding," Juliette said.

"Speaking of Grandville, do you think he'll like Derek?" Greta asked Juliette.

"Yes, I think so. Derek is a nice guy, and he makes you happy. That's all your brother wants for you."

"Juliette, I'm not going to lie. I'm a little worried Grandville is going to be upset when he finds out I'm engaged. He has never even met Derek, and I'm afraid he won't like the fact that I'm going to marry someone he doesn't know. You know how protective he can be," Greta replied.

"Greta your brother respects you and your judgement. He knows if you're with Derek, then he must be a quality person. Also, I mentioned you were dating Derek when I saw him at the extended visit. Let's just continue to pray Grandville is released, so he can get a chance to know Derek before you two get married. "

"Juliette please don't mention to Grandville the fact that I got engaged. I want to be the one to tell him."

"No problem it's your news to share."

"He's always been so down for Rayshawn. I know we've never talked about the visit I had with Grandville. When I went to see him he mentioned Rayshawn had been to visit him on the Anniversary of Jessica's death."

"Grandville told me," Juliette replied.

"Grandville also made me look at my breakup with Rayshawn in a different light. After talking with him I realized Rayshawn and I did not share the same views about marriage, and this ultimately led to the failure of our relationship.

Grandville helped me to understand the breakup was not all Rayshawn's fault, and I have to share some of the blame. I talked to my Priest about it too and this time I'm going to try and do things differently. I want to make sure Derek and I are on the same page spirituality. I think you Baptists call it being evenly yoked," Greta joked.

"Is Derek going to convert to Catholicism?" Juliette asked.

"Believe it or not he grew up Catholic. Although, he isn't' practicing Catholicism right now. He attends a non-denominational church, and he's already told me, I can have any religious ceremony I want as long as I marry him," Greta smiled.

"That's great and makes for less problems,"

"I also wanted to ask if you would be my Matron/Maid of Honor when Derek and I get married?"

"Greta, I would be honored. I want you to know I'm planning to go all out. I'm going to throw you an awesome Bridal Shower and Bachelorette party."

"Okay that's cool, but I'll be giving you the money for whatever you plan for me. I don't want you to spend your money on this event. I have plenty and you shouldn't have to come out of your pocket," Greta said.

"Greta for the last time, I have money and planning and paying for the Bachelorette Party and Shower is my responsibility if I am going to be your Matron of Honor," Juliette scolded at her.

"You're the only person I'm having in the wedding. I had a huge lavish affair with seven bridesmaids when I married Rayshawn. Now, I am going to be blessed with marriage a second time I just want a quiet, small, family affair. As far as I'm concerned having a Bachelorette Party and Shower is really unnecessary, because I just want a small quiet affair. Hell, I really don't even want a party. I would prefer if you, and I were to go to Vegas or Miami and have a girlfriends' holiday."

"Greta, this is your wedding, and I will do whatever you want. I just need notice if we are going out of town, so I can arrange childcare for the kids."

"I'll let you know soon. I'm going to start researching when and where as soon as I get home. I want us to really do it up. I'll hire us a limo with a driver, and I want it to be a five-star experience complete with great restaurants, a luxurious spa and a fabulous hotel," Greta said.

"Like I said we can do whatever you want, because it's your wedding but slow down and take a deep breath. You can start planning tomorrow" Juliette said, and they both giggled together.

"You're right Juliette, but I'm just so excited. After my divorce from Rayshawn I never thought I would be getting married again."

"Remember, God does answer prayers and you deserve to be happy," Juliette said.

"You're so right. I asked the lord to bless me with a husband who will treat me right and give me the kids I want. I prayed for a man who'll be a good father and spend time with them.

"That's a beautiful prayer, and most of the time God gives you what you ask for. Hopefully you and Derek will be blessed with the children you both want."

"Grandville and I never had a father because until recently we never even knew who our father was."

"Grandville already told me the whole tragic story, and I'm sure it's the last thing you want to discuss on this special day," Juliette stated.

"You are so right. I have much more important things to think about like how I'm going to let Rayshawn know I'm engaged and I'm getting remarried."

"You should wait until right before the wedding and have your divorce attorney advise him. Will you stop receiving alimony once you remarry?" Juliette questioned.

"Yes, the monthly alimony will stop, but once I'm married I'll receive a lump sum payment of two million dollars. I'm going to put the money I get from Rayshawn, along with the rest of the money I have already received from him in a trust. Then, I'll only use the interest generated from the money to subsidize me and Derek's cost of living."

"Are you going to ask Derek to sign a Prenuptial Agreement?" Juliette cautiously asked.

"Yes. Last night Derek and I had an extensive conversation about my wealth. I want to be honest, but after all I have been through I can't help but be cautious. I explained to Derek my philosophy regarding marriage and explained to him about some of my wealth. My mother didn't raise no fools, and she taught me to never let the left hand know what the right hand is doing. So, the bottom line is, Derek will never know exactly how much I'm worth. All he really needs to know is that I will fulfill my vows to him."

"Well, did he say he would sign the Prenuptial Agreement?" Juliette asked.

"Yes, he said he wasn't marrying me for my money, and he will sign whatever I asked. This will be the second marriage for both of us. Derek said, no matter what it will be his last time ever marrying again."

"I didn't realize Derek had been married before," Juliette replied.

"Yes, he married his college sweetheart, but she died in a car accident three years after they were married. She was pregnant with their first child when the accident occurred and he lost them both."

"Oh my God that's terrible."

"It really is horrible. Derek like the rest of us have been through a lot, but when we fall down we have to learn how to get back-up again.

"Now, you know I know . . .OMG."

"Derek said, God sent me to him. He even felt this way when we lived in California. He said he respected me for not getting involved with him while I was married to Rayshawn."

"You guys are each other's second chance. Make sure to cherish each other and not take one another for granted," Juliette advised her.

"I'm going to treat that brother like the King that he is. This I promise."

The doorbell rang and interrupted the ladies conversation.

"I wonder who that could be, I'm not expecting anyone."

Juliette went to the front door and looked through the window and saw Franklin standing on the porch. She opened the door and invited him in.

"Hey Franklin, what a surprise. I wasn't expecting you. Greta and I are sitting outside on the sun porch. Go on out and have a seat. I'll be right there."

Franklin headed to the back of the house and Juliette went into the kitchen and got another Champagne Flute. When she got out to the sun porch Greta excited and showed off her new engagement ring while at the same time swearing Franklin to secrecy.

"Ladies, it looks like the celebration has just begun. I hate to barge in on you, but I tried to call you several times Juliette."

"I'm sorry, but I was blasting one of my old school hip hop cd's and didn't hear my house phone, and I left my cell phone upstairs when Greta got here. What's up?" Juliette asked him.

"We just got word Grandville's motion is being granted. He's being released from Oakhill," Franklin explained.

Juliette could not believe her ears. Her prayers had finally been answered, her husband and best friend was coming home. She couldn't stop the tears as they streamed down her face. Greta was also in a state of shock and immediately began to cry. The two women hugged each other as they cried tears of joy.

"Today is one of the happiest days of my life," Greta exclaimed.

"When will Grandville be released and what are the next steps?" Juliette questioned.

"He'll be released in a month and will be transported directly to the Ontario pre-release center which is located on Carnegie Avenue in Downtown Cleveland. He'll stay there for two weeks, and then he will move into his new apartment that's about seven minutes away from A Better Tomorrow. He will be on Parole, and he'll have to do everything the Court has ordered or he can be sent back to Oakhill or another facility.

Greta, I know you just got engaged, and I'm sure you want to move in with your Fiancé, but I renovated the apartment right next door to Grandville for you. Your brother is tripping on you living at the house. He feels the neighborhood is bad, and he doesn't want you living alone. I thought if you moved in next door to him, it would help with his motion. So, I told the Court you would be residing in the apartment right next door to him. It's important the Court know that Grandville has family support," Franklin explained to the both of them.

"I don't plan to move in with Derek until after we're married, so I'll take the apartment. It will only be temporary until after Derek and I buy a house, Greta replied.

"I understand, but please act surprised when Grandville pitches the idea to you," Franklin said.

Juliette got out the champagne and poured the bubbly into their glasses. "I think a toast is in order," Juliette stated.

"To love, family and freedom." Franklin said as they tapped the tips of their glasses and simultaneously sipped their drinks and spoke of their future which would once again include a very special gift, the presence of their loved one, Grandville.

Chapter 31

Home

Grandville lay in his lumpy little bed at Oakhill for the very last time, his mind in a whirl. Tomorrow this time, he would be lying in a new bed, preparing for a new life away from Oakhill.

He had given away much of his belongings to Joe who despite their past conflicts had become one of his friends while they played the game of Chess. Grandville had been true to his word and played the game to win and as a result remained unbeaten against Joe. Grandville reflected back to when he advised Joe about his release. They were playing chess and discussing the grade which Joe had received in Grandville's English class.

"You should be very proud of yourself. You earned an "A" in my class." Grandville complimented Joe in between Chess moves.

"Thanks Teach, I worked hard. I can't wait to take your next class," Joe replied.

"Joe, I have some news," Grandville confided to him.

"What is it Teach?" Joe asked.

"I'm being released from Oakhill. You're one of my only friends here at Oakhill, and I wanted to let you know."

"What a blessing. I'm happy for you Teach."

"I want you to know that though I won't be here at Oakhill, I'm going to be keeping up with you. I want you to promise me that you'll continue with your twelve step programs, that you'll continue taking classes, and that you'll stay out of trouble. That means no more assaulting vulnerable men in the shower or bullying people," Grandville said.

"Teach, I'm a man who is in the midst of a metamorphosis. I promise you, I'm going to work hard to get my life together. I want to go home like you and Montell, and I'm hoping that I'll be released right behind the two of you" Joe confided in him.

"Good that's exactly what I want to hear though, I haven't been released yet," Grandville said.

"You'll walk out of here soon. I've been going to Church for the past few months, and I realize that coming to Oakhill was the Lord's divine intervention for my life. If I had of remained in the community, I would have probably killed someone. Then, instead of coming here to Oakhill, I would most likely be on Death Row."

"Wow."

"Lucky for me, I had a great Public Defender who fought hard for me to have the opportunity to come to Oakhill. He advised the courts about my mental health issues and convinced them I would be better off receiving help for my issues. It seems though I had an extensive Juvenile Record, I did not have a Felony Record in my adult years. This made me a good candidate for the program," Joe said.

"I'm happy you have realized that even at our weakest we can still find strength if we lean on the Lord. It was a long time before I actually believed these words. I was angry at the Lord for allowing me to lose my mind and for the accident that took my daughter's life. I tried to do it on my own and for a time I lost my faith. I was alone without him, and I had to learn that I would continue to fail if I didn't find him. Now, I'm trying to live by the words, a man who doesn't believe in the lord believes in nothing and is destined for failure," Grandville preached.

"Teach, if you're not going to be here anymore who will teach our class?" Joe asked.

"The institution doesn't have anybody lined up to take over where I left off. The English class was borne out of a grant from my Fraternity to Oakhill, but I have made a list of books which I want you to read while your here at Oakhill. You might as well use your time for something constructive," Grandville said.

"Thanks Teach I really appreciate you doing that for me," Joe replied.

"I also want you to take my Chess set." Grandville replied.

"Teach I appreciate the gesture, but I don't have anyone but you to play with and you're leaving. Also, I already have one chess set, so I don't really need another," Joe said.

"I definitely understand where you're coming from but having two sets could come in handy one day. It just so happens that one of the students in my first English class just approached me about playing chess with him. He realized that I played when he saw me playing with you here in the library. I explained to him that I didn't have the time to play with him, but told him that you would love the opportunity to challenge him. I've arranged for him to play against you next Wednesday right here in the library at our scheduled time. Actually, he's going to take my place."

"Okay Teach, I'm looking forward to it. I just regret that I have still not beat you," Joe said.

"Just keep practicing and when you get out of here we'll have a rematch. Who knows, you may get good enough to beat me," Grandville encouraged him.

That was two weeks ago and true to his word Grandville had given Joe his Chess set and most of the belongings he did not want to take with him from Oakhill. Grandville also watched Joe beat Valentino at Chess. When the two inmates played one another, he felt certain the two would continue playing against each after he had departed Oakhill.

Usually time passed very slowly at Oakhill, but for some reason his last month at Oakhill seemed to move at warp speed. He could not believe he would walk out of Oakhill the very next day. He was so excited, he couldn't even sleep for fear he would wake up and find his leaving Oakhill was a dream. He had been incarcerated for almost four years, and he was a little nervous about the changes the world had seen while he was locked up. He couldn't wait to see his sons and his daughters who he had not yet formally met. He also couldn't wait to spend quiet, quality, private time with the love of his life Juliette. He also was looking forward to being able to spend time with Greta, Franklin and Montell.

Franklin had come to visit him a few days before and brought pictures of their new building and his new apartment. With the help of an online catalog he helped Grandville pick out furniture for his new home. He was looking forward to moving into his place and the comforts which came with it, but he wanted more than anything to go back to his own home with Juliette and his children. He told himself, he had to be patient and show Juliette that she could trust him again.

While he lay in his lumpy little bed he racked his brain thinking of ways he could pitch the idea to Greta about moving into the renovated apartment next door to his. He was told, he would be able to have a private visit with his family when he arrived at the Pre-Release center. Grandville was praying that when Juliette came to visit with him she would bring the kids and Greta with her.

He had mailed a letter to Juliette last week requesting just that. However, as he wrote to her he realized this would be the last letter he ever sent from Oakhill and his heart soared. Soon he would be able to talk to Juliette in person and by phone without anyone listening. Grandville had no way of knowing if Juliette would comply with his wishes until he actually had the visit. He didn't know if Juliette considered the Pre-Release Center as a prison. If she did consider it as a prison, he knew that she would not bring the kids. However, he did have hope Juliette would recognize how much he missed them and bring them despite her reservations. He was so excited about the fact that he might actually see his kids he could not sleep.

Time passed as he lost himself in his thoughts when he saw someone standing in front of his cell. After his eyes focused to the dim light he realized it was Emerson.

"Stubbs I know you're leaving Oakhill today, and I wanted to stop by before the lights come on to wish you farewell. You're a good man. While working here at Oakhill I've had the opportunity to see many men and most are not good people, and in my opinion they should never be released back into society. I've been watching you since you came to Oakhill, and even before you hooked my son up I felt like you are deserving of a second chance. I never want to see you again if I have to see you here at Oakhill. Please go home and do exactly what you need to do, so you can be there for your Lady Love and your family. I want you to know you're one of the few inmates I'm actually going to miss," Emerson whispered in a deep but sincere voice.

"Officer Emerson, thank you for treating me fairly and like a human being. Believe it or not I'll miss you too," Grandville said to him.

"Grandville please take care of yourself and your family."

"I will Officer Emerson and you be sure to do the same," Grandville stated.

As soon as Emerson left from in front of his cell Grandville got up and kneeled down on the floor right in front of his lumpy little bed and began praying. He thanked the Lord for allowing him the opportunity to go home. He also asked God for the strength to deal with the new obstacles which would be placed in his life. Lastly, Grandville asked God for his help and protection.

After breakfast Grandville was taken to Mr. Bolden's office where he said his goodbyes. He received his discharge paperwork and two-hundred and fifty dollars. He was then escorted to the Prison Van. As the van drove away from the institution which held his person for almost four years, he burnt the image of Oakhill into his brain to never be forgotten. When life became difficult he would remember the time which he spent in his own private hell that was known as Oakhill and whatever was wrong wouldn't be so bad.

It took more than six hours before the Oakhill van pulled into the Ontario Pre-Release Center located near Downtown Cleveland. He was tired and his legs were cramped but Grandville had no complaints. He would have walked through scalding hot oil if it meant that he would get to go home. He could barely sit still when he spotted Progressive Field and the Terminal Tower, because these landmarks indicated that he was back in the city he called home.

Once at the Ontario Pre-Release Center he was advised of the rules. He was told by the staff the would be expected to take his medication as prescribed, and he would need to do it in front of the staff who would be reporting back to the Courts. Grandville was also advised, he would be expected to participate in numerous classes and seminars aimed at helping him with re-adjusting to living in the community. They told him the classes covered subjects like how to write a resume, finding employment, anger management and living with a mental illness.

He was then placed into a small room which had three twin beds in it. One of the beds was bare so Grandville assumed this was the bed he would be sleeping in. He learned that he would share the room with two other individuals who were already at the Pre-Release center. Grandville was given worn bedding to make-up his own bed, a light blue uniform to wear while in the facility and a schedule of mandatory classes and counseling sessions which he had to attend.

Grandville was putting away his meager belongings after making his new lumpy bed when the two men who were his new roommates came back from their scheduled programs and introduced themselves to him. Their names were James and Sam, and they both seemed like decent guys who were also anxious about going home. All three men were aware that they would be returning to their previous lives with the stigma of incarceration hanging over their heads.

Grandville lay in his new lumpy bed and listened to his new roommate's converse. He was happier than he'd been in a very long time, because being in the Pre-Release Center was an indicator that his time being incarcerated was coming to an end.

Grandville had been resting for one hour when his new counselor Mr. Davis summoned him to his office. The guard that escorted him said very little while Grandville looked around the facility. Once in Mr. Davis's office he sat down at a small table and waited for his Counselor who he had not yet met. Soon Mr. Davis entered the office and sat directly across from Grandville.

"Mr. Stubbs it's good to meet you. I'm Mr. Davis. I'll be your counselor while you are here at the Ontario Pre-Release Center. I know you've had a long trip, and you're probably tired but I wanted to go over a few things with you before you get settled in," Mr. Davis said.

"I'm ready to do whatever is asked of me," Grandville said.

"That's good, because I'm going to be asking a lot of you. I've set you up for an appointment with the mental health clinic which the release center contracts with for tomorrow morning. You'll meet with your new psychiatrist, and he or she will discuss your medications with you. If you have an appointment outside of the building, I'll be the staff who will arrange for you to have a pass so you can leave the facility. Any issues that you're having should be discussed with me first and together we'll find a solution. Do you have any questions?" Mr. Davis asked.

"Yes, I have one question. My counselor from Oakhill Mr. Bolden told me that I would get to visit with my family once I've been through intake here at the Pre-Release center. Is this true?" Grandville questioned.

"Yes, it is true. You'll get to visit with your family tomorrow evening. I've already spoken to your wife and she has assured me that she and your children will be at the visit. The next four weeks will be intense, but at the end you will be granted the opportunity to go home. You'll be on a special conditional release. You'll be randomly drug and alcohol tested to ensure you're complying with the Court's order," Mr. Davis said.

"That's fine. Do you need to test me now?" Grandville asked.

"No, but you will be tested while you're here at the Pre-Release Center and when you go home," Mr. Davis said.

"No problem," Grandville confidently replied.

"Do you have any other questions Mr. Stubbs," Mr. Davis asked.

"No, but I will let you know if I think of additional questions," Grandville stated.

Okay you can go back to your room and try and get some rest. The next few days will be busy for you," Mr. Davis said.

Epilogue

Juliette sat on her sun porch and gazed across her backyard. The rose bushes in her backyard were again in full bloom, and as she breathed in the lovely scents wafting from the flowers she found herself reminiscing about the past year. It was the fourth Anniversary of Jessica's death and Juliette took a deep breath and thought to herself, what a difference a year could make.

With the help and support of her God, her family and her friends, Juliette felt as though she had finally achieved the peace which she had yearned for in respect to coming to terms with Jessica's death and Grandville's role in it. The prayers that she had made to the Lord about putting her family back intact had been answered, and she had finally forgiven Grandville for everything which had happened. She felt as though she was no longer emotionally in limbo now that he had been released from Oakhill and was now home in Cleveland.

Juliette reflected back to three months before when Grandville was first sent home from Oakhill to the Pre-Release Center in Downtown Cleveland. After speaking to Grandville's new counselor by phone, she made arrangements to come to the Pre-Release Center the very next day after Grandville's arrival. However, she did not tell the children they would be visiting with their father. When they arrived and Jabari and Jonah saw their Dad and realized what was going on they jumped into his arms with smiles on their faces and tears in their eyes.

Grandville was so excited to see his sons after more than three years and meet his daughters for the very first time that he couldn't stop himself from breaking down in tears of joy. It was a very emotional time for them. They were all crying together as a family, and Juliette stood by watching as the kids and Grandville kissed each other and cried unstoppable tears. She finally walked over to them and hugged all of them together and joined in on the family's celebration. The reunion which Juliette's family experienced was an epic scene, and even the guard and counselor were almost in tears just watching as Grandville's family poured out so much love from their hearts to him.

Juliette was pleased on how well Grandville appeared to be adjusting to life outside of the walls of Oakhill. She also had to admit that since his release, Grandville appeared to have changed. He was calmer and insisted on spending as much time as possible with his kids. He had established a routine which included helping their son's with their homework and reading to their daughters.

He came over to their house every day and he had resumed all of his fatherly and husbandly duties including making love to her and cooking for her and their family at least twice a week. She had to admit, she was both appreciative and grateful Grandville was working extra hard to rebuild, repair and strengthen his relationships with the people who he loved.

He and Greta were closer than ever, and the twins were spending a great deal of time together since Greta now lived in the apartment right next door to his. Grandville was also getting to know Derek and over the past few months the two seemed to have bonded due to their mutual love for Greta.

The trio also worked together to finish clearing out Mother Stubbs home. Grandville was able to recruit Franklin, Montell and Derek to help him re-paint Mother Stubbs house inside and out. They also updated the kitchen and the bathrooms and the home is now on the market to be sold.

Grandville had also resumed his work with Franklin, and was now making his living preparing taxes. He was making good money and even though he was not residing in their home, he had resumed giving Juliette a monthly allowance to help her with paying bills. He also advised her, his Trust was making a great return on his investment. He told her she could have anything she wanted, including purchasing a new house.

Juliette didn't want Grandville to buy her anything because she had already received what she wanted, Grandville was home. She also decided against them purchasing a new house, she loved her house. Although her family had experienced a tragedy while living there, it was their home. She felt that it would not be in the family's best interest to move right now. However, she wanted to re-visit the idea in the future after more time had passed.

Juliette had also found with Grandville being home she now had more disposable income. She was still doing her Involuntary Commitment hearings in both Cleveland and Painesville, Ohio, and she was making good money and helping her clients along the way. Juliette also assisted the Defense Attorneys who represented the Involuntary Commitment clients whom she fought to have hospitalized, were linked to mental health treatment and social services when they were released from the hospital. Her rooming house, A Better Tomorrow remained full, and she was making a good profit from the house. She was able to hire another former resident to help Viola with keeping the common areas clean, with cooking and shopping, so she could focus more of her time on Grant Writing.

Juliette and her family had been working hard. She was planning a surprise trip to Disney World for Grandville and the kids. She had stashed some extra money from her earnings, and she now found herself with a way to reward them for being such a great family.

Grandville was settling into his new life and was also enjoying playing a weekly game of Chess with Montell, who didn't live too far away from Grandville's apartment. Juliette really liked his wife, Maria, and the two were fast becoming friends due to their shared experience of being married to former Oakhill inmates. Grandville was also preparing his application to the Ohio Bar, so that he could ask to have his law license reinstated. He was also attending as many Continuing Legal Education Seminars as he could find in an attempt to make-up the hours which he was unable to take while he was incarcerated at Oakhill.

Over the past few months with Grandville's release, the couple had engaged in several extensive discussions about his mental illness, and its effects on their family and his relationships. Both had agreed that Grandville's condition had been exasperated due to his Mother's passing, and him learning about the son which he made with Gina.

Juliette had come to realize with the burden Grandville had been carrying, his breakdown was almost inevitable. She hoped with their improved communication, Grandville would continue to be open and honest with her, so this would minimize the risk of him becoming psychotic again in the future.

Juliette also decided she would remain vigilant in watching for signs which indicated Grandville was becoming overly stressed, and when she did see it, she would encourage him to rest. Juliette had taken Emily's advice and had signed up and attended The National Alliance for the Mentally Ill's Family to Family program where she learned about strategies on how to make Grandville's home atmosphere calm and stress free. She also learned first-hand that there were many families who had a member who was mentally ill, and although Grandville was sick, their situation was not near as bad as it could be.

The couple decided they would ask the Ohio Bar to allow Grandville's situation to help raise awareness in the legal community about stress and how it could help to contribute to a manifestation of a pre-existing mental health issues as well as the importance of early detection and treatment. The odds of him actually being reinstated into the Ohio Bar were slim. However, Grandville felt that by telling his story to other Attorneys, he could show the Ohio Bar that he was serious about his commitment to practicing law while helping others in the legal community to avoid some of the heart aches and pains associated with being a professional and suffering with a mental illness.

Since Grandville's return home he and Juliette were spending alone time with each other and with their children. Juliette was happy she had made the decision to grant Grandville the chance to be a part of their family again. Even though they had not been living together, the family still spent quality time together.

Grandville had also convinced her from his actions that he was not a danger to himself or to their family. He was open with her and others about his illness, and he often discussed how he felt due to the side effects of his medications. Since his return home, Juliette had removed all the liquor from her home and made sure not to allow others to drink or smoke Marijuana around him or in their home.

The family had been attending family counseling twice a week and during their last session they made the decision it was time for Grandville to move back home. During the Counseling Sessions the family learned to be open with each other about Grandville's illness and about the accident which took Jessica's life. Juliette's heart was still heavy due to the loss of her oldest daughter. However, Juliette had to admit with each passing day that despite the tragedies they all had been through her family had been blessed.

As Juliette cut rose stems off of her rose bush in her backyard she reflected on the beautiful roses and the quietness in the yard. She could actually feel Jessica's spiritual presence among the beautiful flowers, and in her mind a small little voice said, "I'm glad Daddy's coming Home." Juliette just smiled and shook her head, and said, "Me too." Juliette knew it was a message from God that every little thing would be alright, and she was ready to give it all she had again to make her family whole again.

Her daughters were napping and the boys were with Grandville at his apartment where they were helping him to pack his few belongings so he could return to their home for good. The family had decided that the Anniversary of Jessica's death should be more than a day of mourning. For the Stubbs Family, August 21 would also represent the Anniversary of a new beginning for Grandville and his family, because it would also be the day that he moved back into their house. Her kids were ecstatic Grandville was coming home, and even her daughters were constantly asking for their father when he was not with them. Juliette felt she was making the right decision for her husband to come home again.

With the help of her God and her therapist Juliette had finally found a place in her heart where she truly forgave Grandville for Jessica's death and for not telling her about his past before they were married. She silently vowed to continue to stand by her life partner despite the ups and downs which life would bring to them.

It wasn't long before Grandville and the boys returned with Grandville's belongings and before she knew it, she and her family were placing roses from the rose bushes in their backyard onto Jessica's grave. This was the first time Juliette had ever brought her sons to visit Jessica's grave. She now realized that she should have brought them much sooner. It was also Grandville's first time visiting Jessica's grave as he was still in the hospital during her funeral.

The family prayed together and talked to Jessica like she was still alive and among them. The girls didn't really understand what death meant so Juliette showed them pictures of the big sister they had never met and explained to them that Jessica was in heaven with the Lord. Both Juliette and Grandville encouraged their sons to be open with their family about how they felt in respect to Jessica's death and about Grandville's illness. From the moment Grandville came home from the Pre-Release Center the family had been working with a family Counselor who was helping them to communicate with each other more effectively.

Juliette was happy, the happiest she'd been in a very long time. It had been a long journey and though her family still had a long way to go she felt they would make it if they continued to stick together as a close knit family. The only dark cloud which hung in her sunny sky was that Melinia was still missing. Ironically, the Anniversary of Melinia's disappearance coincided with the Anniversary of Jessica's death. Juliette was heartbroken that August 21 was also the Anniversary which Melinia had gone missing and she had been gone for one year. Melinia's nude images were no longer on the internet, leaving Juliette and her family to again wonder if she was dead or alive. Her family was holding a vigil for Melinia's safe return the next week, and Juliette and Grandville planned to attend with their children.

Even though there was a large reward which could be claimed by anyone who supplied information about Melenia's whereabouts, there had been no new leads. Grandville shared with Juliette while he was incarcerated that he had arranged for Franklin to hire a private investigator in an attempt to help her family locate Melinia. Juliette wasn't angry that Grandville had kept this information from her, but instead she was grateful Grandville was trying to help her even while he was locked away at Oakhill. This confirmed she was doing the right thing in respect to their reconciliation.

After the family was done laughing, crying and remembering Jessica and the joy which she brought to their lives, it was time to go home.

Juliette had planned a small party to celebrate Grandville's move home for later on that day which included Greta, Derek, Franklin, Samantha, Montell and Maria. They would continue to celebrate all they had lost and gained. With true love, nothing can tear a family apart, not even a tragic death of a loved one!

And "Now I Will Show You The Most Excellent Way: Love"

1 Corinthians 13
(Taken from the New International Version (NIV))

13 If I speak in the tongues[a] of men or of angels, but do not have love, I am only a resounding gong or a clanging cymbal. 2 If I have the gift of prophecy and can fathom all mysteries and all knowledge, and if I have a faith that can move mountains, but do not have love, I am nothing.

3 If I give all I possess to the poor and give over my body to hardship that I may boast,[b] but do not have love, I gain nothing.

[4] Love is patient, love is kind. It does not envy, it does not boast, it is not proud. [5] It does not dishonor others, it is not self-seeking, it is not easily angered, it keeps no record of wrongs. [6] Love does not delight in evil but rejoices with the truth. [7] It always protects, always trusts, always hopes, always perseveres.

[8] Love never fails. But where there are prophecies, they will cease; where there are tongues, they will be stilled; where there is knowledge, it will pass away. [9] For we know in part and we prophesy in part, [10] but when completeness comes, what is in part disappears. [11] When I was a child, I talked like a child, I thought like a child, I reasoned like a child. When I became a man, I put the ways of childhood behind me. [12] For now we see only a reflection as in a mirror; then we shall see face to face. Now I know in part; then I shall know fully, even as I am fully known.

[13] And now these three remain: faith, hope and love. But the greatest of these is love.

Grandville's Playlist
While at Oakhill

1. *Tragedy*- Bee Gees
2. *Locked Up*- Akon
3. *It's So Hard to Say Goodbye To Yesterday*- Boyz to Men
4. *Set Adrift On Memory Bliss*- PM Dawn
5. *Shackles (Praise You)*- Mary Mary
6. *Keeping Secrets*- Switch
7. *Can We Talk*- Tevin Campbell
8. *Reminisce*- Mary J. Blige
9. *Tomorrow (A Better You, A Better Me)*- Tevin Campbell
10. *Sooner Or Later*- N.E.R.D.
11. *What About Your Friends*- TLC
12. *Fallin*- Jay Z
13. *Time Will Reveal*- Debarge
14. *Gone*-Kanye West
15. *Back Down Memory Lane*- Minnie Riperton
16. *Find My Way* - N.E.R.D.
17. *Always In My Head*- Coldplay
18. *Bag Lady*- Erykah Badu
19. *Confessions*- Usher
20. *Touch Me Tease Me*- Case
21. *Love's In Need Of Love Today*- Stevie Wonder
22. *Is It A Crime*- Sade
23. *Between The Sheets*- Isley Brothers
24. *Controversy*- Prince
25. *Olivia (Lost and Turned Out)*- The Whispers
26. *Tha Crossroads*- Bone Thugs N Harmony
27. *Hard To Say I'm Sorry*-Az Yet
28. *Clocks*- Coldplay
29. *People Make The World Go Around*-The Stylistics
30. *Let's Get Married*- Jagged Edge
31. *Home*- Stephanie Mills

About the Author

JJ Winston has worked in the area of Behavioral Health for over 20 years and is now employed as a Family Court Magistrate Judge in Cleveland, Ohio. JJ Winston is licensed as an Independent Social Worker and Attorney in the state of Ohio.

An avid reader whose hobbies include fishing, watching movies, writing fiction stories and spending time with family and friends. The Anniversary is JJ Winston's first novel.

The

Anniversary

"What do you do when life has you in checkmate?"

JJ Winston

Made in the USA
Columbia, SC
17 October 2017